SAMURAI WIND

NIGEL SELLARS

Hydra
Publications

ISBN: 978-1-942212-98-0

Hydra Publications
Goshen, KY 40026
www.hydrapublications.com

CHAPTER ONE

"There are no heroes," Ichiro told himself on the morning he planned to die. "There are only those who have no other choice." The knowledge came to him in a dream that night. It brought him quickly awake with the knife-edge of pain in his abdomen.

But in a few hours, he would no longer worry about pain. Soon he would have no worries at all. In a brief moment his life would end, a death of accomplishment without agony. It was a better end than cancer's lingering death, with its rotting and wasting away and pain.

He knelt before the small shrine in the temple and prayed to Hachiman. Although he had long lost his own faith in an afterlife, he did not think the god of war would be offended. His sacrifice would bring honor to his Japan and his Emperor. That was enough to please Hachiman.

Although the morning was hot and wet with steaming rain, the temple was bitter cold. Ichiro found no warmth from his flight suit. He shivered, and the fur lining made him itch unbearably. He set his mind to the task before him, shutting the minor irritations away in the depths of his consciousness. There they would bother him no more.

Despite its chill interior, the temple allowed the only privacy Ichiro could find. Here he could vent his doubts, away from the prying eyes of fellow pilots, bothersome flight mechanics and superior officers.

Each pilot had his own fears and doubts before a mission, but to express them openly was an impropriety.

Every man faced his personal terror alone. Ichiro learned that with much difficulty, and he knew it better than any other man on the airfield did.

He removed his *hachimaki*, the headband of resolution, from inside his flight jacket. He spread it out on the altar and whispered each of the prayers stitched into it. Every word brought more doubt and confusion. Ultimately came despair.

His mother's prayer, delicately embroidered, was calmly resolute and patriotic. It was quite unlike her. His father's prayer was also empty and filled with false hope. As always, words failed them.

The other prayers, from friends and relatives, extolled the glory of Japan, of the kami and of the Emperor. Only the prayer from his beloved Yumiko spoke with genuine pain.

"Though you are far from me, in islands I cannot know, yet you live within my heart, as perennial as the cherry blossoms and as fragile as an orchid."

He lifted the *hachimaki* from the altar and brought it to his forehead. His fingers fumbled with the lacing, but at last he drew it tight.

From his jacket he withdrew three envelopes. Two he placed on the altar. From the third he shook out a handful of gray poppy seeds. The seeds he placed into a small brazier set into the altar. They burned briefly and died. The smoke seemed to rise forever, casting a faint perfume about the temple.

Ichiro regretted he would never again smell such a scent. There was so much he would never again experience: *sake*, rose blossoms, and the fragrance of his Yumiko. All that was his now was the pungency of aviation fuel and hot motor oil, the perfume of salty perspiration and the odor of a damp rubber and canvas oxygen mask.

But he was resolved to that loss now. When the cancer first took root in his bowels, the knowledge tortured him.

Then he had no choice. Now he chose to rejoice in his memories and not wallow in their loss.

The poppy seeds burned to ash; he made his last gesture to the living. He opened the two envelopes he had placed on the altar. Each contained a letter, one written to his parents and other to Yumiko. The letters were scrawled on scraps of rice paper in the calligraphy of a shaking hand. Never well skilled in handling a writing brush, Ichiro found his task of writing so much the harder.

The letters contained a poem and a promise, as was the tradition of the *samurai*. Only one thing remained for him to add.

His knife rested in its scabbard. Though it was not a proper ceremonial knife, it would suffice. His hand trembling, he withdrew the knife and reached to the back of his head. He took hold of his fine black hair and cut free two locks. One lock he placed in his parents' letter, the other in the letter to Yumiko. He said a Buddhist prayer over each envelope and sealed them.

He returned the envelopes to his jacket and replaced the knife in its scabbard. He bowed his head to the floor and said a final prayer. Rising slowly, he turned and walked into the hot and stifling morning air.

Ichiro had not walked far when he heard a noise in the undergrowth. He saw the snake slither from the bushes, its black and orange scales glistening in the sun. His breath caught in his throat and he felt his heart pound in his chest. When had it been? When he was five? He remembered the snake strike his playmate, saw his friend sicken, go into convulsions and die.

After pausing a moment to taste the air, the snake moved on, sliding back into the undergrowth.

Ichiro licked his lips. His mouth was dry.

"Are you all right, Ichiro?" said Major Tagura, coming to Ichiro's side. Pain and concern etched Tagura's face. He was a man who drank another's pain and made it his own. "If you feel unprepared, Lieutenant Esu is willing to replace you."

"No, I am ready," Ichiro replied flatly. "I have nothing further to do."

"Very well. Then it must be done," Tagura said. Anguish colored his speech. Tears moistened his mahogany eyes. He looked at the ground. "I shall miss you, my friend."

Ichiro gently clasped his friend's shoulder. "Please, Genjo, do not cry for me. I would soon be dead in any case. I choose this death. Is it not the *Bushido's* essence, to die in this fashion, as a whole man rather than in agony as an invalid? Would it not be more agonizing for everyone is to see me die a little each day until I become simply a wasted shell?"

Tagura wiped his eyes with his sleeve. "Yes," he said, "but death is always most painful to those left behind, no matter its fashion of exit."

"I have no choice," Ichiro said softly and kindly. "Events chose me. I did not choose them." *Because there are no heroes*, he thought.

A telling silence held the air between the two men.

"I must go," Ichiro said at last. He pulled his flight helmet from a jacket pocket and placed it on his head. Beneath the helmet, the hachi-maki pressed its prayers into his forehead, branding him forever. He turned toward the airfield and walked toward his plane.

"I love you, Minamoto Ichiro," Tagura shouted.

Ichiro paused. " And I love you, Tagura Genjo," he replied. "But even lovers must part. Good-bye, my friend."

Without glancing back, Ichiro continued to his plane.

The airfield was aged and decrepit. It lacked runways, having only yellowed grass verges that flowed into hard earth. Huts replaced billets, and a flimsy wooden platform masqueraded as a control tower.

No fineries were required. Those belonged to combat squadrons needing to maintain pilots, crews and aircraft. But a kamikaze unit needed only rotting huts and rickety platforms.

Before the cancer seized him, Ichiro knew the fineries of a pilot's life. He flew at Pearl Harbor, Midway, Guadalcanal, and at Leyte Gulf. He distinguished himself with twenty kills of American and Australian aircraft.

New ratings on the aircraft carriers would whisper. "See him, the officer with the twisted leg, the club foot? That is Captain Minamoto, the finest fighter pilot in all Japan."

Such ironies filled his life. His clubfoot drove him to become a pilot, although it took so much else from him. The infirmity kept him alone and apart from other children.

He took to building kites. Only in kite flying did he feel free of earthly shackles.

When he reached the age for military service, he saw his decision as simple: become a pilot or rot as a cripple.

He knew his twisted leg was no handicap in an aircraft. Indeed, it was no problem at all compared to a legless English pilot he knew. A man without legs, yet he still flew, Ichiro recalled with admiration. He wondered if that man were still alive.

Ichiro quickly showed his instructors that they were the cripples in the air, not he.

But the worm of disease crawled into him and gnawed away. A crippled man as a pilot was one thing, but a sick and dying man was quite another. Regulations were regulations. His superiors took him from flight duty and gave him an administrative position because they could not bear to simply retire him.

Angered, he fought the petty bureaucrats as fiercely as he had enemy fighter pilots. But he had little or no hope.

Salvation came with the *kamikaze* units. A desperate measure, a futile stopgap, it still attracted pilots. The units willingly accepted men whose knowledge of flying was rudimentary at best.

Ichiro saw an opportunity in this, a chance for honor and self-respect. He begged and cajoled his superiors, requesting they not deny him the chance to die for his Emperor, as befit one born into a samurai family. He told them they lacked any excuse to deny him this right.

Was he not going to die anyway? he asked. His superiors pondered his request. Impressed by his sincerity, they approved his transfer to a *kamikaze* flight.

His transfer, however, first required that he act as flight trainer. He obeyed, but his heart was not in it. His trainees learned quickly under his tutelage before they took off on their first and last missions. For two months Ichiro watched them and despaired. Then he began writing his own name at the head of each new pilot list for the next mission.

Each time Tagura countermanded it. But finally, the major had no choice. There were no more pilots left. He reluctantly approved Ichiro's request for a mission.

Ichiro reached his plane and tried to jump up onto a wing. His foot felt heavy and clumsy. Disease had so weakened him that he almost slipped from the wing. He cursed his infirmities and pulled himself to his feet.

Ushi, his flight mechanic, came to assist him. "Good morning, sir," he said, smiling faintly. The man rarely displayed any signs of emotion.

"Good morning, Ushi. Is the plane ready?"

Ushi shook his shaved head and sighed. "She's cobbled together from bits and pieces, Captain. We'll see a miracle if she can start and taxi. If she flies, it will be a profound shock."

"I see." Ichiro pushed back the canopy of the Zero-Sen and lifted himself into the cockpit. A weakness possessed his body. He would not survive much longer in any case. The disease was entering its final stage.

Sliding his feet into the rudder controls, Ichiro positioned himself in the cockpit. The plane had no seat, just a hard wooden plank. Not even a parachute could have made it comfortable. Like all *kamikaze*, Ichiro wore no parachute. A parachute was an admission of doubt and fear.

He tightened the shoulder harness until it pulled him snugly against the cold metal back of the cockpit. *How reassuring to be in something so familiar,* Ichiro thought. In a plane, he felt secure and confident. No longer was he confined to earth while others spread wings in flight. He was free. It was as it had been, when he and his plane sprang from a carrier's flight deck to engage Wildcats and Dauntlesses.

Twisting his head slightly, he saw the other aircraft comprising the flight.

There were three Zero-Sens like his own plane. In addition, there were three other fighters, two aging Raidens and a battle-scarred Hien that seemed ready to collapse once its engine started. At the far end of the row sat a twin-engine Mitsubishi bomber. Its useful days all but over, it would serve one final purpose. Filled with high explosives, this flying bomb would crash and detonate deep within the bowels of an American aircraft carrier.

The bomber was Colonel Noguchi's plane. The colonel dedicated his life to this act of *jibaku* as revenge for the deaths of his beloved wife and four children, lost to the bombs of an American B-29 Super-fortress raid on Osaka.

Noguchi's motives disturbed Ichiro. Revenge and glory were foolish motives. Even his own motive, a simple, honorable death, now seemed foolish. They were all fools then, flying toward targets they had little chance of destroying.

It was a futile, and therefore noble, goal.

We Japanese are expert at the nobility of failure, Ichiro thought, shaking his head.

Trucks equipped with starting winches backed toward the aircraft. The trucks had already started two planes.

Noguchi's bomber possessed self-starters. Protesting and groaning, its motors turned over, trying to roar into life.

Mechanics attached the starter rods to the other planes' propeller hubs. The winch motors whined as they revved up, turning over the powerful aircraft engines. As the engines caught, the trucks pulled away, allowing the planes to taxi.

Ichiro's Zero refused to start.

Its engine coughed, sputtered and belched thick, oily smoke. The mechanics tossed up the cowling and feverishly probed the engine.

"What's wrong?" Ichiro shouted. He watched Noguchi's bomber lumber into the air while he sat helpless. He feared he would be left behind, never to fly this mission, to finally wither away on a urine and pus-stained cot.

Ushi fiddled with the engine. With the Raidens in the lead, the remaining planes quickly followed the bomber, which was now disappearing into the overcast sky.

Frustrated, Ichiro banged his fist against the side of the cockpit. He cursed his luck.

Ushi slammed the cowling down and scrambled across the wing to the cockpit. He was out of breath and grasped for air at each word. "The fuel line was clogged, Captain," he said. "We haven't started this engine in some time. It's clear now."

"Very good. Thank you, Ushi."

The mechanic clambered from the wing.

"Ushi," Ichiro cried, remembering the envelopes.

The mechanic climbed back onto the wing. "Yes, sir?"

Ichiro extracted the two envelopes from his jacket. "Please see that these are delivered." He handed the letters to the small mechanic.

Ushi took the envelopes and tucked them into his coveralls. He did not speak, but the downcast expression on his thinly bearded face betrayed his emotions. Ushi gave a quick salute and scrambled from the wing.

The starter winch raced, slowly turning the propeller. Cylinders sighed and whined. A brief thunderclap, a white puff of smoke, and the engine was alive.

The truck pulled away. Two ground crew members dove beneath the wings and removed the wheel blocks from the landing gear.

A flight sergeant signaled the all clear. Ichiro acknowledged the signal and began taxiing the Zero toward the grass verge runway.

Wheeling the Zero about, Ichiro saw a man frantically running toward him

The man, a junior officer, flung himself onto the wing and struggled toward the open cockpit. *He must be mad!* Ichiro thought.

The man shouted something, but Ichiro could not hear him above the engine's roar. The man pressed a neatly folded sheet of paper into Ichiro's hand, then slid from the wing. An aileron caught the man at about shoulder height and flung him aside like a rag doll.

Ichiro wanted to stop the plane, but the horror numbed him and the plane was already accelerating for takeoff. He pulled the canopy closed and fastened it. Its reassuring lock separated him from the accident that now lay far behind him. He was in another world where the horror no longer existed. He shut it from his mind. He had no choice.

Its engine racing, the Zero gained speed down the runway. Ichiro pulled back on the control stick, feeling it slick with perspiration. Slowly the plane climbed skyward, caught like a *kami* between heaven and earth.

The other aircraft were already too far ahead to justify his attempting to catch up with them. He lacked the fuel, and he was uncertain the plane could take the additional stress of more speed. He would reach the target only a few moments after the others in any case. Once there, aircraft from other units would join him.

He might not witness Noguchi's death, but he would definitely see its aftermath. And before his own *jibaku* that would break the back of some American ship, he would view the handiwork of his students, his poor noble cherry blossoms.

He remembered the words he told all his students. "Always aim your aircraft for the forward elevators of the aircraft carrier. This will render a mortal blow to the ship, exploding the fuel and ammunition stores. If you cannot hit the forward elevator, aim for the secondary elevators. If that is not possible, then crash where you may cause the most damage. Only after none of these options is left to you should you attack the battleships and cruisers."

All very simple, indeed. There was no accounting of a man's motives for dying so. It gave the illusion of choice where none existed.

He felt a stabbing pain in his abdomen as the worm of cancer took another bite. Compounding matters, he had eaten nothing that morning as the thought of food had nauseated him. Now sharp hunger pangs blended with the agony of cancer.

Ichiro closed his eyes and whispered a Buddhist sutra, hoping to will away the pain. Was this how *seppuku* felt, he wondered, when the sword blade sliced skin and bowels and the intestines themselves spilled forth onto the ground?

His attempt to will away the pain only made it worse. He balled his hand into a fist to aid his concentration. His fingers bit into something. It sounded like crumpling rice paper.

The sudden sound took his mind from the pain. Glancing down, he saw the folded message the junior officer had probably given his life to deliver.

Holding the control stick between his knees, he unfolded the paper. It was a note, written in Tagura's small, precise calligraphy.

"My dearest friend," it began." The pain of your loss is a great burden for me. Our friendship enriched me and fulfilled my desires. But knowing you will be gone forever is a knowledge I cannot carry. Let us then die together, in the manner of true lovers and brothers. The sword is sharp; the pain is undoubtedly great, but not so great as the burden I shall face when you are dead. Forgive me, my friend."

At the bottom was a poem, a traditional blessing for the *kamikaze*:

We are like the cherry blossoms,
*   Doomed to flower briefly and die.*
*   Yet the brevity of our lives burns*
*   More brightly than a thousand suns.*
Ichiro crushed the note in his fist and wept.

––––––––

He sighted the targets after two hours flying. The white wakes of the American ships shone like beacons through the gossamer thin cloud cover. Below him, he saw Noguchi's bomber and the other aircraft diving toward the fleet.

But he also saw American fighter planes rising to meet the *kamikaze*. Some of the inexperienced pilots would shortly fall victim to a Hellcat's cannons. Yet others might still carry out their mission.

Of course, the mission would ultimately end in failure. Even if they sank a carrier or a heavy cruiser, the pilots' efforts were futile. The war was over, Ichiro knew. This was the action of desperate men seeking desperate answers. It was noble only because it was sincere. Sincerity in desperation was always noble.

Ichiro banked the Zero and descended rapidly. The clouds whirled past like memories held in tenuous grasp. Below, the ships' arrow-straight wakes became zigzag lines of evasive maneuvers. Above the ships, the gnat-like forms of aircraft darted like insects skimming pond waters.

There was a bright flash. Smoke and flame trailed toward the sea as one *kamikaze* met his destiny too soon.

On the surface a huge column of flame erupted. Noguchi had found his mark, and a carrier burned its life away.

Black bursts of anti-aircraft fire speckled the sky. A near-miss rattled Ichiro's plane, causing it to buck savagely, and almost ripping the control stick from his fingers.

He fought to regain control as the Zero attempted to twist itself in knots. Ichiro clutched the joystick and wrestled with the rudder controls.

Panic rose in his mind. Could he straighten out the aircraft before it slammed into the sea? He had to control his mind, to force the fear back. Ichiro remember a koan the old abbot of a Buddhist monastery near his home had once taught him: *The hubless wheel turns.*

He let his mind play with the riddle. It soothed him, calmed him as he fought the controls. Forcing the stick and rudder as far over as possible, he still got no response from the Zero. *The hubless wheel turns*, he thought. He let his fear drop away. The plane's nose rose slightly, as though some hand eased it gently upward. He loosed his grip on the stick slightly, felt the rudder grow easier to the touch.

"It is not your place to die, Minamoto Ichiro," said a pleasant voice.

It was the voice of fire and ice and earth and sky. *"Not yet. I still have need of you."*

A burning coldness crept along Ichiro's spine. "Who are you?" he whispered through clenched teeth. The air in the cockpit was dry and choking. Yet he felt like he was drowning.

"In good time, little one," the voice replied. There was a hint of joy and sorrow in its tone. "At that time you will know you have always known me."

"Leave me alone," Ichiro demanded. "I came here to die. Do you not know I am already a dead man? Allow me the dignity of death by my own choosing." He pushed the control stick forward, sending the plane into a sharp dive. *The hubless wheel turns.*

The fleeing form of an American jeep carrier loomed before him. It was the hare, and he was the hound. He concentrated on his task while all around him the anti-aircraft fire grew thicker and more deadly. If he did not hit the carrier, the gunfire would surely hit him.

"Do not be a fool, Minamoto Ichiro," the voice said. Its tone was now severe and harsh. It filled the cockpit with its choking fumes. "This is futility. Your cause, this Japan's cause, is lost. There is no nobility in this death. Why waste your courage when I have use for it?"

Ichiro closed his mind to the voice. The cockpit air was thick and foul. He found difficulty breathing and reached for his oxygen mask.

As he brought it to his face, the odor of decay, not oxygen, greeted him.

"Do not think you are so brave, Minamoto," the voice said. "Behold. Your greatest fear."

Something slithered around his ankle. Perspiration poured from Ichiro's forehead. He looked down and saw the head of a coral snake as it slipped between the cloth of his flight suit and his bare skin.

His scream mingled with that of the Zero as it dove and shook from the turbulence generated by exploding anti-aircraft shells. He battled the controls, keeping the plane on target.

He beat at his leg in fear, but found there was no snake. "Damn you," he cursed. "Leave me alone! I want to die!"

But as he drew closer to the carrier, he found nagging doubt tearing his thoughts. He knew this was written in the *Bushido*, the samurai code. At the moment of death, a man should naturally want life. So close to his own death, he naturally wished to withdraw the hand holding the knife before its blade plunged into him.

But this knife could not be withdrawn. He could not alter the plane's course. Each ensuing second brought him nearer death. His only choice now was to whether to crash into the carrier or the sea. Again, a choice that was only an illusion dogged him.

Did others feel this uncertainty? he wondered. If they did, he would never know. Their fears were hidden from him. He only knew his own.

Below him, the carrier's crew scattered for safety. It was futile. Only Ichiro's crashing into the sea could spare their lives. But his course carried him relentlessly toward the forward elevator and the perfect *jibaku*.

In a shattering moment he would deliver the great beast's doom, consuming the carrier's aviation fuel, munitions, aircraft and men. But this would not end his country's suffering. It would just prolong pain as part of a noble, sincere, and desperate failure.

A voice told him this was not right. But it was his own voice, not the strange being's. "If you wish death, then you must take it," the voice said. "But do not take others. This is your death, not theirs."

He pulled back on the control stick. The Zero's nose rose obediently and the rest of the plane followed. It shuddered slightly, then steadied.

Ichiro did not know if he could clear the carrier.

The anti-aircraft fire abated as he closed in, but the machine guns fired tenaciously. Shells rang off the plane's armor plating. They sounded like temple bells tolling in the wind.

The Zero continued rising, but Ichiro doubted it was enough. The plane and carrier raced toward each other in a death embrace. He would reject it if he could.

The plane shuddered. He kicked the rudder controls and felt no reassuring response. He knew instantly what had happened. The control cables had snapped, either from wear or from anti-aircraft fire. It didn't matter which.

The carrier filled his field of vision. In desperation, he pulled the joystick tight against his groin. The nose lifted a little more.

The Zero skimmed the carrier's deck as though trying to land. But it still wished to crash. Ichiro fought the controls. The plane maintained its altitude, racing over the deck.

The ship's superstructure jumped in front of him. Ichiro clenched his teeth and prayed to Hachiman. He felt the left wing catch the super-structure's trailing edge. *The hubless wheel turns!* he heard his mind shout before he lost consciousness.

The Zero spun about, wildly out of control. It vanished over the deck's edge. The sea's green turbulence swallowed it.

On the carrier deck, seamen and officers raced to the side. Each wanted a glimpse of the crashed Zero, but all that remained of the aircraft were a few bits of debris and a mass of churning white water.

CHAPTER TWO

Ichiro remembered only the wing tip catching. Tearing metal screamed. The world whirled. Icy cold water shocked him. Darkness swallowed him.

He opened his eyes. All around him was darkness and yet not darkness. He raised his right hand to his face and saw it as clearly as he would in daylight. In fact, the hand glowed with its own light.

So this is death, he thought.

Ichiro sat up. He lay on a large bed with golden silk sheets. The bed floated in a sea of black nothing. Glancing at himself, he saw he wore a sky blue kimono. It was loosely tied with a yellow *obi*, or waistband.

Where were his flying suit and boots? he wondered. He touched his hands to his forehead. His fingers touched the *hachimaki's* soft fabric. Still firmly tied, its embroidered prayers reassured him. It was a familiar object in this strange place.

"Good, you are awake," the voice said.

"Am I dead?" Ichiro asked.

Laughter shook the air. "Do you feel dead?"

"No," Ichiro admitted. "But then, how am I to know what death is?"

The laughter deepened. "You are very much alive, Minamoto-no-Ichiro. But in the world of your birth, everyone believes you are dead. Your plane will never return to its base. The American sailors saw it crash and sink. Your wife will receive the death notice soon.

"But you are no longer in that world. And you are not dead," the voice assured him.

"But if I am not in that world, where are am I?" Ichiro asked.

"Ah, my friend, at this moment you are not in any world. You are caught between worlds, floating in the essence of all existence," the voice said.

"That tells me nothing," Ichiro protested.

"Then I will show you."

A wind rose from nowhere, tearing the stillness. It grew to a howling gale. Ichiro raised his hands to his face to protect it from the onslaught. Through his fingers he saw a dust cloud forming in the distance.

The cloud glowed with its own iridescence, changing color at each moment. First it glowed golden, then crimson, then indigo. It billowed to the foot of the bed and coalesced.

Spinning rapidly, the cloud took various forms. It passed through all of Time's primeval shapes. First it was the Void, then it became water thick with tiny creatures. In succession it evolved from a fish to a long, sinuous sea monster, a slimy newt, a sail-backed lizard, a dragon, an eagle, a bear, a dog, a monkey, and at last a human.

The human took on more definite form. Tall and muscular it stood, larger than any living man or woman. It glowed as bright as the sun, forcing Ichiro to cover his eyes.

A thunderclap rent the air. Silence followed.

Cautiously, Ichiro spread his hands and stared out. A huge samurai stood at the foot of the bed. A head and a half taller than any living man, his limbs were large and muscular under thick armor plates. The armor itself was of the ancient *tanko* variety. Blue and gold silk cords bound the plates together.

About the warrior's waist was an *obi* that was a writhing serpent. Ichiro felt his heart skip a beat when he saw the snake, but he grew calm as he saw it quickly altered into a golden chain.

The *obi* held heavily jeweled *daisho*, or paired swords.

A flaming *kirin* decorated the samurai's *kabuto*. The horse-like creature danced about the helmet. It metamorphosed constantly, yet always remained a *kirin*. A *so-men* obscured the samurai's features. The armored iron mask bore a cold visage, with empty eyes, hideous smile and flowing yellow millet straw moustaches.

The warrior's voice gave lie to any impressions of terror. Although it was loud and thunderous and shook the air, it was oddly gentle and friendly. "You have many questions, Minamoto-no-Ichiro. I shall bring you answers. Follow me."

Ichiro moved to the bed's edge. He lowered his feet to the floor. The floor was hard, dark and freezing cold to the touch. His skin goose-fleshed from the sensation. An icy finger ran along his spine.

"You are cold. I ask your pardon for not being a better host," the warrior said. He pointed a long thin finger at the floor.

From the darkness a flickering shape appeared. It formed beneath the floor, growing more distinct as it reached the surface. There it became a pair of sandals woven from rushes and piped in red fabric. Ichiro placed his feet into the sandals. A warm tendril threaded its way into his body.

"Come. I will show you many things." The samurai gestured with a long *nabigata*. The spear's curved blade glinted with sunlight, but there was no sun.

The darkness did not vanish as they walked through it. It was an impenetrable and infinite curtain. Each step Ichiro took drew warmth from him. The darkness fed upon heat. Ahead of him, the samurai maintained a steady pace. At each step a column of cold vapors swirled about his feet. The footprints he left behind glowed red like live coals.

Ichiro, shivering, stepped into the footprints. Although their heat rapidly vanished, the footprints warmed the sandals and drove the cold from Ichiro's body. He suspected the samurai knew this. He wondered if the footprints' warmth refreshed whatever power the sandals possessed to drive away cold.

It seemed they walked for ages and made no progress. The darkness gave no clues by which to judge distance. For all Ichiro knew, they had gone nowhere or merely traveled in a circle, he could not tell.

His body grew tired. A dull pain began in his right leg. The leg throbbed until the ache became unbearable.

He faltered and fell behind. He found difficulty in maintaining a pace that allowed him to reach the footprints before they cooled. Soon he fell so far behind that the footprints were dark and lifeless. Pain lanced his leg at each step he took.

The samurai was now merely a small, fleeting figure, shrinking by the second.

"Wait, I beg you, please!" Ichiro shouted.

He stumbled. His hands stopped his fall, but the instant they touched the floor, they went cold and numb. He tried to regain his feet, but his body ached. He felt heavy, and he could not feel his feet or hands.

He gritted his teeth. The cold killed the pain. He cleared his mind and struggled upright. By now he no longer saw the samurai. Only the dying coals of the warrior's footprints remained. Ichiro wondered if he should press onward or wait for the warrior's return. He looked about him to see where he was.

Shapes lay outside the path. Ichiro walked toward one and bent down to examine it. It was white with hoarfrost and as immobile as a rock. He brushed away some of the frost and gasped in fear.

Beneath the frost was clear ice. Beneath the ice was a man's face, the eyes wide open in terror. Ichiro knew what the other shapes were. He knew also the samurai would not return this way, except with a new recruit.

He started walking.

Although the footprints cooled quickly, Ichiro saw that it took some time before the dark reabsorbed them. He watched them as they vanished, using that as a gauge to mark his progress. But even so, the footprints became fainter and fainter. He began relying on guesswork and faith. He whispered prayers to Hachiman and to Kannon, the *Bodhisattva* of Compassion.

The pain in his leg diminished, but stiffness and heaviness replaced it. With great effort, he dragged it clumsily along the floor.

He kept walking. He felt ice crystals form on his lips, felt the frigid air grasp him. At last, he could go no farther. The last vestige of his strength drained away. He sat down and waited for the cold to take him.

"You are a good choice, Minamoto Ichiro," the samurai said from the shadowy darkness. "You continued. You did not surrender. A rare courage. You cling tenaciously to hope. I knew you would do well."

Light surrounded Ichiro. The color of rich butter, its warmth returned life to his frozen and numbed limbs. He felt like he was floating in hot spring waters and drinking bowls of heated sake. Pain passed from his mind. The iciness drained from his hands and feet. All too soon the light and heat faded, but it left strength behind.

Ichiro felt refreshed. Energy abounded in him. He rose to his feet and found he now stood on a sunlit, featureless plain. He saw no horizon. He looked into the sky and found neither sun nor clouds. The sky itself was azure and bright, but it did not seem like day.

Ichiro lowered his gaze and saw he was in the middle of a circle. The circle was composed of ornate bamboo screens. Dragon motifs decorated the screens, as did paintings of sages, warriors and assorted *kami* and *bodhisattvas*. Wrought gold edged the screens.

An oddly shaped, short-legged *karabitsu* sat in the circle's precise center. Ichiro approached the lacquered box and tentatively touched it. He ran his hand over the surface. Smooth lacquer, carefully waxed and polished, greeted his touch. It felt neither hot nor cold.

Strange translucent levers of green, red, blue and yellow were set into the *karabitsu*. Mysterious dials marked in an indecipherable script blended with the surface. The dials puzzled him. They were clearly part of the elegant finish, but were also alien. In fact, even the delicate pearl inlay *horimono* that defined the box's perimeter were strangely alien. He wondered what the dials measured.

"What is this?" he asked, looking up to see if the giant samurai were there.

"You would not understand, my friend," the warrior replied. The samurai stepped through a bamboo screen, leaving it unharmed by his passage. He came to Ichiro's side. With a huge, armored hand, he reached out and moved a single crimson lever.

A hissing sound issued from the ground. Near one side of the circle, the floor turned to molten metal. From the bubbling mass, a jade ring stabbed upward. When it was completely exposed, the ring stopped. The floor beneath was solid once more.

His curiosity aroused, Ichiro examined the ring. It stood on edge, balanced on a decorated golden triangle. He touched it. Despite having passed through molten metal, the ring's rough surface was cool and moist. Indeed, it was almost slick with moisture. Within the ring, Ichiro saw flickering lights, like the flames of tapers madly dancing in a temple.

"You are correct. I do not know if I would understand," Ichiro said. He turned to the giant. "But then you have not bothered to tell me anything."

The samurai laughed. "That is true." He gestured with the *nabigata*. "Watch the circle, and you shall see."

The warrior swept the spear back to his side and manipulated more levers. Mists obscured the ring's center. Clouds swirled and lightning leaped in its midst, joined by thunderclaps. Slowly the mist coalesced into ghostly shapes.

The shapes were scenes of a mysterious world. Gigantic lizards slid through giant marshlands. Long sinuous necks dove beneath foul green waters and came up with rotting vegetation dripping from huge hideous mouths.

The mists thickened. The picture changed. Incredible aircraft appeared. Formed in various shapes, they flew among the night stars beyond the Earth's confines. They maneuvered in silence. On occasion, a craft spat a thread of light. The beam dissipated if it found no target, but if it made contact a fireball erupted in silence. Without a sound, one ship exploded as two beams struck it. Debris spun away wildly in all directions.

The mists returned. The scene altered again.

A reddish dust cloud blew across a wide desert. A figure struggled against the wind. The figure bore the features of a dog or a wolf. At the figure's side was a large cat-like creature loping on all fours. The creature was as huge as a tiger and unlike any cat Ichiro had ever seen.

The strange beings faded and were replaced by ships. It was the American fleet Ichiro had seen from his Zero. Aircraft battled in the sky above. Damaged, one fell away, trailing a ribbon of smoke and flame.

"I know this place," Ichiro cried. "It is Okinawa."

"All that you see is real," the samurai said. "There are many realities, many pasts, many presents, and many futures. Some are like your own world, differing in only minor ways. Others are as strange as you can imagine and even stranger still."

"Why are you showing me this?" Ichiro asked.

The samurai's masked countenance turned toward him.

"I show these things in part so you will be aware of them. But more importantly, they illustrate a principle.

"In all existence, there is balance. As male and female are equal parts in harmony, so it is in all reality. The *in* and the *yo* battle, power swings from one to the other. Kindness and cruelty are faces of the same force. Nothing can tear them apart.

"In this balance is maintained the precarious order of things. Should one or the other gain absolute power, total destruction would occur. Fortunately, in all these worlds these forces exist in uneasy communion. The pendulum swings and power flows from one to the other. So it is with all the worlds you glimpsed. So it is with your world."

The answer came to Ichiro. "Then there is one world where the balance is in danger."

The samurai nodded. He swept his hands across the levers. Within the jade ring the mists danced, spun and solidified.

A *shiro*, or fortified castle, appeared. Samurai fought on its battlements. A besieging army strove to overrun a paltry force of defenders, but the defenders' tenacity repeatedly repelled the attackers. The ground was crimson with blood. It ran in streams down the castle walls.

Within the city, starving villagers scraped paltry amounts of rice into wooden bowls. Their bloated bellies empty of food, malnourished children tried to cry but could not. In contrast, the Imperial Court was elegant. The young emperor and his family enjoyed watching actors perform a *kabuki* play.

"This world is like your own, Minamoto Ichiro," the warrior explained. "There is much suffering and injustice.

Ichiro started to speak, but the samurai raised a hand and silenced him.

"Yes, I know what you will say," the warrior said. "Injustice in this world is no different from injustice in every world. That is true. To correct injustice is the purpose of existence. What man would do otherwise?"

"But I assure you, this world is different. The outward signs of evil do not betray their source. In many worlds, men's actions alone create both good and evil. Because no man is stronger than all others are, no one gains complete power over the many. Thus balance is preserved.

"But in this world, the cause is more sinister. Many are assisted by outside forces. All those things which you call demons, spirits, monsters, wizards, as you wish, they are real in this world. These are fantasies, dreams, myths you only touch in the darkness of sleep."

"In this world, then, the balance has shifted?" Ichiro asked.

The samurai sighed. "For the moment, there is balance. But the forces of chaos grow stronger each day. The scale tips in their favor. Soon these forces will swallow reality as easily as a fish takes an insect from a pond's surface.

"And it will not stop there. The infection will spread. Other worlds will grow chaotic and collapse. Other worlds will grow orderly and stagnate. The balance will end. Reality will fall in upon itself, and neither chaos nor order will reign. Only vast wasteland and emptiness will remain."

Ichiro turned to the warrior. "Am I to restore this balance? If you have the power to pluck me from my world, surely you can restore the balance."

The samurai shook his head. A sad smile deemed to appear on his *so-men*. "Ah, my friend. I, like many others, may toy with the fabric of universes, but we cannot command them to our will. Chaos and order obey laws greater than the *kami* themselves. The laws are vast and unfathomable. We *kami* have great powers, but we too are part of the universe and must answer to those laws."

"Then how could you bring me here?" Ichiro asked. He grew impatient. He wanted answers and the *kami* only threw out a maze of words.

"I command many things, but those events have little bearing on the ebb and flow of a particular reality," the samurai said. "For example, your death meant little for your world. Events flowed whether you lived or died. Therefore I could remove you as easily as plucking a petal from a rose."

"But were I to directly tamper with your world, keep someone alive when he should be dead, it would prove disastrous. Lives would alter. Events that should occur might not. Possibly it could accelerate the process of chaos, or it might tip the balance in favor of stasis and death.

"Instead, we use agents whose actions can perhaps correct such things," the *kami* said.

"Agents such as me," Ichiro said. He now resented what had happened to him. No longer were events under his control. All of this was forced upon him, and he did not like it.

"So you have chosen me. But what of the others you chose, the frozen ones?"

"They lacked courage. When the time came for them to continue, the urge for death and surrender overcame them."

Ichiro was angry. "So you deliberately abandoned me, to test me."

The kami nodded. "Yes, but I had no choice. I need a warrior who will not surrender, whose urge to live overcomes his urge for death. You embody the balance I seek: bravery, but not foolhardiness. Male and female minds are within you, and you understand both their natures. You love both men and women with all your heart, yet you can hate them as passionately. You willingly accepted death, but you still fight for life. You are the perfect choice."

"And if I refuse?" Ichiro asked.

"Chaos will grow. And order also. They will grow until they destroy each other."

"You can find other agents."

"Perhaps. But so many fail. So few succeed."

"Then there are others."

"Yes," the samurai said. "But so few. They cannot fight the cancer alone."

The word cancer hung in Ichiro's mind. He felt a dull pain in his viscera. He saw a world-cancer, growing, consuming all reality, even itself.

"If I help you, what will you do for me? Straighten my leg? Cure my cancer?" Ichiro asked.

"I promise you nothing. I cannot alter the way you were born. I may slow the disease, but it may kill you eventually. I can give you one blessing. As long as you live in this world, no mortal man can kill you. I offer you nothing more, other than these gifts."

The samurai raised his hand and drew fire from the void. It crashed at his feet, bubbling and hissing like lava. As it cooled, it took shape as a suit of fine armor.

The armor rested on a teak frame. There was a *do-maru*, a cuirass with heavy armor plates bound with cords of crimson, blue and gold silk. There were *kote*, the armored sleeves, and *suneate*, the leg armor. For the feet and hands there were *kogake* and *tekko*. A *kabuto* decorated with hammered gold stars and dragons rested atop the armor.

The kami passed his hand over the neck of the *do-maru*. The *mon* of Ichiro's clan appeared on the armor. The enameled red circle with two pieces of small bamboo told everyone he was a Minamoto, descended from Yoritomo, the first shogun in all Japan.

"These are for you. Put them on," the samurai said.

Ichiro took the cuirass from the stand and strapped it on. The armor for sleeve, leg, hand and foot slipped on easily and became part of him. As he placed the *kabuto* on his head and tightened the chinstrap, he sensed that the armor was alive. So naturally did it fit his body that it felt as if he wore no armor at all.

"Excellent," the kami said admiringly.

"Armor is fine, but what good am I without weapons?" Ichiro said.

"This is true," the warrior replied. He raised his left arm and spread his huge fingers.

Flames leaped at his fingertips. They spread themselves thin and formed a *tachi*, or long-sword.

The samurai raised his right hand. Lightning coursed across his palm and formed a *tanto*, with a blade sharp enough to penetrate an enemy's armor. Together they formed the *daisho*, or paired swords. The *kami* handed Ichiro the swords. He placed them in the waistbands of his armor.

The warrior raised both his arms above his head. The *obi* about his waist reverted to its serpent form. The snake climbed the warrior's arm until its head lay in his left hand. He grabbed its tail with his right hand and held it skyward.

Its body stiffened. Its head spread into huge plum leaf. The plum leaf turned to glistening steel and its body to stout oak. The serpent was transformed to a *nagaki-yan*, or plum-leaf blade spear. The giant presented the spear to Ichiro.

Half afraid it would revert to its serpent form, Ichiro hesitantly took the spear from the samurai's grasp. But it felt light and easily maneuverable in his hands. He slid the spear through leather straps on the back of his cuirass.

"Examine the sword," commanded the kami.

Ichiro withdrew the *tachi* from its lacquered scabbard and examined the blade. Formed into the blade were *horimono*, engravings meant to tutor the sword's bearer. Some were of *sennin*, wise men armed with swords and the flame of knowledge. Near the hilt were the ideograms of the sacred Lotus Sutra. Ichiro turned the sword over and found a name engraved on the other side.

"Read it," the warrior ordered.

"Hachiman," Ichiro whispered.

He lowered his head in shame. "Forgive me, Hachiman. I meant no disrespect to my family's *kami*."

"There was no disrespect, Minamoto-no-Ichiro," Hachiman said. "You acted as I wished. You are my agent in this world. I will help you when I can, but you must fight your own battles. You must rely solely on your own wits."

"Thank you, Lord Hachiman," Ichiro said. He knelt before the *kami* and pressed his forehead to the ground.

He lifted his head and gazed up at the samurai. "Lord Hachiman, I am your servant, but how will I know my task?"

"Patience, Ichiro," Hachiman said. "Do not worry about finding it. It will find you, and you will know it then."

"I see."

"Come. Let me show you more of this world that is now yours."

Hachiman waved his right arm. The bamboo screens vanished. The plain had faded to darkness. Stars surrounded them. All that remained were the *karabitsu* and the jade ring. Within the ring the clouds danced and the world's history rolled away like waves on the angry sea. Emperor Jimmu conquered the barbarian Ainu. The Fujiwaras rose to power by marrying their daughters to princes. His ancestor Yoritomo defeated the Taira clan at the strait of Dan-no-Urra on the Inland Sea. Mongol hordes twice invaded Japan and twice were driven back by the Divine Wind, the first *Kamikaze*. The dwarfish Hideyoshi defeated the Koreans and captured the fertile land for his Emperor.

All of this was familiar to Ichiro.

But some things differed. European Christians watched Vienna fall to the Mongols and then the Turks. The American Commodore Perry did not arrive, for his America was a barely colonized land, squabbled over by the great European powers. Its settlers fought disease, the great Indian nations and each other.

And Japan, the legendary *Nihon*, was isolated. Civil war broke out. Armies ran rampant across the countryside, wielding swords and the power of great wizards. Everywhere was disorder until a new shogun arose and restored peace. But it was only tenuous.

"This is the world now," Hachiman said.

Peasants starved as renegade armies plundered their crops and butchered their livestock. The young Emperor sat impotently in his palace, where concubines, young boys, sycophants and ingratiating courtiers surrounded him. The Shogun's armies tried to maintain order, but they were powerless against swift and mobile bandit forces.

And always, there appeared the shadowy figure of a man, a man whose power controlled more evil than Ichiro knew he could imagine.

Ichiro felt uneasy. He knew this man waited for him. He also knew this man's name.

"The man I must destroy. His name is Taira," Ichiro said, turning to Hachiman.

The *kami* smiled sadly and nodded. "You will meet him when the time is right. Now, you must go." The *kami* stretched a long thin finger toward the ring.

The jade glowed. It expanded until it filled everything Ichiro could see. It drew him toward it. He could not control his actions. Again, he had no choice.

The ring engulfed him. Ichiro felt himself falling, twisting his body about in the air. He called for aid, crying "*Tasukete*!"

But Hachiman was no longer there. Instead he saw an old monk dressed in saffron robes, with a long gray beard and a shaved head. It was another face of the *kami*. Doubtless he was not only Hachiman, but also a Buddha. Or perhaps he was Izanagi, the father of all the gods. Ichiro did not know.

"You will see me next as this old man," the monk said. "But you will not recall me until later."

Ichiro called out, but the blackness overwhelmed him. He drifted for a moment, falling but not falling. Then the blackness gave way to sunlight and the warmth of a summer day.

He stood in the middle of a road. The ground under his feet was moist with a recent rain. A gentle breeze freshened the air with oleander. Green fields of millet and rice surrounded him.

A horse trotted toward him. It was saddled and bridled. Ichiro saw the saddle and stirrups bore his *mon*, the Minamoto clan's crimson crest with the image of small bamboo. The horse, a stallion, was another gift from Hachiman. He pressed his head against Ichiro's arm. Ichiro smiled and rubbed the horse's muzzle. He noticed a small mark between the animal's eyes. A small patch of fur formed the ideogram for "Luck."

Ichiro laughed. "I can't even choose your name then."

He looked toward the sky. "Very well, Hachiman, we'll have it your way. His name is *Luck*. I only hope he lives up to your expectations."

Taking the reins into his hands, Ichiro moved to the horse's side and mounted. Luck did not flinch under the rider's weight. He gently kicked the horse's flanks and started down the road.

Ahead Ichiro saw a formation of riders and *ashigaru*, peasant foot soldiers, coming toward him. Their flag fluttered madly in the wind. Its *mon* identified them as soldiers of the Emperor.

"Hachiman, you arrange strange welcomes," Ichiro said. "Let us meet our new allies, Luck," he said and spurred the horse toward the approaching army. Two years would pass before Hachiman arranged something other than a welcome.

CHAPTER THREE

The warrior charged Ichiro, sword raised high above his head. As he attacked, the warrior released a strangled cry intended to frighten his victim as well as aid his own courage.

It did neither.

The attacker brought his *katana* about in a less than graceful and smooth maneuver. He plunged forward like an onrushing, out-of-control water buffalo, legs and arms flailing about.

Ichiro waited until the warrior's sword swung about in a wide arc. He slipped to his right and parried the blade. Then he dropped to his right knee and thrust out his left leg.

His leg caught the attacker at the ankles, tripping him. Out of control, the man rocketed head over heels across the courtyard. He tumbled to an undignified halt against the trunk of a young cedar tree.

"Enough," the young warrior cried, exhausted. The attacker sat upright and removed his helmet and mask. "I should know better than to press a straightforward assault on you, Ichiro," the young Emperor said.

Ichiro removed his own helmet and mask. He crossed the courtyard to the Emperor. "The attack itself was not a poor one, Emperor. But you revealed your intentions too early. That allowed me adequate time for a defense."

The Emperor laughed. "I should be grateful the swords are only bamboo. I shouldn't like to become the *late* Emperor Saigo."

Ichiro smiled and helped the young man to his feet. "I apologize for my unorthodox defense, but in battle honorable forms of warfare are rarely respected." He rested his bamboo *kendo* sword in the crook of his arm. "I think this is enough for today. There is plenty of time later for lessons."

The Emperor pouted. "But not from you, Ichiro." Humor fled him. Now he was merely a hurt young man. "Do you still insist on leaving the Mikado, to become a *ronin*?

"Not a lordless samurai, Saigo," Ichiro said. "The Shogun is need of generals. The distant lords are always making trouble."

"What if I forbid you to go?" the Emperor said.

"It would do no good, my lord," Ichiro replied. "The Emperor reigns, but does not rule. You may forbid me from leaving, my lord, but you cannot stop me."

He removed his *kendo* armor and handed it to a page, who handed Ichiro his long-sword and scabbard. The page sped off to carry the armor to Ichiro's rooms.

Ichiro returned his *tachi* to its rightful place in his *obi*.

"I could have the guards restrain you," the Emperor said.

"And they would be dead at my feet before their swords could even stir the breeze," Ichiro said.

Dejected, the Emperor capitulated. "Yes, Ichiro. You are right." Frustrated, he slammed his bamboo sword against the cedar. The blade snapped and flew across the courtyard.

"Such anger does not become an Emperor," Ichiro said, gently admonishing the young ruler. He understood Saigo's anguish. He saw the pain in the Emperor's black eyes and the furrows creasing the youthful brow.

Shamed, Saigo hung his head. "It is unseemly, I know," He looked up at Ichiro. "But what am I to do? No one here is as expert at *kendo* as you. Only two or three ride as well, and maybe a handful approach your skill at archery. Life will be intolerably boring when you go."

Ichiro put his hand on Saigo's shoulder. "Emperor, you cultivate those flowers you have in your garden. I cannot teach you forever. Neither can you have a perfect rose forever. Learn to ride from the best riders and to shoot from the best archers. Find masters of *kendo*, of *aikido* and *jujitsu*. Where you had one great flower, cultivate ten."

"But I am so powerless," the Emperor protested. "The Shogun dictates to me. You dictate to me. Even Lord Akiyama dictates to me. I am not allowed to make any decisions for myself. Sometimes I feel like a puppet in a play."

Ichiro understood what Saigo was undergoing, but he could not find more compassion for him. It was not Saigo's choice to be emperor. But the Emperor was trapped by over a thousand years of privilege. He could not extricate himself from an imprisonment imposed by his birth.

Neither was it Ichiro's choice to leave. Ichiro knew if there were a reason to stay, he would have found it, but the day before he met a visitor to the capital, an old Buddhist monk and practitioner of Soto Zen. Ichiro chatted briefly with the man, and the monk said Ichiro should go to Edo because there was much work to be done there.

Ichiro realized afterward that the monk was Hachiman. As the *kami* had said, Ichiro did not at first recognize Hachiman. His appearance was the sign that it was time for Ichiro to leave the court. And as much as he cared for the Emperor, he owed fealty to Hachiman and had to obey the *kami's* wishes.

"We all have our duty, Saigo," Ichiro said. "We are prisoners of duty. We learn to accept our fate and work to change our karma in this life. Now I must go." Gently he pried the Emperor's clutching fingers from his jacket sleeve.

"You will speak to Akiyama before you leave?"

Puzzled, Ichiro stared at Saigo. "A last attempt to keep me here?"

Saigo nodded, glancing at the ground to avoid Ichiro's gaze. "But you will speak to him?"

"As you wish, my lord," Ichiro said. "But then I must go."

"And what will I do when you are gone?" Saigo asked.

"Your duty," Ichiro answered.

It pained him to leave the young man. He loved the Emperor as he loved his beautiful Yumiko and so many other friends and lovers. As he walked away, he heard Saigo sobbing quietly.

Ichiro gritted his teeth and tried to withhold the tears he could feel rolling down his own cheeks.

———

Ichiro waited outside the doorway to Lord Akiyama's quarters.

"Come in, General," Akiyama said flatly. He did not look up from his writing desk.

Ichiro stepped into the room. "I am here as the Emperor requested, my lord."

Akiyama looked up from his work and gestured toward some cushions. "Please, be seated." It was not a request, but a command.

Ichiro bowed and then sat. He folded his legs carefully under him. Because he had no time to change clothes or bathe, he was acutely aware that he was drenched with perspiration. He hoped Akiyama would not notice his unpleasant body odor. No doubt the pungent perfume and incense with which Akiyama inundated his rooms would mask the smell.

"You must forgive me, Lord Akiyama. I was instructing the Emperor in fencing. At his request," Ichiro said.

"I understand," Akiyama replied. "You do not have to tell me, Minamoto." The noble continued with his work.

Ichiro rested his hands on his legs and leaned forward to scrutinize Akiyama. The nobleman made broad brush strokes on a rice paper scroll with his right hand while his left hand absent-mindedly tapped a fan against the desk top. It beat out a tattoo only Akiyama understood.

Lord Akiyama was a tired man, an aging man. He no doubt knew his useful days were long past for the most part. Now he was relegated to playing wet nurse for a brash Emperor a fifth his age. Akiyama reportedly resented Saigo, despised his youth, his love of swordsmanship, hunting, riding and music. In his own youth, the noble was said to excel in those fields, now all denied him.

But if he was quiet on many things, Akiyama made no secret of his displeasure that Saigo had produced no heir. But Ichiro knew the

Emperor loathed his wife, Akiyama's granddaughter. In fact, Saigo loathed most of his concubines as well. Ichiro wondered if Akiyama knew the Emperor preferred the company of young men and of serving maids to that of pretty but all too often empty-headed and tittering noblewomen.

All of this made Akiyama's eclipse deeper and more humiliating. Add to that the make-up the nobleman wore on his face and hands, and he was more and more like the tragic Fool in a *kyogen* play. Of course, other courtiers also wore white powder and rouge, but only Akiyama was hiding the ravages of a skin disease that afflicted his entire body. Assorted quacks professing cures were always bringing Akiyama balsams, unguents and lotions. But the disease remained unchecked. Sooner or later, it would force him to spend his days a complete invalid, immersed in a mineral water bath.

The disease meant that Akiyama grew bitter and more dangerous. But disease or not, the lord was still powerful. He was envious of everyone and trusted no one. That was why he remained so long in power while others perished or were exiled.

"So warm," Akiyama muttered, opening his fan and shaking it briskly before his face. He motioned to a servant standing outside the doorway. "Bring tea. It will cool the body."

The servant bowed and left.

Akiyama adjusted his black *sotai*. He wore the bulky robes of state not just to denote his office, but also because their loose form created air pockets that cooled his skin.

"The Emperor is fond of you, Minamoto," the noble said. "He tells you things in confidence that even I am not party to." He smiled. It was a thin smile through grotesque red lips. "Perhaps that is a good thing. The Emperor is brash and headstrong. In many ways, he is very fool-hardy. He needs discipline to bring his nature under control. You are necessary to such discipline."

Ichiro sighed and rested his weight on one arm. He had not antici-pated this. Although he did not blame Akiyama, he hardly expected the man to present such an apparently sincere case. Ichiro knew Akiyama was otherwise probably quite glad to see him leave. And if he were Akiyama, no doubt he would feel the same way.

"Lord Akiyama, I know you wish me to stay, for the Emperor's benefit," Ichiro said. "But I have reasons for leaving. I have grown tired of the Court. I am a warrior, and I seek a warrior's destiny."

"General Minamoto, you know what the Emperor was like before you befriended him. He was uncontrollable. He acted like a child, not like a divine god on earth. If you had not come, I surely would have strangled him myself," Akiyama said.

No doubt with great pleasure, Ichiro thought.

"It would have been best for all Nihon," Akiyama said. "But since you arrived to command his armies, he has grown calm. Yet there remains much to do. I beseech you to stay."

There was no conviction in Akiyama's voice. What Ichiro first took for sincerity was simple court courtesy. Akiyama mouthed these words, like a competent *kabuki* actor performing his part and making his exit.

"I came here two years ago, Lord Akiyama," Ichiro said. "In that time I have achieved little. Oh yes, I led the Emperor's armies in support of the Shogun's wars. I taught the Emperor *kendo* and archery. But this is all of no consequence. It keeps me from my duty in life."

"And what is that duty? Is it greater than the Emperor's?" Akiyama said. Venom now tinged his voice. Then, aware that Ichiro sensed his contempt, Akiyama changed his tone. The red lips curled back in a smile, exposing blackened teeth.

"I apologize for my disrespect, general. I have many worries. If my darker nature sometimes shows, please forgive me. Nothing is meant by it," Akiyama said.

"No offense was taken, lord," Ichiro said. Such a liar Akiyama was, so deceitful and sly. He could feel the noble's hatred spreading like a poison throughout his body. Ichiro shifted position to more directly confront Akiyama.

The noble flinched. Being placed in a position of weakness did not appeal to him. "Where is that fool boy with the tea?" he said.

"My purpose is long assigned. My karma decrees I must act," Ichiro said.

"Have we not all some purpose?" Akiyama said. Perspiration beaded on his brow. He cooled himself with his fan. "I have a duty to serve the Emperor. Surely yours is the same."

"I swear allegiance to the Emperor, but I owe him nothing more," Ichiro said.

The servant delivered the tea. He poured a bowl of steaming green tea from a cobalt blue ceramic pot and handed it to Akiyama. The noble sipped the tea, then nodded his approval and dismissed the boy.

Akiyama placed the bowl of tea on his writing desk. "Beware, my impetuous friend. In some quarters there are those who think such words as yours are treasonous."

"I mean no treason. But there are things I know that no one else may understand," Ichiro said.

Angered, Akiyama slapped his fan against the desktop. It rattled the tea bowl. "Are you saying I am ignorant of affairs of state?" the noble said.

Ichiro resisted a smile. He had gained the upper hand. Akiyama was flustered. "Oh no, my lord," he said soothingly. "Forgive me if it seemed I implied that. What I meant is there are things I know because I was born in a place you will never see."

"*Yai*, now you tell me fairy tales! I am not a child, general," Akiyama sat back on his cushions and resumed fanning himself.

Ichiro sighed. "Ah, Lord Akiyama, if only it were just a tale. Then I would sleep in my grave as I was intended."

Akiyama stopped fanning himself. "What do you mean? In your grave?"

"In the world of my birth, I am a dead man. I died there two years ago, but was brought here instead." He leaned forward and stared into Akiyama's now uneasy face. "Think back, my lord. I appeared two years ago, but who had heard of me before that?"

Akiyama started to speak but thought better of it. He tapped his fan into his palm. Fretful lines appeared in his brow, made more prominent by his make-up.

"All you have is legend, my Lord Akiyama. Legend, hearsay and outright lies," Ichiro continued. "And remember what the Emperor's soldiers said when they first encountered me. They said I appeared from a whirlwind such as they had never before seen."

Akiyama wiped his forehead with a napkin. "Yes, I see. It is true no one had heard of you. But it was obvious you were of noble birth. You were descended from Yoshitsune, the scholars and priests said. They said you were born in the great fortress he built in China."

Ichiro shook his head. "Oh no, my lord. But in the world of my birth, men travel the sky in metal kites driven by great motors. Iron ships cross the sea, powered by the fire of dragons. In that world, I was a warrior who flew those metal kites. My duty was to die for Nihon, although our cause was lost."

"But Hachiman spared me. I did not die, but I awoke in this world. I was brought here for a purpose,"

"Again, you tell me tales for children!" Akiyama exclaimed. He edged back, trying to avoid Ichiro. "General, I do not understand you. One moment you are reasonable, but the next you prattle like a madman."

"I assure you, my lord, I am not mad," Ichiro replied. He unsheathed his tachi.

Akiyama cried out and jumped backward. He knocked his desk over, spilling tea and ink across the woven mats.

"Do not be alarmed, my lord," Ichiro said. He righted the lacquer desk and placed his sword on it. "Now, pick up my sword," he said.

Akiyama, still startled, hesitated for a moment, but then reached out. His fingers touched the hilt, then he cried out and pulled his hand back.

"Ice! It is as cold as ice!" Akiyama cried, blowing on his frozen fingers.

"True," Ichiro said. He picked up the sword and touched its tip to a bamboo screen.

The screen smoldered and blackened. A wispy tendril of smoke rose from it. The acrid odor of burning bamboo filled the room despite Akiyama's perfume and incense.

"Strange, is it not, how a sword as cold as ice can burn bamboo?" Ichiro said. He returned the sword to Akiyama's desk. "Now, my lord, pick it up. I assure you, it is neither hot nor cold."

Cautiously the noble leaned forward. He grasped the *tachi's* hilt and tried to lift it. The sword would not move. Akiyama placed both hands on the sword and strained to pick it up. Again it refused to rise from the desktop. Defeated, Akiyama sat back on his cushions. Perspiration streaked his make-up.

Ichiro returned the sword to its scabbard.

"I saw writing on the blade," Akiyama said, awed by what he had seen. "Strange *horimono*. And a name."

"There are many names on the blade, my lord. Most prominent is Hachiman, the *kami* of my clan. Mine, for another, because it is now my sword. No other may wield it without dire consequences."

"General, I thought all you said were lies. I was wrong," Akiyama said, wiping his brow with a napkin and smearing his white make-up. He shook his head, still unsure. "*Mah, mah*, I am old and prone to suspect and doubt."

"Lord Akiyama, you have done what you believed you must do. That is your duty, as you have said." Ichiro rose to go. "Now, I must do mine."

"Wait, General," Akiyama said. "This duty… can the Emperor perhaps assist you in its fulfillment?"

Ichiro shook his head. "No, my lord. I do not know myself precisely what it is. I must find it alone. Hachiman told me I must go. I will find my duty when it finds me."

"Will you find it with the Shogun?" the noble asked.

Ichiro smiled. "Perhaps. His armies travel all Nihon and cross the seas to Korea and Manchuria. Perhaps my karma lies there. Perhaps not. But I cannot languish here. And now, farewell, Lord Akiyama."

He gave Akiyama a cursory bow and left. As he left, Ichiro knew he would meet the old noble again under less friendly circumstances. No doubt the lord would say it was for the good of Nihon. Akiyama, too, was a victim of duty, but his duty was to himself.

But all too often such victims became victimizers, Ichiro thought. Behind his white powder facade, Akiyama grew more powerful each day and his machinations became more complex. Ichiro expected trouble from Akiyama again.

———

Saigo was waiting for him outside in the courtyard. He had dried his tears, but his eyes were still red-rimmed.

"I hoped Old Death-Face would talk you out of leaving," the Emperor said, trying to laugh. "I've heard it said he could win an argument with a stone and convince it to move from his path so he would not have to go around it." New tears betrayed his feigned joviality.

"Akiyama did not win this argument, Saigo," Ichiro said softly. He took a napkin from his kimono and wiped a tear from the Emperor's cheek. Then he turned and left the courtyard without a word, but with more pain and sorrow than he had ever known before.

CHAPTER FOUR

I chiro began to regret his decision to leave the safety of the Tokaido Post Road and to journey overland to Edo. But it was too late to change his mind. Nightfall approached, and any attempt to return to the main highway was foolhardy. Certainly the woods teemed with ninja and with *ronin* turned brigands. Even as skilled a swordsman as he was, Ichiro was uncertain that Hachiman's grace would protect him against ten or twenty bandits.

His only option now was to find a bed in the first village he encountered and perhaps content himself with a bowl of *sake* and a meal of rice cakes. That would ease the ache he felt from the long ride. His thoughts of rice cakes vanished as the stench of burnt straw and rice reached his nostrils. It drifted across the foothills and mingled with the moist summer air and with something else, the odor of decay, of rotting flesh. It offended his nostrils, even though they were used to the fetid smells of Kyoto's seamier districts.

Ichiro crested a rise and gazed out on a long, narrow valley. A village lay on the other side, nestled between a meandering stream and a grove of ancient *matsu* trees. The pines stood gaunt and thin above the villagers' huts, as ominous and foreboding as the burnt fields spreading out across the valley.

Obviously this was not a village in which to spend the night, Ichiro realized. But the swift approach of dusk left him no alternative. He drew Luck and Fortune, his pack horse, to a halt and dismounted. After tying the animals' reins to a stunted and twisted pine, Ichiro left the trail and walked toward a scorched millet field. Behind him, the horses grazed on the few stalks of millet and straw left untouched by the fire.

In spite of the evening's warmth, a chill pervaded his body. The air itself seemed possessed by a *mononoke* and that evil spirit appeared intent on controlling all who entered the valley. Ichiro resisted an urge to flee, to return to the main road, ninjas be damned.

He kept walking. His right leg, stiff from riding, dragged behind slightly. It gave him a lop-sided gait. Every so often he stopped and brushed away layers of ash. The dark gray particles billowed like sinuous thunderclouds, then fell slowly earthward.

Even the ground was scorched. The fire had been powerful and intense indeed. *It almost possesses a life of its own,* he thought, *consuming and consuming until nothing is left. And even then it does not seem to have died out.*

Then he saw the blackened trunk of a small sapling thrusting itself from the soil. Ichiro withdrew his *tachi* and gently tapped the tree. Ash fell away and revealed something black and oily. White bone appeared beneath the ash. The sapling's tiny branches, Ichiro now saw, were fingers. Two were curled under, two were twisted and broken. If there had been thumb, it was there no longer.

A round rock lay at his feet. He lifted it free with the tip of his sword. A skull grinned with a mouth of brown and broken teeth, and few of those at that. The skull and arm made it clear that Ichiro's decision to avoid the highway was not fortuitous. He felt an uneasy knot in his stomach, gnawing away at him. It was not fear, he knew, just a realization that only a fool would remain here without good reason.

Then he realized he had more than good reason to remain. Hachiman had drawn him here. If this were Hachiman's maneuverings, then Ichiro would find his purpose. *But what if this is a malevolent kami's doing?* he wondered. Was it intent on his destruction? He did not know.

The samurai's duty was to correct injustice. Clearly something unjust had happened here. Ninjas and brigands now seemed irrelevant. Ichiro chose to stay. He returned to the horses and untethered them. He mounted Luck, eased his sore right foot into the horse's stirrup and rode to the village.

As he rode he saw black mounds lying in the fields. Carrion crows pecked at some, pulling away slivers of red meat. He could not imagine what force had ravaged these people. *Tencho* was unlikely. Divine punishment was far too severe for simple peasants. This smacked of a man's vengeance. *Cruelty is always easier for men than for gods,* Ichiro thought.

He started wishing for help. "Perhaps some winged *tengu*, Hachiman? You spared a few to teach Yoshitsune *kendo* and archery. No?"

Naturally, no such luck. Like all *kami*, Hachiman was being uncooperative when truly needed, except as it befitted his needs or whims.

A small wooden bridge crossed the stream. The stream separated the millet fields and pasture land from the village and the flooded rice paddies.

Ichiro stopped halfway across the bridge. He was weary and ill at ease, and the stillness of the stream did not console him. It was *too* quiet. There were no *ajiro* set upright to catch fish in their nets. There were no boats, no casting lines, no hand nets. There were not even small racks to dry fish.

It struck him as odd. The stream, almost a river, was wide and deep, a most excellent breeding ground for fish. No village could turn down such a blessing. Yet here it was, unused and untouched.

Ichiro continued his journey. He reminded himself to make an offering in the local temple before starting off tomorrow. Some poppy seeds, or perhaps a rice cake, might assuage whatever force had ravaged this land.

The village's flimsy bamboo and straw huts appeared deserted as he rode past, but he saw frightened and suspicious eyes peering from behind shutters or glancing around doorways.

Each gaze felt like it could sear his flesh. He expected this. He was a stranger. The cut of his *kimono* and his bundled armor identified him as a samurai. The villagers probably thought he was a *ronin* and a dangerous swordsman or perhaps a *ninja* lord. By all rights, they should fear him and hide whatever riches they had, even as poor as field mice as they were. The braver ones might harbor thoughts of killing him, either to protect the village or gain his riches for themselves.

He drew up before a small shrine and dismounted, tying the horses to an iron ring projecting from the entrance. The shrine honored the Amida Buddha, the protector of travelers. If the villagers saw him make offerings to the Buddha, perhaps they would not fear him, Ichiro thought.

He washed his face in the water trough set before the Amida Buddha's *shintai*. The Buddha's image smiled beatifically from its wall niche. Ichiro took a drink from the altar bowl and knew he could spend the night within the shrine if need be. There he would have some amount of safety.

Someone had placed rice cakes on the altar, the appropriate offering for the Butsu. It was also understood a needy traveler should partake of them. But Ichiro was not needy. So what to do? He reached into his kimono and withdrew a packet of rice cakes. Breaking one in half, he placed one portion on the altar and ate the other half.

Perhaps the villagers would see this. As he had made his own offering, they might then interpret that to mean he was simply a traveler passing through who had no intention of robbing them. On the other hand, they might think he had some riches and would rob him.

"You are most welcome in our village, kind sir," a voice said behind him.

Instinctively, Ichiro dropped his left hand to the tachi's hilt as he turned to face the speaker.

A bent and withered man faced Ichiro in the shrine's doorway. His head was bald and liver-spotted. Wrinkles creased his face and a whisper of a goatee sprouted from his narrow chin. He wore *hakama* patched at the knees and a thin *karaginu*, or short-sleeved jacket.

"Please, honorable sir, do not draw your sword," the man said in halting tones. Fear was in his eyes. "We intend you no harm, but perhaps you may understand our fears. If you have come to rob us, take what you wish and leave us alone."

Ichiro's hand fell away from the sword. "Old man, I am not a robber, only a weary traveler," he said with a smile. "I am going to Edo and have ridden many hours. All I seek is some food and a place to sleep. I intend your village no harm."

Ichiro adjusted his kimono and sat on the edge of the altar. He suddenly felt weary and tired. "If you wish, sir, I will spend the night within the Butsu's shrine. I will leave in the morning to continue my journey, I promise you."

"Pardon my suspicion, honorable sir," the old man said, bowing slightly. "But much evil has befallen our village. You have seen our plundered and burnt fields and the bodies of those who resisted. Even our stream is robbed of its fish."

The old man's words touched Ichiro's heart. He whispered a prayer to Kannon, the *bodhisattva* of compassion. "You have suffered long enough, kind sir. I will trouble you not. The shrine is lodging enough for me."

The man raised his head. His eyes were sad and rheumy, like those of an aged dog. "I am called Gidayu, most honored sir. I am *jito*, although I have little to be village master of. It would honor me if you would spend the night in my wretched home. What little fish, rice, tea and *sake* I have is yours."

Ichiro bowed, moved at this act of generosity. "I am honored, Gidayu. But let me provide the fish and rice. A bowl of *sake* is gift enough for me."

"*Arigato*, you honor me," the *jito* said. "And what should I call you, honored sir?"

"You may call me..." Ichiro paused for a moment. Something told him anonymity was preferable at this time. *Better let the villagers think I am just a humble ronin,* he thought. "You may call me Kochi."

"East wind? A most unusual name!" Gidayu said.

Ichiro rose to his feet. "I come to your village as unbidden as the east wind. My name is unimportant," he said.

"Very well," the *jito* said. "Now, most honorable Kochi, you honor me beyond all time by staying in my home." He turned slowly and walked from the shrine.

Ichiro followed after a moment. *Why had he chosen to call himself Kochi?* he wondered. *A trick of Hachiman's perhaps, to protect him in this dangerous land?* Certainly it was advisable that few people know he was Minamoto-no-Ichiro, general of the Emperor's armies.

He was now as legendary as was his ancestor Yoshitsune. A warrior, with a twisted leg and club foot, who wields his sword in his left hand was not easily forgotten. And there were plenty of persons willing to challenge a legend. *Yes, the longer I keep my identity a secret, the better it is,* he thought, *at least until I reach Edo.*

———

Gidayu's home was simple, yet more luxurious than the other dwellings in the village. Those were merely hovels, barely resisting the wind and the rain. The *jito's* home was made of strong stone, cut from quarries or carried from the stream. Ichiro could see that skilled *ishidaiku* had cut those stones.

But even it showed the ravages of time and turmoil. Its rice paper windows were torn and only a few were replaced. Holes in the thatching opened to the sky. Ichiro watched the stars through them and worried about rain.

However, the dwelling was spacious, pleasant and dry. A small *hibachi* warmed the home. Rice boiled in an iron kettle above the brazier and a *sake* jar was heating in the coals. The coals themselves burned red hot under a dusting of gray ash. The house offered Ichiro a night with some measure of peace and quiet.

He undid his belongings from his packhorse and carried them inside. He dropped his bundle in a corner.

A piece of oil cloth fell from the *mon* it was covering, momentarily exposing the lacquered symbol. Ichiro quickly replaced it.

He looked up and saw Gidayu watching him. Ichiro hoped the man failed to recognize the clan symbol of the Minamoto, but he had the nagging suspicion that Gidayu was more adept at heraldry than the head of a small village should be. But if the *jito* knew what the red circle and the small bamboo meant, he did not show it.

Gidayu smiled and bowed slightly. "I will get you some *sake*, friend Kochi," he said. The *jito* turned to tend the fire in the brazier.

The man's constant bowing and politeness suddenly bothered

Ichiro. And now the fellow was calling him "friend Kochi," and not just "honorable sir"! Ichiro shook his head, not knowing what to think. There was certainly more to this village master than one would expect to find.

They dined on a meal of rice with radishes and red millet. Ichiro provide rice cakes filled with black bean paste and some strips of dried fish in soy sauce. Gidayu devoured the fish like a starved man. Afterwards, he poured the warmed *sake* into two earthenware bowls.

"I am sorry my humble meal was not worthy of a samurai such as yourself," Gidayu said. He brought the bowl to his lips and sipped some of the rice liquor. "But we have so little, such ills have befallen us."

"Yes," Ichiro replied. He stretched out on a straw mat and drank a small quantity of *sake*, savoring its flavor. It was a fine quality liquor, slightly sweet.

"How did such a terrible fire start?" he asked. "Was it a fire demon?"

"Oh, if it had only been a fire demon," Gidayu said. "A demon the priests could easily exorcise. But a human hand is far harder to drive away."

"*Yoi!* I thought there was some intelligence behind this destruction," Ichiro said. "Who was it, a wizard?"

"It was Lord Taira's soldiers," Gidayu said.

Taira! Ichiro was not surprised to hear the name of his clan's traditional enemy. He had guessed as much in Hachiman's realm. But, still, it was disturbing to think that the Taira, wiped out to the last man in the sea at Dan-no-Urra in his world, could still exist 800 years later in this world.

More disturbing was that Lord Taira apparently controlled great powers. Ichiro ran his thumb across his lips and thought of the consequences of such magic.

"The *daimyo's* men destroy those villages who do not or cannot pay tribute. Resistance is futile. The bodies in our fields show the truth of that," Gidayu said.

"I do not know this Taira. Is his army large? Does he oppose the Emperor?" Ichiro asked.

The *jito* shook his head. "Of that knowledge I am ignorant. His armies ride into the valleys, steal what they need, and leave.

"We were once united against him, but we were defeated. The *daimyo* himself led the attack. He possesses some power that caused us all to flee in the face of battle. We ran in panic, and Taira's forces harvested us like ripe millet. Then he sent his *ryu* to burn our village.

"A dragon?" Ichiro said. He stifled a laugh, remembering how amused he often was when empty-headed courtiers and fraudulent learned men would lecture on how dragons rarely came among men. The force of the earth around human beings often pulled dragons to their death, the self-proclaimed experts said. As for a man to command a dragon, it was unheard of, they added.

"Do not laugh, kind Kochi," Gidayu said. His tone was reprimanding, his expression now stern. "What you know of *ryu* is limited. You are a man of the city, I know, and city dwellers scoff at dragons."

"That is possible," Ichiro admitted, although he was still amused.

Gidayu's burning gaze wiped the trace of a smile from Ichiro's face. The samurai stared at the ground and sipped his sake, now ashamed for his laughter. "I ask your pardon, Gidayu. Indeed, all I know of dragons I learned as a child. I ask you to educate me."

The *jito* adjusted his position on his *tatami*. There was a certain pride in his presentation, like that of an aged scholar attending a student who truly wishes to learn.

"As even a child knows, dragons live in the sky. Their breath creates the clouds that bring rain for the meager crops of poor farmers such as we. Their breath also brings the *inabikari*, and that lightning causes the rice to ripen. In all things, the dragon protects the farmer."

Ichiro set on up and leaned on one elbow. "But if *ryu* protect the farmer, then why did this one burn your crops?"

"Ah," Gidayu said, smiling. He was obviously delighted with the question. The *jito* gestured with a finger. "Although dragons live in heaven, they sometimes come to earth. But when he touches the earth a *ryu* become as mortal as we and may be possessed by a *mononoke*. Then that evil spirit may use the dragon as it wishes."

"Then this dragon is possessed," Ichiro said.

"Precisely, friend Kochi."

Ichiro finished the last of the sake in his bowl and poured himself some more. "Is Lord Taira a *mononoke* then?"

Gidayu brought his fingers to his lips, indicating Ichiro should say no more. "I do not know. But the troubles did not begin until Lord Taira become *daimyo* two years ago. He is a cruel man and dangerous. I do not doubt he already knows of your presence."

The *jito* furrowed his brow and gestured toward Ichiro with a long, thin finger. "Evil follows him, Kochi. Though the wind that brought you here may be as divine as the *kamikaze*, you should not tarry with Lord Taira."

"I see," Ichiro replied. Part of his mind believed the old man's talk was ludicrous. But another part was not unconvinced. Taira's presence was foreordained.

Ichiro felt a chill envelope his body despite the warmth of the summer night. His right leg grew stiff and painful, as it often did in winter. He sensed the presence of something cold, black and foreboding. It touched him, and he felt the edge of fear.

Greetings, Lord Taira, I am pleased to meet you, Ichiro thought.

The presence fled.

Ichiro smiled. Warmth returned to his body.

"You must forgive me, Gidayu," he said. "But I should like to retire. I am weary from my ride and my leg gives me much pain."

Gidayu seemed disappointed that the conversation was ended. "Oh, no, you should forgive me." He rose unsteadily to his feet, warmed by too much sake and too much talk. "I talked far too long. My addled meandering surely bored you."

"Oh, no, far from it," Ichiro replied. "Gidayu, your words were most enlightening. I suspect a *kami* brought me here for a purpose. Now I believe I know that purpose. For that knowledge, you have my grateful thanks."

This pleased the old man. He smiled. "I leave you now. Sleep well." Gidayu passed through a doorway into an anteroom and drew curtains across to separate Ichiro from the rest of the house.

Ichiro doused the lamps and settled down for the night. He stretched out on the straw *waroda*, laid his head on the wooden pillow, and closed his eyes. But he could not sleep. He turned over the events of the day in his mind and examined them for meaning. He had left the Emperor's court and its pleasant decadence to fulfill his duty to Hachiman. But now he was regretting that decision.

"When will you leave me alone?" he whispered to the darkness.

"Not until you are dead, Minamoto-no-Ichiro," came the reply, deep within his consciousness, "and not even then."

Voices in the next room drew his attention. They were whispers, tinged with anger and fear. He lay quietly and listened. One voice he identified as Gidayu. The other he had not heard before. It was an old woman's voice, most likely the *jito's* wife.

"I do not want him in our house," the old woman hissed. Her voice was rich with anger. "He is a *samurai*; worse, he is a *ronin*! He brings trouble with him. Lord Taira will think we have hired him. He will send his dragon to burn our houses this time!"

"Foolish woman, be quiet! You'll wake him!" Gidayu said.

Ichiro smiled. *Poor Gidayu*, he thought.

"I tell you, he is the one," the *jito* said. "He is General Minamoto. I saw the symbol on his armor!"

So, the jito did know more than he let on! Ichiro thought.

"He has the twisted leg and the left-handed sword!" Gidayu continued. "The blood of Yoshitsune flows in him, and Hachiman protects him. He is Minamoto-no-Ichiro, woman. It is said no man can kill him!"

"I still do not trust him," the woman countered. "It is said he is not like other *samurai*. No one knows where he came from, but I have heard his father was his mother's own brother!"

That was a story Ichiro had not heard before. He was intrigued and amused.

"And it is well known he prefers the company of both young women and young men in his bed," the woman said.

"And what of it? Oh, Masako, you act like a superstitious old man instead of a sensible woman. Be reasonable. He comes to us and calls himself Kochi. East wind! Surely that is a sign, a good omen. Hachiman himself has delivered the General to us. We have not been forsaken."

So, my masquerade is over, Ichiro thought. *No longer am I Kochi, if*

I had even been Kochi to these people, Ichiro thought. *The jito under-stood the whims of kami very well.* Hachiman had indeed delivered him to these people. He pondered the situation and rubbed his chin, feeling the stubble of beard.

Ichiro reminded himself to burn a few poppy seeds as an offering for Hachiman. Then he cursed the *kami's* meddling ways. He turned on his side and slept.

———

Taira's men came with the dawn.

Ichiro was waiting for them. He stood in the middle of the road that ran through the village. The tachi rested in its scabbard, but his hand rested on the hilt. His bow and a quiver full of arrows rode high on his back, awaiting use.

There were three samurai riding three large bays. The horses' hooves clattered on the wooden bridge as they crossed the stream.

The riders were fully armored, while Ichiro wore only his kimono. He felt like a schoolboy who had worn the wrong clothing for a special occasion and could not save face without appearing a fool. But Ichiro knew the armor would also slow the warriors down, perhaps enough to give his sword the advantage.

He could detect no expression on the riders' faces. Their features seemed rigid, fixed and cold as stone. As they drew closer, the reason grew clear.

Each warrior wore a *so-men*. The iron masks were painted in the manner of a *Noh* actor's make-up. Their mouths' gaped in silent *banzai* beneath golden horsehair moustaches that sprang out between lip and nostril. The *so-men* were intended to arose fear, and perhaps they would frighten an already terrified peasant. But Ichiro had seen far more ghastly faces on dead comrades. By comparison, the iron masks were merely ludicrous.

The horsemen drew up eight horse-lengths from Ichiro and halted. For a moment time seemed to stand still.

"*Hitocku! Hitocku!*" screamed a thrush in a nearby oak tree.

Yes, indeed, someone is coming, my fine friend. Only you are several minutes too late to be of use, Ichiro thought.

The middle samurai reined his horse forward. The animal moved in a slow, deliberate stride. The rider tugged at the reins and brought the horse to a halt an arm's length from Ichiro. The horse's breath was heavy and strong, its body glistening with perspiration. The odor offended Ichiro's nostrils.

"You are Minamoto-no-Ichiro," the rider said. It was not a question. The rider spoke in a voice that was thick and awkward, as if something were blocking his windpipe.

"I am Minamoto," Ichiro replied. "Who asks my name?"

"I speak for my *daimyo*, Lord Taira." Again, the labored, viscous voice.

Ichiro smelled a faintly acrid odor, like putrefaction, drifting toward him. It seemed to emanate from the rider himself.

"What does your lord wish of me?" he asked.

"To speak to you. You are well known in these islands. Lord Taira wishes only to meet such a famed samurai."

"And if I decline to come with you?"

"We are not to return without you."

"And if I resist?"

"We are to bring you back by force, if necessary."

Ichiro smiled. "And if I still will not come?"

"We are to bring your head. Lord Taira at least wishes to see your face."

Ichiro unsheathed his sword and launched himself at the samurai.

Startled, the warrior's horse reared, throwing its rider to the earth. But not before Ichiro's sword had cut the man in two at the waist. The *tachi* cut through flesh as easily as it would cut rice paper. The sword found the armor's weakness and exploited it.

Indeed, the ease of the attack perplexed Ichiro even as the other riders bore down on him.

He ran toward the horses, cursing his limp. But he used his handicap to his advantage. He ducked beneath the slashing blade of first one rider, then the other. He somersaulted and came back to his feet with the lightness of an acrobat.

In their turn, the riders were slow in bringing their horses about. It gave Ichiro time to unsling his bow. Quickly, he notched an arrow and drew back on the bowstring.

But the riders changed their tactics. Instead of attacking together, they delayed, then one rider alone charged Ichiro. The samurai raised his *katana* above his head, ready to strike at Ichiro's neck. He rose up in his saddle to gain a better position.

Ichiro released the arrow. The razor sharp *ya* shot from the bowstring and went straight through the hideous gash of a mouth in the samurai's iron mask. The rider's head jerked back suddenly and snapped like dry twigs.

To Ichiro's surprise, he watched the head roll away from the rider's shoulders. The sword fell from the rider's grasp and tumbled harmlessly to the earth. His headless body joined it moments later.

Ichiro did not notch another arrow. The last rider was already upon him. The samurai's sword blade whistled through the still morning air. Instinctively, Ichiro dropped to one knee and raised his bow to deflect the sword blow. The *katana* missed the bow, but sliced cleanly through the bowstring as the rider thundered past.

Ichiro rolled over and came to his feet, the *tachi* unsheathed once more. He set himself for the attack.

The samurai wheeled about and charged.

Even as the samurai bore down on him, Ichiro realized there were no sounds save the clash of swords, the thunder of horses' hooves and his own shouts. Despite the intensity of the battle, the three samurai were all eerily silent.

The samurai was upon him, sword glinting in the sun. Ichiro parried the attack and spun about. His *tachi* continued until it found its mark.

With unerring skill, he cut the tendons in the horse's hind legs. Horse and rider crashed to the ground. The animal screamed horribly. Its rider lay motionless beside it.

Ichiro had not wanted to hurt the animal. It was a fine horse, an exquisite mount. But crippling it was the only way to save his life. Now it was his responsibility to end its agony. With both hands, he raised the tachi above his head. The sharp blade fairly sliced the wind itself as he brought it down.

The horse kicked once, then was still.

His grim business finished, Ichiro attend to the prostrate samurai. His body ached, but he remained on guard. The tip of his sword danced a circle in the air.

Suddenly the samurai moved. It was slow, uneven movement, like a puppet. He sprang upright, sword in hand, and lashed out.

For a moment, Ichiro's mind failed to react, surprised by this odd resurrection. But his sword hand was not startled. Almost of its own accord, his left arm rose to deflect the attacker's sword and return an attack of its own.

The blow brought Ichiro back to his senses. He saw the *katana* leap toward his head. But the attack was not swift, and he easily turned it aside.

Again the warrior pressed the attack, his sword dancing over his head.

Ichiro seized the brief opening.

His *tachi* flew toward the samurai's exposed and unarmored armpit. The blade met flesh and bone and divided them as a scythe cut stalks of rice.

The samurai's body collapsed noisily. As he hit the ground, his armor clanked dully. All life had left it. Yet life refused to leave the arm and hand that clenched the sword. It continued forward of its own accord and Ichiro dove to avoid its onslaught.

He parried one attack, but grimaced as the sword slashed the right sleeve of his kimono. But while the sword's blows were easily deflected, Ichiro's own attacks were parried with equal ease by the floating blade. He could not get behind the arm, as it moved when he moved, circled when he circled. It seemed to know exactly what he would do at the very moment he did it.

His own arm was tiring. He suspected the disembodied arm grew in strength with each blow he wasted on it. Was there a way to combat a sword possessed by a *mononoke*? he wondered.

Ichiro retreated as the sword unleashed a flurry of attacks. From the corner of his eye, he saw the shrine of Amida Buddha. A plan came to his mind. If he could perhaps reach the altar, he might confine the blade's ability to move. He eased himself toward the shrine, parrying each of the sword's now relentless blows. Working his way backwards, he pressed himself close to the altar. He waited, saving his attack, hoping. At last an edge of the altar was between him and the sword.

From deep within his chest, he unleashed a tremendous shout of *"Yoi!"* and pressed his attack. Even as the sword moved to meet his blade, he changed his tactics. His mind thought of one attack while his sword did another.

The tip of the *tachi* feinted to the right, then cut over the other sword. The floating arm, moving to counter the attack Ichiro was thinking of, was trapped. The *tachi* caught it above the hilt and smashed it against the edge of the altar.

With a sound like a temple bell, the demon sword broke on the hard stone. The blade tumbled into the water trough, raising a cascade of steam.

The arm hovered for a moment, preparing to strike. Then the life left it, and it collapsed to the shrine's floor, the fingers of the now motionless hand still clutching the useless sword hilt.

Ichiro brought the *tachi* down on the arm again and again, cutting it into several pieces. When he was at last certain it was dead, Ichiro fell back against the altar. The demonic thing had nearly sapped all of his strength. His breath came in heavy draughts. His lungs burning with the effort, he offered a prayer of thanks to Hachiman and to Amida Buddha. After a moment, he felt his strength returning.

He bent down to splash water from the altar trough over his face. But the water was scalding hot and smelled of metal and sulfur.

Under the surface, the broken sword blade glowed red hot. Ichiro eased it from the trough with the tip of his tachi. Once exposed to the air, the blade grew cold and crumbled into bits, its magic at last dissipated.

Ichiro sighed with relief. He sheathed his sword and stepped from the shrine into the warmth of the morning.

"A most excellent display of swordsmanship, General," someone said. "I commend you. You are indeed the finest swordsman in all Nihon."

Standing in front of the shrine was a *biroge*, a small carriage with sides of woven palm fronds. Four *ashigaru* guarded the carriage. The foot soldiers stood at each corner.

A nobleman sat within. He smiled. His face was sallow. A long moustache in a Chinese fashion drooped from his upper lip. Deep-set eyes of obsidian lurched beneath pencil thin black eyebrows. He was dressed in casual finery, a blue silk *hahama* overrobe, an embroidered red kimono and a black lacquered *eboshi* on his head. "I am Lord Taira Mitsuharu," he said.

"These were your men?" Ichiro asked, gesturing toward the dead samurai.

"They were expendable. I had to be certain you were who it was claimed you were." Lord Taira smiled again, exposing teeth as white as porcelain. The *daimyo* seemed not to like the traditional court practice of blackening teeth with strong tea and iron filings. His teeth glistened like a shark's. His smile chilled Ichiro's mind and body.

"Did you get your answer?" Ichiro asked.

"I am satisfied," Taira replied.

"You let me kill three good men, just to prove who I am?" Ichiro said, perplexed.

Taira nodded. "I am an orderly man. I prefer to know who my opponents are. But in any case, you did not kill my men."

Ichiro raised his eyebrows in surprise. *He had not killed them? Then what were their bodies doing lying lifeless in the dust? What was the arm that had nearly killed him?*

"What do you mean, I did not kill them?"

Taira stroked his moustaches and laughed. "Most honorable General, you cannot kill that which is already dead." He gestured with a long, cadaverous hand toward the body of the third samurai lying still in the dust.

"Look for yourself. Remove the so-men and gaze upon your opponent's face."

Ichiro hesitated a moment, then he edged past the *biroge*. He kept his eye on the four *ashigaru* standing guard. Kneeling beside the dead man's body, he reached for the iron mask. An acrid smell, the very odor he had detected earlier, assaulted his nostrils. Then he noticed there was no blood on the ground near the stump of the severed arm.

His curiosity aroused, Ichiro hooked his fingers under the so-men and lifted it from the samurai's face. If the mask had been merely ludicrous, what lay beneath was not.

Maggots crawled over wrinkled gray flesh. Bone and cartilage stuck out where a nose should have been. The lips drew back to expose brown and rotting teeth in silvery gums. Empty eye sockets, seething with worms and maggots, stared back at him.

Ichiro swallowed, tasting bile on his lips. He replaced the mask.

"Satisfied, I trust?" Taira said.

"Why?" Ichiro asked. His body shook with rage as he confronted the *daimyo*. An uncontrollable tremor possessed his tired sword arm.

"Why did you do this?" he asked again. It was as much a gesture to restore his own confidence as it was a question.

"For the answer, you must come to my *yashiki*. There we can discuss certain matters," Taira said. "But now I must leave you. If you will pardon me."

The *daimyo* thrust his hand outside the carriage. In his palm was a ball of light.

The ball grew brighter and brighter. Soon it was more dazzling than the sun, and it seemed three times as large. And with the light came Taira's laughter, horrible, cold and wet.

Ichiro shielded his eyes with his sword arm. The light seemed to penetrate him and its heat was scorching. The awful laughter rang in his ears.

He gasped in wonder. The *biroge* began to melt.

Twisting and spinning, the carriage formed itself into a dragon. Four times as tall as a man, it had a tiger's head, a serpent's body, a bird of prey's legs, and huge leathery wings.

Seated on its back in a silver saddle was Lord Taira. "At my *yashiki* this evening," he shouted. "Unless you are afraid, Minamoto-no-Ichiro." He almost sneered the name. Then he laughed and pulled back on the creature's gold reins.

The *ryu* flapped its huge wings, raising a huge dust cloud. Slowly it rose into the air, filling the sky with smoke and fire. Its wings were so huge they blocked out the sun. Airborne, it turned toward the north and flew off, growing gradually smaller and more distant.

The smoke and dust choked Ichiro and stung his eyes. But a gentle wind came from the east. The *kochi* cleared the square.

An east wind, and he had called himself just that. Would he clear the land of this scourge as easily as the wind cleansed the air? He did not know. He had no answers. All he had were nagging questions.

The villagers, who were hiding, at last came out into the street. They chattered noisily, pointing to the bodies of the samurai.

The undead warriors dried up like cicada carapaces and blew away. Even the disembodied arm turned as thin as rice paper and floated away on the breeze.

"You have saved us," Gidayu cried.

Ichiro shook his head. "No, I have merely won one encounter. There will be more."

Defeating men, even undead men, was easy.

But how does one fight a dragon? That answer, he knew, would not be soon in coming.

CHAPTER FIVE

The sun was sinking below the mountaintops when Ichiro at last reached the *yashiki*. The castle stood nestled against a gentle slope. Trees surrounded it on three sides, dark and dense pines which blocked all sunlight. A series of low earthen walls formed concentric circles around the central house of the *yashiki*. The walls served as the main defenses of the castle.

At the south wall stood a low gate with ramshackle wooden doors. The doors seemed oddly impoverished for a noble so obviously powerful as Lord Taira was. Then again deception was the *daimyo's* specialty, Ichiro realized. Wealth was best protected if disguised as poverty. Thieves would see the gates, deduce the noble's station in life and decide there was nothing worth plundering there.

The main house of the *yashiki* was quite old. It was built in the fashion of the *Heian* period almost nine hundred years ago. That was the period of Taira supremacy, a century before Minamoto Yoritomo and his brother Yoshitsune cast them down and established Yoritomo as Shogun. The house spoke of a simpler, crueler world than the one in which Ichiro was born.

The central section of the building, the *shinden*, faced south. The outer sections, the *hishi no tai* and the *higashi no ta*, flanked it on the east and west. Ichiro could not see the northern wing, the *kita no tai*. In that wing, no doubt, Taira kept his principal wife.

A curious sense of loss struck Ichiro at that thought. He rode toward the gate, each second flowing backward in time, cast loose upon the sea of reality. He thought of his own world, of fighter planes and battleships, of cherry blossoms and of Yumiko. Here, in this world, all that no longer existed. Indeed, it had never existed. The only reality of importance was this world of chaos and order, the reality of a castle from a time that should have been safely dead.

Ichiro felt a chill as he approached the gate. It was like the presence of evil he had felt in the village, only this was more penetrating. He prayed to Hachiman, asking for a little warmth for his aching limbs. He was also pleased that he had arranged lodgings and left his packhorse at the Buddhist monastery he had passed on his way. Although night was swiftly approaching, Ichiro knew spending the night here could mean his death, regardless of Hachiman's blessing.

He drew Luck up before the gate and dismounted. With an armored fist, he pounded the wooden doors. They resounded like drums, echoing off the nearby mountaintops.

A foot soldier appeared at the top of the earthen wall and chal-lenged Ichiro. He lowered his *jumonji-yari* so the lance's cruciform blade was aimed at Ichiro's chest.

"Who asks admittance to Lord Taira's castle?" he asked.

Ichiro dropped his hand to his sword. If he had to fight to enter the *yashiki*, then so be it. "Tell Lord Taira that General Minamoto-no-Ichiro is here as he requested."

The guard raised his lance and grabbed an animal horn that hung from a thong at his side. Bringing it to his lips, he produced a deep, rolling note that shook the air. As the sound of the horn died away, the gates swung slowly open.

Ichiro paused a moment, intrigued. The gates seem to have opened by themselves. He remounted and rode through the gateway.

While the air outside the castle was thick with the heat and humidity of summer, within the earthen walls the atmosphere was cool, almost chilly, and dry.

The *yashiki's* keep, or *tensho*, was filled with tents of the drabbest variety. *Ashigaru* sat around the tents, gambling and drinking sake and rice beer. Their coarse laughter mixed with the smells of cooking fires and broiling meat and vegetables.

A loud commotion sprang from one tent as Ichiro rode past. He reined Luck to a halt as a naked woman fled the tent and ran across his path. She was pursued by a drunken foot soldier dressed only in a flimsy *dhoti*.

The woman appeared confused and frightened. Her hair was tangled and dirty, her face streaked with filth. Seeing Ichiro, she ran toward him and grabbed the bridle of his horse.

"Please, you must help me!" she cried. "He will kill me."

Before Ichiro could act, the drunken *ashigaru* had caught her by the waist and flung her to the ground.

"Little thief! I should cut your throat!" he growled. She tried to get up but was held down by the force of his foot on her back.

Ichiro lashed out with his right leg, his foot catching the drunk squarely in the back. The foot soldier tumbled headlong into the dirt. He came to his feet, sputtering.

"Get up," Ichiro said. He dismounted and helped the woman to her feet. "Now, what has she stolen?" he asked the *ashigaru*.

The man shook his head and wiped his bleeding mouth with the back of one dirty hand. "She stole my purse of gold. Fifty *riyo* I had there," he muttered. "Little bitch, she was going to run away."

Ichiro turned to the woman. "Were you running away?" he asked gently.

She looked at the ground and nodded.

"Going back to her damned husband, no doubt. Not enough of a man to keep me from taking her," the man said contemptuously. He spat at her feet.

"Please," she said, tugging at Ichiro's arm. "He beats me and hurts me. He is a brute." She fell sobbing at Ichiro's feet.

He turned to the *ashigaru*. "You will give her clothes and some money, then let her go."

Rage grew in the foot soldier's eyes. "Why should I? I took her, she is mine!"

"There are plenty of unmarried women to quench your lust. Why take another man's wife?" Ichiro said. He bent down to help the woman to her feet. Out of the corner of his eye, he saw the man grab a sword from a compatriot.

Ichiro's hand went to his *tachi*. It sped from the scabbard and returned as quickly.

The drunkard lay on the ground, writhing in pain. At the side of the road was his severed right hand, still clutching the sword.

"Next time, it will be your head," Ichiro said. He turned to a group of soldiers who had gathered, hoping to see a fight. They seemed disappointed that the battle had ended so abruptly.

"You," he said to one, "help this woman find her clothes and give her money from this *yopparai's* purse. Then you will let her through the gate. If when I return I find she has not been allowed to leave, I will kill the man who has her. Do you understand?"

The *ashigaru* nodded.

Ichiro cocked his head toward the wounded man. "See he gets proper attention."

The woman felt to her knees and clutched his legs. "Thank you, honorable sir."

He gently pushed her away. "Do not thank me, just return to your village." He mounted his horse and rode toward the *shinden*.

A ratty little man with rotting teeth and a scraggly beard waited for Ichiro at the entrance to the house.

"Sir, I am Lord Taira's equerry," he said, bowing slightly. "I am to take care of your horse."

Ichiro nearly declined the offer, but he glimpsed a touch of sincerity in the man. *Surely a few of Taira's servants could be trusted,* he thought. Even the most corrupt man always has aides whose integrity is above reproach.

He dismounted and gave the man Luck's reins. The equerry led the horse to a nearby paddock.

Ichiro noticed a carefully trimmed low hedge that encircled the house. A small wooden gate was set into one section of the hedge. Ichiro pushed it open and stepped into the garden. He walked along the stone path, feeling acutely out of place.

Ichiro was dressed in armor, ready for combat. He even carried his general's horsehair baton, a symbol of his former authority. Yet all around him were quiet, non-threatening things. The garden was filled with delicate *bonsai* cherry trees, sculpted rose bushes and sheltering plum trees. White oleander and apple blossom scented the air.

It was once again the eternal confrontation between peaceful nature and war-like man. That this was Taira's garden seemed more ironic and sad. Ichiro felt an ancient melancholy that such fleeting beauty existed among the evil of men.

Two samurai confronted him as he reached the steps of the *shinden*. Fully armored, each carried *naginata*, the spears' curved-blades glistening red in the dying light.

"General Minamoto, our master Lord Taira awaits within. Please enter," one said, gesturing to the doorway. Then they stepped aside to let him pass.

Ichiro climbed the steps and entered the house. The two samurai fell into step behind and followed him into the main chamber. He halted before a set of latticed doors. The two warriors stepped to the doors and pulled them open. Ichiro stepped through the doorway. The guards did not follow but slid the doors shut behind him.

"General, how kind of you to accept my invitation," the *daimyo* said. Taira sat on several silk cushions of various shades and colors. A short-legged black lacquered table sat before him. On the table was a *go* board and playing stones.

"I trust your ride was pleasant?" he said.

"No ride is truly pleasant, Lord Taira. It is reaching the destination which makes the ride worthwhile," Ichiro said. "But only sometimes," he added.

Taira laughed. "A swordsman and a wit, too! Such a delight!" The *daimyo* gestured to a mound of cushions on the other side of the table. "Please, be seated. I have servants for food and tea. Or would you prefer *sake*?"

"Tea is fine," Ichiro replied. He lowered himself carefully, placing his left leg underneath him and gradually easing his right leg into a comfortable position. Taira, he realized, had provided extra cushions to accommodate his infirmity.

"You must forgive me, my lord, for wearing my armor. But I could not be certain of your intentions," He undid his chin cords and removed his helmet, setting it at his side.

"Think nothing of it," Taira said, gesturing as if to sweep the apology aside.

As he removed his cuirass and leg armor, Ichiro's eyes roamed over the *moya*. The main chamber of the house displayed Taira's elegant taste. The decorations were both modest and attractive. It was quite unlike the vulgar and ostentatious decor of nobles' homes in Kyoto.

Taira waited until his guest was seated, then he clapped his hands twice.

Five musicians entered. They sat down and began to play. These were not *beiju*, professional musicians, but members of the household. Four of them were young women. The fifth was an old man who played the *koto*. He was probably a music teacher, Ichiro surmised.

He suspected the woman were either the *daimyo's* wives or his daughters. They were all young and pretty. Each was dressed in formal attire. Their faces were powdered white, their cheeks rouged, their eyebrows shaved and redrawn high on their foreheads.

But whatever their position, wife, daughter, or concubine, they played most excellently. Ichiro's ear found the sound of *koto, sonokoto, shakuhachi* and *biwa* relaxing.

"Do you play *go*?" the *daimyo* inquired.

"I was quite good once. Long ago," Ichiro said.

He had played some at court, when it was too hot or too cold to move. But the nobles were rarely good players, and he defeated them with ease. The last game he had truly enjoyed was with a pilot named Chiba. That was the night before the young man flew his kamikaze mission. Ichiro took the game less seriously after that. It reminded him all too much of those young men he had trained and set to their deaths.

"I am afraid the game has lost much of its fascination for me," he admitted.

"How unfortunate!" Taira said. "There are so few good players about. Most offer me no challenge at all. I have been studying the great masters' scrolls, learning their strategies and tactics. I had hoped I could test them against you."

"Indeed, it is very unfortunate," Ichiro said. He had to be careful that the *daimyo's* charm did not lull him into a false sense of security. But then he was not so easily beguiled as others might be.

The servants entered with food. There was bleached rice, no doubt stolen from a peasant's fields, pork in a sweet and delicate sauce, assorted vegetables, shredded white mounds of *daikon,* bright yellow pickled radishes and plums, and raw fish wrapped in kelp. One servant poured steaming *ryokucha* green tea from a decorated blue and white porcelain teapot into two wide china bowls.

The two men ate in silence for a few minutes, then toward the end of the meal, Taira once more tried to engage Ichiro in a game of *go.* Again Ichiro declined.

"I apologize for not wishing to play," Ichiro said. He lifted his bowl and the servant with the teapot quickly poured him more tea. "We have more serious matters to discuss."

"Of course," Taira said. "That is why I asked you here." He clapped his hands. The musicians stopped playing in mid-note. The *daimyo* nodded. The musicians rose and left the room.

After they had gone, Taira leaned back against his cushions. He lay his arm across a carved wooden armrest. "First, you wish to ask why I treat the peasants so harshly."

Ichiro nodded. The *daimyo* did not need supernatural powers to know that. "Your army steals their crops, rapes their wives. They kill those who resist. You have reduced them to *eta*, to outcasts. Surely this is not how a noble governs his men."

Taira smiled faintly. "General, you sound like that fool Oshio Meihachiro. All his talk of saving the people produced his unpleasant death at the Shogun's hands. Surely you are wiser than that."

"Nobles rule on a knife-edge, lord. To mistreat your subjects is to hone the blade that will slit your throat," Ichiro said.

"General, you are such an innocent," Taira said. He stroked his sharp chin. "Your years in court have taught you little of the ways of government. The peasant is a child who needs my protection. I only ask their obedience. When a child is disobedient, shouldn't a father reprimand him?"

"So you burn their crops."

Taira sighed. "It is sometimes necessary for a father to apply his willow rod to the child so severely that the child is killed. On occasion, I must discipline harshly, even cruelly, so they will remember I am their superior."

"I have never met a *daimyo* I considered my superior. But in many things I have met peasants who were clearly my better," Ichiro said.

Taira's features grew dark. He frowned, but his voice remained calm. "Enough of this talk, General. There is more important business to discuss."

"Since when do a Taira and a Minamoto have business together?" Ichiro asked.

"My friend, almost nine centuries have passed since your ancestors defeated mine. Then yours too fell by the wayside and lesser men gained power. With that came the dimming of Nihon. You have only to look at the Tokugawa Shogun, shut up in Edo. Armies rise to oppose him, and he sends out proxies in his name. True, they are victorious, but eventually he will lose. For Nihon's sake, perhaps ancient enemies should now be allies?"

Ichiro was puzzled. "I am not sure I understand you."

Taira tapped his forefingers together. A wicked grin crossed his face. "For years I have assembled an army. You have seen it; you know its size, but not its powers. It is my aim to restore Nihon to the ancient glories of our forefathers."

The *daimyo* sighed. "But my men lack discipline. Even my powers cannot command an army as a general does. Then you appear, a famous general, a warrior of incomparable skill. Are you a gift from the gods to lead my armies to victory? I do not know. It is also possible you are test for me. The ancient enemy, once victorious, returns to thwart my family's dreams. If so, then I may defeat the past. Nothing will stand in my way. But which is it to be?"

Ichiro resisted reacting to the *daimyo's* words. "An interesting concept, my lord. Perhaps it is the former. Or the latter. We shall see."

Which is it, Hachiman? Give me a sign, he thought.

"Before you decide, let me show you some trinkets," Taira said. He clapped his hands loudly. The lattice doors opened, and two servants entered. They carried a large oaken chest.

The chest was made of recently cut wood. The wood was oiled and stained to enhance the grain. Large iron bands bound the wood together.

The servants carried the chest to the center of the room and placed it on the floor. Taira nodded. The men undid a thick iron catch that held the lid in place. They lifted the lid with difficulty, then tilted the chest forward so Ichiro could view its contents.

The flickering candlelight struck the inside of the chest and was reflected by one of two objects inside. The reflected light filled the room. Beside it, the second object glowed with power and force.

Ichiro gasped in awe. He realized at once what the objects were and was shocked that Taira possessed them. The first was the Mirror of Ameratsu, the *kami* of the sun. It could bring day to dark night and cast arrows of flame that would burn everything its path. Yet the mirror itself was cool and soothing to the touch.

Beside it was the jeweled Great Seal. With it came the power of all the Emperors since Jimmu, the first Emperor.

Ichiro did not doubt they were authentic. He had seen them often enough. They belonged at the Ise shrine in Nara. Yet here they were in Taira's hands. How had they been taken? Ichiro wondered. The Ise shrine was guarded continuously. Few were allowed entrance.

Was it possible that Taira could have passed unnoticed through the treasure room's thick walls? he wondered.

"Yes, they are what you believe they are. The Sacred Mirror and the Sacred Seal restored to their rightful clan, my clan. Remember, Minamoto, it was a young Taira who was emperor at Dan-no-Urra. A young emperor your clan drowned."

There was venom in his words, though he spoke calmly, even charmingly.

"But I cannot gain power without the third of the treasures, the Sacred Sword *Kusinagi*," he said. Taira seemed disappointed, then he smiled. "But if you become my general, it shall be mine. All of Nihon shall be mine."

He clapped his hands. The servants shut the lid of the chest.

Immediately the light of day vanished. The room returned to the illumination of half-melted, flickering candles.

"So, will you lead my armies, Minamoto-no-Ichiro?" Taira said.

Ichiro did not hear the question. He was impressed and disturbed by the spectacle. Taira was more powerful that he had thought. Yet it was Taira's belief that if Ichiro become the noble's general, the third relic, the sword Kusinagi, would be delivered to him. *But surely Kusinagi was at the bottom of the Inland Sea? And his own sword, that could not possibly be Kusinagi, could it? So what did Taira mean?*

"Your answer," Taira said.

"Forgive me, my lord. I was lost in thought," Ichiro said. "What I have seen is most remarkable. But I cannot consider your offer at this moment. Please, give me time to ponder it. In the morning my mind may think more clearly."

Taira nodded his acceptance. "Very well," he said.

Ichiro rose and gather his armor. "Now, I must ask your leave. It is a long ride to the monastery where I am lodging."

"You will not stay the night here?" Taira asked. He was suspicious.

Ichiro shook his head. "No, Lord Taira. I wish to think. Only in the monastery may I have the solitude to ponder my choice." *And, we Minamoto too have a long memory, as long as your own, Lord Taira.*

"I see. Very well, you may leave," the *daimyo* said.

Ichiro bowed politely, and began putting on his armor. "In what direction should I exit, my lord?" he asked.

Taira smiled, both pleased and surprised. "You know my beliefs well!

"You are fortunate tonight. The western exit of my house is closed to you. The *kami* Hitochimeguri and Nakagami are both in residence there. I would suggest you also not leave through the garden. Dokujin resides at my gates in summer. Like all gods, he is easily offended if you ignore him. And, alas, he is so easy to ignore. My men will show you the way out."

"Thank you, Lord Taira." He turned to go, but halted at the latticed doors and turned around. "A final question, my lord."

"Yes?"

"Do dragons sleep like mortal men?" Ichiro did not wait for an answer. He flung the latticed doors apart and walked through. The doors, on their own, slammed soundly shut behind him.

Outside, he found the old man had already brought Luck around to the gate. The horse had been groomed and fed, but seemed somewhat displeased at the prospect of a night ride. Ichiro stroked the horse's nose and calmed him. "It will not be long. Then we both can rest," he said soothingly.

He thanked the equerry and offered him some coins, but the man refused.

"They are worthless to me, I am afraid. I have no place to spend them," he said.

Ichiro smiled. "You are an honest man in dishonest surroundings. Why do you stay?" he asked.

"Even in troubled times a man must eat, and at least the food here is plentiful," the equerry replied.

Ichiro nodded in sad agreement. The man's words were all too profound. He mounted Luck, bridled the horse about, and rode toward the gate.

At the earthen wall, he halted and demanded the guard bring him the soldier he had told to release the captive woman.

The man came from his tent. He had dressed hastily in *dhoti* and short-sleeved jacket. He sleepily rubbed his eyes.

"The woman. Did you release her?" Ichiro said.

The soldier stifled a yawn. "Yes, General," he muttered. "We gave her clothes and some money from *Kunitaro's* purse and sent her off." He could not stifle a second yawn and shook his head to stay awake. "She left about an hour ago. We have not seen or heard anything since."

"Good. You may go," Ichiro said. "But if I find she has not returned to her husband, you will answer for it."

The soldier nodded and walked away, yawning.

The guards opened the main gate.

Ichiro rode through the entrance and started down the road. He kept alert, half expecting some crazed soldiers to place an arrow between his shoulder blades. But no arrow came.

He could not get away from Taira's *yashiki* fast enough for his liking. The warmth taken from his bones slowly returned. A sense of well being erased the fear he had felt. But his renewed good spirits were rudely shaken as two riders tore towards him.

"Make way," one shouted, brandishing his tachi over his head. "Make way for the lord's carriage."

Behind them a low black *basha* drawn by four gray horses raced down the dusty road. Moonlight glistened on its lacquered sides. On the sides of the carriage, two small lanterns glowed like serpent's eyes. A faint glow crept around the edges of thick curtains drawn across the carriage windows. Nothing could be seen within.

"Can't you hear, you fool?" the other samurai shouted. "Out of the way!" To make his point he lowered his spear at Ichiro.

Ichiro reined Luck to the side of the road.

The *basha* sped past in a cloud of dust. As it went by, its two lanterns bounced like the laughing eyes of a malevolent demon. When the carriage was distant enough, the lanterns disappeared momentarily, as though the demon had winked.

Ichiro watched the *basha* vanish into the night. There was something familiar about it, but he could not be sure. He felt he knew to whom it belonged, that he knew who this mysterious lord was. But he could not retrieve that knowledge from the depths of his memory. It disturbed him. He brought his horse about and continued on his way.

By his reckoning, he was not far from the monastery. He imagined he could see it already, see its lantern fires beckoning like stars, stars one could hold in one's hand.

Unexpectedly, Luck drew up and reared. Ichiro clutched the reins to keep from being thrown. The horse snorted and took a step backward. Ichiro reached down and stroked Luck's neck.

"What is the matter, my friend?" he asked the animal. "What is bothering you?"

Luck snorted again and tried to turn back the way he had come.

Ichiro reined the horse about, soothing him with calm words, stroking his neck. Something ahead was clearly bothering Luck. Ichiro had never seen the horse so skittish.

He dismounted and led the horse to a small bush where he tethered the reins. Luck seemed relieved and displayed his relief by grazing on a clump of thick grass.

Ichiro looked down the road but could see nothing. Yet like his horse, he too began to have the *zanshin* and sensed danger. He unsheathed his tachi and walked slowly and cautiously down the road. His eyes scanned all the road, looking for anything unusual. His sword arm was tense, fully expecting a ninja or bandit to leap from the darkness.

But still he saw nothing.

Then his foot struck something. He stumbled and almost fell before realizing it was there.

A large bundle lay at the side of the road. It was wrapped in dark cloth and difficult to see now that the moon had ducked behind the clouds.

He knelt beside the bundle and lifted it. His fingers encountered warmth and softness, like human flesh. He brought the bundle onto his lap, and it emitted a low moan.

He pulled the cloth away, exposing a young woman's face. She was obviously hurt. A dried streak of blood ran from her forehead, down her cheek and onto her neck. There were small bruises on her chin and on one arm.

Her face was familiar. *Ah, yes*, he recalled. This was the woman in Taira's camp, the one he'd rescued from the drunkard. Gently Ichiro laid her down. He rose and went to Luck, where he retrieved his water flask from the saddlebag.

He tore a small piece of cloth from the woman's clothes. Soaking it with water, Ichiro washed her face, sponging the blood from her cheek and neck. Then he raised her head and poured cold liquid through her dried and swollen lips.

She drank, then coughed when she was unable to swallow fast enough. Liquid poured from her mouth like drool and ran down her chin. But the water revived her. She sat up suddenly, as if awakened from a nightmare.

Ichiro eased her back down. "It is all right," he said soothingly. "You have had a bad accident. You must rest."

"I...I do not understand," she said. Then she recognized Ichiro. "You...you were the one at the castle, the one who cut off Kunitaro's hand."

"Yes," he said, smiling. "It seems I am fated to keep rescuing you."

He stoppered the water flask. "I thought you were told to return to your village."

"Honorable sir," she said, somewhat indignant, " I was going back to my village. But it is two days' walk from Lord Taira's *yashiki*."

"It is dangerous to travel at night. Bandits are everywhere," Ichiro said. "They could easily have killed you instead of just leaving you here."

"Oh, no, my lord. It was not bandits who attacked me," she said.

"No?"

She shook her head. "Oh, no. I travel at night because I have no choice. There is no place here for me to stay, and Kunitaro's friends would kill me if they found me near the castle.

"So I was walking when two riders appeared from a strange mist. They carried spears and swords and shouted. When they were near, I heard them shouting, 'Make way for the lord's *basha*'," she said.

The two riders and the coach that passed me, Ichiro thought.

"I ran to the side of road to avoid them," she said. "Their horses were so huge I feared their hooves might trample me. Then a *basha* came from the mist, pulled by four even larger gray horses. The carriage had lanterns like eyes. They might even have been eyes for all I know because I saw no driver.

"As the *basha* passed me, a gust of wind blew open one of its curtain and I saw its passenger," she said.

The woman closed her eyes and shivered with fear. "He was horrible," she said. "He was wrapped in heavy black robes and continually fanned himself with a wicker fan. But his face - his face was white, whiter than anything I had ever seen, whiter even than newly fallen snow.

"I took him for a ghost, he was so pale. But his lips and cheeks were deep red. I thought perhaps he drank other's blood," she said.

"After the carriage went by me, one of the riders returned. 'What are you staring at?' he demanded, but I was too shocked to answer. He struck me across the head with the staff of his lance. I remember falling, striking my head on the ground and that is all."

"Akiyama!" Ichiro said. Now he knew why the carriage was familiar. Akiyama used it so rarely, but Ichiro had seen it enough to remember it. He spat at the thought. "So he is Taira's guest."

"Who is Akiyama?" the woman asked.

"An old enemy, who is friendly with a new enemy," he said.

Everything was making sense now. It explained why Taira knew about his sword, why the *daimyo* had the Sacred Mirror and Sacred Seal. Akiyama had easy access to the treasures of Ise. Like Taira's game of *go*, the moves slowly revealed the *daimyo's* goals.

Ichiro helped the woman to her feet. "Come, I will take you to a Buddhist monastery where we can spend the night. I will take you to your home in the morning."

"Thank you, sir," she said.

"What is your name?" he asked as he helped her onto his horse.

"I am called Shizuka, lord."

Her name surprised him. Shizuka was the name of Yoshitsune's beloved mistress, the one who bore him a son. Was Hachiman's hand in this, too? he wondered.

"Well, Shizuka, you must forgive me. It is partly my fault you were hurt. If I had known you lived far from here, I would not have let them just throw you out their gate."

She lowered head, seemingly embarrassed. "You gave me freedom. I thank you. Never apologize to anyone you have just freed."

Ichiro smiled. "You are wise, Shizuka." He mounted Luck and spurred the horse toward the monastery.

Shizuka slipped her arms about his waist, holding on as Luck maintained a lazy trot. But Ichiro barely noticed the warmth and softness of her body against his own. The chains of two enemies weighed on his mind.

CHAPTER SIX

The light from the Jimmukei monastery's lanterns appeared as tiny, glowing blossoms in a dark night, a night steamy with humidity. They beckoned to Ichiro, offering welcome rest. Shizuka was already asleep. Her head rested against his back. He realized he too would relish sleep.

The monks of this monastery were humble in appearance and generous to worthy travelers. But beneath their gentleness were the skills and mind of *hoekke*, warrior monks. Over many centuries they repeatedly demonstrated their abilities as messengers and assassins for various factions, but held a particular fondness for the Minamoto and its allies.

Centuries earlier the Taira had tried to break the monastery and had nearly succeeded. The monks had never forgiven the Taira and took great pains in aiding their enemies.

Ichiro held a strong affection for monasteries. As a young boy, he served for a year as a *chigo*, a page boy, in a Zen monastery near his home in Tokyo. It had been his father's idea, and he always thanked his father for it. It was a time of great joy in Ichiro's life. The abbot had taken an immediate liking to Ichiro, in part because of his infirmity.

The monk taught Ichiro the rudiments of Zen meditation, calligraphy, poetry and *kendo*.

But the greatest pleasure he gave Ichiro was instruction in kite-making. Often they would stand on the monastery walls and release a kite into the swirling warm air currents that rose along the wall face. In flying kites, and later planes, Ichiro thought he might eventually solve the *koan* the abbot had given him. *The hubless wheel turns.*

Ichiro did know if he would ever solve the riddle, but he felt obligated to pay off his debt to the abbot by visiting other monasteries, even if only as a guest.

As he dismounted he took great care not to waken Shizuka. He leaned her forward on his saddle so she rested across Luck's broad back. He led the horse to Jimmukei monastery's high cedar gate and rapped on a small entrance door.

As he waited for admittance, he sniffed the air. A scent of burning wafted through the night. It smelled of sulfur, and it reminded him of the burned millet fields in the village. In fact, it seemed to come from that direction. The odor worried him, but his tired mind pushed it back in the depths of consciousness.

Once safely inside, Ichiro lifted Shizuka from the horse. The abbot provided them each with a small, uncluttered room. In both rooms, there was fresh straw on the floor and a simple wooden headrest.

Ichiro placed his bundle on the straw and laid her head on the headrest. She stirred once but did not awaken.

Before retiring, Ichiro received permission to examine the volumes in the monastery library in the morning.

"A true scholar is always welcome," said the abbot, whose name was Kobori. He was a *roshi*, or Zen master.

"I am no scholar, only a humble warrior," he said.

The abbot laughed. "General, he who seeks knowledge is a scholar. Some of us are more modest than others in what we wish to learn."

In return for the generosity, Ichiro burned some poppy seeds at the monastery altar. He said a prayer to Kannon to guarantee Abbot Kobori's health and secure the blessing of his ancestors. Then he prayed to Hachiman for guidance. No answer came. At last his own tired body overcame his thoughts and he slept.

The alarm sounded in the hour before dawn.

Ichiro awoke to the stench of sulfur filling the air. It was the same odor he had sensed at the gate. The sound of conflict filled the courtyard. Outside Ichiro's door someone screamed.

In the darkness, Ichiro fumbled for his bow. Finding it, he notched an arrow. Carefully he opened his cell door and peered out.

Three armored samurai stood in the center of the courtyard. They were fending off determined but decidedly futile attacks from the monks, who were armed only with farming implements and wooden *kendo* swords. The feeble weapons were no match for tempered steel. Several monks already lay dead at the warriors' feet.

Ichiro knew instantly whose men these samurai were.

Even though he was too far distant to use his sword, his bow would raise the odds in the monks' favor. Bringing his mind and body into total concentration, he drew back on the bowstring. The tension built in his body until he could not hold it back. The arrow leaped from bow with the same ferocity as the yell that sprang from his lips.

The *ya* found its mark in the gap between the chest plates of one samurai's armor. The warrior staggered, driven back by the force of the arrow, then fell face forward into the dust. The ground drove the arrow through the attacker's body. The arrowhead glistened in the moonlight.

For a moment the other samurai seemed confused. They had seen the arrow fly from the darkness but could not guess its origin.

Darkness was in Ichiro's favor. He notched another arrow and drew back. But before he released the arrow, bright light flooded the courtyard.

Ichiro shielded his eyes from the blinding glare. He choked on the sulfurous fumes. High above Ichiro in the night sky came a familiar laugh. The dragon's breath had started several fires and exposed his position. Taira's warriors drove off the last of the monks and were nearly upon him.

He remembered the arrow. He drew back on the bowstring and released. Aimed for the legs of one samurai, the *ya* deflected off the warrior's shin armor and caromed harmlessly away.

Ichiro drew his sword and prepared to face both samurai. But something moved in the shadows.

The *samurai* had no time to react as the *shuriken* whistled from the darkness and caught the warrior in the right shoulder. As the *samurai's* hand went to remove the nine-pointed star, a black-clad figure attacked.

The creature grabbed the warrior's helmet and snapped it back. The chin strap of the *nigiryuno kabuto* began to strangle its wearer. Nimbly, the dark figure grabbed the samurai's own *aikuchi* and drove the armor-piercing knife blade into the warrior's back.

With a feeble strangled cry, the samurai collapsed. The attacker leaped aside as the regrouped monks fell on the wounded warrior and finished the task.

The last samurai faced Ichiro.

Ichiro thought the warrior seemed oddly small and fragile. But whatever the size, the samurai maneuvered the *tachi* with great skill. Ichiro beat back two attacks and returned a flurry of his own, only to have the blade glance ineffectually over the armor plates.

But his major advantage was his left-handedness. His opponent found increasing difficulty in countering his attacks, which always seemed to come from the wrong side. He exploited the advantage. The *tachi* sang and found its mark just above the left elbow. The warrior's blood dripped down the armored sleeve and onto the ground.

The samurai was more cautious now, but still baffled by the wrong-handed swordsman. The warrior pressed an attack, almost running with the sword blade pointed down like a lance. Ichiro deflected the blade and felt his own sword meet flesh.

The warrior grabbed a wounded right shoulder. In the fire light Ichiro saw blood flow between the fingers of an armored glove. The samurai could now barely raise his sword. He tried one more attack, but it was feeble. Ichiro easily turned it aside. Arms drooping, losing blood rapidly, the warrior could hardly stand.

Ichiro placed the tip of his *tachi* against the samurai's breastplate. He pushed gently.

The samurai sank slowly, tired legs folding under like an over-weighted table. The fall was as soft as that of a cherry blossom from a wind-swept bough. The warrior tried once to rise, but fell back.

Ichiro sheathed his *tachi*. He knelt beside the fallen samurai and undid the warrior's *kabuto*. As he pulled the helmet away, a cascade of black hair spread itself across the ground.

Now Ichiro knew why the samurai seemed small.

The warrior was a woman.

The black-clad figure came to his side. A dark cloth covered its face. A spiked fist removed the cloth.

"The others are also women," Shizuka said. She still held the *aikuchi* she had used on one samurai. "Does that make sense to you?" she asked.

Ichiro shook his head. "I don't understand it at all."

A raw wind swirled about them, accompanied by the leather of wings and a thunderous laugh.

"You are clever indeed, Minamoto!" came the cry of Taira from high above the monastery. "But even you may find it hard to decipher this puzzle. And by then I shall find a way to stop you!"

Taira pulled back on the dragon's reins. The creature raised itself upright and filled the night sky with flames.

The monastery roof ignited. Several small buildings were already aflame, and the library was also blazing.

"You seek answers, General!" Taira taunted. "Well, now I give you more questions!" The necromancer's laughter grew more hideous until both the dragon and its rider were engulfed in a blinding ball of light and vanished.

Ichiro ran toward the library. Taira's threats meant the fire endangered little now that the knowledge he sought. Some of the monks and *chigo* had realized the danger and were already carrying out armloads of precious scrolls. Other monks were pulling burning wood and straw from the rooftops.

Shizuka grabbed a pitchfork and scrambled to the rooftops to help.

Ichiro pushed his way past the novices and entered the burning library. Many of the rice paper scrolls were already aflame. Other scrolls were starting to scorch despite the monks' best efforts.

Undoing the front of his jacket, Ichiro began filling it with scrolls. When he could fit no more, he piled others into the crook of his right arm. He slowly made his way back to the entrance. The burning scrolls, furniture and wooden beams produced a thick suffocating smoke. Ichiro hacked at the flaming timbers with his sword and armored fist.

His lungs ached and burned as he battled for breath. His eyes watered freely. Once outside he handed the scrolls to a frightened young novice and then reentered the library.

By now the smoke was so heavy he found his way using the tip of his sword. He brushed away straw and timbers until he made a path to the scrolls. Two young monks followed him into the library and aided him in gathering the last of the scrolls. Ichiro tasted ash. It scorched his throat. Tears nearly blinded him.

"Is this all the scrolls?" he asked.

"Yes," said one monk.

"Then let us get out of here," Ichiro said.

"I can't see. The smoke is too thick!" the other monk protested.

"Hold onto the sleeve of my jacket," Ichiro said. "I'll get you out."

The first young monk grabbed Ichiro's sleeve while the other held his compatriot's robe.

"Now, down on your knees! We must crawl," Ichiro said.

The monks obeyed.

The trio inched their way toward the door. Ichiro beat back a timber that fell across their path. He fanned his sword to clear away the smoke. A pocket of clear air rushed in from the doorway.

Not understanding how he could still move, Ichiro stumbled through the entrance into the open. He rolled onto his back, his lungs stinging. At each breath his body ached. His head spun wildly.

"Toki!" a voice cried. "We have lost Toki!"

Ichiro turned toward the voice and saw that only one of the monks had escaped the building.

"He must have let go of my robe!" the monk said. Tears rolled down his sooty face.

Ichiro staggered to his feet. It was madness to go back into the inferno. He knew that, but reason did not control him now. He shoved his way past a cluster of monks and staggered into the library. The smoke was thick as ink. Waving his sword did not clear it.

Ichiro dropped to his knees and let his other senses take over. With his sword he pushed aside flaming wood. He felt his way by tapping his sword on the ground ahead of him and by reaching out with an armor fist. His ears listened for the faintest sign of life.

The sword nudged something soft. He reached out, and his hand touched the young monk's body. Ichiro sheathed his sword. He gathered Toki into his arms then slung the monk over his back.

He tried to remember the path he had taken. His senses did not betray him. He moved with speed, yet fully conscious of the conflagration trying to block his path.

Suddenly the air was cool. Voices chattered in amazement. Ichiro felt the monk being lifted from his shoulders. He collapsed, then raised himself on one arm. Someone pressed a water bowl into his hands. He was uncertain if he whispered any thanks, but it did not matter. Lifting the bowl weakly to his lips, he let the water trickle down his dry throat.

The water revived him. "The monk? How is he?" he croaked.

"He will live," Abbot Kobori said. "He is badly burned, and he has breathed much smoke. But he will live."

Ichiro tried to rise, but lost his balance. The abbot took his arm and steadied him. He led Ichiro to the edge of a stone water trough and made him sit.

The abbot dropped a cloth into the water, wrung it out, and washed Ichiro's face.

The water was cooling. The skin on his face throbbed. By morning he knew he would find the areas burned, each glowing an angry shade of red. But now he was too exhausted to feel pain.

"You are a remarkable man, Minamoto-no-Ichiro," the abbot said. "You do yourself and your ancestors honor by your courage."

"I will do them more honor by defeating Taira, *roshi*," he replied. He grimaced as the cloth rubbed a particularly sensitive spot.

"That can wait, my friend," Abbot Kobori said softly. "It is almost dawn. You must sleep. When you are rested, then we may talk."

Ichiro felt the strong arms of two burly monks lift him to his feet. All strength to resist them fled him. He let them guide him back to his room. He recalled the softness of straw and odor of ash and nothing more until morning.

———

The early morning sun filtered through the tiny slit windows of the abbot's room. It cast a buttery glow over everything, including Ichiro.

"Sit, my friend," Abbot Kobori said. Ichiro did so only too gratefully.

Before he came to the abbot's cell, Ichiro washed himself in a basin of water a monk had thoughtfully provided. He removed the soiled kimono he had worn and dressed in a loose pair of *hakama* and a *karaginu*, a short jacket with long sleeves.

From a low shelf the abbot took three scrolls and placed them before Ichiro.

"I took the precaution of removing these from the library. Perhaps it was a premonition on my part, but I also wished to discuss them with you."

"Hachiman's doings, no doubt," Ichiro said with a faint smile.

The abbot nodded his shaved head. "Or the Buddha. Perhaps. Both *bodhisattvas* and *kami* do not forget those who serve them well." He unrolled one scroll and spread it out between them. "But to the matter at hand. You have said the *daimyo* follows the *Shinto* codes of the *Heian* Emperors. It is called *ritsuryo*. And he also obeys the traditions of those ancient gods."

"That is true."

"Then you should know Taira must spend one night in sixty in wakefulness. Poisons accumulate in his body and he must purge them. These poison are a result of the magic he practices. It is the price he pays for his powers."

"On that one night he is weak and vulnerable," Ichiro said. *At last,* he thought, *here is the opening I need to defeat Taira.*

"Ah, so one might think. But that is not quite true," Abbot Kobori said.

"Each spell the *daimyo* performs increases the poisons in his body," the abbot explained. "Because he must spend one night in sixty expunging these poisons, he will eventually be vulnerable. His body will be tired. However, it is also possible to drain so much of his strength that he could not overcome those poisons. That might prove dangerous to everyone if he cannot control his powers."

"But which night in sixty is it?" Ichiro mused. "Tonight? Tomorrow? Twenty days from now, or thirty or even sixty days? How am I to know?"

Abbot Kobori smiled. "General, if Hachiman has picked his agent well, you will have your answer."

Of course, Ichiro thought. *There was an easy way. An astrologer, given the vital information about Taira, could undoubtedly determine when Taira Mitsuru must spend a night in sleeplessness.*

"Do you know of any astrologers nearby?" Ichiro asked.

The abbot shook his head. "If there is one, I suspect he is in Taira's employ. Those who live in this valley are mostly poor peasants. They have neither money nor need for such nonsense as an astrologer. Most are lucky if they have time to pray to the *Amida Buddha*. I cannot help you there, my friend."

"Oh no, dearest master. I should apologize for imposing. But I will seek Hachiman's aid in this matter," Ichiro said.

The abbot nodded. "As you wish," he said.

Ichiro felt uncomfortable. Kobori's gentle demeanor and calm words belied the troubles surrounding the monastery around him. The Buddhist *dharma* gave the abbot strength. But the presence of evil left Ichiro uneasy. The *dharma* held sway within these wall, but he needed to travel in a world beyond the monastery, a world far less than pure.

He rose to go. "Again, most honored *roshi*, I thank you for your kindness and offer my humble apologies for the harm I brought to the monastery," he said.

The abbot laughed. "If you feel it is necessary, I accept your apologies. But I must thank you for saving a young monk's life and for helping preserve the life's work of many generations. Now, I ask you to stay. Read these scrolls alone. The mind functions best in solitude, undistracted."

Abbot Kobori rose stiffly. "Now, I will leave you to your work."

Ichiro bowed his head in respect. "Thank you, venerable *roshi*. I also have one other request of you. I should like to question the woman who attacked me."

A frown crept over the abbot's face. "I will tell you now, Minamoto-no-Ichiro, that may prove futile. She is in a deep sleep. We tried to revive her, but an evil presence surrounds her. I cannot prevent you from speaking to her, but I give you warning. Decide wisely, my son."

Ichiro nodded slowly. Taira's hand was apparent in the woman's condition, that was certain. "Thank you for your concern, *roshi*."

"You have an arduous task, Minamoto-no-Ichiro. I cannot believe one as sincere as you will fail."

"I trust I will not disappoint your belief," Ichiro replied. He prostrated himself at the abbot's feet, pressing his forehead to the floor. Ichiro felt the abbot's hand on the back of his head. It reassured him.

When he rose, Abbot Kobori was gone.

Ichiro sat and unrolled the first scroll. Inside he found a thin sheet of rice paper. It was a note. The writing, in a firm hand with fine brush strokes, was obviously the abbot's. It was placed in the scroll only a short time before because the ink was barely dry.

He lay the note across his leg and read it. It was a statement made by the Buddha in a *sutra*: "Like the discerning man who stands on a rocky promontory and sees the distress of those below him, so then does the sage, having banished ignorance through enlightenment, look down on suffering mankind from the heights of wisdom he has attained."

To that the abbot had added: "Those who attain such heights must use their wisdom to lift all from darkness, lest evil pull everything that is good into the depths."

Ichiro pondered this. The self-centered games he had indulged in at court were unimportant now. He, as himself, was unimportant. He was now a creature of destiny. Until Hachiman released him, any choices he made were no longer just his own.

"There are no heroes," he whispered, recalling another time, another space, "only those who have no other choice."

He read the first scroll.

———

It was well past noon when Ichiro finished the scrolls. He had disciplined himself to concentrate solely on the scrolls. He forced all distractions from his mind.

When a monk brought him a bowl of vegetables and rice, Ichiro sent him away with unthinking curtness. He made a mental note to apologize to the monk.

At last he rolled the final rice paper scroll back onto its wooden spindle and tied it fast with a thin ribbon. His head swam with what he read. Ichiro leaned forward and caught his head in his hands. He rested a moment. His eyes ached and his body was stiff from having remained in one position for so long.

A loud growl issued from his stomach. It reminded him that he needed food. However, now he had some answers. A meal would be ample reward for his efforts.

As he left Abbot Kobori's quarters, Ichiro saw a young monk crossing the monastery courtyard. He recognized him as the young monk whose companion he had rescued from the fire. Ichiro called out to the monk. The monk turned and came toward him.

"What is your name?" Ichiro asked.

"Yukio, Minamoto-san," the monk said shyly. He stared at the ground, avoiding Ichiro's gaze.

"I trust your friend is better?"

Yukio raised his head. "He still feels some pain," the young monk said. He smiled broadly. "But Abbot Kobori said the pain will pass."

"I am glad to hear that," Ichiro said. "Now, Yukio, I have some errands that must be done. Would you be so kind as to aid me?"

Yukio's eyes brightened. "I am honored, Minamoto-san," he said eagerly.

"First, tell the abbot I have finished with the scrolls he provided me and express my deepest gratitude. Then tell him I will need a monk to help me question the female warrior. You must bring that monk to my cell. Very well?"

"Of course, General," he said. Even before Ichiro had finished talking, the young monk was racing toward the main temple, his robes whipping about his thin legs.

Ichiro smiled and shook his head. Yukio was far too innocent and child-like. *He will need to control that youthful energy if he wished to be a good monk,* Ichiro thought. And yet the young man's exuberance impressed Ichiro. He knew he would find a use for the young man, and he suspected Yukio would willingly renounce the monastic life, if just for a short time.

Ichiro returned to his room. The atmosphere of the monastery was conducive to meditation. His mind, both weary and exhilarated by his findings, needed time to absorb that information.

He tried to recall what the monk taught him as a pageboy. To his surprise it returned easily. He slipped into the contemplative state of *zazen*, and once more tangled with the *koan*. Gradually his mind and body fell. His eyes closed, Ichiro was deep in the mindless mind when he heard the slap of Yukio's bare feet outside the cell door.

He opened his eyes but did not turn to look at the young monk. "You must learn, Yukio, not to walk so loudly. Mask your movements. A monk should move through this world like a shadow. Only a fool or a samurai announces his presence like a thunderclap."

"Forgive me, Minamoto-san," the young monk said.

Ichiro rose. A slight edge of pain passed through his leg. It was the result of having sat far too long. "Do not worry, Yukio, the skills will come in time. If you let them. Now, please take me to the monk who will aid me."

"There is no need. I am here to help you, Ichiro," said a voice outside.

Abbot Kobori stepped into the room. He walked to Yukio and placed his hand on the young monk's shoulder. "You must listen to what our guest says, Yukio. There is wisdom in his words." The abbot smiled gently.

Humbled, Yukio lowered his head.

"Come on then," the abbot said. "Let us see what we may learn from our prisoner." He turned to Yukio. "Yukio, we will need your help."

The monk's flagging spirits instantly rose. "I will do whatever I can, venerable *roshi*."

The abbot led Ichiro to an old stone structure across the courtyard. The building had been useful, once. Now its four walls stood inelegantly against the higher monastery walls. Its thatch had long vanished to the ravages of wind and rain, exposing naked roof beams to nature's fury.

It now served as an impromptu stable and punishment area where disobedient novices could consider their errors of behavior. The pungent odor of animal waste permeated the air.

"What kept you?" Shizuka asked. She stepped from the shadows. She wore the dark clothes of a *ninja*, a black *dhoti* and a long-sleeved jacket. Straw sandals clad her feet. The sandals were cushioned with heavy cloth to dampen any sound. A *katana* in a black lacquered scabbard was thrust into a wide black *obi* about her waist.

"Where did you come from?" Ichiro said.

"I've been watching the monks from my room," she replied. "I saw them bring the woman warrior here."

The sudden change in Shizuka puzzled Ichiro. When he rescued her, she was the picture of a frightened woman. Now there was confidence to her movement and manner. She carried herself with the sureness of a master of *ninjutsu*.

"You did not have those clothes or that sword when I found you, Shizuka. If that is your name," Ichiro said. "Where did you get them?"

"I did not steal them, samurai, and my name is Shizuka, if that matters," she said sharply. "Some of you think we *ninjas* are nothing but common thieves. These clothes are mine. I cached them in the woods. I retrieved them last night while everyone was asleep. That was how I raised the alarm when the women warriors attacked."

"So it was you who jumped from the darkness and killed that one samurai," Ichiro said.

"Yes," she answered. "I knew even with that sword of yours, Minamoto, you would have been hard pressed."

"I would have prevailed, in the end."

She stared at him a moment, then smiled. "Yes, no doubt you would have. Now, shall we tend to this business?"

"Very well," Ichiro said.

"Are you certain you wish this?" Abbot Kobori interjected.

Ichiro nodded. "Yes, I am," he said.

"Then let us proceed," the abbot said.

The aging monk led the way into the building. It was larger inside than it appeared, Ichiro noted. Stalls lined the sides and in the center was a wide, flat table of stone.

The stone protruded from the earth, as if it had grown there. It was as thick as three severed heads placed atop each other and as wide as a person was tall. Its length was half again as large. Sculpted prayers and *sutra* covered the surface. Handholds were cut into each corner.

"I will need your assistance," the abbot said. He went to one corner and grasped the handhold there.

Yukio took the corner next to Abbot Kobori. Ichiro grasped the corner across from the abbot, and Shizuka the remaining corner.

"Heave!" the abbot ordered.

They lifted with all their strength.

At first there was resistance. The stone refused to move. Then it rose slowly, only to slide back into place.

Ichiro grit his teeth. He remembered a Buddhist prayer from childhood, a portion of the *Lotus sutra* he used to aid his concentration.

"*Nom-myoho-renge-kyo*," he whispered. "*Nom-myoho-renge-kyo*." Glory to the *Lotus sutra*'s law, he thought.

Abbot Kobori smiled, nodded once and took up the prayer. Yukio and Shizuka also took up the chant.

The stone began to rise.

"It's moving!" Yukio shouted.

But the more they exerted, the heavier the stone was. Ichiro's arms felt like wet cloth, heavy and limp. They grew numb. Sweat stood on his brow. He chanted with more determination.

A gap appeared between the stone and the rest of the table.

"Quickly, move it to one side," the abbot ordered.

The stone slid aside easily. Once taken from the table, it barely weighed anything. They laid it down on the bare earth floor.

From the hole it covered came a foul odor, a stink of decay. A faint orange mist drifted through the opening. It dissipated slowly in the fresh air. The stench made Ichiro slightly nauseous.

"Come, follow me," Abbot Kobori said. He stepped onto the table and descended a narrow stone staircase.

Small torches illuminated the stairs. They glowed brightly and warmly. Narrow openings beneath the torches directed fresh air from above. An occasional blast of cool air issued from the openings, and the torches grew brighter.

"During the civil wars we used these catacombs to hide from enemy soldiers," the abbot said. "They would enter the monastery, find no one about and make camp for the night. While the soldiers slept, the monks would slip out and cut the enemy's throat."

"Hardly the behavior of a gentle monk, *roshi*. I would expect that more from a *ninja*," Ichiro said. He watched Shizuka for a reaction. If the remark angered her, she did not show it.

"A dead monk cannot help all sentient beings. They prayed that the dead soldiers would be reborn in the Pure Land," Abbot Kobori said. "And I was," he added with a laugh.

Ichiro smiled. The abbot was more enlightened than he had thought.

The staircase curled downward as they neared the catacombs themselves. The odor of decay was distinctly stronger and more penetrating. The mist was now an orange fog. Moisture ran down the walls, accompanied by the steady drip of water from the ceiling. Ahead of them a rat scuttled quickly away, diving into a narrow crack in the wall.

At last they reached bottom. The stone floor was covered in pungent standing water. Clotted with algae, the water was not deep, but it sloshed over their feet. It was slimy and slick underfoot.

The abbot led them down a brief corridor. It stopped at a short flight of stairs which led into a large room. In the room four torches danced brightly to their ultimate destruction. The light they cast was harsh and yellow, flickering like existence itself. The carved tiled floor was dry. So was the air, which was freshened by vents along the lower part of walls.

The woman warrior lay strapped to a heavy lacquered table. She was barely alive, suspended between the conscious and unconscious worlds. Her eyes were open but unfocused. Unmoving, she stared at the portrait of Kannon on the ceiling. Occasionally she blinked. Her stomach rose slightly at each breath she took, and the breaths themselves were infrequent.

The monks had removed her armor and dressed her in a thin blue kimono. They had bathed her, cleansed her wounds, and bound them with soft white linen. Without her armor, she seemed as fragile as an eggshell. She was thin and spare, yet Ichiro knew she must possess considerable strength to wield a *tachi* as she had.

"Do not touch her," the abbot warned. "A force surrounds her and protects her."

"A *mononoke*?" Ichiro asked.

"Perhaps," Abbot Kobori said. "But the demon does not possess her body. It lies elsewhere and merely guards her."

"Then how did the monks change her clothing and bind her wounds?" Shizuka asked. "If this force protects her, surely it would have attacked them?"

"I do not know," the abbot said. "The demon, if it is a demon, knows who threatens her and who does not. It lets us feed and bathe her, but nothing else."

He gestured toward the woman. "See, even now it rises to protect her. It knows there are enemies here."

A soft red aura formed around the woman. It was a hazy mist, ululating, pulsing with energy. As Ichiro approached it, it grew brighter and harsher until it was the crimson of fresh blood.

Anything they might try, even just questioning the woman, would prove futile, Ichiro realized. The demon would only allow those concerned with her welfare to touch her.

Yet Ichiro knew the woman held a key to Taira's power. With the right questions, he could discern the *daimyo's* thoughts and perhaps plan his own next move. He had to counter the nobleman before Taira gained an unassailable advantage.

"How long has she been in the trance," he asked.

"Almost since you were attacked," the abbot said. "My monks noticed it after you removed her helmet."

"Have you tried to rouse her?" Ichiro asked.

Abbot Kobori nodded sadly. "Yes. We have tried all that we know of potions, balsams, herbs and strange roots. But our knowledge of such things is sadly limited. We have no apothecary and what little knowledge we possess is limited to treating simple sicknesses."

"*Roshi*," Yukio said quietly. He seemed almost afraid to speak.

"Yes, Yukio?" the abbot said.

"In the village where I was born is a fine apothecary," he said shyly. "Perhaps he has the knowledge to rouse the woman."

Ichiro grabbed the monk's left arm without thinking. "Where, Yukio?" Where is your village?"

Yukio grimaced with pain from Ichiro's grasp. Realizing what he had done, Ichiro relaxed his grip. "Forgive me, Yukio, I was not thinking."

The monk smiled, rubbing his arm. "There is no need for apologies, Minamoto-san. I know it is important to you. My village is called Kata. It is perhaps a day's ride from here to the north. It sits on a hilltop overlooking a river valley."

Ichiro turned to the abbot. "*Roshi*, can your monks prepare my horses for the journey?"

"There is no problem, but it would not be until morning."

"Good. That's soon enough. I will also need to have the woman prepared for the journey."

The abbot frowned. "As you wish, but it is dangerous."

"I am aware of that," Ichiro said. "But I am sure you will find some way to keep the demon in check."

Kobori smiled.

"And I will need to borrow Yukio to guide me."

"What about me," Shizuka said. "Do you think to leave me here, to sit around doing nothing while these monks chant their *sutra*s all day?"

Ichiro still was unsure if Shizuka were an ally or merely one of Taira's ploys. He also knew she would never willingly tell him much of anything.

"No," he said. "I do not intend to leave you. And I think you would come regardless of my wishes. But I need your skills and sword."

Satisfied, she smiled. But her hand dropped to rest on the *katana's* hilt.

"Ho ho, Minamoto," a thundering voice suddenly said. "You deceive yourself, fool samurai, if you think your journey will be an easy one."

The voice came from the woman's mouth, but it was neither her voice nor the voice of a demon. It was Taira's.

Ichiro smiled. If it was intended to scare him, it failed. In fact, it was ludicrous. He mused on how much more convenient a telephone might have been for the wizard. "Speak your mind, Taira," he said. "I have things to do."

"Ah, such arrogance!" the voice said, laughing. "All you Minamoto are so self-important."

"Get on with it, Taira."

"Very well. I know you mean to travel to a village called Kata. There you seek an apothecary."

"So not only does your woman speak with your tongue, she listens with your ears," Ichiro said.

"I am master to the *mononoke* who guards her. He tells me what I need to know. But enough. You think if you destroy the demon you will learn information that you can use against me. I will tell you, you are quite correct. And I will tell you I cannot allow you to reach Kata."

"You cannot stop me, Taira."

"Ah, how wrong you are, samurai." The voice seemed to spit contempt. "Already I have begun. Go to the monastery parapets and look for yourself.

From far above came a sudden cry from several monks.

"Already the monks have seen my handiwork. Go, look for yourself."

Without hesitating, Ichiro turned and ran down the steps into the flooded corridor. His feet tossed up great gouts of water as he ran. As he went up the stairs to the surface he knew something was desperately wrong. The cries of the monks were confused and frightened. The sound of their running feet reverberated down the narrow confines of the catacombs.

When he reached the surface and entered the courtyard, his eyes were momentarily blinded by the bright sunlight. As his vision cleared, he saw a cluster of monks gathered at a parapet on the far northern wall. Their robes fluttered in the wind. They were chattering and pointing over the wall into the fields beyond.

Ichiro climbed a thin wooden ladder to a ledge that ran along the wall to the red tiled rooftops. Forcing his way past the monks, he found an opening and looked out into the valley.

His heart skipped a beat at what he saw. *Was Taira right? Can I be stopped?* Ichiro wondered.

He was suddenly unsure of what to do. His confidence drained away as water from a cracked jug. All he could do was shake his head and watch in amazement as huge black trees forced themselves fully grown from the earth. There were such great numbers they quickly surrounded the monastery and covered the land from horizon to horizon.

CHAPTER SEVEN

By morning the forest surrounded Jimmukei monastery. The monks on watch reported seeing strange shapes lurking at the edge of the woods, but nothing came into the daylight.

Ichiro slammed the hilt of his *tachi*. How was he to get through those trees? The woods were incredibly dense, so much so that no sunlight penetrated the branches. But he had to reach the apothecary. Remaining in the monastery was accepting inevitable defeat. Taira's minions could easily besiege them and there would be no escape.

"Have you decided, my friend Minamoto?" Abbot Kobori asked, climbing the stairs to the battlements.

Ichiro leaned against the top of the battlements. "What decision have I, venerable *roshi*, that has not already been preordained for me?" He stroked his chin, felt the rough stubble of fresh beard under his fingertips.

"Taira has forced my hand. He knows I need the apothecary's help. So he sends a forest to stop me. And he knows that I must enter that forest." He stopped and looked out over the battlements. A frown crossed his face. "Now he taunts me," he said, shaking his head. "Look for yourself, abbot." He pointed to the forest.

In the midst of the trees a path began forming. The trees moved apart, forming an archway over the path. The path itself ran directly toward the apothecary's village.

"No," abbot Kobori said, "he does not taunt you. He is challenging you, Minamoto. He knows you will take that path and confront whatever is there. He would taunt you only if he knew you would not go."

"But I will go," Ichiro added softly. "He is after something I have." He fingered the lacquered handle of his *tachi*. "I cannot help but think it is my sword. And somehow Akiyama is tied into this." He paused a moment and reflected. "A mirror, a seal and a sword to rule a nation. Come, abbot, I have preparations to attend to."

The monks had brought the horses into the courtyard. They placed provisions on the packhorse's backs. In addition to Luck and Fortune were the three horses that had been ridden by the female *samurai* and the monastery's plow horse. Ichiro wanted to protest that the plow horse was too important to the monastery, but Abbot Kobori pointed out that plowing had long since passed. The horse was useless until the harvest. Better to have it work than have it remain idle, penned in a stall while its muscles went thin. It would know when to return, the abbot explained.

"There is much danger in those woods," the abbot commented. He folded a section of his robe over his arm to keep it from dragging the ground. "I have taken the precaution of having prayers painted on your horses' foreheads. This will protect them from any *mononoke* that dwell in the trees."

Three monks went from horse to horse. Two held the horse's reins and quieted it while the third carried a small pail and drawing brush. He dipped the brush into the ink pail and painted a line of *ganji* characters from the horse's forehead down the snout to just under the eyes. The prayers were protection against demons, a wish for good luck, and a prayer for blessings from Hachiman.

All went well until the monks reached the third of the female samurai's horses. The two monks held the horse's reins, but it jumped and struggled in protest. With great effort the two monks pulled the animal's head down so the third monk could apply the prayers.

No sooner had the monk completed the first prayer, the protection against demons, when smoke began to rise from the prayer. The horse screamed in pain and broke free of the grasp of the monks. The prayer burst into flame on the horse's forehead and began to burn its way into the animal's skull.

Frightened and in pain, the horse raced madly about the courtyard. Monks jumped out of its way, but even so some were knocked to the ground. Ichiro knew what to do. He drew an arrow from his quiver and notched it into his bow. Pulling back on the bowstring, he waited until the horse came around once more, bucking madly.

The arrow jumped from the bow and entered the horse's front right shoulder. Crippled, it tried to run, but collapsed. It thrashed the air with its back legs, tossing up a cloud of dirt. But exhaustion and pain soon brought it to silence.

Ichiro slung the bow across his body and withdrew his sword. With deliberate slowness, he approached the animal.

There was wildness in the horse's eyes as it saw Ichiro. It tried to regain its feet, but could barely lift its head. Blood flowed down its nose and mixed with phlegm and saliva that foamed at its mouth and nostrils. The area around the prayer still smoked faintly, the flesh cooked black and the bone of the skull shining death white underneath.

"I am sorry, horse," he said softly. He reached down and stroked its head. Reassured, it lay its head down. The wildness fled its eyes.

Ichiro raised the *tachi* and brought it down with both hands. It cut cleanly through the horse's neck.

The headless body spasmed once, the legs flailing uncontrollably about, forcing Ichiro to step back from the deadly hooves. But without a brain to guide them, the legs collapsed like broken twigs.

Hot red blood boiled from the neck and flowed over the earth and stones. Steam rose in sheets from the blood as it ate rocks and soil like acid. It bubbled and cascaded as it flowed. As it cooled, the blood began to form the shape of a creature. It was almost human in form, yet seemed hideously deformed, with claw-like hands with three fingers and a huge, grossly misshapen head. The blood cooled quickly, turning black and leaving the shape like a shadow without a source.

Ichiro stared at the form on the ground at his feet, then looked at his *tachi*. The engraved *horimono* glowed red-hot, while the remaining metal was barely warm.

"You have not only slain the horse, Minamoto," Abbot Kobori said as he came to Ichiro's side, "but you have slain the demon which possessed it."

Then the abbot saw the engravings on the sword blade and nodded with understanding. "No, it is your sword that has slain the *mononoke*."

Suddenly disturbed by the sword, Ichiro sheathed the sword. "*Roshi*, why did the prayer injure this horse and not the others?" he asked, hoping to distract the abbot's attention from the weapon.

"I do not know. I can only guess," Abbot Kobori replied. "This is surely the horse of the woman we hold captive. Horse and rider both are held together in a demonic bond by means of the *mononoke* that undoubtedly Taira has placed there. The prayer to drive the demon out proved efficacious."

"But that does not explain the other horses," Ichiro protested.

"There were no demons to possess them," the Abbot stated. "Now the answer should be apparent to you, Minamoto."

Ah, yes, he realized. The demons bound the horse and rider to Taira's control. But with their riders dead, the horses would be useless. The demons had fled accordingly. All except the third, for it still lay waiting for the woman to recover.

But Ichiro's *tachi* had driven it out, feeding somehow on the force that kept the demon alive.

"Yes, I see, Abbot," Ichiro said.

A scream tore the air.

"The woman," Ichiro realized. He ran toward the room where she was held.

He burst through the door in time to see two monks trying to restrain her. She was sitting bolt upright, her mouth open in soundless terror and her eyes round in madness. Ichiro's eyes saw the *hachimaki* lying on a small table. Quickly he grabbed it and tied it to the woman's forehead.

Almost immediately, her body went limp and she collapsed onto the bed. Her face was still pale with terror, but the prayers stitched into the headband were keeping at bay whatever she had seen in her fear.

"The demon that possessed her is dead," Ichiro said, thinking aloud. "Yet what still controls her?"

"Lord Taira still controls her," Abbot Kobori answered.

"Yes, in some fashion. No longer by the *mononoke*, but the spell is still strong." Ichiro hoped that this apothecary Yukio knew would have the potions to break the spells.

"Can she ride?" he asked one of the monks attending to her.

The monk nodded. "You will have to tie her to the saddle."

"Very well." Ichiro turned to the abbot. "*Roshi*, it is now even more important that I reach this apothecary. This woman is the key, and I must open the lock."

"We will prepare her for the journey," Abbot Kobori answered. "But beware, Minamoto," he cautioned, "she is still in Taira's power and he may use her as he pleases. And the woods you must enter are his creation. You will not be safe."

Ichiro dropped his gaze to his *tachi*. "Yes, abbot, I know. But my sword is of value to Taira, and somehow I think it will not let me die so easily."

———

They left the monastery near midday.

Ichiro wore his armor, although he let his helmet dangle by the chinstrap, dancing on his back. Luck sensed the imminent danger and let his master know by pawing the ground nervously.

Shizuka was at Ichiro's side, mounted on one of the female warriors' horses. She remained dressed in the black trousers and jacket of the *ninja*. A black *eboshi* rested on her head. The *katana* was sheathed at her side. Yet despite the martial trappings, she retained the simple humanity of her womanhood. But Ichiro knew she was his equal, and he did not resent it.

The loss of the possessed horse meant Yukio had to share Fortune with some of the supplies. As a packhorse, Fortune was used to weight. Yukio, however, seemed uncomfortable on horseback. It was apparent from the manner in which he held the reins that his experience in riding was very limited.

The woman warrior was tied to the saddle of her horse. Her head lolled forward on her chest. Her arms hung limply by her side. The reins of her horse were tied to the back of Shizuka's saddle.

The monastery plow horse brought up the rear. Laden with baskets of food and jars of water as well as a suit of armor that Shizuka had taken from one of the dead warriors, the poor horse seemed very forlorn. The cast in his eyes gave the impression that he preferred being hitched to a plow in a stony field to being laden with supplies.

"I wish you well," Abbot Kobori said.

"I thank you, abbot," Ichiro replied. "But I do not think wishing me well will matter much."

"I do not comprehend your point, Minamoto."

"My friend," Ichiro said with a smile, "you and I are in a game of *Go* which lasts for eternity. There can be no end in this game, for victory for either player would result in the destruction of them both. Instead, the players maneuver pieces so that one side may occasionally gain the advantage. But never is this advantage so great that victory is assured. The advantage is always ultimately lost, for as one piece is lost, another piece replaces it.

"Yet now, dear and honored *roshi*, something has happened to the game. The balance has been tipped. One side nears victory and guarantees destruction."

The abbot nodded sadly. "You comprehend the nature of things well, my samurai friend." Then he smiled. "But the game is not over. And like a master of *ju-jitsu*, you must use your opponent's strength to your advantage."

"I will remember, *roshi*," Ichiro replied, the wisdom of the abbot's words sinking in into his mind. He reined his horse about. The party rode through the monastery gate and down the path into the forest.

Although the day was warm, the forest air was distinctly chilly. Ichiro was glad he had worn his armor, as it kept him warm. He glanced at the others. There was no discernible reaction from Shizuka, who now seemed more mysterious than ever. He could not fathom what she was, and it bothered him. Yukio, on the other hand, was shivering in his thin monk's robes.

"Cold, my little monk friend?" Ichiro asked.

Yukio nodded. "Do you think it will be this cold all the way into the forest?" he asked, his teeth chattering.

Ichiro shook his head. "That, I am afraid, I do not know. But we will get you warm clothes, if you wish." He gestured with his head. "The wicker basket to your left has a quilted jacket. Put it on if you are cold."

All too soon the air became hot and humid. The sun bore down on the trees, forcing the leaves and the earth to surrender what little moisture they possessed. By late afternoon, the woods exhaled a sweltering miasma.

The heat did not seem to bother Shizuka at all . Beneath her black clothing, she appeared relaxed and at ease, as though on a casual ride in the country and not a potentially dangerous forest.

Yukio still struggled with riding the horse. Occasionally, he would hold onto the reins with one hand as he wrung moisture from his perspiration-soaked robes.

The woman still remained immobile, her head bouncing on her chest at each step of the horse. Ichiro thought he perceived a slight movement of her lips, as though she were trying to speak, but he was uncertain.

Ichiro perspired under his armor. His skin crawled with discomfort, and he wished he could stop to change clothing. But something told him stopping meant disaster.

At the outer edges of the path, he sensed the movement of...things. Their shapes were not discernible, but they loped and shambled with the motion of predators. Ichiro did not wish to make their hunting any easier.

They passed from under the forest canopy into a wide clearing. A stream of foul-smelling water, choked with green and yellow scum, ran through the clearing. A fish, silver with decay, floated belly-up in strings of red algae.

On both sides of the stream lay the scattered bones of men and horses. Rusted armor dressed many of the skeletons. Faded tatters of clothing clung to some bones, streaming in the breeze like tiny battle flags. In many of the bodies stood an upright spear or the broken shaft of an arrow. Skeletal hands often clutched the corroded and rusted remnants of *tachi* and *katana*.

"There was a battle here," Ichiro announced. He pointed at a skull which lay at his horse's feet. "You may see how the *tachi* cracked the skull here, how the serrated blade of a *su-yari* pierced a foot soldier's lungs."

He imagined the scene easily: blade against blade, a thrust of the lance to the chest bringing death. The same scene repeated eternally. Perhaps it had been a clash of armies after the death of the great general Hideoyoshi; the supporters of Hideoyoshi's son and those of the regent fighting for a cause that, if not lost, was at least unclear.

For the living, a smattering of glory. For the dead? Well, what did it matter now? he thought.

"How long ago was this battle?" Shizuka asked suddenly. It was the first thing she had said since the journey started.

"Two, perhaps three centuries." Ichiro replied.

"That long?" Yukio said in awe.

"How do you know?" Shizuka challenged him.

"The armor, for one thing." Ichiro answered. "The style is that of the time of Hideoyoshi. But the rust and decay would seem to say it happened long ago, much longer even than that."

Time, he thought, *what a curious thing.* The bones and weapons revived the memories of his own warriors. Friends and students plunging to their deaths in the tinfoil and bamboo aircraft. Only Hachiman knew why Ichiro had been saved and the others allowed to die.

"Come," he said, "let us be off." He reined his horse to one side. "The water should not be too deep."

As he approached the brook's edge, he heard a rattling sound. He reined Luck to a halt. Across the river was a pile of skulls. Apparently they were trophies presented to the victorious general. The wind whistled through them, a disturbing low-key whistle. But that was not the sound Ichiro had heard.

The pile seemed to shift. The rattling sound repeated. The wind picked up and dislodged the topmost skull. It rolled down the pile and across the ground until it reached the water's edge directly across from Ichiro. Coming to a halt, it righted itself. Grinning, it stared at Ichiro.

The skull's eyes glowed with a blood-red light. Then it rose slowly until it was almost level with Ichiro's own head.

Frightened, Luck reared back, nearly throwing Ichiro. He quickly calmed the animal, but he too felt its fears.

"Well, samurai," the skull said with a booming voice. It was Taira's voice. "You still see fit to challenge me. You are brave, Minamoto, and no fool."

"What do you want, Taira?" Ichiro said coldly. "These tricks of yours quickly bore me. Why not face me in the flesh as a human being?"

The skull laughed heartily. "Come, come, my friend Minamoto, why should I do so foolish a thing as that? I must consider my safety, you know. This forest is quite dangerous."

Ichiro grew angry. "Do not taunt me, Taira. You are here for a purpose. Tell me what you want or go from my sight."

The skull appeared to frown. "Such discourtesy, Minamoto, especially when I merely intended to direct you to a fine dwelling in which to pass the night. This is my forest, and naturally I must make certain that my guests have excellent accommodations."

"We have no use for your accommodations, Taira." Ichiro tugged on his reins, urging Luck forward.

"Though you are a discourteous guest, I will at least tell you, Minamoto, that crossing the brook is ill advised."

Ichiro brought the horse to a halt. For all Taira's deceit, this advice was not to be taken lightly. After all, this was his forest, and Taira had spared no expense to populate it with less than amusing things. Ichiro dismounted. Leading his horse by the reins, he walked upstream along the bank. Then he saw it.

A human leg bone protruded from the dark earth. The sun bleached part and another was blackened by decay. Ichiro reached down and pulled it from the soil. It came free with little effort, leaving only a small depression behind.

Cautiously, Ichiro approached the water's edge. He knelt on the bank and stuck bone's tip into the stream. The waters hissed and bubbled furiously, giving off a gas that stank of rotten eggs.

Ichiro withdrew the bone. As he expected, the portion that had been in the water had dissolved.

"And that is not all, friend Minamoto," the skull said. "Behold the fish."

Ichiro looked across the water toward the dead fish floating amid the algae and scum. A hideous hand emerged from the water. Red as blood, it was, with three fingers ending in hawk-like talons. One finger appeared decayed. A shaft of white bone shone against black meat.

The hand grasped the fish and pulled it under the water. A moment later, the severed fish head bobbed neatly to the surface. Ragged teeth had separated it from its body. The hand reappeared, located the head, and pulled it down as well.

"Satisfied, Minamoto?" the skull said. "You cannot cross my tiny stream. It might as well be the Inland Sea itself!"

Ichiro did not replied. He walked back to the pack horse. From a wicker basket, he pulled out something wrapped in an oil-cloth.

"What do you intend to do about the stream?" Shizuka asked, riding up to his side.

"I intend to cross it," he said flatly. He removed the leather thongs that bound the package and unwrapped it. He held up the woodcutter's axe and examined its blade. The abbot thought they could use it, and now Ichiro was appreciative of the man's foresight. He looked up at Shizuka.

"Do you know how to use an axe?" he asked her.

"Yes," she said, somewhat perplexed. "But why do we need the axe?"

"To build a bridge," Ichiro replied. He handed Luck's reins to Yukio and trudged toward the trees.

He selected a tall thin tree. As the axe bit into the tree trunk, Ichiro knew that it would be harder work than he had anticipated. His right leg found difficult footing, and as a consequence he could not get the leverage he needed.

"You will be ages," Shizuka told him. She had dismounted and tied her horse to a nearby bush.

He did not comment. The axe came back and then forward. Chips of wood danced into the air as the blade struck.

"I can handle the axe as well as any woodcutter," Shizuka stated. "Let me cut the wood."

Ichiro stopped cutting and leaned on the handle of the axe. Perspiration rolled down his face, reddened with exertion. He wiped his face with the back of his hand. He knew she was right, but he saw a chance to get some information from her. "You could strip the branches from the tree with your sword," he said.

"As can you," she replied. "But if I cut the trees and you trim the branches, we can save valuable time. Even you know you cannot use an axe with a leg like yours."

He smiled, nodding slightly. "Very well," he said. He handed her the axe and removed his sword.

"Tell me," he said, slashing a branch from the trunk. "Who are you?"

"My name is Shizuka," she answered, grunting as the axe head bit into a new tree.

"No," Ichiro stated, "you are more than that." He hacked another branch free. "What were you doing in Taira's camp?"

"My village was attacked by his army, and I was carried off."

The axe thudded against the wood.

"That I seriously doubt. You move with too much skill. The sword you carry is well scarred from use."

"It is Gito's. Without a hand, he didn't have much use for it. And I needed it for protection."

Splinters spun away. The tree trunk groaned.

"If any bandit saw you use that *katana*, he surely would give you wide berth. You were born to that weapon."

Shizuka pushed against the tree. The wood screamed as the tree went over. It hit the ground solidly in a cloud of dust and decay.

"Why were you in Taira's camp?' Ichiro asked again. His *tachi* split branches with a single stroke, emphasizing his impatience.

"I was there to kill him," she answered. She selected another tree and began cutting.

"Taira?"

"Yes."

"For what reason?"

She stopped cutting and stared at him. "You would not understand, samurai. They are reasons of my own."

"They certainly must be good ones then. For you have taken time to learn the skills for murder. Others attempt to kill an enemy in the heat of passion, flinging themselves madly upon their foe. Taira must certainly have wronged you if you take time to plan this murder." There was a hint of considered sarcasm in his voice, a mocking. He hoped she would react to it.

"My father taught me his skills," she replied. "How many trees will we need?"

"Your father was a *ninja*?"

She spun around to face him, the axe raised in her hands.

Ichiro remained impassive. "Was he?"

"Yes!" she spat. "Now, how many trees?"

He had one answer. The others would come as easily, with patience. "Eight, at least. But let us take ten, to be cautious."

"You are always cautious, samurai," she said, "even when you seem reckless, you are still cautious and careful."

"My caution has kept me alive," he answered flatly. He flung aside a severed branch. "So your father taught you the ways of the *ninja*. Did he teach his sons also?"

"He had no sons," she said. "So he taught me the traditions and skills of his *tan*."

"A woman warrior is a fearsome thing," he said, hacking off another limb as he spoke. "Your father taught you well."

"That is why I must kill Taira."

"To avenge him?"

"Yes. Taira killed my father. He betrayed him to the Emperor's soldiers, after he had hired my father to assassinate some high minister in the Emperor's Cabinet."

"Lord Toita," Ichiro said softly.

"Yes. Did you know him?"

"He was my first friend in this world."

"I am sorry. My father had been paid to kill him. He asked no questions of his employer."

So, Ichiro thought, *Taira's machinations have been occurring for some time.* With one step, he had eliminated the sole voice of reason in the cabinet and Lord Akiyama's major opponent, and with it destroyed one of the most powerful *ninja tans* in all Japan.

"So what were you doing as Gito's woman?" he asked.

"A role to play," she replied. The axe bit wood, and the tree began to fall. "That's six. Four more to cut. Hurry up, samurai. I'm two trees ahead of you."

"Don't worry. I'll soon have them done." He grasped a long branch in one hand, bent it back, and separated it from the tree trunk with a single stroke. "But continue with your story."

"A role," she said. "I pretended to be the frightened female. I submitted myself to one man's indignities, and then to Gito's after he had killed the first man in a brawl."

"Over you, no doubt."

"Exactly. I had hoped to attract Taira's attentions. He likes pretty girls, particularly those trained to his personal tastes." She lowered the axe a moment and rested on it. "But Gito got drunk one night and decided to teach me a lesson. He was going to whip me until you appeared." She stared at him coldly. "I must thank you for saving my life, but you ruined my plans for Taira."

"Your plans would have failed," he stated. He caught her gaze. "Taira is not one to be trifled with. You have seen his powers. It will take great effort to defeat him."

She frowned. "Unfortunately, yes." She picked up the axe and swung it hard into the tree, venting her frustration.

The tree gave way and fell.

"That's nine," she said.

"That should suffice," Ichiro responded. "Help me trim the limbs."

With a length of rope, they dragged each log into the clearing and up to the side of the stream. Carefully, they raised each log until it stood upright, then they slowly lowered the logs across the stream.

Carrying the axe and two wooden stakes, Shizuka crossed nimbly to the other side.

"Are you ready?" she called to Ichiro.

He nodded and took hold of the end of the first log. Together they rolled the log around until it butted firmly to the log next to it. They repeated it with each log. When they had fitted the final log, Shizuka drove an anchoring stake into each corner of the wooden rectangle. The stakes would prevent the logs from rolling apart under the horses' weight.

"Not a permanent bridge," Ichiro remarked. "But it will do."

He turned to Yukio. "Start the horses across."

The young monk took hold of Luck's reins and led the horse onto the log bridge. At first the animal seemed frightened, but quickly became resigned to its fate. The logs moved only slightly, although once just enough to give Yukio a start. But they were soon on the other side.

Ichiro and Shizuka led the other horses across with no incident until the last horse. The old monastery plow horse was plainly not used to all this fuss and excitement. He resisted all of Ichiro's efforts to pull him across the timbers.

"Damn you, horse," Ichiro said through clenched teeth. He felt the reins slipping through his fingers. Wrapping the reins around his arm, he suddenly realized he was now at the mercy of the skittish animal. Snorting and whinnying, its nostrils flecked with moisture, the horse moved back toward the bank of the stream. It slipped and dislodged a timber.

The horse screamed as its right back leg slipped between the logs, and it stumbled and fell.

Ichiro released the reins and went to the horse's side. He cursed the animal's stupidity but was still concerned for its safety.

Ichiro examined the leg. It did not appear broken, but it was badly lacerated and abraded. A trickle of blood ran from the knee down the furrow between the bones of the leg to the hoof. "Give me a hand," he called to Shizuka and Yukio.

Yukio took the reins and began to soothe the horse by stroking its muzzle. The horse seemed calmed by this attention and relaxed somewhat.

"Help me with the leg," Ichiro said to Shizuka.

They got on opposite sides of the leg and carefully took hold of it. Slowly they eased the injured limb from between the logs.

Shizuka ran her hand over the leg, checking for breaks. "We are fortunate," she said. "It is not broken. But it will be tender. We may have to shift the supplies to another horse."

"I see." Ichiro sighed. "Another delay." He looked across the stream to where the skull bobbed merrily in the air. "Damn you, Taira," he whispered.

He turned to Shizuka. "Get him up and across."

The horse hobbled to its feet and limped across the bridge as Yukio led it. Ichiro followed, slowed by his own crippled leg.

He took a step and discovered his left leg was not supporting him. His club foot took the brunt of his weight and he fell heavily. He was being dragged toward the edge of the bridge. The same hideous claw he had seen in the stream now had a hold of his left leg. His hands fought for purchase between the logs, but the creature's strength was incredible.

Then he saw its head. Its scaly skull was the color of dead kelp. Huge browridges loomed over tiny red eyes. It had no discernible nose. The sight spurred Ichiro's courage. He grasped his ceremonial knife and drove it into the log. It held fast, keeping him from moving further.

Angered, the creature began to climb onto the bridge, but it was slow and moved with too much caution, perhaps fully aware of Ichiro's sword. It did not see Shizuka.

She brought her *katana* down on the claw clutching Ichiro's ankle. The creature screamed as its hand was severed. It fell back, staring at its missing hand, watching ochre colored blood cascade down its arm.

Ichiro snatched his knife from the log and flung it at the thing's head. The knife lodged squarely between the creature's eyes, buried to the hilt. A trickle of the ochre blood rolled down between the eyes and curled around the lipless mouth. But it was far from dead.

The creature reached up with its good hand and plucked the knife from where it had landed. It shook its head with rage and climbed onto the bridge. Fully upright, it was nearly twice as tall as Ichiro.

By now Ichiro had his *tachi* from its sheath. He hounded the creature from one side while Shizuka attacked it from the other. The bridge was slick with the creature's blood, and footing was hard to find. Ichiro pressed an attack and stumbled. As he tried to regain his balance, he caught the back of the creature's claw, which knocked him down on his back.

His armor imprisoned him, weighing him down. He was trapped like a tortoise. The creature loomed above him, oblivious to Shizuka's attacks as she slashed at its body and legs. It cuffed her aside as if she were a doll.

It stood over Ichiro, its mouth open, exposing its shark-like teeth. Saliva glistened on them. It raised its good hand, the claws exposed, ready to gut him.

Someone screamed.

The creature took a step back, reeling from the blow. It plucked at the spear embedded in its side.

Ichiro spun onto his chest and saw Yukio standing at the end of the bridge. The monk, now trembling from fear and exertion, had thrown the spear.

Ichiro forced himself to his feet. His legs ached, but he drove himself forward. His left hand gripped his *tachi* more tightly than he ever recalled. His breath came in short, quick, burning gulps.

The creature staggered, still trying to pull the spear free, but with only one hand, it did not have the leverage to do so. The spear's barbed blade, buried deeply in the creature's flesh, held it fast.

Wounded and struggling, the creature did not seem quite so tall any more. It looked at Ichiro, its red eyes glowing dully.

Ichiro thrust his *tachi* into the animal's chest. It screamed and swung a claw at him, a feeble attempt to attack at best. Still, it refused to acknowledge defeat. It swung its wounded arm at Ichiro, but he managed to duck under the blow. Frustrated, the creature opened its mouth to scream, but nothing came out.

The *tachi*'s blade grew red hot as it drank the creature's life. The metal sang shrilly, as though the sword were not just a sword but a living being. The creature fell to its knees, then rolled onto its back.

Ichiro pulled the sword loose. The blade cooled instantly.

Still alive, the creature crawled slowly to the edge of the bridge.

With a final effort, it propelled itself into the stream, as if the poisoned waters would restore it.

"You let it get away!" Shizuka shouted, coming to his side.

"No," Ichiro replied. He gestured with the sword. "Look."

The liquid in the stream began to boil furiously. The creature's skeleton bobbed briefly to the surface. Other taloned hands reached up and tore away shreds of black meat. Then the bones themselves slowly melted and drifted away, now just white froth on the scummy green liquid.

"Let us go," he said softly. "We still have a distance to travel."

Once they were on the other side, they were greeted by the skull.

"An excellent performance," the skull said jovially. "Rarely have I seen the *tachi-mawari* performed with such energy and grace. Most exciting."

"You talk like we were nothing but performers in the *kabuki*," Ichiro said angrily.

"Ah, dear Minamoto, but you were performing," the skull replied. "It was my play, written, directed, choreographed by me, with you as my actors. And Minamoto, you are giving the greatest performance since Yoshida in *Benten-Kozo*. I commend your skill."

"I want no part of your play, Taira," Ichiro said. "I wish to destroy you."

"Ah, but that must wait until the final act, where it will surprise us all, no doubt." The skull bobbed about, its voice gleeful. "But now we must hurry. The accommodations I have arranged for you cannot be kept waiting."

The skull dodged a pebble that Yukio threw at it.

"Leave us alone, skull!" the monk shouted, still trembling. "Go away, go away!" He grabbed a handful of stones and flung them in rapid succession.

Ichiro grabbed Yukio and fastened his arms. "It's futile, little monk. Pebbles will not hurt him. You are spitting into the wind."

Yukio's emotions finally broke down. "I want to destroy him," he sobbed, tears streaming down his cheeks. "Because he tried to hurt you." He slid to the ground, resting on his knees.

Ichiro gently lifted the young monk to his feet. "Come," he said, "we must be going. It is almost evening."

As they remounted, Shizuka turned to Ichiro and asked, "So, samurai, what do we do now? For myself, I do not intend to spend a night here."

"We have no choice," Ichiro replied. He gestured toward the skull. "He controls the actions at the moment." Ichiro kicked his leg over the saddle and fitted his clumsy foot into its stirrup.

"But what about tonight, Minamoto?" Shizuka asked, riding up to his side.

"We will have to devise something when the time arises."

Shizuka shook her head. "Sometimes you are a fool," she said disgustedly. "And sometimes so am I," she added.

Ichiro did not reply. He urged his horse forward, keeping his eye on the skull which now drifted with purpose down the narrow path through the woods.

Everyone remained quiet for some time. Ichiro noticed that Shizuka rode behind him, while Yukio and the packhorses lay further back. He detected a hesitation in the way Shizuka rode, as though she wished to come to his side but something held her back.

"Her fears, no doubt." he told himself. And why not? His own fears certainly could cause indecision. It was the warrior's fatal affliction. To think was to hesitate. To hesitate was to die.

Ichiro wished the woods would end. He could see the sun slowly dropping behind the tall spires of the black trees. The sunlight trickled through in thin and delicate shafts, slicing between leaves and branches.

Night approached and that made Ichiro uncomfortable. One of Taira's creations had nearly killed them in broad daylight. Darkness was Taira's domain, and there was no telling what things the wizard could unleash then.

The skull had said accommodations waited, prepared especially for them. An obvious trap, yet Taira was not such a fool as to display his plots so openly. Just more trickery and deceit, that was apparent.

Perhaps, Ichiro thought, *the creature at the bridge was a test. No, there had been ample tests with the other traps Taira had laid. Then what? A diversion, perhaps? Or a delaying action? Ah, now that seemed far more likely.*

The skull was adamant when it talked of the lodgings prepared. Indeed, now that Ichiro considered it, he realized there was an urgency as well. *Did it mean he was close to his goal? Or was Taira's trap too well set, so finely planned that the slightest mistiming would send it awry?*

Ichiro scratched at his moustache and beard and pondered a moment. They had been making excellent time since entering the woods. Taira's creations stayed away from them for the most part. *Why? Fear? Not likely. Anxiety? Impossible, if the creature at the bridge was any indication.*

The sword.

Yes, there was something about the sword, the way the *horimono* blazed after slaying first the demon and then the creature. That bothered him. The sword had never done that before. Its powers were formidable, naturally, and they made his skill even more considerable. But this new power was disturbing. The *tachi* seemed alive, feeding off the things it killed.

Yes, perhaps the creatures were afraid after all. He would fear it too, if it were not his weapon and almost a part of him.

So the demons held back, fearful, hesitant to attack. That fear allowed Ichiro's party to make good time through the woods, perhaps such good time that they would be long past Taira's trap before the *daimyo* had the chance to spring it.

Obviously a delay was necessary, to consume time so Taira could finish his plot and guarantee Ichiro would not reach it before nightfall. *All it took was a creature foolish enough not to know better. If it killed him, then excellent. If not, it would force him to spend precious time combating it. Either way, it served Taira's purpose and was expendable.*

"That is it," he said to the skull, "that is precisely it, isn't it?"

The skull, which floated four horse lengths in front of them, appeared to bounce delightedly. A small chuckle issued from its bleached jaws.

"Yes," Ichiro said, "I was right, wasn't I?"

"Thinking?"

He had not noticed that Shizuka had ridden up to his side.

"In a fashion," he said. He nodded his head toward the skull. "About him."

"What about him?"

He told her.

"Interesting," she admitted. "We shall have to see about that. He's quite ugly, don't you think."

"Everything here is ugly."

"Even me?"

He looked at her and saw that she was serious. "I did not mean you, obviously. You are not one of Taira's creations." He paused. "Or are you?"

"You doubt me?" she said. Her voice was flat and unemotional.

"I have learned to doubt nearly everything," he replied. "There are even moments when I doubt my own reality."

He looked directly at her. She seemed puzzled. "I have no control over the existence of this world," he said. "But I must accept it and act upon it because my mind accepts it."

"You still did not answer me," Shizuka said.

"I doubt you, true," Ichiro stated. He looked back to Yukio. "I also doubt him. And the abbot as well. Does that satisfy you?"

"I am not one of Taira's creations, even if you don't believe me."

"They can lie as easily as anyone."

She quickly changed the subject. "I have been talking to Yukio."

"Yes."

"He cares very much for you."

"And you don't?"

"I said nothing of myself. Let it stay at that."

"Very well." There was an honesty in her speech, he admitted to himself. Truthfully, he could not believe that she was Taira's agent. But his intuition ran counter to what his eyes could and did see. And that seed of doubt produced a slight, dull ache in his mind, an ache of uncertainty and suspicion. He still could not trust her. Not yet.

"Tell me," he said, "what do you mean that Yukio cares for me?"

For a moment, Shizuka seemed dumbfounded. Then she tossed

back her head and laughed. "You fool," she said, "Can't you see, oh wise samurai? The boy is in love with you."

Ichiro found himself unmoved by the revelation. His own emotions had been strained too often by love and his mind grew preoccupied with more pressing matters. He had learned to shut out such feelings.

Shizuka was puzzled by Ichiro's lack of response. "Why don't you react, samurai? Doesn't this disturb you?"

"As a boy," he said calmly, "I was in love with my teacher. I thought him the most beautiful man in all Japan." He let his gaze burn into her for a moment. "Are you perhaps offended by this, *ninja*?"

She lowered her head slightly, obviously affected by his suppressed anger.

"You are jealous of the boy, aren't you?" he said.

She did not answer him.

"No, not jealousy," he said. "Envy. You envy his feelings, that he can love someone." He paused a moment. "I envy him too."

"You, samurai?" she snapped. "What have you to be envious of?"

"I told you that I loved my teacher." he said gently. "It was a deep, romantic love. All young samurai are expected to love their mentors. But what I had not anticipated was that he did not love me."

"Someone else?"

Ichiro nodded. "I hated her. She was very beautiful, and I thought she had seduced his love from me. Such is the folly of men. We do not see the world as clearly as women often do."

"So what did you do, samurai?"

"I grew older and wiser," he said with a smile.

"That is not an answer."

"No, you are right, that is not an answer."

"So?"

"I could not have his love, and I could not hate her forever. So I married her daughter."

He glanced at Shizuka and noticed her perplexed expression. "An odd thing for me to do, you think? Quite wrong, Shizuka. I learned that the world expects a man to take a wife, if only for appearances. But I learned also that a part of him was a part of her. If I could not have him, I could at least have a piece of him."

"That is still not an answer," she said flatly.

"There are never any answers," he replied.

"Where is she now, your wife?"

Ichiro pulled on his reins and brought Luck to a halt. He felt suddenly sad and laden with loss and grief. "She is alive, somewhere."

"Will you go back to her?"

He smiled wanly. "No, she lives in a world where I no longer exist. Do not ask me to explain what I mean, Shizuka. There is an answer for this, I assure you, but no one but me may understand it." He gave Luck a gentle kick to the flanks. The horse resumed trotting slowly along the road.

"I feel sorry for Yukio, in a way," he admitted. "He will have to learn that every one he loves will not always love him."

"I am sorry for all of us," Shizuka said. She looked up and the expression on her face changed to one of apprehension. "Look," she said, pointing

The path opened into another clearing. In the twilight, shadows danced madly around the trees and played along the side of a small house that sat in the center of the clearing.

"Your accommodations," the skull said with glee. It glowed with a soft white light, like sunshine reflecting on mother-of-pearl. The light emanated from within the bone.

"I promised you lodgings," Taira laughed. "Here they are. Warm beds, a fine meal, jars of hot *sake*, all await you."

Ichiro brought Luck to a halt and dismounted. "Yukio," he called over his shoulder, "take the horses and tie them to that willow."

The young monk dismounted, grabbed the horses' reins and lead them toward the tree.

"Well," Shizuka said, coming to Ichiro's side, "what do we do?" There was more than a trace of unrest in her voice.

"For the moment, we do nothing," Ichiro replied. "We will spend the night here and go on in the morning."

"In the house?"

"No, of course not. It is obviously a trap, and I do not intend to give Lord Taira the pleasure of springing it. If we have to, we can enter it in the morning. It should not be so dangerous in daylight."

They made ready for the night. Ichiro gave the horses oats, and then had Yukio draw a circle of prayers around them for protection against any of Taira's spells. As an added precaution, Ichiro had a prayer carved into the willow tree's trunk. The tree, fortunately, was simply a tree, and not another of Taira's tricks.

Shizuka had a fire going and cooked a quick meal of fish, rice, and some green vegetables. After the meal, they unrolled wicker mats and thin blankets to sleep on. Yukio drew another prayer circle around them again as a precaution.

While Ichiro and Shizuka took care of the still unconscious female warrior, Yukio played a pleasant melody on the *samisen*, accompanying himself in a skilled voice.

"We will keep watch in turn," Ichiro said.

"I will take the first watch," Shizuka said.

He nodded. "Very well. I will take the second."

Ichiro lay on the wicker mat and pulled the blanket over him. He was too tired to even remove his armor. From the corner of his eye, he could see Yukio was already asleep.

The young monk lay curled up on his mat like a small boy. One arm lay outside the blanket, the hand clutching the neck of the *samisen*. Yukio had displayed a great deal of endurance in the ride, but his tired body had at last caught up with him.

Ichiro unbuckled the armor from his hands and arms and turned on his side to sleep. Sleep came quickly.

And all too quickly he felt Shizuka rousing him.

"Your watch," she said tiredly.

Ichiro brought himself awake as best he could. His back ached and his arms felt like heavy rocks. His mouth was dry, so he picked up one of the ceramic water jars and swallowed several mouthfuls. It did little to clear his head and still left his mouth dry.

He sat before the fire and rested his *tachi* across his lap. Shizuka was already asleep, snoring peacefully.

Ichiro resolved himself to his vigil. The fire flickered brightly before him. Tongues of fire leaped from the wood and curled away, subsiding.

"How can you stay awake, Minamoto," the voice of Taira taunted him, "after you have ridden so far and so long?"

"Go away," Ichiro mumbled. He tried to shake off the weight of slumber from his mind.

"Why do you sleep outside," the skull asked, "when I've provided such fine lodgings for you? You insult me with your refusal."

"And you insult me with your presence," Ichiro shouted. "Leave me alone." He hurled a clod of dirt toward the grinning skull.

The skull remained out of reach and laughed gleefully.

Ichiro returned his gaze to the fire. Its flames were spiraling and swirling hypnotically. His tired mind relaxed its hold on consciousness and fell into sleep. He shook himself awake and found himself outside the circle. The house was before him now, and he stood at the foot of the rickety wooden steps.

Laughing skulls, all with the voice of Taira, orbited the house. They were challenging him, taunting him.

Three huge spiders were spinning webs from the roof to the ground. Suddenly, a strand of the web wrapped itself around Ichiro's legs and pulled him to the ground. The spiders began slowly to drag him into the house. He slashed at the web with his sword, but it was moist and resistant. It took several blows before it severed.

The spiders came toward him. Venom glistened on their mandibles, and their eyes reflected a hundred full moons. A quick movement of the *tachi*, and one spider was cut in two. It lay on its back, its legs twitching feebly. Its severed head thrashed feverishly about, trying to strike something that was not there.

Carefully, Ichiro lured the second spider about, pulling it farther and farther from the house. It followed him cautiously, never taking its gaze from him, its jaws clacking to and fro. Its resolute action was its downfall.

It did not see the severed head of its companion until it was too late. The jaws of the still struggling head touched the soft underbelly of the second spider and struck, injecting venom deep into its companion's abdomen. The second spider shuddered, struggled momentarily, but the poison was strong. It collapsed and rolled on its side, its eight legs curling up into its body.

The third spider was not so easily deceived. It held back and waited for an opening. At last it attacked, but Ichiro was prepared. The spider retreated, minus two legs on its right side.

Again it charged, only to retreat minus another leg. It stumbled, and Ichiro counterattacked, striking the legs from the spider's body. Unable to move, it tried to drag itself along by its jaws. It tried to reach the safety of its web.

Ichiro was weary, and he could hardly lift his sword. But he could not let the creature escape. He walked up behind it. With one careful thrust, his sword pierced the spider's abdomen and pinned it to the ground.

It screamed once, a long shrill sound, then bent at its middle in a final, futile effort. Then it, too, was still.

Pulling the sword free, Ichiro turned and started back toward the safety of the fire and the circle of prayers. Still dazed and tired, he felt something touch his shoulder. He whirled about, sword ready to strike.

His wife Yukiko stood before him. She was as he last remembered her, before he had left for the airfield. Her face was white with make-up. Her cheeks were delicately rouged and her eyebrows darkened in the manner of an aristocratic woman.

She wore a yellow flowered *kimono*, bound with a heavy green silken *obi*. A formal crested *haori* and an elaborate *marumage* coiffure completed her attire. She took his hand and placed it on her breast.

"No," he shouted, pulling his hand away. "You are not real. You are a dream! Get away from me!"

Ichiro tried to run, but stumbled on his crippled leg. He caught his balance and got to his feet. The circle of prayers and the safety of the fire were within reach. Sanctuary was as close as a few steps. Then he heard the voice.

"Do you wish your wife to die, Minamoto?" Taira said.

Ichiro turned around and saw Taira himself and not the skull. The *daimyo* had his arm around Yukiko's waist and held a thin dagger to her throat.

"She is an illusion, Taira!" Ichiro shouted. "She is just another of your tricks!"

"But can you be sure, Minamoto?"

"What do you mean?"

Taira smiled slightly. "You know my power, Minamoto. All around you are my works. Could you then deny me the power to bring this woman whom you call your wife to you?"

"You're lying!"

"You cannot be sure." Taira smiled again. "Perhaps a demonstration will persuade you." He drew the edge of his knife across Yukiko's cheek. A trickle of red blood ran down her face. But she did not make a sound nor show any sign of pain.

Ichiro's suspicion was stronger now. Yet he saw an opportunity as well. Taira had appeared himself, disdaining to use any masks. Perhaps if he could play the game as Taira wished, the wizard would make a blunder.

"Are you convinced?" Taira asked. "Or do I have to cut off one of her pretty fingers?"

"I am convinced," Ichiro replied. He stepped toward the nobleman. "What do you want of me?"

Taira took a step backward, dragging Yukiko with him. "Ah, not so fast, my friend."

"What do you wish?"

"Is it not obvious, Minamoto?" Taira said. "I need your sword."

"Why, Taira?" Ichiro asked. "Of what good to you is my sword, you who controls magic far greater than any man?"

"Do not play the fool with me, Minamoto," Taira snapped. He pressed the edge of the knife closer to Yukiko's throat. "Or perhaps you would prefer to see her die?"

"Answer my question, Taira," Ichiro said, almost spitting the man's name. "Or you shall have my sword -- in your heart." His hand fell to the *tachi's* hilt and he took a step forward, deliberately provoking the necromancer. Ichiro wondered if Taira would act on his threat.

But the nobleman took another step backwards toward the house. Taira was obviously a man of words and not deeds.

Ichiro took another step toward Taira and started drawing the sword from its scabbard.

"I warn you, Minamoto," Taira said, his voice now wavering slightly, "I will not hesitate to kill her."

"Why do you want my sword, Taira?"

"Folly, my friend, what you do is folly!" the nobleman replied. "Have you not seen the sacred relics, the mirror and the seal?"

Ichiro nodded and took another step.

Again, Taira retreated. By now he and his hostage were on the edge of the steps. "I warn you, Minamoto," he said, "come no farther." He stepped onto the stairs and pulled Yukiko after him.

"Taira, are you afraid of me?" Ichiro asked. "Or are you simply afraid of this?" He withdrew the *tachi* and held it ready in his left hand. The *horimono* pulsed red with life, growing brighter when aimed at Taira.

"That sword commands the power of Nippon," Taira said nervously. "With it and the other relics a man would have absolute control over all of Japan!"

"And you expect me to give it to you?" Ichiro taunted. "If you believe that, you are the fool, Taira, not I."

"I did not think you would give it to me, Minamoto," the *daimyo* answered. He was now on the porch, almost at the entrance to the house. "Now no farther, samurai!"

Ichiro took another step.

Taira flung open the door and dragged Yukiko inside with him.

Ichiro sprinted after them. The door slammed in his face. He flung it open ran inside. In the half light, he could see little but flickering shapes. His eye caught movement to his left, and he sprang toward it.

He found Taira standing in the center of the house. The *daimyo* stood bathed in moonlight which poured through a gaping hole in the roof. In his hand was the knife, red with blood.

But there was no Yukiko.

"What have you done with her?" Ichiro demanded.

"She was an illusion," Taira said. "Or have you changed your mind, Minamoto?"

"Do not trifle with me, Taira!"

"Give me your sword then, and I will tell you." The *daimyo* put out his hand to take the weapon.

"If you are so powerful, wizard," Ichiro said, "then you must take it from me." He lunged toward the nobleman, his sword poised to deliver a *kamitatewari*, a cut downward through the neck and into the breast.

Taira stepped back. "Fool," he said, "do you think you may kill me so easily?" He threw the knife at Ichiro.

Ichiro easily deflected the small projectile, which lodged deeply in a bamboo shutter.

"No, Taira," Ichiro replied. "I did not intend to kill you. If I kill you, as you know, I have no guarantee that I have stopped the evil you have unleashed. Now, where is my wife?"

"She is not here."

"Liar!" Ichiro said. "I saw you bring her into the house." He lunged at Taira's head.

"She was an illusion," the nobleman said, taking a cautionary step backwards. "A ploy to help me dispose of you."

Ichiro realized he had walked directly into the trap. Taira had laid it out perfectly, from the forest itself, to the delaying action at the stream, to the house itself.

"I will have your sword anyway, Minamoto," Taira said, laughing. "Then no one shall stop me from ruling all of Japan."

The *daimyo's* laughter angered Ichiro. He swung the sword across his chest, slashing Taira's face. The *tachi* sliced through both cheeks, widening the *daimyo's* laughing mouth into a hideous grin.

Taira fell to the floor, choking on his blood. It pooled about his head as he gasped for air. He spat a gobbet of saliva and blood.

"You shall pay dearly for this, Minamoto," he said.

Ichiro smiled. "So I shall, Taira, but remember what I have done. Remember what Lord Asano said: 'If you hate your enemy, let him live.' I have let you live, Taira, and you will not forget it."

Fear crossed the mutilated face of the *daimyo*. He suddenly thrust up right hand and produced a glowing ball of light. It grew quickly until it engulfed the wizard.

Ichiro shielded his eyes from the dazzling brilliance. When he looked again, Taira had vanished. Only grey shafts of moonlight trickled onto the ground. A dark pool lay on the ground, quickly soaking into the earth.

Kneeling, Ichiro touched his fingers to the pool. The blood was still sticky and warm, moist on his fingertips. So it had not been an illusion of Taira at all. But although he had temporarily disposed of the treacherous noble, Ichiro had other problems.

First and foremost he had to escape this house, which was clearly a trap. But where was the entrance? Ichiro couldn't recall, and now it seemed the room had changed. He saw three doorways. The one at the left end seemed closest to where he remembered he had entered.

He chose it.

As he reached the doorway, he heard a voice, sobbing. It came from the middle door. *Yukiko!* he thought, *it had to be Yukiko.* Forgetting where he was, he opened the door and ran in.

He ran down a twisting corridor dimly lit by small oil lamps. Although he suspected another trap, he followed the corridor until it opened onto a small room littered with dust and broken furniture. In the middle of the room a figure lay curled on the floor.

It was Yukiko. Her *kimono* was soiled and tattered, ripped at one shoulder. Her hair was in disarray and tumbled across her naked back, which was streaked with crimson scratches.

Ichiro went her. "What has he done to you?" he asked, placing his arm around her. He lifted her to look at her face and fell back in horror.

In Yukiko's place was a hag with skin the grey as death, sunken eyes, dried-up dugs and long, thin, needle-sharp teeth. She laughed and grabbed him, drawing him to her breast. Her breath was thick and foul. Saliva glistened on her teeth.

Ichiro pushed her away and scrambled to his feet. He held his sword ready and pressed his back against a rotting wall.

The hag came toward him. Her breath was a thin, stinking fog that permeated the air. She reached out her hands, beckoning to him, calling to him in a thin, reedy voice. "Ichiro, come to me. I hunger for you!" she cried.

Her breath was choking him, making his head spin. His fingers tightened on the hilt of the *tachi* and his arm acted for his mind.

The blade sang as it cut the air, passing completely through the hag. She screamed once and vanished into mist.

But his sword was swung with such force it buried itself into the floor.

A hideous shriek split the air. Like a bolt of lightning, it passed through the *tachi*. Ichiro could not release the weapon, his fingers glued to the hilt.

The shriek grew more intense. It began to shake the sword, then took hold of his body and shook him like a large dog shaking a kitten. But it could not separate him from the weapon.

He fought against it, trying to pull the *tachi* free. A milky substance flowed up the length of the blade. It was like white blood.

Ichiro planted his feet and pulled. The sword slid free. He stumbled backward, crashing against a wall which collapsed from the blow. He heard the shriek a final time and darkness overwhelmed him..

CHAPTER EIGHT

S unshine fell on his face and woke him.

Ichiro opened his eyes. He sat up and looked around him. A thin mist hung over the land, but that was not unusual. What was unusual was that the house had vanished.

In its place were burned timbers, still smoldering in the misty morning air. Bits of broken rock and bamboo stood as mute testimony to the house's demise.

Ichiro saw a thin line of white running from the edge of his sword to the center of the house, where it suddenly stopped. He followed the line, probing each inch of ground. He quickly found the gap between the hard-packed earth and a thinner, hollow area. *It was like the hiding place of the trap door spider,* he thought.

He slid the *tachi* into the gap and levered open the gossamer thin cover. He peered into the gaping hole that was now exposed. At the bottom of the pit lay a huge black spider, curled on its back. An ulcerous white gash ran the length of its grossly distended abdomen. Dried white blood formed a thin line from the wound up the sides of the pit to where Ichiro's sword had entered the floor of the house.

"Help me," it said feebly, "help me or I will die."

Ichiro looked at the spider's huge jaws and knew his answer to that plea. All around the spider's head were the skeletal remains of those unfortunates who fell victim to its trap. Stripped clean of flesh, the bones seemed like bits of pearl. Skulls were piled together, their tops crushed like eggshells where the spider had sucked out the contents.

"Help me," the spider cried, its voice thin and reedy, like the old hag in the house. Ichiro suspected the creature lured its victims to their doom by projecting images of things they loved or desired.

He sheathed his *tachi* and went to the horses. He found what he wanted in one saddlebag.

"I will help you," he said to the spider.

The axe smashed the spider's head directly between the huge mandibles. The blade split the head and came to rest buried in the spider's thorax. The spider screamed once, a frightening and pene-trating wail. Its eight legs twisted violently, then curled inward as creamy white blood oozed out across the ground.

Assured now that the spider could do no more harm, Ichiro lowered himself into the pit to retrieve the axe. He intended also to destroy any eggs the creature might have laid. He carefully avoided stepping in the blood as he recovered the axe. Placing his foot against the spider's body, he tugged at the axe handle and eased it loose.

He nearly had the weapon free when he felt the spider stir.

Startled, he dropped the axe and jumped back, pressing himself against the wall of the pit. He unsheathed his *tachi*.

As Ichiro watched, the huge distended abdomen of the spider began moving. A small bulge appeared on its surface, growing quickly larger. It seemed occasionally to wriggle. Stretched to its limit, the abdomen burst, spattering thin green fluid against the pit wall.

From the hole appeared a long chitinous leg, then another, and then a third. As the forth leg appeared, so did a small round head with large mandibles. The small spider emitted a squeal and began to consume its mother.

A second and third bulge appeared. Soon there were at least eleven bulges, each spattering the pit wall with the green liquid as a young spider appeared. The spiders seemed more concerned with their meal than with Ichiro. It was the opportunity he needed.

Using the axe to cut hand- and foot-holds, Ichiro climbed from the pit. Pausing to catch his breath, he looked back into the pit. The tiny spiders had eaten nearly half of their mother. Her carapace was now thin and translucent, like old rice paper.

Ichiro knew he could not allow the spiders to survive. But there were too many to kill with a sword or an axe. They would easily overwhelm him. The longer they stayed in the pit, the better. But once they escaped, they would be loosed upon the nearby villages.

Quickly he roused Shizuka and Yukiko.

"Gather some dried grass and firewood," he said curtly.

"What?" asked Shizuka. "Have you gone mad, *samurai*?"

"I cannot explain yet," he replied. "Please trust me."

Mumbling, Shizuka got up and slapped herself about the arms to get warm. "Damn you, Minamoto, it's freezing!"

"If you gather the wood, we'll soon have a fire to keep you warm," Ichiro said.

After they all had armfuls of tinder and wood, Yukiko and Shizuka joined Ichiro at the pit. Yukiko dropped his wood, screamed and stepped back when he saw the spiders.

"Where did they come from?" Shizuka asked. "Taira?"

Ichiro nodded. "He hoped to lure me into the house to kill me. I suspect he wanted me to feed his pet."

"He got you into the house?"

"Oh yes," Ichiro said, "but as you see, the spider has become food herself. Start throwing the grass and bits of wood into the pit."

Shizuka heaved an armful into the pit. "What do you intend to do?"

"Burn them," he replied flatly, "burn them all."

They soon had the pit filled with dried grass, sticks, and branches. The young spiders were unconcerned, mindlessly finishing their meal. Occasionally, two or three would attack a smaller one and consume it.

With a piece of flint and her knife Shizuka ignited a small pile of grasses and sticks. When it was ablaze she thrust three oil-soaked torches into it. The torches crackled loudly in the morning mist, hissing and popping.

Shizuka looked at Ichiro. "Now?"

"Yes."

The three torches sailed into the pile of tinder and kindling. The grass caught fire quickly and soon ignited the branches.

The spiders, sensing they were trapped, wailed madly and tried to scamper up the pit's walls. But they were too slow, and the walls were too steep. Ichiro tossed a few more branches into the fire, but it was apparent by now the flames would reduce everything in the pit to ashes.

"Let us go," Ichiro said, "we have an appointment with this apothecary friend of Yukiko's."

The apothecary's village rested against the side of a small rounded hill. It was surrounded by green fields of millet and flooded rice paddies. Peasants drove heavily

laden ox-carts along the narrow path from the fields into the village.

"Your village is oddly prosperous," Ichiro said to Yukiko, "when one considers what Taira has done to the rest of his domain."

"The *daimyo* have tried to bully us before. But we have always beaten them," Yukiko said proudly. "Kichija the apothecary knows many spells to counter the Lord Taira's magic."

"He must be a powerful man," Shizuka said.

"Yes," Yukiko said, "Why, it is said Kichija can bring dead animals back to life and make old people young."

"Have you seen this?" Shizuka said.

"No," Yukiko admitted. But he quickly added, "I know those who have seen it, though, and they say it is so."

Shizuka shook her head and laughed. "Superstitious peasants. They will believe any trickster's slight of hand."

"Trickster or not," Ichiro said, "this Kichija is an ally we can ill-afford to lose."

Kichija's hut was at the far edge of the village. It was a modest dwelling, but a strong one as well. Instead of the usual wooden huts, the apothecary's was made of carefully mortared stones with windows of oiled paper and bamboo shutters. It was quite different from most

Japanese dwellings, and no doubt added to the mysteries surrounding the fellow.

Ichiro dismounted and tied his horse to an ornately carved wooden pole, a totem dating from before the days of legendary Jimmu, a time when only barbaric tribes inhabited Japan. The totem disturbed Ichiro, as if a being from the depths of the past were challenging him. For a moment he almost untied the horse's reins, but decided that the totem was meant to frighten away evil spirits.

"The totem won't be offended?" Ichiro asked Yukiko.

The monk smiled. "Kichija made it to scare away children. He says it is harmless."

Ichiro left the reins in place, but felt foolish for having been bothered in the first place.

Shizuka dismounted and tied her horse to the totem without hesitation. *Ninja*, it seemed, feared nothing, least of all ancient spirits.

"I will have to go in first," Yukiko said. "Kichija is a little suspicious of strangers, but he's friendly once you know him, and then he accepts you."

Ichiro and Shizuka waited as Yukiko knocked on the door and was given entrance. Moments later, Yukiko returned.

"Kichija says you may enter," he said. "He has been expecting us."

They followed the monk into the apothecary's hut.

It took some time for their eyes to adjust to the relative darkness of the hut. The light entered only through three slit windows with oiled-paper panes. Just enough light appeared to allow Kichija to get on with his work.

"You are welcome," Kichija said. "Those who are friends of Yukiko are friends of mine."

The apothecary stood in a corner, his back turned toward them. He seemed intent on checking shelf upon shelf of ceramic jars. The jars themselves covered each wall of the hut almost to the ceiling. The only spaces bare of shelves were the windows and the doorway.

Ichiro had to stifle a laugh when he realized that, given time, the doors and windows too might be covered up, and Kichija would be trapped by his own potions, unable to find any exit.

"Kichija," Yukiko said solemnly, a sign of respect for the apothecary. "This is Minamoto-no-Ichiro and the woman-warrior Shizuka. They desire your knowledge on a matter of some importance."

Kichija turned from his work and faced Ichiro. With a grim visage, he eyed Ichiro up and down.

The apothecary was an old man, immeasurably old. He had pouch-like jowls resembling a macaque monkey's, and sunken eye sockets. Within those sockets, two black eyes burned fiercely with an energy more of youth than of age.

His skin was as brown as a nut and as dry as old rice paper. It was, in fact, more like skin broiled by the sun than bleached by a hut's dim confines.

Kichija's facial expression and actions reminded Ichiro of a pet macaque he had as a child. The animal, too, was mistrustful of strangers. Unlike the monkey, Kichija seemed not likely to bite those he didn't like.

The apothecary drew a thin, liver-spotted finger across his lips and then scratched his chin. "I like you, *samurai*," he said with a smile. The smile made years melt from his face.

Ichiro was relieved. He returned the old man's smile and bowed slightly. "You do me honor. Yukiko has spoken highly of you."

"And no doubt does me disservice," Kichija said, "by making wild claims about my powers." He turned to the young monk and repri-manded him gently. "Modesty is a virtue that is most difficult to learn, particularly modesty about a friend."

"I am sorry, Kichija," Yukiko said, suitably chastised.

"You are forgiven," the apothecary said.

He turned to Ichiro. "You have a request of me." it was a statement, not a question.

Ichiro nodded. "I need a spell broken."

He explained his encounter with Lord Taira and with the woman warrior. "Can you break the spell over the woman?"

Kichija frowned. He scratched his chin and pondered a moment. "This *daimyo's* magic is very strong. To fight it is an arduous task. I can only be of some small help, I fear. But bring the woman in."

"Yukiko, Shizuka, please," Ichiro said.

Yukiko went to fetch the woman. Shizuka hesitated a moment, then she bowed politely to Ichiro and left.

"Kichija," Ichiro said, turning back to the old man. "What of my other request?"

Kichija shook his head. "I will examine my writings for help. But I know so little of dragons."

The apothecary went to his shelves and took down three ceramic jars. Ichiro watched silently as Kichija carefully measured quantities from each jar and poured them into a small bowl. From a jar on his work table he added a small amount of an amber liquid and stirred. The substance boiled slightly, releasing a rich, spicy odor which soon filled the hut.

By now Yukiko and Shizuka had returned, supporting the woman between them. She was half conscious, mumbling incoherently and blinking her eyes, trying to focus upon the world.

"Put her on those *tatami*," Kichija said, gesturing toward a small pile of mats and blankets set against the wall across from the doorway. After they had laid her down on the mats, Shizuka and Yukiko joined Ichiro.

Kichija now added substances from two other jars. From one he withdrew a blackened object which resembled the overcooked paw of a snow monkey. From the other, he measured white powder.

"What is that?" Shizuka whispered to Ichiro.

"Ground bones," Yukiko said, "from the great giants who lived before men were placed on earth."

Ichiro smiled. He recalled similar such potions being sold in the shops of Tokyo. Ground up bones, rhinoceros horn, foul-smelling plants, all guaranteed to cure or restore something.

"It is very potent magic," Yukiko said.

"It is said to cure many things," Ichiro added with a smile.

Yukiko nodded his head in agreement.

Kichija now poured the thick substance into a glowing fire-pot. Into the center of the fire-pot, he added sticks of charcoal. Soon blue flame leaped from the fire-pot, tossing tendrils of smoke toward the ceiling. The smoke curled and twisted in the cool air.

The pot boiled madly now, releasing a heavy grey fog. The fog had a spicy, cloying odor.

Ichiro wrinkled his nose in disgust. "It smells terrible," he said.

"It is a strong potion," Kichija replied. "It breaks down the will and exposes the demons dwelling in the mind."

Yukio ran to the window and began to retch. His body was racked with the spasms, but at last he regained control of his stomach.

"Horrible," he said, gasping for air. Flecks of vomit were on his chin and lips. "I saw creatures running through my mind and they were burning like firewood."

Kichija turned to Ichiro. "The boy got a brief whisper of the effects of the drug. He has seen for himself what powers it possesses." He turned to Yukio. "But the sensation has passed?"

The young monk nodded.

"Good."

Ichiro breathed deeply. Although he had not experienced the sensations that Yukio had, the fumes made burned his lungs and stung his nostrils. A cool breeze had by now driven the fumes from the hut and Ichiro was thankful for the fresh air it brought. However, he could still smell the substance and taste it on his tongue.

Kichija turned his attention to the firepot. With a pair of tongs, he lifted the hot metal from the white-hot embers and tilted it into a small ceramic bowl. Instead of a yellowish paste, a fine powder, red as blood, fell into the bowl.

"This is to be administered in a bowl of sake," Kichija explained, "as its effect are weak unless mixed with alcohol."

"How long does the drug take to have an effect?" Ichiro asked.

The old man frowned. "I cannot say for certain. An hour, perhaps two. The drug is fickle and each person is different. I have known those who have waited the entire night for the drug to work its magic."

"An entire night!" Shizuka said. "Well, *samurai*, I hope you don't loose any sleep over this."

"I won't," he said. "I intend first to have a meal. Then I shall wait until I am summoned." He turned back to the apothecary. "I thank you for your efforts, most honored Kichija." He bowed to the apothecary.

Kichija returned the bow and went to open the door of his hut for them. "There is an inn a short distance down the road. The food is most excellent, and the accommodations sparse, but not uncomfortable. I shall send a boy to you when the woman begins to be affected by the drug."

"Again, thank you, Kichija-san."

"Are you angry with me for talking so much?" Yukio asked, looking up from the bowl from which he was eating.

"No," Ichiro replied. "I would have done the same thing when I was your age." In fact, he recalled, as a page-boy at the monastery near Tokyo, he had hidden himself behind some screens in order to hear a traveler discuss a journey to the Ainu. He never regretted eavesdropping, but he was embarrassed when the abbot smiled the next day and told him not to be so timid when the next traveler arrived.

"I trust you learned something," Ichiro said.

"You must learn discipline," Shizuka said. Oddly, there was a surprising softness to her voice and a friendliness Ichiro had not perceived before.

"I am sorry," Yukio said, shamefacedly. "But I find Kichija very fascinating. Did you know some say he is over five hundred years old? Not that I believe it," he added quickly. The wonder and awe in his eyes, however, betrayed him.

"You believe that, little one," Shizuka said, sounding like her old self.

"Please, do not call me 'little one,'" Yukio said.

Before Shizuka could respond to her small error in courtesy, Ichiro interrupted, hoping to avoid a conflict. "How is it then that Kichija is so old?" he asked.

Yukio's enthusiasm returned. "It is said he has potions which purge the poisons of death from his body. They know he is so old because it is written he fought at the side of Tokimune when he drove back the invading armies of China."

"If it is so, then he is more than six hundred years old," Ichiro said. He took a bit of fish from the plate and watched the look of awe on the young monk's face.

Ichiro smiled and shook his head. After his meal, Ichiro rested in his room.

The sun was setting in the west. While the superstitious thought it took its light from the world of the living and delivered it to the land of the dead, Ichiro knew better, but his weary mind found some truth in that belief. He lay back and rested his head on the wooden pillow. His body ached, something he had not realized until this moment. His legs throbbed, particularly his right one, which felt more twisted than ever. Both of his arms were sore and his back hurt.

Ichiro wondered if he had not betrayed himself. He almost wished he had died in that *kamikaze* attack. War and adventure were pointless, and he did not want the responsibility. By his own choice, he could leave such foolishness to younger men who didn't know better. Then he remembered the faces of his young recruits, boys barely able to climb into an aircraft, let alone fly it.

He could betray himself, but he could not betray them.

He felt suddenly old. He was tired of his armor, tired of his sword, tired even of the glory. Yet, here he was, once more the aging warrior drawn into battle against his will. Or was it unwillingly? After all, this world gave him a second chance at life.

And for that chance, he was expected to destroy Taira Mitsuyu and the evil the *daimyo* created.

Did he still have choice in the matter, though? Could he mount his horse in the morning, ride to the Tokaido Post Road, ride to Edo or Kamakura or north to Hokkaido, and leave all of this strife behind?

Yes, he had that choice.

He would not take it. Deep within his conscience voices spoke of duty, of honor. He was the *samurai*, son and grandson of *samurai*, and the code of the *bushido* was explicit.

To make any other choice would disgrace him not only in the eyes of others, but in his own inward eyes, eyes more penetrating than any other man's.

"You seem weary, *samurai*."

Ichiro opened his eyes and saw Shizuka sitting beside him. She too appeared tired and worn. For the first time he felt kinship with her. He knew at last he could trust her.

"I have the weight of the world upon my shoulders," he said with a sigh.

"It is not an easy load, I take it," she said. She stretched out and supported herself on one elbow.

"Everyone must bear the load at least once in their lives," Ichiro replied. "It is price we pay for life. But at this moment my load seems so much greater." He turned toward her. "Why did you come here?"

She smiled and shook her head. "I could lie and say a thousand things. *Ninja* are very good at that. But, to be truthful, I was lonely and wanted to talk to someone."

"Why not Yukio?"

Shizuka laughed. "Him? He's only a boy, with boyish enthusiasms. When he talks, you cannot get a word in edgewise. And he is oblivious to what the other person says."

Ichiro smiled. He had to admit that Yukio was not exactly a good listener. The young monk did initiate many conversations but once started, it was hard to stop him.

"He will learn," Ichiro said, "when he acquires some discipline. Kichija knows that."

"Do you think he will succeed?" Shizuka asked.

"Who? Yukio?"

"No. Kichija."

Ichiro shook his head. "I do not know. I hope so, for all our sakes, even if all it gives us is some time."

He noticed Shizuka gazing out the window.

"You did not come here to talk about Yukio or Kichija, did you?"

She shook her head. "No."

"What then?"

"Myself, I suppose." She looked at the floor of the sleeping platform and idly dug at a nail embedded in the wood. "I have begun to wonder if it is all worthwhile."

"Strange. I was thinking the same thing."

She looked up expectantly. "What did you decide?"

"That I had no choice," he admitted. "It is worthwhile because it is all I have."

"And that is what you decided?"

He nodded.

"I thought you were wise, *samurai*."

"I never said I was."

She still seemed troubled.

"Are you still jealous of the boy?" he asked. Ichiro expected an angry look and flow of words, but to his surprise she smiled.

"Yes, it is true. I am jealous, " she said, " But that is not why I came."

"I see."

"No, you do not." She sat up and resumed staring out the window at the stars. "Shall I tell you then what bothers me?"

"If you wish."

A knock on the door interrupted them.

"Yes?"

A small boy entered the room.

"Pardon, honorable sir, but I am sent here by Kichija, the apothecary. He tells me to say the woman awakes, and you may talk to her."

Tapers flickered in the hut, casting dancing shapes across the walls. Censers released clouds of cloying incense to purify the air. The odor was overpowering, but Ichiro tried to ignore it as he entered.

He saw Kichija hovering over the woman warrior. The apothecary had her tied up and propped against a wall. Ichiro did not know if the woman was bound for her own protection or for Kichija's.

"Ah, you have arrived," Kichija said, turning toward them. He held a ceramic *sake* jar and a small cup decorated with blue flowers.

"The drug is at last taking effect. I have given her a slight amount more to guarantee a result." He gestured for them to come nearer.

"Come, in a moment you may ask your questions."

Ichiro and Shizuka approached and sat down in front of the woman.

The woman drifted between sleep and wakefulness. Every so often her eyes would flicker and she would move her mouth to speak, but she strangled on her words and lapsed back into unconsciousness.

"How long will I have to ask her?" Ichiro inquired.

"The drug is not perfect," Kichija admitted. "You may have a good amount of time, or you may not. Choose your questions carefully."

Ichiro turned to Shizuka. "What should we ask?"

"You know as well as I."

He nodded.

"Look," Shizuka said, taking his arm, "she awakes!"

The woman raised her head and blinked. She appeared groggy, in part from the *sake*. Her eyes blinked, tried to focus on the world, but failed. She became aware of the bonds and tried to struggle free. But the apothecary's knots were strong, and she could do nothing but fall on her side and scream in frustration.

Ichiro and Shizuka raised her to a sitting position. "Who are you?" Ichiro asked.

"I might well ask the same of you," she replied angrily. "What have you done to me?"

"It is for your own safety."

She spat in his face.

Shizuka slapped the woman. Stunned, the woman fell back against the wall and glared at them.

"That was not necessary," Ichiro told Shizuka.

"Nevertheless, you would not get any answers without her attention," she said. "Now, you have her attention."

Ichiro wiped the saliva from his beard and continued calmly.

"You know things I must know. And you will tell me."

The woman struggled. He grabbed her shoulders and brought her face to face with him. "Now, who are you?" he asked.

"If you don't answer, I will have Shizuka cut your throat. She is a *ninja* and can make it very painful."

The woman now seemed to realize how serious her inquisitors were.

"My name is Tamika."

"Thank you, Tamika." He gestured to the apothecary and Shizuka.

"This is Kichija and this is Shizuka. I am called..."

"Minamoto-no-Ichiro," she said. "You do not have to tell me. I always know the names of those I am to kill."

"As you tried that night."

"Yes," she admitted sullenly. "If it had not been for her," she gestured with her head toward Shizuka, "we would have succeeded."

"What were you after?"

"You know."

Ichiro shook his head. "Pretend I am a fool. Tell me what you are after."

She remained silent.

"My sword," he said. "That is it, isn't it?"

She stared at him, but again did not answer.

Ichiro realized that getting her to respond would require more effective methods. He drew his *tachi* from its scabbard and placed the edge to Tamika's neck. "I have changed my mind. If you don't answer, Shizuka will not cut your throat. Instead, if you do not answer me, I will cut your head from your shoulders so swiftly you will have time to see your headless body before you die." To prove his point he pricked the skin below her eye drawing a trickle of blood.

Tamika cried out in pain. Fear filled her face, and she pressed herself against the wall, as if trying to be absorbed by the stones.

"Will you answer me?"

"Yes, yes, we were after the sword!" she exclaimed.

"Why?" Ichiro asked, resheathing the weapon.

"You don't know why?" she exclaimed, genuinely surprised.

"I know that Taira believes my sword to be *Kusinagi*," Ichiro said. "Why does he believe this?"

"Because it is *Kusinagi*!" she exclaimed.

"No, it cannot be," Ichiro said, shaking his head. "*Kusinagi* was lost at sea. Only the fishes may reach it."

"It is *Kusinagi*!" Tamika protested.

"No!"

"Pardon, good samurai," Kichija said, "but the woman speaks the truth."

Startled, Ichiro turned to the apothecary. "What do you mean?"

"Your sword bears engravings."

"Yes, what of it?"

"I saw them as you drew the weapon. They glowed bright red."

From around his neck he drew a small talisman. "The pattern is like this." He handed the talisman to Ichiro.

Ichiro's heart skipped a beat as he saw the talisman. Carved into the cold flat metal was the identical pattern of the wise men and the sayings. And the talisman was glowing. In fact, the nearer to his *tachi* it was, the brighter the talisman glowed.

"Where did you come by this?" he asked excitedly.

"They are old, Minamoto," Kichija said. "It is said that Prince Yamato Takeru, to whom *Kusinagi* was first given, had them made because of a kindness our village gave him. The royal armorer made them. Yamato said if the village were in trouble, we should send a messenger with a talisman. The talisman would guide him to the Prince because it would glow when it was near *Kusinagi*."

Ichiro stared at the shining metal.

"And it is near *Kusinagi* now," he said softly.

The apothecary nodded.

What a fool I've been, Ichiro thought. *All this time I have had Kusinagi and did not know it. No wonder I was able to defeat the Emperor's enemies. And no one recognized the sword because it has been lost for centuries.*

"A fish may find the sword at the bottom of the ocean," he said, thinking aloud, "and so may a *kami*. Damn you, Hachiman. And damn me, too, for being so thick-headed."

He turned back to Tamika. "So Taira sent you to get the sword from me. Why?"

"He wishes to be Emperor of all Japan," she replied.

"And so he has stolen two of the great relics, the mirror and the seal, and wants the third."

"He who has all three is the true emperor."

"How did he know I had *Kusinagi*?"

"He didn't, but someone told him."

"Who? Lord Akiyama?" He placed his hand against her throat. "Answer me."

"Yes," she hissed through clenched teeth. "Akiyama thinks the young Emperor Saigo is incompetent. And he thinks the *Shogun* is an upstart and usurper of Imperial power."

"I see," Ichiro said. "So why does he back Taira?"

"Lord Taira has a claim to the throne by descent from the uncle of the Emperor Antoku," she said, "and because he has a large army."

"Many pretenders and tyrants have had armies," Ichiro said. "It does not automatically give them claim to all of Japan."

It did, however, raise more than a few problems, he admitted. Taira's desire for the throne was understandable, but now the *daimyo's* desire for the sword was greater. After all, it was in the hands of a traditional enemy of the Taira clan, an enemy so hated the mother of the boy Emperor Antoku threw him into the sea to drown rather than let him become the prisoner of the Minamoto clan.

"Tell me," he asked, "what does Taira plan to do with his army?"

She did not answer him.

Ichiro threw her against the wall.

"Tell me," he said sharply.

Tamika dropped her head to her chest, breathing heavily. "Please, I am weak. Please, let me rest."

"Let her rest, *samurai*," Kichija said. "The drug is taking her strength. You have what you need to know."

"No," Ichiro replied, "I don't have enough. Now, what does Taira plan to do with his army?"

Tamika raised her head. Her face was drawn and pale, her eyes were red. "He has two plans. The first is to attack Edo and the Shogun's army."

"The second?"

The woman was wracked with a coughing fit. She fell on her side and coughed up a mouthful of phlegm and sputum. After she spat, she tried to sit up, but was too weak.

"I warn you, *samurai*," the apothecary said, helping Ichiro to sit her up, "taking a risk with her life is not wise."

Ichiro saw the wisdom of the apothecary's words. He would get no more from the woman this night. "Yes, very well," he said, getting to his feet. "I thank you, apothecary. Your drug works quite well. Let her rest and give her whatever she needs to recover."

He pressed a few bars of money into Kichija's hand. "Forgive my treatment of the woman, but the safety not only of the Emperor but of the world depends on my obtaining this knowledge."

"Do not justify yourself," Kichija said. "And I will not take your money, but I will tend to the woman."

For the first time, Ichiro felt shame. He had abused the woman because he needed the information. He still did not know the second plan. But perhaps there were other ways to obtain it.

He turned to Shizuka. "I am tired, let us go back to the inn."

———

Back at the inn, he ordered a jug of warmed *sake*. He drank the milk-white rice wine as he sat and stared out the window at the stars.

"You should not despair," Shizuka said as she entered. "Go away," he said.

"No," she replied, "I will not. It is not healthy to brood alone."

"I am not brooding," he said. He tilted his head back and poured a stream of the warm liquor down his throat.

"If you are not brooding," she said, "then what is it you are doing?"

"Thinking." He stoppered the jar of sake. "I told you before that I did not have any choice. Remember?"

Shizuka nodded.

"I was wrong," he said. "I have always had a choice. But I thought I had none because I always chose what was obvious to me. It was against my principles to surrender, so any choice which involved it was not a choice at all."

"So? What of it?"

"Now I clearly have a choice." He unstoppered the jar and took a drink, wiping his mouth with the back of his hand after he finished.

"Tell me," Ichiro continued, "what would you do? I may choose two roads, but either choice may lead to disaster. If I fail to choose a road, that, too, could be fatal. Should I go to Edo, get aid from the Shogun, and prepare an attack on Taira, or should I ride back to Kyoto and try protect the Emperor?"

"Does the Emperor know he is in danger?" she ventured.

"Do we even know he is alive?" He stared out the window.

A storm was breaking on the horizon. Dark clouds rolled across the mountaintops toward the village, bringing thick curtains of driving rain. A flash of lightning raced across the sky like a jagged lance, to be followed moments later by a shattering roar of thunder.

"It's not a real storm," Shizuka said softly.

"How so?"

"Kichija says that every so often Taira attempts to send storms or fire to destroy the village," she replied, "but the talismans always protect the village."

Even as she spoke the storm came to an abrupt stop, battering itself against an invisible barrier until it broke and scattered across the heavens. Gentle rain began to slap the roof of the inn.

"See," she said, "the storm is tamed."

"What an amazing talisman!" Ichiro remarked. "It protects you against a magician's vented spleen. But if the storm is a natural one, you will be washed away all the same."

He rubbed his chin, feeling the beard growth, stiff and rough at his fingertips. The storm had given him an idea. With a bit of luck, it might perhaps fool Taira long enough to gain the upper hand.

There were two choices. If he chose first to rescue the young Emperor, he could be playing directly into the *daimyo's* hands. Taira expected that Ichiro's loyalty to the young man would overrule his reason and send him back to Kyoto.

And yet Taira had protected himself by planning to engage the *Shogun's* armies. This meant Ichiro would be cut off in the capital with possibly inferior forces. A fine plan, on both counts. Its only flaw was a simple one: there was no accommodation for the unexpected, and Ichiro had something very unexpected planned.

"Shizuka?" he asked.

"Yes?" She was placing opium into a small pipe.

"Have you been to Edo?"

"Once," she said, "why do you ask?"

"How long will it take us to reach there, do you think?"

"Two days, perhaps three." She lit the opium with a taper and exhaled cloying smoke. "So you intend to go there?"

He nodded. "I wish to find a good sword maker."

"A sword maker?" Shizuka asked with puzzlement. "Why do you need a sword maker."

"I wish to have a sword made," he said smiling. "a magic sword." He started to laugh.

Shizuka shook her head and did not understand. She sucked at the slender opium pipe, as though seeking enlightenment in its dreams.

CHAPTER NINE

The journey to Edo took them three days. They followed the shoreline of the southern coast for the most part, passing Suruga and Sagami provinces and entering Mushashi province where Edo sat at the head of a deep bay. In Edo Ichiro and his companions were given a warm welcome by the Shogun, who provided them with rooms and meals.

But despite the warm welcome and the courtesies, Ichiro was uncomfortable. It had been almost too easy to reach Edo, and that fact troubled him. Had Taira expected him to reach Edo? Had he in fact played into the *daimyo's* plans after all? Were there things in Edo already in Taira's control? Events in a city, even murder, often go unnoticed. In Edo, Taira could pursue his plans as secretively as he wished. Or had Taira turned his attention elsewhere, to Kyoto and the Emperor?

Ichiro realized there was little he could do. He now had to complete his own plans and hope they would be enough to stop Taira. And if they weren't, well, he had no choice. All in all, a most uncomfortable dilemma.

With Shizuka and Yukio, he tried to appear peaceful on the outside.

But, like Edo itself, a city bustling with merchants, fisherman, farmers, soldiers, and nobles, he was seething underneath.

Edo itself somehow seemed apart from his problems. It was not the industrial city of Tokyo which Ichiro knew in childhood. Shogun Tokugawa Yoriyoshi's capital was once a humble fishing village and might well have remained so had not the mighty Hideyoshi given the provinces surrounding the village to his ally Tokugawa Ieyasu in 1590.

Hideyoshi had suggested to Tokugawa that Edo would make a lovely seat of power from which to rule the provinces. Tokugawa had agreed. Had Hideyoshi known what was to pass, he would have had Tokugawa assassinated.

That Yoriyoshi was Shogun fully three and a half centuries after the death of his ancestor was tribute and testimony to Ieyasu's skills and forceful personality. Among other things. But an army that has no one to fight save occasional upstarts such as those Ichiro had dispatched has little need for generals. And a Shogun who has the needs of a nation to attend to has little need of being a general. Tokugawa Yoriyoshi therefore devoted his skills to diplomacy and the administration of the state bureaucracy. At that he was even more adept than his notable forbearer.

Those were skills Ichiro appreciated.

"I wish," said the Shogun, placing his writing brush on its stone rest, "that I could spare the troops for you, Minamoto."

Tokugawa was a lean man, broad shouldered and well muscled. His hair and beard were both well kept, framing a gaunt face. It was a face which seemed stretched over his skull, with crow's-feet at his eyes and folds along the corners of his mouth as the only disturbances in that smooth plane. It was a serious face which hid a gentle mind.

The Shogun dusted sand across the rice paper to dry the ink. He emptied the sand into a black container. "My problem is a curious one. I have an army which survives so long as it stays in one place because there is not enough food for any campaigns nor the funds to raise for such food," Tokugawa said.

"Additionally my best *samurai*, as you well know, are either engaged in fighting pirates along our coasts or in the pay of the Emperor of China as advisors to his army conquering Nam Viet.

"I am left with only enough troops to defend Edo. And most of them are *ronin* who decided it was better to be a palace guard and eat rather than pawn their armor to maintain their expected high lifestyle."

Ichiro sighed and shook his head in disappointment. "So you cannot help me, Shogun."

"I did not say that," the Shogun replied. "I will issue an order, requesting *ronin* and *ashigaru* who so desire to join you. And I will ask the village masters of the provinces to spare food for your armies."

"Will it be enough, do you think?"

Tokugawa smiled, but shook his head. "I cannot say. The Taira's reputation proceeds him and there are many young men who see in facing him a chance for glory, as well as an escape from plowing furrows or netting fish."

"I fear it will not be enough," Ichiro said. For the first time, he felt discouraged and uncertain. He wondered if he had run out of choices.

"Do not underestimate the *ashigaru*. They are only foot soldiers, as you should know, but most of them are well trained, particularly the village militia. The Kanto provinces are filled with such men."

"Men I do not worry about," Ichiro said, "but food and weapons, even with the village masters' aid, will be hard to come by."

The Shogun handed Ichiro the rice paper scroll. "This will introduce you to many people in Edo, particularly those who are not sympathetic to the Taira and wealthy enough to be of assistance to you."

"Thank you, my Lord Tokugawa."

"Do not despair, Ichiro." The Shogun unrolled his fan and began cooling himself. "There are many things to be done. Hachiman watches over you. I will talk to the other *daimyo* and some merchants today. I am having some attend a tea ceremony. I will try to get support for you then."

Ichiro rose to go. "I thank you again, Lord Tokugawa, for all your kindness. I hope I can prove myself worthy of them."

Tokugawa fanned himself. "You underestimate yourself, Ichiro. The power of the Minamoto name is still considerable. Never hesitate to use it."

Ichiro bowed and left the Shogun's offices.

Shizuka was waiting outside. She was amusing two of the Shogun's children by performing sleight-of-hand tricks with two boiled eggs she had begged from the castle cook. Seeing Ichiro, the two children stopped giggling and ran off toward their mothers' quarters.

Ichiro knew his ambling gait and twisted leg had scared them. His grim visage probably did not assure them either.

Her audience now departed, Shizuka stretched her body, and yawned. She peeled the shell from one egg. "Well," she said, "what help can we expect from the honorable Shogun?"

"The Shogun is a busy man," Ichiro replied.

"Which means he can give you nothing," she said, tossing bits of eggshell aside and stuffing the entire egg into her mouth.

"He can give us what he can and no more," Ichiro answered. "He has offered to issue an edict requesting *ronin* and *ashigaru* to form an army. And he gave me a letter of introduction to people who may have money to contribute to our cause."

"A piece of paper," Shizuka scoffed, spitting out an overlooked piece of eggshell.

"Nevertheless," Ichiro said, "he has offered what he can. It is more than any other person has done."

"His rooms are clean and his servants pleasant, that's all I will say," Shizuka replied.

"In any case, we have business to attend to. Are you coming?"

"Why not. There's nothing else to do," Shizuka said. She peeled the second egg, bit in, and swallowed it whole.

They walked together out of the main gate and into the street outside the castle. The thoroughfare was filled with farmers and fishermen buying and selling their goods and haggling with merchants. The merchants in turn either refused to pay what the farmers and fishermen demanded or were claiming their own wares were the finest in all Nippon, used personally by the Shogun himself.

Ichiro mused that if the Shogun used those goods, then Edo was indeed in a very sad state.

"Where's Yukio" he asked, noticing the young monk was not with them.

"He's at the temple, *samurai*."

"The temple? Whatever for?"

"You've forgotten," she said. "Today marks the first day of *Obon*, the festival of the dead."

Damn, Ichiro thought. It was difficult enough trying to pawn items in an unfamiliar city, but during a festival it was next to impossible. And should Taira decide to attack Edo now, the slaughter would be horrendous.

Not the best of prospects. No, not at all.

———

Ichiro dealt with several pawnbrokers before finding one who met his needs. He realized the pawnbrokers were in business to make profits, but he found their begrudging, stingy attitudes offensive.

"Times are difficult, *samurai*," they all would say. "So few people can afford to buy such things. Now, for that sword you have, I could pay you handsomely, say several hundred *riyo*."

Always he would have to stifle his anger, suppressing his urge to tell them that he knew they would sell his "worthless" rings and jewels at four, five, perhaps six times what they had given him.

The pawnbrokers, he knew, preyed on the poor and fed the rich -- at substantial profit. That was, when they weren't accumulating gold so their daughters could marry impoverished *samurai*—thereby raising their family's status from licensed thief to loyal noble.

But at last Ichiro found a man sincere enough to admit to the value of the jewels. He was small, shrew-like man with thin moustaches. He dealt heavily in jewelry, all of high quality, which indicated that nobles who had overspent their stipends often came to him for loans.

Ichiro suspected the man could afford generosity when two young nobles came in to pay back their loans. He knew they were sons of a *samurai* family by the cut of their clothes.

The pawnbroker's largesse was soon explained when he exacted a heavy interest payment from the two. Ichiro realized the pawnbroker was thus able to keep the nobles coming back because they could never save enough to avoid needing loans and the interest destroyed whatever they could save. It was harsher than the other pawnbrokers, but also more honest, if in a deceptive fashion.

"Three hundred *riyo*," the pawnbroker said. "I can offer you no more, but to offer you less, honored sir, would be an insult, not just to you, but to these jewels as well."

Ichiro readily accepted the offer. Three hundred *riyo* was easily twice the amount offered by the other usurers.

As the pawnbroker counted out the gold bars into a small linen purse, Ichiro noticed the two young nobles were staring at him. When he glanced their way, they feigned interest in the items the pawnbroker was offering for sale. They pretended to examine a suit of armor, commenting on the poor quality of the lacings, but every time Ichiro turned away from them, he could feel the icy steel of their eyes burrowing into his back. He knew, instinctively, that they meant him no good.

Thanking the pawnbroker, Ichiro placed the purse into his *kimono*, where it joined two other purses. Then he left the shop.

"How much?" Shizuka asked. She had been outside, waiting and watching.

"Three hundred," he said.

"Pittance," she said, and spat into the dust to show her disgust. "A curse on all pawnbrokers. Those jewels were precious, I could tell. A child could tell! Any *ninja* would gladly give his little finger to steal them"

"It is enough for our purposes," Ichiro replied. He cocked his head toward the door. "Do you see those two young nobles?"

"Yes, I saw them come in. A surly pair, I must say."

"As we walk away, I want you to notice if they follow us."

As they mingled with the throng of peasants and merchants who were buying and selling and quarreling, Ichiro turned to Shizuka. "Look over your shoulder," he said, but do not be obvious. Pretend you're looking for things to buy."

Shizuka stopped at a stall and admired a gaily decorated lady's *kimono*. "I see them. They are looking this way."

"Yes?"

"Now they're coming toward us."

"As I suspected." Ichiro looked up and saw a narrow pathway between two of the stalls.

"Quickly, this way," he said.

As they turned down the narrow pathway, the crowd parted to let them through and just as swiftly closed behind them, leaving them swimming in an ocean of people. Ichiro knew the crowd would do the same for their two pursuers, but he hoped the pursuers' impatience would aggravate someone just enough to delay them.

He and Shizuka maneuvered around a market stall, taking care not to knock over the merchant's stack of *sake* jars. A flurry of cries and shouts and curses moments later indicated their pursuers were not so lucky.

One of them, in his haste, crashed into the stack of jars, sending them careening into the street. Several had smashed open, spilling their heady contents. The merchant grabbed the clumsy miscreant by his jacket and was demanding payment for his losses.

The other man was having difficulty rescuing his friend as he tried to work his way past the crowd which had gathered around the smashed jars. Several drunkards were using the opportunity to lap up pools of rice wine from the street or to lick dry the liquor-soaked shards of the jars. The more enterprising merely helped themselves to unbroken jars while the merchant was engaged with the young nobleman, who was now trying to push and kick himself free.

The merchant, however, held fast. It was more than enough diversion for Ichiro and Shizuka to gain a head start.

"We've lost them, the stupid louts!" Shizuka trumpeted with glee.

"For the time being," Ichiro said. "For the time being."

"You do not expect to see them again, surely?" Shizuka asked.

"Yes, I do," he replied.

He knew the two were compelled to complete their task or they would die, either at his hands or those of Taira and his black agents. Taira had seen to that, of course. There was no need to resort to potions or spells all the time. Some men are all too easily swayed by the promise of money, especially those who are accustomed to its presence and equally accustomed to having spent more than they have.

Such men were not evil, Ichiro knew, but are willing to do much evil, and willing, however grudgingly, to accept the punishment for failure because they believe they cannot fail.

After all, it should be simple for two men to steal a sword from a single man, especially a *samurai* with a crippled leg. But they would not have that pleasure, Ichiro knew, not if he could help it.

"Come," he said. "We must find the residence of Setsumu the sword maker.

They hastened their pace and did not look back.

The dwellings and workshops of Setsumu Kobe, the acknowledged master swordsmith of Edo, were both spacious and sumptuous, as befitted a gifted and wealthy artisan. His status, true, was less than that of a peasant in the eyes of the nobility, but it was well above that of a mere merchant, no matter how wealthy that merchant was.

Setsumu was respected, indeed, almost revered by those who saw how he breathed life into a shaft of steel and transformed it into a smooth, swift, and deadly weapon. As Ichiro knew, there were other swordsmiths--cheaper, quicker, and almost as reliable--but none could produce a blade with the grace and skill of Setsumu.

"You honor me with your request," Setsumu said. He sat cross-legged on a woven rice fiber mat, or *tatami*, with his forearm resting on a carved jade armrest brought from China centuries before. His simple clothes, a light brown *kimono* and a rough peasant's jacket, contrasted with the luxury of his home.

"No, Master Setsumu," Ichiro said. "It is you who do me the honor of granting my request for a sword."

"There must be an end of amenities, I fear, or we shall never make that sword," Setsumu quipped, laughing at his own wit. "May I see the sword I am to duplicate?"

"Of course." Ichiro drew Kusinagi from its lacquered sheath and placed the sword before Setsumu.

The swordsmith tried to suppress a gasp of surprise and awe, but failed. "It is truly remarkable," he said softly.

"Hachiman himself gave me this sword, rescued from the depths of the sea at Dan-no-ura," Ichiro explained.

Setsumu reached out to touch the blade, but drew his hand back as the blade grew red hot.

"Only I may handle it," Ichiro said.

"That poses a problem," Setsumu said.

Ichiro's hopes fell. He realized that if the swordsmith could not handle the sword, there was no way to duplicate the sword. "Is there no solution?" he asked.

Setsumu stroked his thin, wispy white beard and became lost in thought.

Ichiro expected the man to refuse to do the job, but he saw a smile cross Setsumu's face.

"I will need to make a mold of the blade so I may duplicate the *horimono*," he said. "The handle is simple and should pose no problem."

Ichiro was relieved. "It shall be done, then."

"Very well," Setsumu said, rising to his feet. "If you will come with me."

Resheathing Kusinagi, Ichiro got to his feet and followed the sword maker into the workshop. Within the workshop, men slaved over white-hot metal. Hammers rang freely like bells, folding strips of metal back onto themselves again and again. This process reshaped the crystalline structure of the metal, making it both flexible and strong. Such a blade would have a razor-sharp edge, an edge which could slice a man in half and leave only a thin red wound as evidence of its work.

Apprentices and journeymen, dressed in thin breechcloths, stood next to forges. They attended to fires which had to remain hot enough to keep the steel glowing a soft whitish-orange. Perspiration rolled down their strong brown bodies, but the heat evaporated it almost immediately and replaced it with new rivulets.

The entire process, as Ichiro knew, was laborious, tiring, and time-consuming. But the gratifying end came after the heated blade was plunged in cold water and its

edge sharpened by hand. That was when the master swordsmith would draw the sword from its sheath and with a single stroke slice through a thick bundle of millet and not disturb a single grain.

In the past, criminals felt the first bite of such blades, but society grew sick of such bloody baptisms. Of course, prisoners expected to face death were in short supply of late, in part because *seppuku* allowed them to save face.

As Ichiro watched the sword makers toiling, he could smell the hot metal and he almost believed that the steel itself could drive away all the evil he had faced or would face.

Setsumu continued to lead the way through the workshop, stopping at last next to a wooden rectangle filled with wet, red clay. "If you please," Setsumu said. "We normally use this to make designs we might wish to cut into a sword. If there is a mistake, we can erase it and start again. Much better than having to make a new sword."

Ichiro withdrew Kusinagi again and pressed the flat of the blade into the soft clay. The clay hardened almost immediately when the sword touched it. When Ichiro lifted the blade, a perfect impression of the carving remained. He repeated the action on the other side of the blade and returned the sword to its scabbard.

Setsumu explained that a lead casting would be made and the engraver would use that as his pattern.

"How long will it take to make the sword?" Ichiro inquired.

"Seven, perhaps, eight, maybe ten days," Setsumu replied.

"Too long. I need it tomorrow."

"But that is impossible!" Setsumu protested.

"No," Ichiro said. "You will use the sword your men are just completing. It has the same shape and form as mine."

"Lord Mishima's sword? He will be angry if it is not delivered."

"His lordship will wait," Ichiro replied slowly. "You will tell him the metal proved brittle and flawed. You are already making him a superior sword, but it will take time."

"But..."

Ichiro withdrew his purse from his *kimono*. He had put almost all the money he had gathered into it.

"Here is a thousand *riyo* for your work. I am quite sure it will ease any pain caused by the wrath of Lord Mishima."

Setsumu took the purse and weighed its contents in his hand. "Yes," he said, now smiling. "It is unfortunate about Lord Mishima's sword, but the metal dealers will sell

inferior material at times. I am sure his lordship will understand."

"Most assuredly," Ichiro replied. "I shall return in the morning with five hundred additional *riyo* if the sword is ready. If I must wait till afternoon, you will receive one hundred less *riyo*."

"We will work the night through," Setsumu assured him. "It will be ready by morning, since you have made it so profitable for us."

"*Arigato*," Ichiro said with a bow. "It has been a pleasure doing business with you."

"For a noble *samurai* general as yourself, the pleasure is mine, I promise you," Setsumu said.

Once outside, he was greeted by Shizuka. "Well? How much did he gouge you for?" she asked.

"A thousand *riyo*, and five hundred more on delivery."

Shizuka shook her head in disgust. "Sometimes I wonder if it is more profitable to be a so-called honest artisan than a *ninja*."

"He would have taken less, I admit," Ichiro said, "if I had offered less. But I gave him what I feel is fair for his troubles." He changed the subject. "Any sign of our two friends?"

"Not a thing. It was so quiet I could hear my hair grow. It was enough to drive me mad, alone out here," she said. "Maybe they have given up the chase."

"Do not be so sure."

They had just stepped through the gateway of Setsumu's house and into the street when the attackers struck.

CHAPTER TEN

They leaped out from behind the pillars of the gate. The first attacker knocked Ichiro to the pavement and went flying over him as Shizuka grabbed the man's jacket and flung him aside. Ichiro felt a searing pain in his right arm and he knew the attacker had slashed him.

The assassin regained his feet and rushed Ichiro, his hand grasping a dagger that glinted in the sun, ready for the fatal blow. But the man was too eager.

Ichiro deflected dagger with a forearm and delivered a two-fingered blow to the attacker's abdomen. As the man wreathed on the ground, gasping for air, Ichiro unsheathed *Kusinagi*.

Before he could deliver the killing blow he saw Shizuka struggling with the second attacker. He had her pinned to the ground, his knee on her chest. He was trying to stab her with a short sword, but she held his wrists fast in a defensive grip, and he could not get the sword's sharp edge any nearer her throat. At last, she twisted a leg around her body and, placing a foot against the attacker's chest, pushed him away.

Kusinagi sang.

Before his body stumbled back against the wall that surrounded the house, the attacker's head went bouncing down the street like a football.

"Behind you," Shizuka yelled.

Ichiro turned, brought the sword up to his waist and lunged, impaling the first attacker, who had regained his breath only to lose his life.

The man dropped his dagger. It clattered noisily on the stone pavement. His face turned pale and white as Kusinagi sucked him lifeless.

Ichiro pulled the sword from the man's body. The attacker collapsed, clutching his wound with cold, clumsy hands, trying vainly to stop the flow of blood.

"Who paid you?" Ichiro demanded.

"Ah! Ah!" the man cried, blood and air bubbling from his ruined body.

"Tell me, and I shall end your pain."

"Taira. Lord Taira," the man gasped. He coughed, bringing thick black blood to his lips.

Ichiro grabbed the man and pulled up upright. "What about Taira?"

"Your..sword...Taira would...pay our debts...if we killed...you...and brought...him...your sword."

Kusinagi was quick and merciful. The attacker's head rolled down the street to join his companion's.

"I'm sorry Taira left you to your fate, friend," Ichiro whispered. "But you have paid the price, and so shall he."

A crowd had gathered. Drawn by the commotion, but now appalled by what it had wrought. Still, the scene of death held a fascination for some people, who gawked and pointed at the severed heads.

"Does anyone among you know these two?" Ichiro asked.

A small, wizened man in fine robes came forward.

"They are my nephews," he said flatly.

"I apologize for the harm I have done you, but they tried to kill me," Ichiro explained.

"They were drunkards, gamblers and wastrels, a disgrace to our family name. You have done their dead father and me a service, *samurai*. *Arigato*, I thank you profusely and beg forgiveness for the harm they intended you," the old man said.

"Who are you, honored sir?" Ichiro asked, puzzled.

My name is Kadayu Nori, honored sir. I am a mere merchant, though my father was a *samurai*."

Ichiro took a purse containing the last of his funds from his *kimono*. "I wish to pay for their funerals," he said.

"Oh, no," Kadayu said, aghast. "You must not deprive me of this pleasure." He smiled. "My money will be gladly spent to be rid of those two. And you will need your money, General Minamoto."

Ichiro was taken aback. "How do you know me?"

"By reputation only, general," the merchant replied. "A *samurai* with a twisted leg who carries his sword in his left hand. Only you could be that man, General."

Kadayu turned and called out into the crowd. A band of men came forward pulling a wooden ox-cart. Quickly, they gathered up the bodies and severed heads and tossed them rudely into the cart.

"It is fortunate that business brought me this way, general," Kadayu said, "or I would not have had my men and cart with me."

He turned to the men. "Take them to the waste ground. That's fitting burial for those two rogues."

The cart rumbled off. Its slightly eccentric wheels bounced as the men pulled it along toward the place where the discards from Edo's opulence found rest.

Kadayu turned to Ichiro. "We shall meet again soon, General. I will try to be of more help to you then."

Before Ichiro could reply, the little man was off down the street, following the ox-cart. Ichiro could tell that Kadayu was taking great pleasure in the deaths of his nephews, and he found it almost distasteful. The dead, after all, deserved respect despite their crimes in life. That was especially true during *Obon*.

"The shit-yard is a good place for them," Shizuka said, "even their blood reeks of it."

Her clothes and face were streaked with the dead men's blood, which was drying to a rust color.

"These clothes are ruined," she said, wrinkling her nose in disgust. "I'll probably have to burn them. And I'll need a bath to rid me of their stench."

"Yes, I suppose you will," Ichiro said with a grin.

"What are you smiling for, eh, *samurai*?" Shizuka asked, puzzled. "We've spent all our own money on a silly sword, we have no army to aid us, and now every common criminal and drunken *samurai* is bound to try his luck in killing us for your sword. And yet, you stand there and smile at a little old man who is glad you have killed his nephews."

"I'm smiling because of what Kadayu said," Ichiro explained. "He said he will be of help, and somehow I suspect he will help us."

"You're bleeding, *samurai*," Shizuka said quickly.

He looked down at his right hand and saw a bright red trickle of blood flowing past his wrist and down his fingers. It dripped slowly to the ground. Now that he remembered he was wounded, he felt the throbbing pain in his shoulder.

"Come, let's go back to the Shogun's palace," he said, clenching his teeth as a white hot shaft of pain lanced his shoulder. "My arm hurts like a crazed dog."

But he still managed a smile. If Kadayu lived up to his promise, then perhaps the cause was far from lost.

———

A servant laid out the clothes Ichiro would wear for the Shogun's *chanogu*, or tea ceremony, while the Shogun's personal physician attended to the general's wound.

It was a long gash, about the distance between the elbow and the shoulder minus a hand's width. The skin was quite red and swollen, but the wound itself was shallow for the most part, being deepest at the point of the shoulder. Although not dangerous, it was still very painful, and

Ichiro resisted the urge to howl each time the physician touched it.

The doctor first bathed the wound in an herbal wash which deadened the pain. Then he began to sew the lips of the wound together with strands of boiled silk and a thin steel needle. Ichiro jumped when the needle first pierced his skin. He was unsure of which hurt more, the wound, or its treatment.

After sewing the lips of the gash together, the physician applied a sweet-smelling herbal poultice to the wound and bound the injured arm loosely with clean linen. Ichiro felt the poultice burn his skin at first, but it quickly exuded a cooling, numbing effect that drove the pain from his injury.

"You are lucky," the physician said, "that you are left-handed, or you would be unable to handle that sword of yours for some time."

"*Arigato*. I thank you for your kindness," Ichiro said.

"There is no need for amenities, Lord Minamoto," the physician replied as he gathered his tools. "I should be thanking you."

"How do you mean?" Ichiro asked. He began to dress himself in the solid red *kimono* with five family crests which he would wear for the Shogun's tea ceremony.

"I have so little chance to attend to interesting ills or to utilize new ideas," the doctor said. "Most often I treat stomach complaints or minor cuts and bruises, or the heavy head that follows a bout of ill-advised drinking. You have given me my first chance for some time to try this new sewing technique for wounds."

"Yes, I noticed," Ichiro replied. He fastened a blue *obi* about his *kimono*. "Where did you learn it?"

"A stranger, a Dutchman he called himself, came to court but ten days ago. He said his ship had been damaged and he wished to put his ship into Edo Bay for repairs," the physician said.

"The Shogun granted him a month and he had promised the Shogun a weapon to destroy cities. And from his ship's physician I learned many things. We discovered we both understood Chinese, though his speech was, I admit, superior to mine. He showed me this way of sewing wounds."

"I am glad his knowledge proved useful," Ichiro said. He flinched at a slight pain in his shoulder.

"That is not all," the physician said. He reached into his bag and withdrew a small stone which he handed to Ichiro. "The physician gave me this."

Ichiro closely examined it. It was smooth, like a stone, but it was not a true stone. It seemed more like strands of cloth or fur bound together by a strange glue. As to its purpose, Ichiro could not begin to guess.

"What is it?" he asked.

"A means of neutralizing poison placed in food or drink," the physician said. "Simply place it into your food or drink and it will draw forth the poison into itself."

"Why are you giving this to me, then?"

"I fear for you, General Minamoto," the physician said, a look of genuine concern on his face. "You are safe among the Shogun's men, but outside the palace walls your life is in danger. You have enemies, I can tell. Today, they use knives and swords, but tomorrow it could be more subtle."

"I see." Ichiro rolled the object in his hand, noting how it caught the light. It seemed translucent, like the finest porcelain. It gave no evidence that it could absorb poisons. It appeared like a harmless river stone.

The physician, though, was an honest and sincere man. Sincerity required that Ichiro accept the gift. Courtesy, after all, was inexpensive.

"I thank you now for your gift, honored sir," Ichiro said. "Should it save my life, I shall thank you even more."

The physician bowed courteously and left the room.

Ichiro rolled the stone into the folds of his *kimono. Later,* he thought, *I shall perhaps have it mounted on a chain.*

He finished dressing for the tea ceremony by placing white *tabi* on his feet and stepping into woven fiber sandals. A small folded fan bearing his family *mon* and a small pad of paper napkins called *kaishi* completed his needs for the ceremony.

He joined the other guests in the waiting room.

The six other guests were a varied lot. Five were merchants with some noble blood, including Kadayu Nori, who acknowledged Ichiro's presence with a huge grin and a polite nod of the head. Of the other four merchants, most were old and balding like Kadayu. The other was a young man of striking features who seemed uninterested in the matters of business which the older men were discussing most animatedly, but politely.

The sixth man was quite different.

He was young as well, but far from handsome, although his features, too, were striking. One pock-marked cheek, half hidden by a thick black beard, told of a childhood illness. Thick and tousled hair indicted that he was from a rural area and not from the city, where a well-groomed appearance was essential.

A black eye patch covered his right eye, giving a sinister look to his features, but the remaining eye sparkled with vitality and humor as it watched the merchants and their conversation. He appeared to find their talk as amusing as a comedic interlude in a *Noh* play, but courtesy and decorum kept him from laughing aloud.

From the crests on the man's *kimono*, Ichiro ascertained the young man was a member of the Date clan. His ancestor Date Masamune also had possessed just one eye. If his temperament were like his ancestor's, he would be a good general and one not averse to dispatching his own men if they were too tired to move.

The young Date came toward Ichiro.

"Pardon me," he said, bowing slightly at the waist. "You are General Minamoto-no-Ichiro, are you not?"

"Yes, that is correct," Ichiro replied, returning the bow. "But you have the advantage of me."

"A thousand pardons. I am Date Matsuo, the son of the *daimyo* of my clan."

"I am honored to meet you," Ichiro replied.

Date smiled. "Not half so honored as I am to meet you. Even in the North we have heard much about your exploits. A general of your skill has not been seen since the great Hideoyoshi."

"He and I have more in common than just a general's skill," Ichiro said softly.

"Oh. Yes, the leg," Date said, embarrassed. "I did not mean it as an insult."

Ichiro smiled. He liked this young man. "It was not taken as insult. It is just a fact."

"You are too kind, General," he replied. "Others would have commented on my eye if I had hurt them so. And justifiably." He clasped Ichiro's wrist and leaned toward him conspiratorially. "Most people believe I lost my eye in battle," he whispered, "defending my family's honor."

"And you didn't?"

"No," Matsuo replied, shaking his head. "I was drunk with friends one night and as we staggered down the road, I went to relieve myself in a copse of trees. As I was about to let some of my troubles pass, I tripped over a root and fell onto the stump of a newly cut tree. A single shaft of wood stuck up from the stump like a spear, and I fell right onto it."

Ichiro winced at the thought.

"I didn't feel a thing," Matsuo said. He raised his voice slightly so the others could hear. "Everyone said it improved my appearance. Some say it makes me look dashing, like my great forebear Masamune."

Matsuo resumed talking to Ichiro privately. "Did you know Masamune had his eye knocked out in battle? For years it simply lay on his cheek like a swollen fruit. Finally, he tired of people laughing at him or being repulsed by it, so he took his sword one day and just cut it off."

Ichiro noticed the others in the room had stopped conversing in order to eavesdrop on Matsuo's story. As they heard it, they were appalled. But Date Matsuo was taking obvious delight in his gruesome tale and the others' reactions to it.

Ichiro suspected the tale had been well-told several times and polished precisely to elicit the very response it drew.

Matsuo had a faint smile on his lips. "I must confess I'd rather have the eye back," he said, "but I make the best of things. At least women seem more attracted to me, but then again, that might be because I am older now and not because I have one eye."

Ichiro felt a moment of pity for the young Date. He realized the man's injury was more than just physical, and that Matsuo had adopted his brash posture as a defense.

At that point, the Shogun entered the room.

"Welcome, my friends. Forgive me, I was delayed and had to attend to some pressing business."

The others murmured politely.

Tokugawa smiled. "Come, let us return to the tea house."

The guests followed the Shogun down the flowered and multicolored garden path to the *sukiya*, the tea house where the ceremony would take place. Before entering the *sukiya*, each guest washed his hands and rinsed his mouth with fresh water from a white stone basin set among the red chrysanthemums next to the entrance.

Then each one fell to his hands and knees in order to crawl through the small entrance way. The entrance was built so to require all the guests to humble themselves automatically as they entered. Once inside the tea room proper, they each knelt in turn before the *tokonoma* alcove, where a hanging scroll and an ornate incense holder were located. They placed their folded fans before them and said the proper obeisance, admiring the scroll and the incense

holder. They took time to admire the intricate ironwork on the brazier before taking their seats.

––––––

Each action had to be follow in form, or the proper mood of the *chanoyu* would be disrupted and the calming effect of the ceremony on the mind would be lost.

As principal guest, Ichiro sat next to the Shogun while a light meal, the *kaiseki*, was served. After sampling a concluding sweet--made from black bean paste--the party retired to the small inner garden of the tea house while the main ceremony of *goza-iri* was being prepared.

Ichiro, however, could not let his mind be soothed by the tranquility of the ceremony. Something about the young merchant disturbed him. The man's disinterest in simple conversation was not haughtiness or disdain. There appeared to be an underlying furtiveness about the man. He averted his eyes whenever Ichiro looked his way, as if his eyes might betray some dark inner secret he held. Ichiro was certain the man was up to something.

"That fellow Fuseya is an odd one," Matsuo whispered.

"Is he the young one?" Ichiro asked.

"Yes," Matsuo replied. "I can't say I care for him much. Something about him sticks in my craw."

Before Ichiro could ask further questions, a gong sounded five times to indicate the start of the tea ceremony.

"Come, gentlemen," the Shogun said, turning to his guests. "Let us retire to the tea house."

Each guest repeated the cleansing ritual at the basin and re-entered the *sukiya*.

Red and yellow flowers of several types were now in the *tokonoma* and black- and red- lacquered bamboo screens which had covered the windows had been removed to brighten the room. The tea caddy and fresh water receptacle were already in place.

The Shogun left the main room and entered the service room. He returned carrying the ceremonial tea bowl, a teaspoon, and a bamboo whisk.

Each of the guests were required to examine the tea bowl and comment on its artistic beauty. Ichiro found most of the comments flat and forced. He almost wished for the sincerity of the ancient warrior who had been so moved by the beauty of a tea bowl he had gasped and nearly dropped it. Ashamed that he could face death silently, but had uttered an involuntary sound of surprise just on seeing a tea bowl, he rose and smashed the bowl at his feet.

The participants, Ichiro knew, were more likely hypocrites and status seekers, perfectly willing to lie and flatter if it meant the sale of more goods or a position in the government for a son or brother. He did, however, take particular care to listen to what the young merchant Fuseya said about the bowl.

There was a nervousness to Fuseya's praise. When Ishido, one of the older merchants, took exception to one of Fuseya's comments, the young man was quick to change his mind to agree with Ishido. After he passed the bowl, he slid his hand across the front of his kimono and a look of relief came to his face.

When the bowl came to Matsuo's hands, he composed a witty, impromptu poem regarding the beauty of the bowl, comparing it to the city's *geisha* houses. While everyone else laughed politely at the poem, Ichiro noticed that Fuseya could manage only a forced grin. The man displayed an increasing urgency and discomfort.

The Shogun now brought out a tea dipper, a waste-water receptacle, and a stand for the lid of the kettle. An assistant then brought out a cake container, which was set before Ichiro, as dictated by his position as principal guest.

Now the Shogun began the tea ceremony proper. He wiped the tea caddy and the spoon with a pale blue *fukusa*, a soft cloth. With hot water from the kettle, he washed the bamboo whisk. After cleaning the whisk, he emptied the water into the waste water receptacle. Finally, he dried the bowl with a piece of white linen.

The procedure was proper and precise, dictated by centuries of use and refinement. Each action was admired by the guests in the same manner as one would admire the movements of a dancer or a performer in the *kabuki*.

The Shogun opened the tea caddy and put three spoonfuls of powered green *matcha* tea per guest into the bowl. Carefully, he put the dipper into the kettle and poured a third of the water from the dipper into the bowl, returning the rest to the kettle. Taking the whisk, he whipped the mixture until it was thick and frothy, the color and texture of pea soup.

While the Shogun prepared the tea, Ichiro removed his cake from the container and passed it along. The cake, he noted, was quite delicious and he hoped its sweetness would mask any bitterness that the frothy tea, called *koicha*, might possess. Frankly, he preferred the thinner *usucha* tea drunk in the second part of the *chanoyu* ceremony.

The Shogun now placed the bowl of *koicha* onto the hearth of the brazier and moved aside. The servant came forward on his knees and brought the bowl of fragrant tea to Ichiro.

Ichiro bowed to each guest and took the bowl in his left hand, supporting it with his right. Hiding his dislike for the tea, he raised the bowl to his lips and took a sip. The tea was sweet and fragrant, not at all bitter.

"I must commend you, Tokugawa Yoriyoshi, on both the excellence of your tea and the manner of its preparation," he said. Feeling the moment was appropriate, he recited a haiku he had composed as a youth.

"Fragrant as the sea breeze,
And sweet as the cherry blossom,
Is the flavor of this tea,

Incomparable in all Nippon."

The Shogun was clearly charmed by the poem, but a smile and a nod of his head were his only departures with formality.

Ichiro took two more sips of tea. Finishing, he wiped the spot where he had drunk with the *kaishi* napkin and handed the bowl to Matsuo.

Matsuo repeated the ritual, reciting a fine poem afterwards, worthy of the great poet Basho, but which was inferior in sincerity to Ichiro's.

———

As the bowl passed among the guests, Ichiro kept his eye on Fuseya. The young merchant was up to something, of that Ichiro had no doubt. Perhaps an assassination attempt? They were not unheard of at *chanoyu* ceremonies. But, if so, who was the target and what could be the reason?

Ichiro could not simply challenge the man. It would not only be dangerous and perhaps incorrect, but it would also disrupt the dignity and grace of the ceremony. He could not face such disgrace even if his assumption that the man was a threat to someone proved true.

There was no choice. He watched quietly as the bowl moved from Fuseya's hands into those of Ishido.

But as Fuseya passed the bowl, the folds of his *kimono* fell open slightly to reveal the handle of a small *tanto* dagger. As he turned back, his eyes caught Ichiro's gaze.

For a moment, Ichiro was afraid that Fuseya realized his weapon had been seen. Instead, the merchant glanced toward the Shogun, who was receiving the bowl from Kadayu. Ichiro saw the man's hands go to the dagger, and as Fuseya started toward the Shogun, Ichiro grabbed the tea kettle and swung it.

The blade of the *tanto* deflected off the side of the kettle, giving the Shogun time to avoid the thrust aimed at

his heart. The kettle continued its journey, striking Fuseya high on the right shoulder. Hot water cascaded from the metal vessel. Fuseya screamed as his arm and chest were scalded by the boiling liquid.

Acting quickly, Matsuo knocked Fuseya to the floor and pinioned the merchant's arms.

But the young man was strong. Despite his own injured arm and Matsuo's weight, he knocked the *samurai* off balance and scrambled to his knees. Seeing the *tanto* on the floor, he leaped for it.

Ichiro was quicker. As Fuseya's hand grasped for the dagger, Ichiro brought his foot down firmly on the merchant's fingers.

Howling in pain, Fuseya fell back to the floor.

Matsuo reacted quickly. Grabbing the knife, he sat on the merchant's chest, his knee in position to crush Fuseya's ribs. He brought the blade of the dagger up to the man's throat, ready to cut it if the merchant resisted.

Fuseya, knowing this time he was defeated, did not resist. He began to sob softly, hugging his scalded arm close to his body in the way a child might protect a favored, broken doll.

There was an odd moment of silence, a quiet filled with fear and confusion. Ichiro saw the other merchants pressed

back against the walls of the tea house. Fear was clearly etched into their sallow features. He could see the beads of perspiration, like tiny pearls, on the forehead of Matsuo as he held Fuseya down. The young *samurai*'s heavy, labored breathing was the only sound in the room.

He glanced at the Shogun and was surprised to see what he swore was a thin smile on the man's lips.

"An outrage!" the Shogun cried, as if on cue. "I invite a man to my dwelling for tea and he tries to kill me!"

The Shogun stared coldly at the other merchants. "My friends, If I, the Shogun, am not safe in my home, then none are safe."

Ichiro had the odd feeling that what he was watching was carefully planned and prepared like a sword dance in the *kabuki*. *But if it were,* he thought, *to what purpose? It seemed a deadly dance if it were a charade.*

The Shogun rose and came to stand above the pinned Fuseya.

"Who paid you to do this?" he asked the merchant.

"No one," Fuseya said through clenched teeth, holding back the pain from his injured hand and arm.

"You are lying," the Shogun said calmly.

Ichiro was certain the man was in pain, it was obvious. Yet there was no cold wave of evil as he felt whenever Taira's treachery was afoot. Whatever the *daimyo's* plots might be, they had nothing to do with Fuseya's act.

"He is telling the truth," Ichiro said. "If someone has paid to have you killed, my lord, surely he would have chosen a better agent than this clumsy wretch."

"That is correct, yet," the Shogun said with a nod. "Yet we cannot be so certain. Why would you say that no one paid Fuseya?"

"The skilled assassin hides his intentions and his weapons. One moment, he praises your tea the next, he has cut your throat," Ichiro said. "He betrayed himself, my lord. Fuseya carried his intentions and desires on his face and his weapon was even less carefully concealed. At first, I thought he was just a nervous guest, but I saw the blade of his *tanto* and I knew."

"So that was why you reacted so quickly," remarked Matsuo, truly impressed.

Ichiro nodded. "My lord," he said to the Shogun, "If you wish to know why he tried to kill you, simply ask him. I believe he has no reason to lie."

The Shogun pondered the thought a moment, then turned to Fuseya. "Why did you want me dead?"

"You killed my father!" the merchant shouted.

"But your father was Fuseya Abe, the merchant," the Shogun said matter-of-factly. "He died of the fever, not by my hand."

"He was not my father!" Fuseya declared.

There was a murmur of surprise from two of the merchants and Matsuo, but the Shogun was unperturbed.

"My father was Hsuyami, the pirate, brother of Fuseya Abe, my uncle." Perspiration speckled Fuseya's brow and his face paled. "He wished his brother to raise me, so I would not know who he was. But I found out the truth after Abe died.

"Then I learned he had been captured and executed by you. When I inherited my uncle's wealth, I gained his position and his access to you. It was only a matter of time before I had my opportunity.

"And I have wasted it," he said, sobbing. "Kill me now, at least let me have that honor!"

The Shogun called to his servants. "Take Fuseya to my physician and have his burns attended to. Then provide him with food. But keep an eye on him and make certain he causes no harm to himself. I shall deal with him later."

After Fuseya was led from the tea house, the Shogun turned back to his guests. "Come, come, gentlemen, let us

finish our tea," he said, addressing them as if nothing had happened. "We have much to discuss."

The Shogun returned to his seat and, with deft skill, began preparing the tea for the *usucha* ceremony. He took precise care with each bowlful. "Yes, gentlemen," he said, passing the first bowlful to Ichiro, "none of us are safe as long as pirates like Hsuyami and rebels like Lord Taira are afoot."

"Fortunately, Hsuyami is dead," Ishido said pleasantly.

"Yes," the Shogun said. "But he was a small danger compared to Lord Taira. The fear the *daimyo* brings drives the sanest men to acts they would not normally contemplate."

"Yes, yes, we must stop him," Kadayu said.

"But how, gentlemen?" Tokugawa said. "In order to stop him, we must have an army, and armies must be armed and supplied. To be sure, *ronin* and *ashigaru* will volunteer to join such an army, but they are a mere drop in the bucket."

"The Shogun is correct," Kadayu said. He turned to Ishido. "We merchants must do something to help."

"But we are only merchants," Ishido protested. "And just four of us at that."

"Ah! You just don't wish to part with your money, you old miser!" Kadayu said. "And what good will it be if Taira succeeds? He'll just kill us and take it for himself!"

"Yes, but..." Ishido said.

Ichiro was watching the conversation with interest, realizing that Kadayu had promised him help and here it was, although in quite an unexpected form.

"Surely you both know other merchants?" the Shogun asked

"Of course," Kadayu said. "And unlike Ishido, they will be willing to give to save their income!"

"I agree, I agree!" Ishido said, almost shouting. "Lord Taira is bad business, it is obvious! I will be more than willing to give!"

The Shogun smiled. "Then we are agreed?"

"No, not quite," Ishido said quickly. "If we raise money for an army, then who will lead it?"

The Shogun sat back, surprised. "Surely you cannot come here to drink my tea without recognizing my honored guest, General Minamoto-no-Ichiro?"

"Oh, no, of course not," Ishido blurted. He turned to Ichiro. "You must pardon me, General. My eyes are old, you see, and I did not recognize you. But your name is well known throughout Nippon!"

"And Ishido, you old cheat, you should be more than willing to contribute to the man who will save all our

skins--even your leathery hide--from Taira's magic and madness!" Kadayu said.

"Of course, of course," the old merchant cried.

Ichiro, tired as he was, could not help but smile at the comic scene before him. Kadayu had done as he said he would. *How odd,* Ichiro thought, *that I should kill a man's own flesh and blood and he should thank me, indeed, reward me!*

The universe does not need Taira's necromancy to create chaos, Ichiro thought. The minds and motives of humans were chaotic and inexplicable enough for all the universes. And he could not help laughing to himself.

But his revelry was cut short by a messenger who burst into the tea house. The man looked wild, his jacket and trousers torn and blood-stained. His face was a mask of exhaustion, with perspiration cutting thin lines into the dust which caked his features.

"My lord," he said, gasping for breath. "Kyoto—Kyoto has fallen to Lord Taira's army!"

CHAPTER ELEVEN

The Shogun ordered the servants to bring water while Ichiro and Matsuo helped the messenger sit down.

"Gentlemen," the Shogun told the merchants. "Please go to my offices. I will join you later to discuss the means of financing the army. But now I must hear this man's news in private."

When the merchants left, the Shogun sat beside the exhausted messenger.

Ichiro, thinking quickly, raised a bowl of tea to the messenger's lips. The man gulped the liquid greedily. Then his body shuddered with thick coughs. A wad of phlegm burst at his lips. Ichiro wiped it away with a *kaishi*.

They let the man rest and drink some water before they question him.

"What happened?" Ichiro asked.

"Taira's army was seen approaching the city," the man said. "We were preparing the defenses. But as the enemy came into view, an unearthly darkness fell upon the city. Only Taira's men could see. Most of the Imperial Guard were dead before they could resist."

"Have any escaped?" the Shogun asked.

"A few, my lord. Those who are not already in Edo will be here soon," the messenger said.

"And the Emperor?" Ichiro asked.

"He is captured," the man said. "Taira holds him prisoner in the Imperial Palace. We were protecting him, and he would have escaped, except..." The man hesitated.

"Yes?" Ichiro asked.

"Lord Akiyama betrayed us, General," the messenger, almost spitting the noble's name. "The Emperor had disguised himself as a lady-in-waiting, but that traitor Akiyama raised the alarm as the Emperor's coach reached the edge of the city."

Ichiro cursed under his breath. Now it was obvious what Akiyama had done that night the coach nearly ran him down. The conspiracy could not have been more blatant.

"I will personally have Lord Akiyama's head," Matsuo declared. "And I'll spread his entrails out for the dogs and crows."

"A fine oath, and I have no doubt you'll fulfill it," Ichiro said to the young *samurai*. "But there is a long path we must travel before that happens."

The servants arrived with the physician, who ordered the messenger be taken to his quarters for treatment. The doctor also ordered them to bring food, drink and fresh clothes for the man.

"My doctor is happy today," the Shogun said after they left. "Three patients in one day, and not one complaining of a hangover. He'll be so delighted, he'll probably achieve *satori*."

Matsuo laughed, but Ichiro's thoughts grew dark. The Shogun noticed almost immediately.

"Excuse me, Date Matsuo," the Tokugawa said. "But I must speak privately with the general."

"Of course, my lord," Matsuo said. He too had noticed Ichiro's bleak mood. "I will just entertain our merchant friends with some amusing stories," he said.

"No doubt about your own escapades," the Shogun said.

"Naturally. I relate no second-hand tales," Matsuo said with a grin.

After Matsuo withdrew, the Shogun sat down and poured himself some tea. "It seems the messenger ruined my little drama, but it achieved its aims, don't you think?" he said.

"I suspected as much," Ichiro said.

"I was not certain of its success," the Shogun said. He sipped his tea. "I trust you approve of my little deception?"

"Am I supposed to approve, my lord?" Ichiro asked.

The Shogun frowned. "I suppose not. It was meant to impress our guests, not you. In particular, I wanted to impress Ishido, that damned old pinch-fist."

Tokugawa smiled. "And you played your part quite well."

Ichiro felt uncomfortable about the deception. He disliked it and the need for it, but if it raised money for an army, he had to be pleased. Especially now with Kyoto fallen.

"No, I am not offended," Ichiro said. In fact, I have a gambit of my own to play."

"Good," the Shogun said.

"This Fuseya, who is he?" Ichiro asked.

"A merchant's son, and an aspiring *kabuki* performer," the Shogun replied. "His father is an old friend of mine. Fuseya learned of your plight from his father and proposed a command performance. Old Kadayu was already invited to the tea ceremony, but also offered his help."

"And Ishido?"

"Probably the wealthiest man in Edo, and the most miserly to boot," the Shogun said. "But he's easily manipulated if the circumstances are right and if it means protecting his precious gold."

"I must apologize to Fuseya for injuring him," Ichiro said.

"Yes, you did give him rather a bad scald," the Shogun said. "Yet he remained true to the character he played. He should make a fine *kabuki* and *noh* artist."

"If we all survive this," Ichiro muttered. *But if I myself could use deception as skillfully as the Shogun had, we indeed might survive,* he thought. He remembered the exploits of his own ancestor Kusunoki Masashige. He was a master of deception in his support of Emperor Go-Daigo against the Shogun and the forces of the *Bakufu.*

Yes, deception is a useful tool, he thought. Already a plan was forming in his mind.

"Your physician said there are foreigners in the harbor," Ichiro said.

The change of subject surprised the Shogun. "Why, yes, there are. They call themselves Dutchmen. They say they come from Europe, which is beyond the western borders of China."

"I should like to meet these Dutchmen. I believe I may make use of them and their vessel, " Ichiro said.

The Shogun smiled. "Ah, I expected you would soon have a plan of action. I can arrange the meeting within the hour."

"No, that is too soon," Ichiro said. "Make it two days hence. I want to see what sort of army I have before I make demands of them."

The Shogun saw the wisdom of the delay. "As you wish. I will order them to appear, but I will also explain the need for a religious ritual to purify them before they appear in our presence."

Ichiro's dark mood lifted briefly and he smiled. The Shogun, at least, found these events part of a grand and delightful game.

He wished he could do the same.

Ichiro bided his time before the meeting. He collected his sword from Setsumu, finding it more than adequate for his plans. Three times he strolled to the harbor to take stock of the Dutchmen's ship.

It was more than adequate for his plans. It was primitive by his standards, as used as he was to the "steel dragons" of his own world. But this was a modern vessel for this world. Her masts and rigging were sound. A single smokestack, ringed with soot, spoke proudly that she ran on steam and burned coal, though she no doubt did both inefficiently. *But she will suffice*, Ichiro thought.

Only her captain was an obstacle.

By the morning of the second day, Edo was welcoming hundreds of warriors from Kyoto and the environs. Many were eager to rejoin the battle. Others were too weary even to stand. But the ranks were swelled by the forces sent by Date Matsuo's father, as well as by *ronin* and *ashigaru* looking for adventure. Even some *samurai* saw fit to leave their *daimyo* to lend aid.

"Children, old men, fools and cutthroats, the lot," Shizuka sneered when she saw them.

"You're a fine one to speak, *ninja*," he chided her.

"We shall see, *samurai*, who fights and who runs away at the first sign of trouble," she replied.

He had to admit she was right.

By evening a loud commotion echoed throughout the Shogun's *yashiki*. The Dutchmen had accepted the Shogun's offer, the gossips said. They were coming to discuss trade arrangements and would arrive that night.

A palanquin was sent to the harbor to fetch the ship's captain. The sedan chair bearers waded into the harbor to greet the captain and bear him from his skiff. It was done so that the foreigner's contaminated feet would never touch and, therefore despoil, Japanese earth. Every step of his journey was marked off with fresh *tatami* mats. When he left, each mat would be burned. Only in that way, the Shinto priests and sages had pronounced, could the European contagion be controlled.

The Dutchman was ushered into the Shogun's offices. The captain was named Rijs Van der Lieuw. The amount of energy expended in placing the mats amused him. He remained amused until he learned he would have to sit on the floor, since there were no chairs.

From the start, this placed the large, bluff man on the defensive. Already, consternation reddened the man's face, a face Ichiro found curiously pale and drawn rather than properly bronzed and weathered by years spent on the deck of a ship.

Van der Lieuw surveyed the scene. He rubbed his thick bird's nest of a black beard. With a sigh, he lowered himself to the thick mat, resigned to the situation.

"A daring man, this Van der Lieuw," the Shogun whispered to Ichiro. Tokugawa was confident of the Dutchman could not understand Japanese. He continued, "My physician learned from the ship's doctor that the captain possesses the natural resistance of a merchant who is forced to accept demands that will benefit others and not fatten his coffers."

"He certainly knows he can expect little reward from my venture, my lord," Ichiro said. "But I suspect he has already found some way to profit from it. Merchants usually do."

Ichiro also knew that the Shogun held the upper hand in any event.

Should the Dutchman refuse to transport a portion of Ichiro's forces to Osaka, he might awaken the next night to find a score of black-clad figures dispatching his crew. That would be just before a *ninja*'s dagger cut his throat.

How Shizuka would love such an opportunity, if given the chance, Ichiro thought.

The Shogun's physician and the ship's doctor translated. It was a long a laborious task, with a proposal first presented in Japanese. The Shogun's physician then translated it into Chinese, with some minor problems involving dialect, to the ship's doctor, who in turn rendered it into Dutch. Counter-proposals reversed the path.

Van der Lieuw would on occasion nod, run his large white hands through his lank and greasy black hair, or puff irritably on a long clay pipe. Blue clouds of tobacco smoke swirled continually round Van der Lieuw's head. They were especially thick when the negotiations did not go his way.

For Ichiro, the tobacco brought back memories of his last night in the barracks. He recalled that long and lonely night when he prepared himself for what he thought was his final assault. He knew now that his true final assault would yet await him.

After an agonizing seven hours of debate, both sides at last understood each other fairly well. At least that was the impression the two physicians gave.

Van der Lieuw obviously understood he had but one choice. That was a position with which Ichiro was all too familiar. "You leave me no alternative," said the Dutchman.

A surprised look went about the room. Van der Lieuw was speaking Japanese. His speech was a trifle clumsy, but made it obvious he had understood the conversation all along.

"I will accept your offer of a guaranteed trading port," Van der Lieuw said.

"In exchange for transporting General Minamoto's army to Osaka and not setting foot on the sacred soil of Nippon," the Shogun said.

The Dutchman broke into a broad smile. "Agreed."

"You will sail tomorrow," the Shogun said. "We are already preparing to provision your ship for the journey."

The Dutchman balked at the news. "So soon? " he said angrily. "My men have hardly had time to recover from six long months at sea. And now you expect them to sail again, you who won't let them off the ship for even the shorted moment?"

The Shogun raised his hand to stop the conversation. "We cannot waste time. You will sail tomorrow. If you refuse, my *samurai* are ready to board your ship and take your crew."

Van der Lieuw bristled. "My guns will destroy this paper-and-wood farce you call a castle," he said. His anger improved his fluency with the language.

Ichiro's distrust of the man was growing. It was possible Van der Lieuw could acquire a language quickly, but he doubted it. He knew the Dutchman was hiding something, and it made him uneasy. Van der Lieuw's nature was lust for profit, and his nature was not easily thwarted, Ichiro realized.

"Your guns may destroy the city, Dutchman, that is true," Ichiro said softly. "But we may rebuild our city. Once your ship is gone, so is your life. From that, you cannot recover, merchant."

Van der Lieuw ran a hand over his mouth and cursed under his breath. He clenched his teeth so tightly on his pipe stem that it was a wonder it did not shatter. "Very well," he said finally. "Tomorrow. But full provisions, mind you. Meat, wine, and fresh water, not just your sticky rice and salted fish."

The Shogun nodded with satisfaction. "It is so. You will sail by mid-day?"

"I will weigh anchor when my ship is provisioned. Two to three days out and back. For that I will need firewood and coal," Van der Lieuw said.

"It will be cut," the Shogun said.

"Good."

"Then this conversation is ended."

Ichiro watched as the Dutchman and the physician rose and the room. Outside, palanquins awaited to return them to their ship. Servants followed behind, gathering up the *tatami* on which the Europeans had trod. The reed mats would be whisked away to the kitchens and consigned to the cooking fires. Every trace of European contamination would be reduced to smoke and ash.

Ichiro wished he could reduce the encounter with Van der Lieuw so easily. This captain was a calculating man and not to be taken lightly, Ichiro knew. For like a slave, such a merchant was easily sold to the highest bidder.

CHAPTER TWELVE

The next day, grim and wet, almost confirmed Ichiro's ill-will toward Van der Lieuw. The sky was steel gray. A bank of storm clouds drifted in from the south, from the direction of Kyoto.

Drizzling rain kept everyone inside, except for the porters loading the Dutch ship. Their backs were bent beneath rice sacks and barrels of salted meat as big as themselves. Their meager wicker rain capes were thoroughly drenched and offered no protection from the downpour.

Ichiro shivered in his own clothes as the skiff rowed his party toward the ship. Shizuka seemed implacable in her black jacket and trousers. She reminded him of the scene changer in the *kabuki* who is always there, but who is almost never noticed.

Yukio huddled under a rain cape, his drenched persimmon robes clinging to his small body. His teeth chattered loudly and he appeared positively miserable.

Ichiro's heart went out to the monk. Yukio had spent the last five days in devotions at the temple. Now he was cast out into the painful world once more. But Yukio would not complain, Ichiro knew. That was considered unseemly behavior for a monk, even a novice.

Tamika sat in the bow of the skiff. The female *samurai* stared out at the cloudbank and at the ship. Apparently impervious to the weather, she did not speak.

The skiff's other occupants were a pair of Dutch sailors who manned the oars. Dressed in oilskin slickers and caps, they did not mind the weather. At each stroke, one or the other would grunt with exertion, or curse or tell a joke in Dutch. The listener always replied with a vulgar laugh.

Ichiro wondered how many of the jokes were about the Japanese. Most, he suspected.

The skiff eased slowly next to the ship. A metal and canvas gangway was lowered to let the passengers aboard. Ichiro's skiff was the last to unload. Twenty hand-picked soldiers were with them. These were the strike force Ichiro estimated he needed to enter Kyoto and free the Emperor. Date Matsuo was leading the remainder of the army to a previously-planned stronghold.

Ichiro knew twenty men was probably too many, but he expected to lose several to Taira's treachery. He would not run the risk of having too few men when the critical time came.

Van der Lieuw, dressed in a yellowish slicker and a broad black hat, stood at the head of the gangway to greet them. The captain did not seem pleased to see them.

"About time you showed up," he said.

"It is still early," Ichiro replied.

Van der Lieuw grunted. "Perhaps," he said flatly. "But I preferred not to have to deal with things at the last moment." He stalked off toward the ship's bridge, rain sliding down his slicker and boots.

Odd. Clearly the man does not like water, although he seems a veteran sailor, Ichiro thought.

The first mate, a dour and cadaverous man, showed them to their quarters, which were near the ship's bow. Shizuka and the female *samurai* were to share one room, while Ichiro and the young monk shared another. The 20 men were quartered in four other rooms, rooms not designed for five men apiece with their armor and weapons.

Worse, the rooms felt awkward. European furniture seemed continually underfoot to Ichiro and the others. Even more agonizing was the roll of the ship as it left the calm waters of Edo harbor and the bay and entered the rough sea.

Ichiro had sailed on aircraft carriers. The continual rocking disturbed him little. Yukio, when he was not resigned to lying on the cabin's hard bed, spent much of his time staggering to the single port-hole and releasing the meager contents of his stomach into the sea.

"Are you all right?" Ichiro asked.

"No," the young monk said, groaning. Beads of perspiration rolled down his head, recently shaved and blue with stubble.

"Is this why the Shogun has forbidden us to leave Japan? Because the *kami* will strike us with this sickness?" Yukio asked. He staggered back to the bed.

Ichiro laughed, something he had not done in a long time. "No, little monk, many people find the sea's motion doesn't agree with them," he said.

He rummaged through his belongings and found a stoppered jar. It contained a potion that the Shogun's physician made for him.

"Here, drink this," Ichiro said. He unstoppered the jar, lifted Yukio's head, and brought the contents to the monk's lips.

Yukio drank the potion. He grimaced, and he tried to spit it out. But he was too weak, and the medicine was strong. Within moments, the young man was asleep, untroubled by a queasy stomach.

Relieved, Ichiro went up on deck.

The sun had set, but the afterglow still cast a crimson sheen across sea and sky. The acrid, salty odor of seawater and earth rode the wind from the shore. It put Ichiro in mind of another place, another time.

That grim December morning on board the carrier *Akagi* now seemed unreal. He barely recalled the odor of aviation fuel and hot oil. Could he fly a plane now? Perhaps. Like riding a bicycle, it was a skill not easily lost.

Did Hawaii smell different from this odor? he wondered.

It was so far away, out of sight beneath the horizon. That sea, too, had sparkled with sunlight. But that was the light of dawn and not evening. The world was new that day.

The attack was a blur. Exploding American ships and lines of burning fighter planes lost their individual identity against the vast canvas of war. He had seen many burning ships and planes since then and had lost too many friends.

Yes, Hawaii did smell different, he recalled. His wingman, Lt. Oyama, swore he smelled the odor of pineapple farms and blooming flowers drifting on the wind that morning. Everyone laughed, but no one dared argue because a few others also thought they smelled pineapple. Oyama had spent several years on his grandfather's farm on Oahu. If anyone knew the odor of pineapples, it was Oyama.

Oyama's death grieved Ichiro. A good friend, the likable lieutenant was shot down over Midway. His wife of less than a year took poison when she heard of his death. She said she could not live as a widow, dependent on unfeeling relatives. It was said she was three months pregnant at the time, Ichiro recalled. *Three lives lost. Such was the law of karma*, he thought.

"Good evening, General," Van der Lieuw said.

Ichiro was startled, but quickly recovered. "Good evening to you, Captain," he said.

The Dutchman ambled up to Ichiro's side. He puffed energetically on an old clay pipe.

"I am surprised to see you take to the sea so well," Van der Lieuw said. "Most of your men are sick in their beds, but you seem like a man familiar with the sea."

"I have sailed before," he replied. "On bigger ships."

"Ha!" Van der Lieuw snorted. "None of your country's ships is bigger than my *Anna der Wentz*."

"True," Ichiro replied. "But in the land of my birth I sailed on steel ships that could swallow your boat."

Van der Lieuw laughed. "You are mad, General. Steel ships? They would sink like a rock!"

"In your lifetime, Captain, you may see them. If you and your world survive. If I am able to see that it survives," Ichiro said.

"As may be, General," Van der Lieuw said. The captain tapped out the ashes from his pipe onto a deck railing. He blew into the pipe stem like a whistle. Once he was certain the pipe was clear, Van der Lieuw put it into his jacket pocket. "But I am concerned with profits, something your expedition is reducing considerably."

Behind him, Ichiro thought he heard a whistle in reply to the captain's. But he saw nothing.

"Without my expedition, Captain, you would have no profits at all," Ichiro said.

"Perhaps. But I am a businessman. I deal with whoever offers me the best return for my investment," Van der Lieuw said. He pulled the pipe and a leather pouch from his pocket. The pipe bowl ducked into the pouch and emerged packed with dark tobacco. "I might have chosen to wait for this Taira fellow, if your offer had not been so immediate and pressing."

"On your life, you mean?"

Van der Lieuw smiled around the stem of his pipe as he struck a match and lit the tobacco. His fine white teeth glistened even in the dying light. "As you yourself noted, if I had refused, you would have killed me and my crew. How can I profit when I am dead?" The captain shook out his match and tossed it into the sea.

"Would you have made deals with Taira, then, if he had made you an offer?" Ichiro asked.

"I will make deals with whoever wins your war," the Dutchman said. "In all manner of politics, I am neutral, unless it costs me money."

Van der Lieuw paused and looked out toward the horizon.

"Do you see that?" he asked. He used the stem of his pipe as a pointer. " A firedrake."

A thin vector of light moved parallel to the horizon and the ship. Its tail stretched toward the north, standing out clearly against a clear black sky that was strangely devoid of stars.

"A comet," Ichiro said.

"*Ja*, a comet. A firedrake," Van der Lieuw said. he sucked at the pipe, then exhaled a stream of smoke that mimicked the comet's tail. "In my homeland, a comet portends the death of a king or the fall of an empire."

"A superstition," Ichiro said.

"I do not know," the captain said. "But a comet appeared in the sky the year we Europeans finally drove the Turks from Vienna, and we killed their Sultan. I was there, twenty-five years ago. We drove them back through the Balkans and Romania. There I was...wounded."

"Was that where you learned your trickery?" Ichiro asked. He noticed the comet was staying even with the ship. No, it actually seemed to be coming closer.

"Ah, no doubt you mean my ability with languages," Van der Lieuw said.

Ichiro nodded.

"I learned much on my travels, General. I trade much with the Chinese. Often we have rescued fisherman from your land, blown of course by storms. They told me of your country, and from them I learned your language."

"I saw no fishermen with you. Did you return them to their homes before you came to Edo?" Ichiro asked.

"Regrettably, no. They told me it was death for them to return home. They would be thought to have fled. Alas, they destroyed themselves with knives and fish poisons. They were dead before my crew could stop them," the Dutchman said.

"But you still saw us as a new market," Ichiro said.

"True," Van der Lieuw said, relighting his pipe. "The Portuguese ran me out of Macao. The British had signed a treaty for Hong Kong with the Chinese Emperor. I was not welcome there, and the Emperor would have killed me if I came to Shanghai. That meant my only other market, besides those wretched tribesmen in the Philippines, was Japan.

"Oh, I confess, I made some friends in Kyushu before I came to Edo. I made a tidy sum selling some unimportant weapons to those petty lords, but I also added to my knowledge of your language and etiquette," he said.

"You played the Shogun for a fool," Ichiro said.

"Far from it, General," the Dutchman answered. "You got what you wished. I received something I desired. We're both satisfied."

Van der Lieuw tapped out his pipe into his hand and tossed the ashes across the rail. "Now, if you will excuse me, this sea air brings out a mighty thirst in me."

Ichiro watched the captain walk away. There was an air of malice and contempt about the man. The amoral, self-possessed Dutchman was not trustworthy, yet Ichiro had to rely on him.

There was, as always, no other choice. The *Anna der Wentz* was the only way to reach Osaka and fulfill the plan. But his talk with Van der Lieuw only increased Ichiro's ill feelings. He had to be more cautious than ever.

Ichiro turned to go below. The comet's tail now stretched from pole to pole. It was not a good sign.

But if it was an ill omen, he thought, *then whose doom was foretold? Taira's or the Emperor's? Was victory to be gained or was everything lost?*

If the comet knew, it gave no answer.

———

In his cabin, Ichiro prepared for sleep on the thin *tatami*. He had barely settled down when he sensed Yukio's body next to him. Although wrapped in a woolen blanket, the young monk still shivered from the chill sea air.

Ichiro drew the young man close and pulled another, worn blanket over them. Yukio sighed contently, then was soon asleep. Ichiro, too, quickly found rest.

He dreamed of long summer days in his youth. He was a fresh-faced student quoting poetry in the long hours of sunlight and warmth. His refined and distant voice won him the respect of men and women both. He had many lovers then.

Now he had none, except a wife in another world who thought him dead and mourned him, and a young monk with a childish infatuation. In his dreams, he wept for all he had lost and all he had gained.

He awoke with a start when he felt a hand cover his mouth. Instinctively, he reached for his sword.

"Quiet, *samurai*," Shizuka hissed. "Or you'll alert them."

"What do you mean?" he whispered.

"The captain is with Taira," she said.

"You're lying!" he said through clenched teeth.

"No. I saw them together in the captain's rooms."

"Take me there," he said, grabbing his short jacket and trousers. He dressed quickly, then picked up Kusinagi by the scabbard.

Moving on silent feet like a cat, the *ninja* led Ichiro to a small closet adjoining the cabin. She pointed to a small crack between the planks of wood. Thin light from several oil lamps filtered through it.

Ichiro kneeled and peered through the opening. Taira's back was toward him, but there was no mistaking the *daimyo's* voice.

"So it is agreed then," Taira said. "You will kill the *samurai* and his men and bring me the sword. In return, I will grant your request for a trading port."

"And as many young women as I need. No questions asked," Van der Lieuw said.

"If you are certain you can kill him, there is no request I cannot grant. But remember, he cannot be killed by any living man," Taira said.

"You underestimate me, my lord Taira," the captain said. The tell-tale odor of the Dutchman's pipe tobacco wafted through the opening.

"No, I do not underestimate you. But I have tried many schemes already to break that spell. None have worked," the magician said.

"I will not fail."

"Good then. Deliver the sword to me in Kyoto, and I will make you a wealthy man in both gold and women."

"Done," Van der Lieuw said. "Now, Lord Taira, the night is near gone. I am in need of nourishment."

"You will destroy General Minamoto tomorrow night."

"And the sword will be in my hands by morning when we dock at Osaka," Van der Lieuw replied, a hint of exasperation in his voice.

Taira nodded. " In three days time then, in Kyoto. If not, then I will know you have failed."

"I never fail where a good profit is to be had," the Dutchman said.

"Good," Taira said. "In three days time."

The necromancer's body began to glow. Slowly it melted into a golden ball. The ball rose from the floor, drifted through the open port-hole, and rose swiftly into the sky.

So Taira was the comet! Ichiro thought. *No wonder it kept such a steady pace with the ship.*

He returned his gaze to Van der Lieuw. The Dutchman rose, and for the first time Ichiro saw there was third figure in the room. It lay supine on the captain's bunk.

It was a young Chinese woman. She was pale, ghostly, and naked., but her appearance was far from sexual. Her arms were like matchsticks, and her breasts were tiny.

"It is late. I am hungry," Van der Lieuw said to the woman. He spoke perfect Cantonese. He climbed onto the bunk and hovered over the woman.

She tried to push him away, but her arms were too weak and thin.

"Oh no, my lovely, it is too late for that," Van der Lieuw said, laughing. He buried his face against her neck. Her mouth uttered a soundless scream.

Her black eyes, sunk deep in their sockets, stared wide open with terror. For Ichiro, it was a stare that would never end.

Van der Lieuw raised himself upright. His body shook with an almost sexual shudder. There was blood on his lips. The hairs of his beard were stained with crimson flecks.

Twice more he sank his mouth to the woman's neck, then he was sated. The captain wiped his face with the back of his hand and rose from the bunk. He disappeared briefly from Ichiro's view, but the *samurai* heard the ring of a small bell.

Van der Lieuw returned and sat on bunk. He reached over and snapped off one of the woman's arms. It made a sound like a dried branch. The captain began to chew the flesh from the bone, relishing each bite.

Soon after, the ship's doctor appeared.

"This one is finished. And a fine one she was, so young and tender," he said mournfully.

"Shall I bring you another, Captain," the doctor said.

"Yes, the dark fat one you procured in Macao. I'll have her," he said. "And give this one to my crew." He lay the dismembered arm on the bunk.

"Yes, Captain."

"Now I will sleep. Much needs to be done tomorrow."

The doctor left and Van der Lieuw doused the oil lamps.

———

"What do we do now?" Shizuka whispered once they were out of the closet into the safety of the corridor.

"I have a plan," Ichiro said. "Come with me."

In his cabin he unrolled a bundle from his belongings. Inside the bundle, each wrapped in rice paper, were 25 medallions bearing the *horimono* from Kusinagi.

"Give one to each man, and then you and Yukio must wear one," Ichiro said.

Shizuka frowned. "Is this all there is to your plan?"

"No," he said. "Tell the men they must not leave their quarters after sunset. They must wear their armor and carry only essential items. Also, they must not go out alone. Always two or more men together."

"I see," Shizuka said.

"Good," Ichiro said. He was pleased she understood. "Tomorrow I will stroll around the boat. There is some information I need. When I have it, I will tell you what else to do."

———

Ichiro rose at dawn. He met the ship's doctor on deck and inquired of the captain's health.

"I notice he prefers to walk at night and disdains the day. Most unusual, I should think," Ichiro said in Mandarin. He had learned the language while stationed in Formosa and was pleased he remembered so much of it.

The doctor was startled to be addressed in Chinese. "Ah, yes," he said, his own face paling visibly. "It is part of a recurring illness, you see. He acquired it fighting the Turks in Romania."

"He said it was a wound."

"Oh. Oh, yes! It was a wound, a wound which festered and let in the disease. On occasion he becomes ill, and finds he cannot stand the light of the sun."

"How unfortunate. Perhaps I shall see him before we reach Osaka, so I may wish his quick recovery," Ichiro said.

"Yes, that would be most courteous," the doctor said. He fumbled with a pocket watch. "Well, I must go. I...I must attend to some sick sailors. If you will excuse me."

The doctor scurried away below decks before Ichiro could speak.

Alone, Ichiro paced the steamship deck, noting the placement of the lifeboats and the location of the several breech-loading cannon. He collared a Chinese crewman who described the range and accuracy of the guns. The crewman spoke with great pride of the gun's destructive power, obviously trying to impress Ichiro.

Ichiro smiled. He recalled the way ratings described the weapons on the aircraft carrier to new seamen. He wondered, how strongly would the Chinese sailor pontificate if he knew of the destructive power of those otherworldly weapons? He then convinced the sailor to give him a tour of the ship, especially the engine room.

Around the boilers the air was hot and filled with a mist of water and oil vapor. The stokers were stripped to the waists. Sweat rolled down their bodies, cutting shiny, wet rivulets in the filth coal dust coating their skins.

The engineers' faces were dark with grime and dirty lubricating oil. They busily checked valves and gauges, making certain there was sufficient pressure to drive the huge reciprocating steam-driven pistons which turned the ship's two paddlewheels.

It was a wonder the continual strain from the engines did not rip the ship apart and sink her. *Perhaps they eventually would, if other factors did not intervene,* Ichiro thought.

A shrill whistle rent the air. An engineer ran to check a pressure valve. He barked an order, telling the stokers to back off the furnaces and vent the excess steam.

"Pressure build-up," the Chinese sailor said knowingly. "The steam was too hot, and the boilers could have exploded like a thousand fireworks."

"Yes. A dangerous thing," Ichiro said. He smiled. Now he had his answer.

The evening came none too quickly. Dying shafts of pink light illuminated the silver underbellies of storm clouds as the sun fell below the horizon. A cold wind rose from the sea, and the sailors raced about the deck preparing for a heavy storm they knew lay ahead.

Ichiro had sent Shizuka ahead to carry out the first part of his plan. But even if she succeeded, it was no guarantee they would reach land alive.

He felt cold and alone. He gripped Kusinagi's hilt more tightly. Van der Lieuw would be stirring now, renewed by the swiftly falling darkness.

Ichiro eased his way down the corridor, listening for any movement. He paused at the hatchway to the deck and prepared to call out. His men had already dispersed themselves about the ship. Now they awaited his signal.

But another shout broke the still night air. A heavy baritone voice barked an order in Dutch.

Lamps suddenly illuminated the entire ship, leaving not an inch dark. Ichiro's men, no longer hidden, went to the defensive as Van der Lieuw's crew attacked.

"Banzai!" Ichiro cried as he leaped from the hatch. Two crewmen saw him and charged with spar and gaff. The sailor with the spar aimed for Ichiro's chest, but the *samurai* merely stepped inside the weapon.

Kusinagi sang. The sailor's dead body crashed into his shipmate with the gaff. Out of control, the pair tumbled overboard.

Ichiro did not have time to notice. To his left came the repeated sharp crack of gunfire. He saw a *samurai* stagger backwards in a cloud of gunsmoke. Blood engulfed the man's chest.

A bullet gouged the deck at Ichiro's feet, sending up a cascade of splinters. He ducked behind a mast. He saw the riflemen standing on the forecastle. There were four of them, each equipped with breech-loading, single-shot weapons. Only two fired at a time while the others reloaded.

Ichiro wished he had his longbow now. He had only one choice, to attack.

A shot whistled past his head.

"To the boats," he shouted to the other *samurai*. The men were engaged in furious hand-to-hand combat with the more numerous sailors. Only the *samurais'* superior abilities in handling sword, lance and *naginata* kept the battle even.

The riflemen were hesitating now, afraid to shoot for fear of hitting their own men. It did not keep them from firing at Ichiro, however.

He needed a diversion. A lamp flickered near his head.

It was an oil lamp, Ichiro saw, intended as a running light to signal other ships at night. Ichiro grabbed it and flung it toward the forecastle.

The lamp broke on the railing, sending out a cascade of orange flame. One rifleman cried out, his clothes afire. The other retreated or tried vainly to put the flames out.

Ichiro climbed the ladder to the forecastle, but one man looked up from the flame long enough to see him.

The sailor raised his rifle and fired.

Ichiro turned aside. He saw the orange flame from the barrel, heard the sharp crack like a thunderclap, and felt the bullet rip through a loose fold in his jacket.

Ichiro charged the man while he reloaded. He caught the man in the chest, sending the sailor tumbling over the railing to the deck below.

An explosion knocked Ichiro to the deck.

Smoke filled the air. It was tinged with the odor of gunpowder.

Ichiro struggled to his feet. Through the haze of the smoke and the oil lamps he saw what remained of the other three riflemen.

The burning man's ammunition pouch had exploded while the others tried to extinguish his clothing.

Ichiro ran to the railing. Everywhere he looked was aflame. The sailors were now more concerned with fighting the fires than with fighting the *samurai*.

Through the flame and smoke, he saw Shizuka and the remainder of his men lowering a longboat. No one tried to stop them.

"Your men fight well," a voice said.

Ichiro turned to face Van der Lieuw.

The Dutchman carried a long cutlass. In the flickering light from the fires the captain's eyes appeared wild and mad. Fresh blood, moist and bright crimson, glistened on his lips and ran down into his black beard.

Van der Lieuw had feasted before the battle. It was clear he wished to feed again, this time on a *samurai's* blood.

"My men are well trained," Ichiro said, tightening his grip on Kusinagi.

"No matter. They will die soon enough. It is your death I desire," Van der Lieuw said.

The Dutchman leaped to the attack, his sword aimed for Ichiro's head.

Ichiro parried the blow easily, but found his counterattack parried swiftly in turn by the Dutchman.

Van der Lieuw possessed enormous strength. Ichiro could feel the force of each blow rattling Kusinagi. His fingers stung. His own attacks seemed to crash into an immovable iron fortress.

"Give up, *samurai*," Van der Lieuw said. "You cannot kill me. I am already dead."

The Dutchman was inexhaustible. The captain's incessant hammer blows placed Ichiro totally on the defensive. Each attack drove him backward across the deck and into the inferno raging all around them.

"Why resist, General?" Van der Lieuw taunted. "Your spell will not protect you. Why not let me kill you? You will be resurrected to live forever." He drew back for a killing blow.

Ichiro grabbed the opportunity. The tip of Kusinagi danced in the light as it slashed Van der Lieuw's wrist.

The sword fell from the Dutchman's useless hand. Thick purple gore flowed from the wound, exposing the thin tendrils of ruined tendons. Surprised by the blow, Van der Lieuw now stared blankly at this injury.

Without hesitation, Ichiro drove Kusinagi deep into the Dutchman's chest. The captain staggered backwards, almost falling, but quickly regaining his footing. A great roar issued from his bloody mouth. He swung his ruined arm like a club, catching Ichiro in the chest and knocking him to the ground.

Ichiro landed heavily on the deck. He came to rest against the corpses of a sailor and a *samurai*. The breath was knocked from him, and he gasped for air.

Van der Lieuw tried desperately to remove the sword from his chest, but his uninjured left hand could not find a good grip. Each movement widened the wound and brought forth more blood.

Van der Lieuw turned toward Ichiro, his face a mask of rage. "No matter. Your sword is but a minor inconvenience," he said. "I will dispatch you with my bare hands."

He started toward Ichiro.

Something pressed Ichiro in the back. He reached for it. It was the dead *samurai's naginata*.

His hands clutched the weapon. Lungs screaming for air, Ichiro staggered to his feet, swinging the lance with all his remaining strength.

Van der Lieuw raised his left arm to stop the blow, but he was too late. The weapon's sharp hook-shaped blade severed the arm at the elbow. The lance carried on into the demon captain's neck. His severed head rolled across the deck. Van der Lieuw's vicious mouth and wolf's teeth grimaced in pain.

Ichiro was still not sure the Dutchman was dead. He jabbed the severed heard with the blunt end of the *naginata*.

The head growled and sank its teeth deeply into the wood, a final act of defiance.

Even without a body, the Dutchman was strong. Ichiro smashed the head against the deck until it released its grip. Then he then impaled the ghoulish head and flung it and the lance into the sea.

Ichiro had to hurry. If Shizuka had done her work, he had precious little time. He pulled Kusinagi from Van der Lieuw's body.

As the sword slid free, the Dutchman's remains turned paper-thin, like the abandoned exoskeleton of a mayfly. Flames ignited the body, which shriveled into powdery ash.

Ichiro sheathed Kusinagi and went to the railing. In the moonlight he saw a single longboat already rowing away from the ship. He hoped he could reach it in time. Taking a lungful of hot, acrid and oily air, Ichiro dived into the sea.

With a roar like a thousand thunderclaps, the boilers of the *Anna der Wentz* exploded.

CHAPTER THIRTEEN

All around Ichiro was smoke and flame. He could not recall where he was. His head hurt, and he coughed up seawater. Burning wood floated past, as did several corpses. He saw a large wooden crate bobbing ahead of him. He swam to it and climbed aboard.

Everything seemed familiar. It reminded him of Midway. Yes, he remembered, he was aboard the carrier *Akagi*. American planes had torpedoed her. He recalled swimming to a lifeboat and climbing aboard. They had searched for survivors, but had only heard their screams as sharks pulled them beneath the surface.

Were there sharks here? he wondered.

A corpse a few meters away was sucked under. Part of it bobbed back to the surface, then it too vanished. Ichiro had his answer.

Water lapped at his feet, and a huge bubble burst beside the crate, tossing spray everywhere. The crate was sinking, he realized. The sharks might soon have more dinner for their feeding frenzy.

"There he is!" he heard a woman's voice say. Ichiro turned toward the voice and saw a longboat rowing toward him through the darkness and haze. A pair of lanterns glowed warmly at its bow.

Ichiro could make out Shizuka's face in the lamplight. He had never seen a more welcome sight. The boat pulled along side the crate. The crate gurgled suddenly and went under. He leaped for the boat and felt himself sinking.

A hand grabbed his wrist. He kicked with all his might, his lungs straining. His fingers caught the side of the boat, and other hands pulled him aboard. He lay gasping in the bottom of the boat.

"You're alive," Shizuka said, a huge grin on her face.

"How could I be otherwise?" he said and belched up a bellyful of seawater. A coughing fit racked his body, but it quickly passed.

"You did a good job on the boilers," he said finally.

"It wasn't difficult," she said. "The sailors were occupied. Doing what you told me to do was child's play."

Ichiro smiled. A safety valve was so simple to sabotage, especially on old-style boilers. Just clog it up and by the time the damage is discovered, it is already too late. He would ask her later what she had used on the valve.

A storm was coming, Ichiro could tell. They needed to reach shore soon or risk being swamped.

"How many of us are left?" he asked, sitting up. His head still throbbed, but the pain was abating.

"Ten, counting me, the monk, and the woman," Shizuka said.

Ichiro closed his eyes. Thirteen dead. Was it worth the cost? He did not know. He whispered a prayer to the Amida Buddha, asking that the warriors be reborn in the Pure Land.

"Yukio?" Ichiro said.

"Yes?" the monk said.

"You must say prayers for the dead."

Yukio nodded. He slipped past the others and said in the gunwale. There he assumed the lotus position. His voice chanting the name of Amida was barely audible above the roar of waves.

"You've given the monk a job. So what about the rest of us? What do we do?" Shizuka asked.

"We row. With luck, we'll reach shore by dawn," Ichiro replied.

When they reached shore the sun was a swollen red pearl breaking free of the ocean. But this morning it offered little warmth or hope.

Already wreckage from the *Anna der Wentz* was rolling into shore.

The wind carried the faint odor of burned wood, further evidence of the night's destruction. It seemed to grown stronger with each gust.

Then the first bloated, shark-ravaged body washed onto the beach. Hordes of tiny crabs quickly covered the corpse, hungrily finishing the sharks' work. For the crabs, the beach was a feast. For Ichiro it was another reason to be rid of this place.

Ichiro surveyed their situation. He was not pleased, even though they had saved all their weapons, including his armor.

There was food, if each of them were to eat but a single bowl of rice for the three-day journey he expected they would make.

If the journey took longer, they would be too weak to rescue the Emperor. Finding horses clearly was also a necessity.

He went to the boat, kicking aside a few crabs who were groping for tidbits, and grabbed his armor, lance and a single bag of rice. "Get your weapons," he told the others.

"Well, what next?" Shizuka said.

"We go to Kyoto," Ichiro replied.

"And how do we do get there?"

"On foot."

Shizuka spat in disgust. "We'll all have blistered feet by then, *samurai*. Or, worse, we'll be in Taira's hands."

"If we stay here, we can be certain Taira will take us. No doubt he already knows Van der Lieuw's ship is destroyed. His agents are everywhere."

"So, what's your suggestion?"

"We take the first horses we find. Then we ride."

Shizuka shook her head, but finally resigned herself to the situation. "All right. So we walk." She picked up a back and some army. "At least I can get some sightseeing done. They say the scenery around here is beautiful."

———

By midday they reached a farmhouse.

At first Ichiro thought it was abandoned. There were gaping holes in the roof thatching. Thick briars and bushes overgrew the yard.

Great clumps of mugwort covered the walls, almost hiding it from view.

It reminded Ichiro of the childhood home of Prince Genji and of the merchant Katsuhiro's manor left in ruins among the thickets in Lady Murasaki's tragic tale. Was there an aged woman living here, unable to fend for herself, like Genji's grandmother? he wondered. Or had the owner simply abandoned the house, letting it go to ruin because his farm was no longer profitable?

There was no way to know.

"It appears deserted," Shizuka said.

Ichiro was about to agree when he heard a sound just inside the door.

"Someone is in there," Yukio said.

Ichiro raised a finger to lips to silence the monk. "Possibly," he whispered. "But it could easily be the wind blowing dead leaves or an owl in the rafters or a wild pig foraging for food."

"Or a *mononoke*," Shizuka added snidely.

The door of the farmhouse opened. A thin, haggard man walked into the sunlight. He wore a breechclout of faded blue linen and an old flaxen jacket. A pair of leather pails were in his hands.

As he turned he came face-to-face with Ichiro. The pails fell from his grasp and clattered noisily on the dried earth.

"Oh, please, go away!" he cried, his face pale with fright. "Haven't you taken enough? I have so little rice and almost no millet. You've left me nothing. My livestock will starve this winter. Please, go away!"

Sobbing, he fell to his knees.

Ichiro helped the farmer to his feet. "Who do you think we are?" he asked.

"You are not Lord Taira's men?" the man said.

"No," Ichiro said. " I am General Minamoto. I am from the Shogun's army. We go to Kyoto to rescue the Emperor from Lord Taira."

Tears of joy rolled down the farmer's face and he took hold of Ichiro's arm. "Please, please, you must come in and share some tea with me."

He led them to the house and inside. If the outside of the house appeared overgrown and abandoned, the inside was worse. Greasy ash from the cooking fire stuck to the walls like mold. The floor was bare dirt with only a few worn *tatami* for sitting.

"Times have been bad," the farmer said. "I had so little and then the soldiers took even that. Now I have few

pigs, no chicken, just an ox too old to pull a plow and too tough for the stewpot."

He passed out old, chipped earthenware cups all around. "My *sake*, I must confess, is not of the best," he said, drawing a jar from the edge of the fire pit where it was warming. "But I have plenty, and it is all I have left."

The farmer poured out the *sake* into the small earthenware cups.

A woman screamed.

Everyone turned toward the noise, except the farmer. He continued measuring out liquor. "It is my wife," he said. "Since the soldiers came she has been quite mad."

The door to the back room burst open, and a tall, slender woman danced in. She turned twice around the room and then threw her head back and laughed. It was a high-pitched, eerie laugh.

The woman wore a stained kimono. From the look of its cut, it had once been expensive but now was little more than rags. Her hair was disheveled and hung down her back. She wore make-up, but it was poorly applied. Her face was caked with powder, her cheeks heavily rouged. Her eyebrows were a single thick black line across her forehead and her lips were so reddened her mouth resembled a bloody gash.

Ichiro felt a wave of evil, dark and grossly inhuman, flow from her.

She stopped laughing and turned her wide, dark eyes toward her husband. "Husband! You did not tell me we were expecting guests. How thoughtless of you. I could have prepared them a fine feast."

The farmer sipped his *sake*. "Go back to your room. My guests do not wish to see you."

The woman pouted. "How cruel you are to me," she said. Her eyes fell on the young *samurai*. "And jealous. You want me to go to my room, and you deny me any comfort from these pretty boys."

"Go to your room," the farmer said.

She walked over to one soldier, who sat frozen in fear. She slipped a thin white hand into his jacket and caressed his chest. "Such a strong boy, someone one who can satisfy me more than you can, husband. What a weak old man you are."

Her hand slid into the *samurai's* trousers. The man sprang to his feet, stumbling to get away from her. She tilted her head back and unleashed a deep, cruel laugh.

Unable to take any more, the farmer leaped to his feet and struck his wife across the face.

Stunned, she stopped laughing. The woman glared at her husband with malevolence, then her eyes rolled back into her head and she collapsed into his arms.

Ichiro and Shizuka helped the man carry her back into her room. They laid her on a pile of *futon* and Shizuka fetched a cold, wet cloth. The farmer thanked her and placed it across his wife's forehead.

"I am so sorry for my wife's behavior. She is young and we were married only a short time before the soldiers came." He lowered his head to hide his tears.

"They raped her and took her away. She was gone a week before she returned, quite mad. Now all she thinks about is possessing every young man she sees and guarding that old block of wood she found." The farmer gestured toward a misshapen log wrapped in cloth and lying on the floor.

The log had an almost human shape. Ichiro thought he saw it move ever so slightly and felt his heart skip a beat. He glanced at Shizuka.

"Yes," she whispered. "I saw it, too."

"She treats it like her child," the farmer said. "Some nights she cradles it in her arms and will not let it go."

"I see," Ichiro said.

"She will sleep now," the farmer said. "And I will find you food and quarters."

"Thank you, you are most generous." But Ichiro doubted he would sleep much this night.

The six remaining *samurai* slept in the farmer's barn, or what passed for one, while Ichiro and the others slept in the house.

Although Ichiro welcomed the warmth of the fire against the cool night air, he found himself almost wishing he were sleeping in the barn. Something about the farmer's wife bothered him more than he could explain. Perhaps its was not her as such, but the wooden child which bothered him. There was evil there, an evil more intense and malevolent even than that of Taira. Knowing she was but a short distance away did not calm his mind.

In the barn I might be safer, he thought, but exhaustion overcame him and he slept.

The scream woke him about midnight.

Ichiro sat upright.

"Did you hear that?" he said.

Shizuka propped herself up on a elbow. "A scream, from outside."

Ichiro grabbed his sword. "You check the woman's room, I'll check the barn."

Outside the house the air was unusually cool and misty. Dim starlight floated down through the overcast sky, illuminating everything with a bluish-gray light. Ichiro could see nothing moving. Everything was preternaturally silent.

A fox cried nearby. Ichiro looked up and saw it a few feet away. Its eyes had a greenish cast and its lips were moist with blood from a fresh kill. It yipped once, then curled its black lips, exposing sharp white teeth, challenging him.

"Not tonight, little fox. I'll challenge you some other day. Be on your away." He picked up a rock and hurled it at the creature, hitting it just above the shoulder.

The fox cried out with pain, an almost human cry which set a shiver up Ichiro's spine. Then it ran off into the underbrush.

Ichiro heard footsteps behind him. He turned, sword ready and saw Shizuka. "Not your light-footed self, I see," he said.

"The woman is missing."

"The wooden thing?"

"Still there."

"Then she hasn't gone far. Maybe it was her screaming."

"Have you checked the barn?"

"Not yet."

Ichiro reached for the barn door and felt something warm and moist drip onto his hand. Then another drop, dark and thick, struck his fingers. He looked up.

The body of a foot soldier lay broken, like a *bunraku* puppet, across the roof of the barn. The soldier was naked, his throat and belly torn, crimson masses. Blood rolled down one twisted arm to the man's fingers and dripped slowly to the earth.

The inside of the barn was a charnel house. All the remaining *ashigaru* were dead, their throats savaged. Only the man on the roof had fought, and he too had died.

Ichiro tasted bile in his mouth and suppressed the urge to vomit. "The fox," he said.

"What?" Shizuka said, entering the barn.

"I saw a fox. It had blood on its lips. His blood, I think."

"A little fox could not throw a man onto a barn roof."

"Perhaps, but what if the fox is not a fox?"

Shizuka opened her mouth to ask him what he meant, then she comprehended. "Yes, I see," she said finally. "The woman."

A scream issued from the house., then a cry for help, which seemed to have come from the woman's room.

Ichiro, sword ready, ran to the house and kicked open the door.

Tamika and Yukio stood in one corner of the room, holding the farmer's wife at bay with a *naginata*.

The woman stood naked over the dead form of her husband, his throat torn from his body. She looked up at Ichiro with cold green eyes filled with hate. Blood ran from her lips down her neck and between her breasts. Her arms, from elbow to finger were stained crimson.

Ichiro could see the angry red gash where he had hit her with the stone.

The woman shrieked. Before their eyes she turned into a fox and leaped from a window. Ichiro ran to the woman's room.

The wooden child was missing.

"Outside, quick," Ichiro ordered. "We have to kill it before it alerts Taira."

He stepped outside.

The creature leaped from the rooftop, knocking Ichiro down. He rolled with the blow and managed to toss the fox-thing across his shoulder.

Shizuka struck the werefox with the butt of the *naginata*, but the creature sloughed off the injury. It

picked up the *ninja* and threw her across the yard. Shizuka crashed into a stone well and did not grow up.

Ichiro got to his feet and found he had lost Kusinagi. He was now defenseless against the creature.

She was a grotesque thing now, a naked woman's body, but with the head of a fox. Auburn fur ran down her shoulder and along its arms, which ended in fingers tipped with ebony claws that glistened in the moonlight.

"Surrender, *samurai*," the werefox said. Her voice was thick and cruel. Its eyes burned with an unearthly glow. "No mortal man may kill you, I have heard, but I am not a mortal man. You are powerless."

Ichiro knew the fox might be correct. Without his sword he probably was powerless. But he was not yet beaten. He recalled his *kendo* teacher's words. "An angry opponent is a defeated opponent."

"You sound so proud, Madame Fox," he taunted, "but you're just another of Taira's servants, obedient to your master like the good dog you are."

The fox howled in anger. She leaped toward Ichiro, her teeth bared, her claws exposed.

He caught her at the shoulders and fell backwards, his left planted firmed in the creature's belly.

The fox went tumbling over him, crashing into some nearby brambles. But she was quickly on her feet. "Clever man, *samurai*," she hissed, "but I have claws and teeth and you still have only your hands."

She did not attack, but held back, cautiously circling around him. Ichiro watched her eyes glow in the moonlight and realized she was trying to find a spot of darkness from which to strike. He turned with her, pacing her, not giving her any openings.

"Look out!" cried Tamika, who was tending to Shizuka.

Something struck Ichiro from behind, throwing him across the yard and against the barn. For a moment he was dazed, but his eyes cleared enough to see it was the wooden child which had attacked him.

Ichiro did not have time to think before the fox was on him. He saw her as she sprang, and he reacted instinctively. She pinned him against the barn, her cruel yellow teeth trying to tear into his neck. Her breath was foul and putrid, like death itself.

He kept one fist pressed hard against her neck, holding her back, while he battled her claws with his free hand. He gritted his teeth as one claw gouged his already injured right shoulder.

The pain surged through his body, and he felt warm blood trickling down his arm, mixing with the sweat of fear. In desperation he kicked at the creature's hindquarters. His foot found the soft underbelly of the fox and she howled in pain. They wrestled in the dirt and Ichiro grabbed the creature about the waist.

Scrambling to his feet, he picked the fox up and raced headlong toward where he remembered the house to be. The fox howled and clawed at his back, but his mind was too maddened to notice the pain.

Ichiro and the creature crashed into the house, colliding with a large beam. He ran the werefox into the beam again and again until he felt her back break against the stout wooden beam.

The fox shrieked once, then died.

Exhausted, Ichiro dropped the creature. Pain stabbed his leg and something yanked the world from under him.

He tried to get up but felt something tearing at his left leg. It was the wooden child, now growing hideously larger, its sharp fangs buried in his calf.

Ichiro drew back and brought the heel of his right foot against the creature again and again, feeling each blow send a crackling agony through his leg. A third blow dislodged the creature, sending it rolling in the dirt.

He clambered to his feet, hoping to set himself before the creature attacked again. He was breathing heavily, blood and perspiration rolling down his body. In the moonlight he saw the *naginata* near the farm house door.

He grabbed it and turned to face the wooden thing.

It was now taller than he was. It was a hideous parody of a human, with thick limbs and a heavy ox-like body. Two red eyes burned like embers in its distorted head. Its mouth was a row of razor-sharp teeth like a shark's.

Ichiro kept it a distance with the spear. He jabbed its iron-like hide and felt the *naginata's* tip glance off harmlessly.

He circled slowly about the yard, the creature following him step for step, almost parodying a *noh* play. Ichiro kept probing with the spear, hoping to find some crack in the creature's armor, hoping also to find Kusinagi. He knew the sword could defeat the creature, but he did not dare look for it. The creature, too, was probing for an opening.

Something glistened in the moonlight near the well. "Kusinagi!" he said without thinking and took his eyes from the creature for just an instant.

With one heavy hand the thing snapped the shaft of the *naginata* as if it were summer straw. The blade flew off,

harmless, into the underbrush. With the other hand, the being knocked Ichiro to the earth.

But the thing held back. It was toying with him, Ichiro realized, taking pleasure in the prospect of a kill, holding off to savor each moment.

Ichiro realized he stood no chance now. He was too exhausted to rise. Even if he were to rise, the wooden thing was between him and Kusinagi. "Well, you may have won after all, Taira," Ichiro said, knowing the necromancer was not far off.

Ah, samurai, why spoil the suspense? a voice said in his ear. It was Taira's voice. *Don't give up so easily now. Let me enjoy my little drama.*

Suddenly the creature screamed.

"Free! I am free!" someone shouted.

Ichiro looked up. One of the creature's arms was lying on the ground. The thing was trying to fend off Tamika with its other arm as she systematically hacked away at it with a sword.

But it was not just any sword. It was Kusinagi. The sword's *horimono* glowed red as it absorbed the wooden thing's energy. As each blow, splinters jumped into the air.

Ichiro did not understand how Tamika could handle Kusinagi.

Everyone else was either burned or frozen by the sword. Yet she was untouched, and the sword sang for her.

He watched in awe as she brought the sword down on the wooden creature's head. The blade split the being in half, like an ax would split a log. The two halves fell away and something came out of the creature's head.

It was a *mononoke*, an ephemeral thing that was as thin as silk with the moonlight shining through it. It was trying to escape, but could not flee. Kusinagi had hold of it. The demon screamed as the glowing *horimono* pulled at it, sucking it into the sword itself. Then the *mononoke* collapsed like a pilot's parachute with the wind taken from it. It rolled up into a ball and was consumed by the sword.

"Free! I'm free of Taira and his demons! " Tamika cried. She danced about wildly, whirling Kusinagi over her head. The heavens crackled with lightning, as if responding to her triumph.

Ichiro marveled at the spectacle. Then, in his own head, he heard someone laughing with delight. He had no problem recognizing the voice.

It was Hachiman's.

CHAPTER FOURTEEN

I chiro lay back in the large wooden keg the farmer had used for a bath. The warm water eased the aches in his bones, and he breathed a sigh of relief. Although his wounds were small, mostly scratches and a number of bruises, his muscles almost screamed from the beating he had received from the werefox and the wooden thing.

He watched the female *samurai* boiling water for the bath. She tossed a few pieces of the wooden creature on the fire. The bits caught fire quickly and burned with a warm, pleasant flame.

Yukio prepared rice and vegetables from the farmer's remaining stock. He was singing as he worked. Shizuka, on the other hand, sat sullenly against a house timber, a bottle of sake at her feet. A blue-black bruise as large as a chestnut could be seen at her left temple. Every so often she would reach up to touch it, wince, then quickly down another cup of rice wine.

The woman warrior took a pot from the fire and carried it to the bath. She poured the hot liquid in near Ichiro's feet.

"*Arigato*," he said. He gently clasped her wrist before she could move away. "Who are you, and why is it you can handle Kusinagi?" he asked.

She pulled her wrist free and smiled. "When you get out of the bath, Minamoto-no-Ichiro, then I will tell you."

Ichiro eased back into the tub. The woman was serious, he realized. She would not talk now. In that case, he elected to enjoy the bath a little longer.

Ichiro used some old cloth as a towel, drying himself thoroughly. From his few possessions, he managed to find a clean *kimono*. The farmer also had a pair of reed sandals which fit Ichiro's feet reasonably well.

He sat by the fire and accepted a bowl of rice and vegetables from the bubbling iron pot. He would have liked a cup of warm *sake*, but Shizuka seemed reluctant to share hers. *No matter*, he thought.

The food was hot and nourishing. Ichiro, his chopsticks clacking, greedily spooned it into his mouth, letting it warm his insides. The fire crackled noisily as its flames warmed the rest of him.

"Now, general, we can talk," the woman warrior said. She sat beside him with her own bowl of steaming food. "Rice wine would be nice, too," she said to Shizuka.

The *ninja* looked up at her, grunted once, then poured another bowl for herself. But after a moment's hesitation, Shizuka got up and reached into the ashes, pulling out a fresh jar of sake. She poured the liquor into two cups and handed them to Ichiro and the woman. Then she returned to the house timber and sulked.

Ichiro picked up the bowl and sipped. The *sake* was warmed perfectly. "Who are you?" he asked the woman.

"My name is Tamika," the woman said, beginning her tale. "My father was a *kendo* master from Nara. He had three daughters, but no sons, so he taught us how to be warriors. A woman must protect herself in terrible times, he told me.

"When we were old enough, he sent us to masters to learn many arts. I was apprenticed as a *geisha* in Edo, but received training in the martial arts. It was there I met Lord Hishikawa, an old *daimyo* with a fondness for young women. He took me back to his home province where I became his mistress and taught other women warriors. I am afraid you killed two of my best pupils at Jimmukei monastery."

"So how did you become involved with Taira?" Ichiro asked.

"Lord Hishikawa died without heirs, so we thought. Then Lord Taira appeared some years ago. He claimed he was the noble's nephew and claimed all rights to the land. Taira had a will he said was in my lord's hand. Lord Hishikawa's head retainer questioned the will and called in two scholars to judge the will. One said it was a forgery, that he knew our lord had no heirs or siblings. But the other swore the document was authentic.

"With two opinions, the retainer asked a visiting noble from Kyoto to act as judge. The noble examined the will and proclaimed it authentic."

Ichiro had an uncomfortable thought. "Who was this Kyoto noble?" he asked.

"His name was Akiyama, and he had a terrible skin disease."

Ichiro slammed his fist into the ground. So that was how Akiyama had allied himself with Taira. The old noble had seen what a powerful man Taira was and contrasted him with the Emperor, who seemed weak and effeminate. "Damn him and his treachery!"

"You know him?" the woman asked.

"Too well. He is the one who betrayed the Emperor to Taira."

"Yes, that would seem like something he would do," she said with a nod. "After he had established himself as *daimyo*, Taira placed his iron fist on things. He forced the head retainer to commit *seppuku* and had the dissenting scholar beheaded.

"He replaced most of Lord Hishikawa's best *samurai* with his own men, thugs and criminals, and he forced the wealthy landowners to wed their oldest daughters to him. When they saw who was to lead them, many of my lord's other men simply left. A few were found outside the castle gate, disemboweled by some creature. That discouraged the others who wanted to leave.

"I tried to resist, to convince others to revolt, but my plans were found out. Taira had me brought before him stripped naked and bound and gagged. While his men watched, he raped me. 'She is strong and independent now, but she will soon obey me willingly,' he said. Then he had me beaten and thrown into a deep pit near the main house.

"I lay in the pit, knee-deep in water, for three days. I became ill and then my belly began to swell. Taira had impregnated me.

"For six months I carried Taira's child. I was in delirium and fever, dreaming horrible things, feeling the child moving in my womb. I knew it was not a natural child, that it was a *mononoke*. But I could do nothing to stop it.

"Finally, I went into labor. Taira's wives held me down as I screamed and pushed. The pain was so horrible I wanted to die. But then I felt it slid from between my legs. One of the wives screamed as she saw it. Another picked it up and held it. I saw it was a creature made of wood with horrible little eyes and sharp teeth. It looked at me and smiled. I tried to scream but I lost consciousness.

"When I recovered, the baby was gone. When I asked one of Taira's wives, she said the *daimyo* had taken the child away and given it to a strange woman.

"The fox woman," Ichiro said.

"Perhaps. I am not sure," Tamika said. She sipped her *sake*. "But this I do know. The child held my soul in its power. As long as it lived, I was under Taira's control.

"Taira also knew that if I found it, I would kill it and free myself. So he sent it away, under the protection of one of his minions, to be sure nothing could harm it. From then on, I was his obedient slave. I killed for him, I tortured and robbed for him, and I shared his bed when he desired me. I was unable resist him. Or perhaps I had forgotten how. And worse, I came to enjoy it, to be pleased when a farmer begged for his life before I beheaded him, or when a monk screamed under my tortures, to relish feeling my lord within me. Then you appeared, and everything changed."

Tamika's voice trailed off for a moment, and she stared into the fire. She tossed a piece of wood cut from the creature, from her demon child, on the coals. It sizzled and burst into flame.

"How did it change?" Ichiro asked.

"He sent me to kill you, as you know. I came with my two best students, whom I had loved more passionately than anyone. They obeyed him because they also were possessed by Taira's power. To assure our loyalty, even our horses were under the control of *mononoke*. We should not have failed, but we met an old Buddhist monk along the road. He said 'I know you, Tamika the swordswoman.

Once you were wise, but now you bring bad karma to yourself and this land. So I tell you now. Your mission will end in failure, with your compatriots dead and you in the hands of those you seek to kill. It is then that you will see who is your true enemy.

"I drew my sword to kill him, but my blade met only empty air. He had vanished, but I heard his laughter pounding in my ears."

"Hachiman," Ichiro whispered.

Tamika looked up at him for a moment, then she nodded. "No doubt, *samurai*, for I heard his laughter again last night. Your *kami* protects you well.

"Not so well as to keep us from the fox woman and your child. Did Taira use you to bring us here?"

She shook her head. "No, Ichiro, it was by accident. Taira never wanted me to find my child. He knew I would destroy it. But no doubt he saw the opportunity to destroy you first."

"He failed."

Tamika smiled. "And I succeeded."

Ichiro frowned. "But that does not explain how you can handle Kusinagi. Only I am supposed to be able to touch the sword without harm."

"You handle it because you are a Minamoto," she said. "But I share that with you."

He stared at her in disbelief. "What do you mean?"

"I am descended from Kusonoki Masashige, who died for his emperor and whose castle you seek. Masashige, too, was descended from Yoshitsune and the Minamoto. Hachiman is my *kami* as well. I am your cousin, Minamoto-no-Ichiro" Tamika smiled. "You understand, now, don't you."

Ichiro nodded and smiled. "Welcome, cousin," he said, and took her into his arms.

CHAPTER FIFTEEN

"So we are back to four," Shizuka said.

"That is more than enough," Ichiro lied. To tell the truth, he now feared more than ever that he would not succeed. But he had to go forward.

He placed a torch to the old barn. The thatching caught easily and flared up.

It was not a proper funeral pyre for his men and the old farmer, but it would have to do. He regretted taking money and weapons from the dead men, but those items could no longer serve them in this life, and he would need funds in Kyoto. He also recovered the remaining medallions from the men.

And once more Yukio chanted the prayers for the dead. Ichiro knew it would not be the last time.

"So?" Shizuka asked.

"So we walk to Kyoto, if we have to."

By the third day, the weather had grown chill and gray. As Ichiro and the others neared Kyoto, they saw lines of weary and dazed refugees trudged down the narrow roads leading to Osaka or Edo. Half-naked men, filthy and with torn breechclouts about their loins, dragged crude carts down the dry and dusty paths. The carts contained all their earthly goods. Behind them walked their wives and children, pale and malnourished. Thieves were everywhere, preying on this misery like the vultures they were.

But Ichiro was not prepared for the sight that came into view beyond the dark and foreboding pine forests that surrounded the capital. Virtually all that remained of the beautiful city was the Emperor's palace. Temples and shrines in the mountains were reduced to charred ruins still smoldering even in the heavy rain, which began to pelt everything. Other buildings were patched with boards and strips of bark in a futile effort to keep out the cold winds and driving rain.

The odors of burning buildings and unburied bodies drew only the notice of carrion crows and hungry dogs. Reveling in their debauchery, Taira's soldiers were too busy to notice. They were more concerned with looting what they could and in quenching their lust. The whore-houses and *sake* shops were spared destruction. They had uses for the warriors' hungers. Soldiers openly copulated with young girls in alley-ways. Even gapped-toothed and palsied old prostitutes were much in demand by the soldiers of Taira's army.

Drunken soldiers brawled in the streets, arguing over trivialities. Some lay in the streets, never to rise again, dead from drink or from the hands of fellow soldiers they had thought were friends. But dead or alive, they did not notice three warriors and a monk walk by. Nor did they notice that the leader had a clubfoot or that tears rolled down his cheeks. Ichiro wept and vowed to Hachiman that he would not fail.

They made camp in an abandoned building, taking shelter behind its cracked clay walls and gray slate roof. The building lay across the river from the Imperial palace.

"What do we do now?" Shizuka asked.

"Tamika and Yukio will look for horses and some food," Ichiro said. He took out his purse and weighed it in his hand before handing it to the female *samurai*. "They should be enough there. If not, steal what you can."

"And if someone tries to stop us?" Tamika asked.

"You have a sword. Use it," Ichiro said. He handed a *tanto* to Yukio.

The monk, who wore a red quilted jacket over his robes to keep warm, sat shivering next to the fire. He did not take the weapon.

"You may need this," Ichiro said, pressing the weapon into Yukio's hands.

"I have taken a vow of non-violence," Yukio said. "I cannot kill."

Ichiro smiled sadly and nodded. "If Hachiman protects us, you will not need to kill. But take the sword, for my sake."

Yukio looked up at Ichiro. The monk was silent for a moment, then took the weapon and tucked it into the folds of his jacket.

"Be back here before sunset, and we will see what we need to do then."

After Tamika and Yukio left, Shizuka turned to Ichiro. "So what do we do then?"

"We try to find a way across the river to rescue the emperor."

———

Ichiro walked along the banks of river, carefully surveying each inch. The only way across the river were two bridges, and both were heavily guarded. The guards seemed more disciplined that most of Taira's men. In fact, their behavior seemed highly deliberate, almost mechanical. Their weapons, both sword and *naginata*, were nothing to trifle with, either.

Ruling out the bridges as a way to cross, Ichiro looked for boats along the riverbanks, but there, too, he was discouraged. The small boats that had plied the river in gentler days were gone. All that remained were the charred remains of one or two turned upside down on the riverbank.

The sight did not encourage him.

"The bridges are all either burned or heavily guarded. There appears to be no way across," Ichiro said when they all returned.

"So do we go back to Edo?" Tamika asked.

"Bridges and guards are trifling matters," Shizuka said. She cut off a piece of pickled daikon and popped the radish into her mouth.

"You have a way across?" Ichiro said.

"We *ninja* always have a way," she said. "But first I will need some empty sake barrels."

"Considering the amount of drinking hereabouts, those should not be too difficult to find," Ichiro said.

———

The river glistened blackly in the moonlight. Occasionally light from the fires, which still raged along the river, flickered like luminous insects in the water. The only other light came from torches along the bridges.

Shizuka and Ichiro slipped along the riverbank, fearful of meeting other human beings. But they only encountered three prostitutes and their customers, all too drunk on *sake* to notice a pair of black ghosts. They froze when one of the customers stumbled toward them. But he went past them and proceeded to vomit noisily in the thick grass nearby.

When they were across from the palace, they halted, hiding in the thick rushes at the river's edge. Everything seemed quiet.

A single guard walked across a bridge some distance downstream. He seemed less disciplined than the men who had guarded the bridge during the day. In an off-key voice he sang a popular ditty extolling the virtue of Osaka women in the kitchen and of Kyoto women in bed. No doubt he had sampled the latter in the orgy of destruction his compatriots had unleashed.

Shizuka passed Ichiro a pair of *ukidaru* made out of *sake* barrels she had procured from a *geisha* house. Each barrel had been cut in half, and fitted with leather thongs. She began tying the barrels to her feet and legs. "Quickly, we haven't time to lose," she said, handing him a long bamboo staff.

Ichiro followed her lead, making sure the thongs were especially tight about his twisted foot.

"Now we just go for a stroll," Shizuka said. She stepped out onto the river, using her staff to steady herself and to pole her way across the water.

He followed, although he could not move nearly as fast as she. She was nearly completely across before he had even reached halfway. Ichiro steadied himself at each step. It was an unnatural feeling, to say the least, rather like ice-skating on melting ice. One barrel insisted on wandering to one side. He judiciously guided back it back into line, whereupon its compatriot decided to seek its own destination.

Ichiro quickly found a rhythm which gave him some control. Then he discovered there were obstacles in the river. The trip became a journey of fits and starts to avoid the obstructions. A dead ox, its belly bloated with the gases of decomposition, slowly floated past until a jagged branch sticking from the riverbed impaled it. Ichiro gingerly eased himself around the obstruction.

Then he saw something move across the water and he froze. The snake was less than a meter in front of him, its body swimming in a graceful sinuous motion.

Ichiro felt his mouth go dry. His heart raced. Cold sweat broke out on his forehead and upper lip. It was an irrational fear, he knew, but his rational mind could not penetrate to the depths where that fear dwelt to eradicate it.

"Hurry up," Shizuka hissed. "This is no leisurely excursion to view cherry blossoms!"

"Coming," Ichiro said. He watched the snake continue on down the river and breathed a sigh of relief when it vanished. He resumed poling across the dark waters.

Ichiro was almost to the riverbank when he heard loud splashing and cries for help from the other bank.

"What's happening?" he whispered.

"One of those drunken louts has fallen in. The guards will be here soon. If we're lucky, saving that fool from drowning should keep them occupied," she said.

Ichiro hurried his step. The barrels found purchase on sandy ground and he walked clumsily onto the riverbank. He steadied himself, and then removed the barrels from his feet.

The path to the castle was clear, but they made their way carefully. Cloaked in black, they pressed themselves against the wall, hiding like specters in the ghostly darkness.

Guards came toward them. They chattered noisily, the rattling of their lamps and *naginata* keeping time to each step they took. An officer barked orders.

No doubt they'll be angry when they find they've given up their beds for a drunken comrade, Ichiro thought. *And doubtless the drunk would be spared, only to be executed later for his behavior.*

A trailing guard tripped. His lantern skittered across the ground. It came to a halt at Ichiro's feet, its dull yellow glow outlining him against the wall.

The guard clambered to his feet. The others were already well ahead of him. Cursing, the man grabbed his lantern. He stopped when he saw feet before him. He raised the lantern and saw its light reflected in Ichiro's eyes.

The alarm cry rose to the guard's lips but did not emerge. The only sound he made was a loud gurgle as a bubble of blood came to his mouth and he collapsed.

Shizuka wiped her dagger on her sleeve.

"We'll have to hide his body before the others come back," she said.

"Over the wall," Ichiro said.

"He's too heavy!" she protested.

"There's no alternative. Someone will find him if we leave him here. Putting him over the wall will buy us some time."

Shizuka did not argue further. "All right," she conceded.

They hoisted the man to the top of the wall and pushed him over. The body hit the ground on the other side with a sound like a sack of rice.

"Now," Ichiro said, "let us hope there are no more delays."

The path to the Imperial palace was now clear, except for one guard. Bored, he leaned forward, supporting himself on his naginata.

Shizuka slid toward the guard. He stifled a yawn. When the yawn was half completed Shizuka struck.

She kicked the *naginata* aside. Startled, the guard tumbled forward unable to control his fall. Halfway down his jaw collided with Shizuka's knee as it came up to meet him. He collapsed like a wet rag.

Shizuka dragged the man to one side. "See if there is a *sake* jar in the guard-hut," she said to Ichiro.

Ichiro reached into the hut. The jar was just inside the doorway. "This is no time for a drink," he said.

"It's not for me, it's for our friend here," she said. Shizuka propped the guard up, his back resting against the guard-hut wall. She carefully placed the lance next to him. Taking the sake jar, she poured its contents over his clothes and into the guard's mouth, letting it dribble down his chin. Then she placed the jar in his lap, covering it with his hairy, calloused hand.

Ichiro noted the alcohol did a lot to reduce the man's unpleasant natural odors, which were a fair stench of perspiration, dirt and oily, spicy food.

"That should hold him. Now, shall we go?" she asked.

"By all means," Ichiro replied.

———

The palace corridors were unlighted. A sharp, almost unnatural chill coursed down them. The only warmth came from lanterns and braziers in rooms hidden by paper walls and sliding screens.

"I'll search the east wing. You search the west," Ichiro said.

"Agreed," Shizuka said, sliding noiselessly past him and disappearing into the darkness.

Ichiro edged slowly along the corridor. His eyes scanned every crack and crevice before him; his ears were alert for any noise. He had not gone far when he heard familiar voices coming from behind one paper wall. He crouched down low to listen and to avoid being seen.

"The Dutchman failed you. So did the fox woman," Lord Akiyama said.

"No matter," Taira replied. "Minamoto and I will meet again. But the emperor is still in my control and even Minamoto cannot stop me."

"I have word he has a large army coming from Edo led by young Date. Can you stop that?" Akiyama said.

"The army is nothing. I will crush them like a moth," Taira said.

"We shall see." Akiyama said. "You are certain there is no chance for Emperor Saigo's rescue?"

"None whatsoever."

"Let us hope so, for both our sakes," Akiyama said. The nobleman did not sound assured by Taira's promises.

Ichiro felt a tug at his sleeve. He looked up and saw Shizuka mouthing words. "I think I have found the emperor," she said silently. She gestured with her head toward one corridor.

He followed down the corridor toward a ghostly red glow, a glow that seemed to pulse and throb like a heart beat. Shizuka pushed open the sliding panel, exposing the light source and the emperor.

"May the Buddha protect us," she whispered as she saw what lay before them.

"I'm not sure anything can protect us or the emperor," Ichiro said.

The room was large and spacious. In the middle was Emperor Saigo. He was encased in a large reddish crystal. The crystal pulsed, occasionally growing brighter. When he saw Ichiro and Shizuka, Saigo tried to cry out to them, but there was only silence. In frustration he beat against the crystal's walls, but it seemed to grow a more brilliant color and pulsed more rapidly. Finally he weakened and the crystal paled.

Ichiro realized the crystal pulsed with the Emperor's heartbeat. Somehow Saigo's own body powered his prison. The more he resisted, the stronger it became.

But escape from the crystal was a minor problem, Ichiro realized, compared to just reaching the Emperor. For guarding Saigo were four huge *oni*, giant horned demons with pig-like snouts and skin the color and consistency of raw fish.

The *oni* sat on their haunches in a circle around the crystal. Two picked parasites from their hairy chests and crunched the lice between huge jaws. The other pair sharpened their wicked-looking axes with whetstones.

"Now what do we do?" Shizuka whispered.

Ichiro reached into his jacket and withdraw a small oilcloth. "Here are four of the talismans we have left." He handed them to Shizuka. "I will draw their attention, and then you can make use of them."

"You must be joking. Bits of metal against these brutes?" Shizuka said.

"It's the only choice we have," he said.

Ichiro stepped into the hall and unsheathed Kusinagi.

"Behold, I am Minamoto-no-Ichiro! No living man may defeat me, for I possess Kusinagi, the Grass-mower. Its blade shall uproot you from life like the weeds you are."

The demons stopped their activity and looked up.

"Go away, little general, or we shall make mincemeat of you," one *oni* said nonchalantly.

The demon resumed picking lice and ticks from its belly. But this time it crushed them between its horny fingers before tossing them down its throat.

"Perhaps you did not hear me the first time," Ichiro said. "If so, I shall repeat it for your convenience."

The *oni* looked up, then turned to the demon beside it that was slicing a hair along the length of its axe blade. "Brother," the first demon said, " take care of this prattling little man. My own axe is not yet sharp enough."

"Indeed, it shall be my pleasure," the second *oni* said. It ran a claw over its axe blade. "But I do hate to dirty my axe on such thin bone and gristle."

The demon rose from its haunches.

Ichiro swallowed hard. He had not expected the thing to be so big. Fully erect, it was almost twice Ichiro's height. *Well,* Ichiro thought, *I have no choice now but to fight the damn thing.*

The *oni* started toward Ichiro, moving with a slow, ambling gait, its body hunched forward like someone suffering with back pain.

"Be gone, little man," the demon said. Its voice was rough and raspy. "Or I shall have your meat for my *sushi* mixed with cold rice!" It raised its axe to strike but Ichiro struck first. Kusinagi sliced through the demon's axe handle as if it were young bamboo. The axe head flew across the hall and imbedded itself in a roof timber.

"Brother, give me your axe," the *oni* cried. "The little man has destroyed mine."

"If I give you my axe I will be defenseless," the other demon replied.

"Very well, then I will just tear him apart with my bare hands," the *oni* said.

The *oni* swung its talons hard toward the *samurai*, but Ichiro ducked under the blow and slashed toward the demon's now exposed legs. Kusinagi found purchase under the creature's scaly hide. The sword bit into muscle and tendon.

The demon, hamstrung, tried to turn but crashed face-first to the floor. Its fall raised a cascade of dust and dried bird droppings. "Brothers, help me!" it screamed.

Surprised at how easily Ichiro had defeated their comrade, the other *oni* rose to aid their injured brother.

"Now!" Ichiro shouted.

Shizuka burst from her hiding place and leaped onto the wounded demon's back. She whipped the talisman over the creature's horned head and around its thick neck.

The talisman glowed. The *oni* shrieked once and vanished. The medallion clattered to the floor. A wall of air rushed in to fill the vacuum created when the demon blinked out of existence.

Ichiro was knocked to the floor. He felt himself being sucked toward the vortex of air. Paper screens and lacquered tables tumbled past him, smashing themselves to kindling.

The demons, ungainly and unbalanced, lost their footing. They careened across the floor, crashing into each other. One demon smashed his axe into the floor to halt himself.

Ichiro slid against a collapsed roof beam. He steadied himself, then saw the talisman tumbling toward him. He grabbed it. "The talismans! Get them around the demons' necks," he shouted.

"But the wind!" Shizuka protested.

"Damn the wind!" Ichiro said.

Almost as he spoke, the wind spent itself. But the palace still shook from its force.

The demon nearest Ichiro rose unsteadily and tried to pull its axe from the floor.

Ichiro quickly tossed the talisman over the *oni's* head. It grabbed the medallion and screamed, but only for a moment. The demon's body turned to stone, the talisman it had tried to pull from its throat still wrapped in its long bony fingers.

Then Shizuka screamed.

Ichiro turned to toward her. The *oni* she had attacked had turned to ice, but she had not been quick enough to escape. Her foot was trapped in its frozen hand.

Ichiro moved to free her, but the last demon stepped between them.

"You have killed my brothers, little man," it said angrily. "For that I must kill you."

Its long axe raced toward Ichiro's head. He ducked and rolled away as the blade struck the stone demon. A shower of sparks filled the air.

"Stand still, so I may kill you and avenge my brothers," the *oni* yelled, saliva flying from its thin black lips.

The axe split the air and buried its head in the floor. The demon cursed and tried in vain to free the weapon.

Seeing his chance, Ichiro raced past the *oni* to free Shizuka. He had little time, he knew. By now the palace was in turmoil, and soon the demon would have human reinforcements.

"Stand back," he told the ninja.

Shizuka pushed herself aside as Ichiro hacked at the frozen demon's wrist. Ice shards skittered across the floor.

"Look out!" Shizuka shouted.

From the corner of his eye Ichiro saw the glint of steel. He dropped to the floor and rolled away just before the axe smashed into the frozen *oni*, decapitating it.

The momentum of the attack left the demon off-balance and gave Ichiro an opening. He sprang toward the *oni* and slashed its exposed side. A great spout of steam burst from the wound. The demon howled in pain. "Damn you, little man," it said.

Steam now filled the hall. It extinguished all the torches, leaving only the crimson glow of dying coals and the pulsing redness of the Emperor's crystal prison.

Ichiro strained to see the demon. A huge shape loomed before him in the mist. He stepped back just as the axe crashed into the floor in front of him.

"Don't move, *samurai*," the *oni* said, " or you will make it more difficult for me to find you."

Ichiro needed to trap the demon, to force it into a mistake. *But how?* he wondered.

Then he remembered.

"A talisman! Give one to me!" he shouted to Shizuka.

She fumbled inside her jacket and tossed one of the remaining medallions toward him. It came to rest against his feet.

"What about me?" she asked.

"If I succeed, I'll free you. If I fail, it won't matter," he replied. He clasped the talisman firmly in his right hand and he ducked behind the frozen demon. The crystal's red glow silhouetted the last *oni*. It was searching for him, but it could not see him.

So it's not only stupid, it has poor eyesight, Ichiro thought.

It turned away from him, slicing the air with its axe. He slipped behind it and slashed its buttocks. The demon howled in pain and grabbed its wounded behind.

"Dirty little trickster," it shouted. " I'll get you for that!" It swung the axe wildly, the blade glancing dangerously off the crystal.

Saigo screamed in silent terror.

Ichiro ran toward the stone demon for protection, but in the foggy air he did not see the half-melted bits of ice from the frozen *oni*, which were strewn across the floor. His feet tangled together and he landed heavily. The fall tore Kusinagi from his grasp.

"Ah-ha!" the demon cried in triumph. It tested the sharpness of its blade. "Now you'll pay. I'll cut you in two."

Ichiro, knocked breathless, felt something cold against his hand. His fingers closed around it.

The *oni* stood over him, cackling with laughter. "Here is your end, *samurai*."

As it raised the axe to strike, Ichiro rifled the sharp piece of ice toward the demon's face.

The ice struck the *oni* in the right eye. Startled, the demon dropped the axe and staggered backwards before collapsing in agony to its knees. Its taloned hands covered the injured eye. Bright yellow liquid oozed between its fingers.

Ichiro struggled to his feet. His cold fingers clutched the warm talisman. He limped forward, looped the medallion over the creature's neck, and flung himself aside.

For a moment the demon froze. Then it glowed like a torch and exploded in a fountain of flame that rolled across the floor and consumed everything in its path. In les than a moment the walls and roof timbers were aflame.

By the fire's light Ichiro saw Kusinagi propped against the stone demon. He grabbed the sword and went to free Shizuka. Ichiro would not have long to act, because already he could hear guards calling out alarms and other voices shouting in panic.

"No, save the Emperor first," she said.

"He is safe enough for the moment," Ichiro replied, raising the sword over his head. Kusinagi whispered and shattered the frozen demon's hand. "Can you walk?" Ichiro asked.

"I can manage," she said. She rubbed the numbed flesh. "Now free the Emperor."

Ichiro ran to the crystal. It looked formidable, he had to admit, but he hoped Kusinagi's magic was stronger than Taira's. Ichiro swung the sword with both hands and felt it crash into the crystal. A throbbing, electrical pain climbed up his arm and shook him, but he did not release Kusinagi.

The sword tasted the crystal's energy and found it pleasing. The prison seemed to weaken. A crack formed in the crystal, then it split in two and each half shattered.

Saigo tumbled out, collapsing into Ichiro's arms. "Ichiro! I knew you would rescue me," he said, managing a feeble smile.

"Quiet, my lord, you are weak, conserve your strength." Ichiro picked Saigo up and flung the young emperor across his left shoulder.

"Surely that's not the proper way to carry the divine god on earth," Shizuka said, hobbling to Ichiro's side.

"One does what one can," Ichiro replied. "Now, which way is the exit?"

"This one. It's the only corridor not on fire," she said.

Before they could move one step, a phalanx of guards armed with lances confronted them, and Taira was with them.

"So, Minamoto, you managed to destroy the emperor's jailers," Taira said. "Impressive, though admittedly, they were inferior demons. Nonetheless, you will not escape with Saigo."

"You are still mortal, Taira. And the spell Hachiman placed on me is still effective."

"True, but spells may be broken, even those of a *kami*. I will find a way to kill you, once you are my prisoner," Taira said.

Ichiro whispered to Shizuka. "The last talisman. Throw it."

She reached into her jacket.

Taira saw the movement. "The woman, stop her!" he shouted.

Shizuka flung the talisman like a *shuriken*. It lodged itself into the floor at Taira's feet. There was a blinding flash, and Time stood still.

CHAPTER SIXTEEN

"What happened?" Shizuka asked. "Are they dead?"

"No, I do not think so," Ichiro replied.

Taira and his guards stood motionless, as rigid as statues. Even the flames from the torches seemed motionless, barely flickering, at as Ichiro watched, he could see slow, subtle movements in both the men and the fires. Somehow the talisman had slowed the passage of Time for everything and everyone but Ichiro, Shizuka and the emperor.

"Are we dead, then?" Shizuka asked.

"No, I doubt that," Ichiro replied. "I do not know what happened, but I do know we must hurry. If it is a spell, it will not last long, I'm sure."

The trio ran past the guards and into the corridor. The corridor led to a courtyard just off the palace.

Guards, frozen in motion, covered the grounds. Most were occupied in fighting the blaze consuming the palace. Their movements were eerily, painfully slow.

As he watched, Ichiro thought the flames seemed to flicker more rapidly. Then he saw a guard wrap his fingers about a leather fire bucket.

"The spell is wearing off," Ichiro said. "We'll have to hide."

"Where, then?" Shizuka asked.

Ichiro had no quick answer for that. His eyes scanned the court-yard. The guards seemed to be moving faster now.

A strong odor greeted his nostrils. *Of course!* he thought, *the honey-pots the gardeners used to collect fertilizer for the imperial gardens.*

"Over there. We can hide in those," he said, pointing to the vats.

"Good idea," Shizuka said.

But Saigo protested. "You must be mad, Ichiro, if you expect me to go into that!"

"My lord, you've just escaped imprisonment and likely death at Taira's hands, and you find hiding in a honey pot objectionable?" Ichiro said.

The emperor dropped his gaze, chastened. "I'm sorry," he whispered.

"Do you want to talk, or do you want to live?" Shizuka said, racing toward the honey pots.

Ichiro and the emperor followed.

"Hurry, we have little time," Shizuka said as she climbed into the vat. She pulled three opium pipes from her waistband and handed one each to Ichiro and Saigo.

"Breathe through these and just keep your eyes above the surface," she said.

The pot's contents-- thick, golden and unpleasant-- exuded a rich and overpowering odor. But Ichiro noticed how quickly the smell vanished when one's mind was preoccupied with avoiding death.

Shizuka covered their heads with dried grass and leaves. "Don't move. I will tell you when to leave," she said.

Ichiro suddenly realized how quiet it was. Noise, like everything else, stood still. In the silence he heard his heart pounding in his chest and the blood pulsing in his eardrums.

Slowly the sounds of the world returned. The fire grew from a dull rumble to an intense roar. The wind whipped past overhead, feeding the inferno. Men's voice barked above the dim.

"Water! Get water and axes!" they shouted.

Ichiro looked over the honey pot's lip. Black shadows frantically danced against the backdrop of fire and night. Everything was chaos, panic and disorder

But buried to his neck in human waste, Ichiro felt an understanding of the universe. He began to comprehend what the Buddhists meant about the essential suffering of the universe. Certainly it was absurd and pointless, but only to those stumbling about in the darkness of mental night. The awareness of this absurdity could lead to enlightenment. *So here is how the hubless wheel may turn*, he thought.

A curious calm came over him, like nothing he had ever before experienced. He felt--changed.

But his glimpse of *satori* was rudely shattered.

"The shit vats! They'll burn if we don't drain them!" one soldier cried.

"Just what we need, burning shit!" another voice said. The voice came from nearby. Footsteps drummed along the wooden stairs. A shape raced past Ichiro. His hand tensed on his short sword. No need to use Kusinagi, especially when in this confined space.

A noise to his left caught his attention. A sluice gate lifted. The honey pot's contents began draining. There was no choice now. He grabbed the rim of the vat and lifted himself out.

Ichiro clutched his short sword as he crept toward the guard, but before he could draw the weapon, the man turned around and faced him.

What the guard saw was a dark shape dripping with fetid water and covered in feces. Blood drained from the man's face. His mouth opened wide, as if to cry out, then he fainted dead away.

That was easy enough, Ichiro thought.

"What a sight you are!" Shizuka whispered.

"Well, we can't stay now. Someone will miss this idiot before long," he said.

"To the river, then?"

"Do we have a choice?"

———

The fire's rapid spread added to the confusion in the palace. That enabled them to reach the river unnoticed. At the river's edge they quickly strapped the *ukidaru* to their feet.

"My lord," Ichiro said to Saigo. "I am afraid you will have to ride. Which do you prefer: a small, but strong mare or a crippled stallion?"

"A crippled stallion is fine," the emperor said eagerly.

"Very well, my lord, but I warn you, it will be slow," Ichiro said.

Steadying himself with the bamboo pole, Ichiro stepped out onto the water. Saigo clambered onto Ichiro's back. The ukidaru briefly dipped below the surface, and touched bottom. Ichiro nearly lost his balance as the barrels bobbed back to the top.

"Can you manage?" Shizuka asked.

"We shall see," Ichiro replied. He took his first step.

If the first journey was awkward, Ichiro thought, *then this is nearly impossible.* He now had to compensate for Saigo's weight as well as his own, as well as for the higher center of gravity they also possessed.

The *ukidaru* seemed to sink deeper at each step. The cold, numbing waters in the bottom of the barrels soaked his feet and ankles. Ichiro could not feel his toes. All he sensed was the continual dip and rise. His legs ached.

His hands slipped on the bamboo pole and he felt himself falling. Water poured over the lip of one ukidaru. Saigo gasped with fear. Ichiro braced himself for the shocking drenching, but Shizuka's strong hands caught them and steadied them. Ichiro regained his grip on the bamboo pole.

"I think it takes both a stallion and a mare to get this rider safe ashore," Shizuka said.

Ichiro was about to thank her when something whistled loudly overhead.

Ichiro knew immediately it was a warning arrow. They had been spotted.

"On the river!" a guard cried from the bridge.

"They're walking on water! How can they do that?" another cried.

Ichiro heard a dull thud and felt the *ukidaru* on his left foot shift slightly. He looked down and in the moonlight saw an arrow embedded in the barrel. Its shaft rested gently against his foot. The arrowhead had also sliced the leather thong holding the *ukidaru* to his foot.

The barrel shifted slightly. Ichiro steadied himself with the pole, but now he found each step was increasingly steady. He also knew that the thong would eventually tear loose and he would be dumped into the river.

More arrows whistled through the air. While some crashed harmlessly into the water, some came dangerously close. One or two screamed overhead.

"Boats! Find some boats!" a guard shouted.

"What boats, you fool? We burned them all!" another replied angrily.

"Not much further," Shizuka said reassuringly.

The pain in Ichiro's legs grew at each step, even as his feet became more and more numb. Each movement was torture. Saigo seemed as heavy as lead. Ichiro was uncertain he could go further.

An arrow whisked past his right shoulder. He saw it just ahead in the moonlight. It had buried itself half in and half out of the water.

They were near shore.

"Hurry!" Shizuka called.

He felt the *ukidaru* touch bottom. Shizuka eased the emperor from Ichiro's back.

"Here, over here," Yukio called from a short distance away. He was waiting with five saddled horses. At the monk's side, Tamika launched burning arrows at some guards who were rowing across in a small boat they had somehow located.

One arrow lodged in the side of the overloaded boat. Two guards fought to remove the arrow. Their struggles only caused the boat to capsize, sending the men tumbling into the river.

Ichiro cut the thongs with his *tanto* and staggered onto the beach. His legs hurt and his lungs fairly screamed with pain.

Shizuka brought a horse to Ichiro and helped him mount.

"Time to go," Ichiro said as he took hold of the reins. Now it was Taira's turn to mount the offensive. Ichiro hoped he was prepared to stand the assault.

"Where do we go?" Shizuka asked.

"To Mount Kongo," he replied.

CHAPTER SEVENTEEN

The five rode in silence until just before dawn. They did not stop to sleep or eat, but it was not until mid-morning that anyone spoke.

"That was too easy," Shizuka said. "It was as if Taira wanted us to escape."

"I don't know," Ichiro replied. "If Taira wanted us to escape, I don't think he would have set up such an elaborate trap. Then again, he may have known we would escape."

"Do you think he knows where we are?" she asked.

"Perhaps," he said. "We should not underestimate Taira. I think he knows where we are heading. But something tells me that since the fox-woman and the creature died, Taira's spies are more in the dark than before."

"He's weakening, then?"

"That I didn't say."

Tamika rode up alongside of Shizuka and Ichiro. "We need to stop and rest. The emperor and Yukio are almost falling out of their saddles."

Ichiro gritted his teeth to suppress a yawn. He knew they were all tired, but delays could prove fatal. "We rest at Mount Kongo, and not before," Ichiro said.

The others did not protest.

They reached the plains of the Ishikawa River just before evening. The road to Mount Kongo had been clear both of refugees and of soldiers.

Ichiro knew that few refugees would flee in the direction of Taira's native fiefdom. That would have been foolish.

But he also knew that if his forces stood between Taira and his lands, then the *daimyo* would be forced into what amounted to a retreat to counter the threat to his rear. That would delay Taira long enough for the Shogun's forces in Edo to build up even further. The Shogun's men would then await Ichiro's word to sail for the north

Joy and relief filled Ichiro's heart when he at last saw the walls of Akasaka Castle across the river. Admittedly, *castle* was a rather grand name for the earth and wood battlements. Rather than a proper *yashiki*, it was really more of a *chiro,* or fortified position. The castle walls were only two hundred meters in circumference, with about twenty defensive towers composed of bamboo. It had no moat for defense.

But although it had been built in a hurry and looked it, the fort was still a beautiful sight, Ichiro thought. He could see copies of the *horimono* from Kusinagi painted on the outer walls. From the parapets flew the banners of every clan who had come to his aid.

A bamboo horn sounded, its high-pitched cry slicing the mountain air. "They have come! They have come!" a lone voice shouted.

A thunderous cheer burst from within the *chiro* walls.

Tears poured down Ichiro's cheeks as the gates opened and a throng of young warriors rushed out to greet them. He wept for brave young warriors who trusted him and would die for his cause, and he wept because he knew he was unworthy of their trust. *How many will live to see this through?* Ichiro thought as he wiped the hot tears from his face with a dirty sleeve.

Date Matsuo, a broad grin across his face, was the first to reach them when they entered the fort. "Remarkable! You did it!" he said, shouting to be heard over the cheering warriors.

Matsuo turned to the Emperor. "Your majesty, surely no man, commoner or noble, has such a friend as Minamoto-no-Ichiro."

"Truly, I have no others as faithful," Saigo said.

The emperor managed a tired smile.

Ichiro noted the weariness on Saigo's face. "We have ridden long and hard, Matsuo. We are all tired. The emperor especially needs food and rest."

Ichiro dismounted and felt his own legs nearly crumble beneath him. He held onto his horse's saddle to steady himself. "After we have eaten and bathed, tell the commanders I wish to discuss our defenses."

"It is done already," Matsuo said.

The cheering continued, but Ichiro did not feel worthy of it.

———

A bath and hot food restored Ichiro's strength. Dressed in a fresh blue kimono, he greeted his five commanders, Date Matsuo among them, as they entered his tent.

Ichiro knew all five men as loyal, honorable and respected *samurai*. Two were also known as fine poets, and one was a renowned musician and composer.

He waited until all five were seated before speaking. "So, how many forces do we have to operate with?"

"Two hundred in the castle," Matsuo said. "Another three hundred, including cavalry, in the hills and forests. They have your standing orders to retreat when the fighting becomes too fierce."

"Good," Ichiro said. "How are the other defenses?"

Matsuo nodded toward a black-haired young man in a red and blue kimono. "Takemitsu Yori has been working on them continuously since we arrived."

"The outer walls are prepared as you suggested," Takemitsu said. "Lord Taira's men will be quite surprised when they try to scale them."

"Excellent. My ancestor Masashige Kusinoki would be proud of you," Ichiro said. He then turned to a heavy, taciturn man named Noshida. "How are our supplies?"

"The keep is filled with rice and pickled fish and we have hidden further supplies in tunnels beneath the castle," said Noshida. "We also have foragers skilled in gathering wild roots and berries and in hunting. As for water, we have dug a well and built bamboo conduits to bring spring water from the hilltops, but it will take another day to complete."

"That is not good enough. Have the men work through the night with torchlight. Each drop of water is a precious jewel we must spend wisely," Ichiro said.

Noshida bowed his ahead. "It will be done."

"Good." Ichiro turned to the final two commanders. They were two brothers, alike in all but temperament. One was brash and mercurial and friendly. The other was cold as a glacier and cautious without being irresolute.

"And what of you?"

"We are prepared," said Dojo Hiroshi, the younger and more temperate. "My archers are ready and have spent extra time in preparing their arrows and themselves."

"The *ashigaru* are a rough lot," his brother Yomiyoshi said. "But I have got them beaten into shape. Most of them like your plans. Already I have two forces ready to use them, but we are a little short of spare armor for just one ploy."

"After a few days of fighting, I fear we will have plenty of spare armor and weapons," Ichiro said.

"True, too true," Matsuo said. "But may those who fall for the emperor be reborn in the Pure Land and be assisted on their path to Nirvana."

"May we all have a thousand lives for the emperor," Yomiyoshi declared quickly.

"It will do little good if we waste the ones we now have," Ichiro said.

Yomiyoshi blushed with embarrassment.

Ichiro noted the young man's response and smiled. "Honorable Yomiyoshi-san, I too wish we had a thousand lives. But one will serve us well enough for now, I think, especially if your men are as well trained as I trust they are."

Yomiyoshi, his honor redeemed, smiled slightly and gave a quick nod. "Thank you, general."

"Then we are prepared. May Ichiro grant us victory or the Buddha will find the Pure Land a trifle overpopulated," Ichiro said.

All the commanders except Matsuo rose, bowed and left.

Ichiro waited a moment after they were gone before speaking. "Do you trust them, Matsuo?"

"They are good men."

"I know their reputations as well as you do. But a reputation is not the man. Tell me, what do you think of them?"

"Noshida and Takemitsu are excellent leaders. They were both very resourceful when they served with my father in Korea. Takemitsu is a fine singer and composer, for what that's worth, but he is a brilliant engineer who can make your wildest plan a reality."

"And the Dojo brothers?"

Matsuo sighed. "Hiroshi seems wise beyond his years. But I fear he is too cautious and may not seize an opportunity when it presents itself. Yomiyoshi, on the other hand, may rush in too boldly and be unable to escape. But together they inspire their men to brave actions and usually succeed."

"I will see to it that their worst qualities are restrained."

"Good, because they *are* brilliant, and I would hate to lose them," Matsuo said.

"It is settled then, so let us rest. I suspect by tomorrow we will find sleep in precious short supply."

Ichiro retired to his tent and fell quickly asleep on his sleeping mat, his head resting lightly on a wooden pillow. He had not slept an hour when he awoke. Someone was in the tent. "Who's there?" he said.

The tent was pitch dark. Ichiro cursed, fumbling for a lantern, which had gone out. His fingers had found the lanterns handle when he felt a hand touch the back of his neck. He froze.

"My, you are a cold fish," a familiar voice said.

A flickering candle appeared and in its glow Ichiro saw Shizuka, kneeling beside him. She was naked.

Shizuka took the lantern from his fingers and lit it with her candle.

In the lantern light, Shizuka's skin shone like cool porcelain, her nipples stiff in the chill mountain air.

"What are you doing here?" he asked.

"Let me in under your blankets, it's far too cold here," she said.

Obligingly, he lifted the top cover of the *futon*, and she slid in beside him.

"Ah, much nicer," she said. Her voice was soft and relaxed, quite unlike her normal gruff tone. It was more like the first time he meet her in Taira's camp. She was naked then, too, he remembered.

"You still have not told me why you are here," Ichiro said.

"I wanted to be alone with you," she said.

"I am tired," he protested. "You are welcome to sleep here, but nothing more." He turned on his right side, his back to her.

"You are a strange man, *samurai*," Shizuka said. "You turn away when a willing woman offers herself. Other men would not hesitate."

"I am not other men."

"So I see," she said. "Oh, of course, the monk. Well if you would prefer those pleasures, then I can oblige." Shizuka rolled over onto her stomach and raised her buttocks. "Pretend I am a boy. I'm used to it."

"Don't be insulting," he replied. "I know you are jealous of the monk, but he does not attract me."

"Then what attracts you, general?" she asked.

Ichiro licked his lips. He could not deny he desired her. It had been so long, far too long. "My body desires you, but my mind is troubled and confused."

"So indecisive, Minamoto-no-Ichiro, quite unlike you," she said haughtily.

"I have a wife, somewhere," he said.

"So? Many men have wives. That does not stop them from enjoying other women." She massaged Ichiro's shoulders, his neck and his back.

At Shizuka's touch, Ichiro felt the pain of regret. *True*, he thought, *a samurai was not expected to love his wife, and yet he did love his Yukiko.*

"My wife is far away, in another time, another Nippon, another world" he said.

"There are no other worlds, and so she is not here," Shizuka said. She slid her hand across his hip and into his kimono.

"I will tell you a story," he said, feeling his loins stir in spite of himself. "There was once a man who had been away from Japan --"

"No one leaves Japan," Shizuka interrupted. Her hand grasped his manhood. "Ah," she said, pleased.

He tried to restrain the long-suppressed urges and felt himself failing. "Nevertheless," he whispered, "a man returned to Japan after a long absence. People asked what he missed most while in other lands. He said he missed his wife most."

"Scandalous," Shizuka said. She rolled him onto his back and he did not resist. She swung a leg over his hips and straddled him.

He gasped as her fingers caressed him. "Yes, to others," he managed to say. "But he was truthful and sincere. The real scandal was that he removed his mask so the world could see his real face."

"And you?" she asked. She raised her buttocks slightly to accommodate him.

"I have no mask. That is my tragedy," Ichiro said. He felt himself enter her and his body shuddered, both from desire for Shizuka and from longing for his Yukiko.

"Ah, yes!" Shizuka said, rocking slowly.

The long-suppressed ache was unleashed. Ichiro surrendered to it. He grasped Shizuka by the hips and rolled her onto her back. Ichiro thrust himself savagely into her.

"Yes, general, I see now you are an *otoko-rosh-otoko*, a great swordsman," she said. "Ah! Ah!"

Ichiro lost himself in the act, unleashing his pain and anguish, his sorrow and pleasure, until it seared his brain and leapt from him. His head throbbed and then blossomed. Spent and empty, he collapsed onto Shizuka's breast.

"You are a great warrior, Ichiro," she said, caressing his head. "You take what is yours."

"And you?"

"I take what I want," she replied.

"I see, I see." Exhausted, but relieved, he rolled from her. Sleep quickly came to him.

Ichiro awakened to the sound of running feet and the cries of a sentry sounding the alarm. He sat up and felt the frosty air form goose pimples on his bare back and arms.

"What's all the ruckus?" Shizuka said drowsily, rubbing her eyes.

"I am not sure," Ichiro said, grabbing his trousers and short jacket. "But I think the sentries have spied Taira's forces."

Ichiro dressed quickly and began to draw on his armor.

Shizuka sat up and pulled the *futon* over her breasts. "What an ungodly hour to attack," she muttered.

"You had better put on your armor. Now I must go," he said, tightening his helmet chinstrap as he went outside.

Chaos ruled the courtyard as soldiers, man just roused from sleep, scurried to their posts. Ichiro saw Matsuo directing men to the ramparts. "What's happening?" he shouted.

Matsuo looked up. "You'd better see for yourself, General."

They climbed a bamboo ladder to the ramparts and crossed to where Noshida was using an ancient spyglass to scan the horizon. "What is it?" Ichiro asked.

Noshida handed him the spyglass. "Out there, to the southeast."

Ichiro raised the glass to his left eye and screwed the right one shut. The sun was just now peeking over the mountains, bathing everything in a soft, diffuse yellow light.

Then he saw something moving in the distance. A black cloud, darker than the blackest India ink, rolled from the horizon toward them. Nearly opaque, the cloud contrasted sharply with the bright morning light. Ichiro suspected the cloud was probably dense enough to blot out the sun, as it had done at Kyoto.

"Did you see it, general?" Noshida asked.

"The cloud? Yes," Ichiro replied. He smiled and handed the spyglass back to Noshisa. "Well, I do believe Lord Taira is getting weaker. I would have thought him more original than to repeat one of his tricks."

"What do we do, then?" Matsuo asked.

"Tell Yukio to burn some mustard seed incense and have the men keep their lanterns and torches burning," Ichiro said. He paused a moment, and added "If any of them know any *sutras*, have them chant as loud as possible. I suspect the Buddha's law will protect us, at least for a while."

The orders were obeyed quickly. Torches flared back to life, spitting bright flames. The odor of mustard seed wafted everywhere as soldiers carried censors into every corner of the castle.

Soon a symphony of chants rent the air. Older, more educated warriors with plans to become monks in old age chanted from the Great Sutras. Some younger *samurai* repeated the Lotus sutra, *"Nom myoho renge kyo!"* Others, mostly *ashigaru* from rural areas, repeated prayers to the Amida Buddha, and asked for rebirth in the Pure Land.

The chanting grew louder as the black cloud, like a *tsunami*, rolled the castle. The multitude of voices took on a life of their own, vibrating everything within the castle walls.

Ichiro felt the chants drumming in his ears, louder even than the beat of his heart. He did not know if any of it would work, but he knew it would keep the men's minds occupied and keep fear from their thoughts. And, in fact, the chanting and the incense almost seemed to lift him above the world, above pain and suffering.

"I hope this works," Matsuo said.

"So do I, so do I," Ichiro heard himself say.

A cold wind howled from the black cloud. It was like the screams of a thousand damned souls. The wind whipped banners along the parapets and ripped some from their stanchions. Dust swirled in the valley below. Trees rocked and were torn from the earth, snapped as if they were mere twigs.

The air itself grew hot, thick and suffocating like ash from a volcano. The cloud, like a curtain of night, swallowed mountains before it. It began to eclipse the sun.

But even as its winds roared and shrieked, it could not drown out the chants.

As the cloud drew nearer, the men's voices grew louder and more intense. Then Ichiro thought he saw the cloud hesitate for a moment. It seemed to shake, to tremble, but then it resumed its course, engulfing everything in its path.

"Did you see?" Matsuo said, grabbing Ichiro's arm. "Tell me I am not mad!"

"Yes, it slowed just for a moment!" Ichiro said. He turned to the men. "Louder, louder!"

And as he turned, Ichiro saw a lone bowman sitting cross-legged nearby. The man was chanting diligently and, in a steady hand, he was writing a prayer onto a small sheet of rice paper.

Ichiro suddenly knew how to stop the cloud.

"You there!"

The man stopped his work and looked up.

"Yes, you. What are you writing?"

"A prayer, general. To the Lord Buddha and to Hachiman, asking them to protect all followers of the Law." The archer nervously lowered his head. "But it is not a very good prayer."

"It will do. Do you have a whistling arrow?" Ichiro said.

The man withdrew the arrow from his quiver.

"Tie your prayer to it, and fire it into the cloud," Ichiro ordered.

The archer obeyed. He quickly fastened the prayer onto the arrow with a length of thread from his jacket hem. Then the man notched the arrow into his bow and raised the bow above his head. He breathed slowly in and out, bringing his mind into clarity.

"Now, release the arrow into the cloud!" Ichiro said.

The arrow slid gracefully from the archer's slender fingers. It sang shrilly as it arched across the sky like a sparrow hawk chasing its prey. Then the arrow struck the wall of darkness and was swallowed.

"I don't understand. What are you doing, General?" Matsuo asked.

"I am whistling in the dark," Ichiro replied.

As Ichiro spoke, he saw the cloud falter. Where the arrow had struck a grayish whirlpool now appeared. The whirlpool swirled briefly, then stopped. A shaft of sunlight poured through the space where the arrow had struck.

Ichiro was elated. "Quickly, have every man who can write a prayer or the Buddha's name. All archers stand ready. And keep chanting!"

Those men who had them frantically drew out ink stones, callig-

raphy brushes and rice paper. As quickly as prayers were written, they
were torn from sheets, wrapped around arrows and launched.

The cloud thinned with each arrow. Sunlight poured through like
moth holes in a black blanket. Trees and land swallowed by the cloud
could now be seen again. But also visible was a huge army, marching
relentlessly toward the castle. It was long and sinuous--*like a snake*,
Ichiro thought, and shuddered--and stretched as far as the eye
could see.

"It's working!" Shizuka cried out from a rampart.

"Archers to the walls!" came the cry.

Every archer not already on the ramparts scrambled up the ladders
and stairs. Their arrows rattled in their quivers. "Wait till they are
range," Ichiro said.

The legion continued its march, apparently oblivious to the disinte-
grating shroud that protected them.

That fact puzzled Ichiro. *Can't they see their shield vanishing?* he
thought. *Well, perhaps.* Ichiro recalled that the messenger in Edo had
said the darkness had affected only the emperor's troops and not
Taira's. It was possible that the *daimyo*'s men saw only sunshine while
their foes stumbled in darkness. Still they marched on, for although the
dark cloud disintegrated, they could not see it.

The cloud, much weakened, reached the castle's outer perimeter.
There it suddenly halted, apparently stopped by the *horimono painted
on the walls. Now as thin as gossamer, the cloud crumbled and tore.
Shreds were caught by the wind and blown away until nothing
remained.*

But still the ignorant army pressed forward. They were about one
hundred meters away, Ichiro estimated. "Take aim!" he ordered.

Several hundred arrows were notched into an equal number of
bowstrings. Men sang and chanted as they raised their bows and drew
the arrows back.

"Now!" Ichiro shouted.

A cascade of arrows whistled from the battlements and rained
down on Taira's men. The first row of soldiers collapsed to a man
beneath the arrows. The second row, pierced as quickly, also fell, as
did the third row.

The remaining soldiers, apparently unable to stop because of the ranks behind them, pressed ahead. Too late they found themselves entangled in their comrades' bodies and were unable to flee. A second volley of arrows dispatched those enemy troops. A third volley drove the survivors back, even as their own archers returned the fire. A fourth volley caused the vanguard to break ranks at last. Their courage shattered, the enemy troops scattered madly across the hillsides or crashed back through their own forces. But the sheer bulk of men, still unable to stop their forward motion, crushed many of the fleeing underfoot. Soon many of the enemy commanders realized a retreat was in order, and most withdrew their men without too much disarray.

As they watched the enemy flee, the archers cheered. The rest of Ichiro's men soon joined in.

"A great victory," Matsuo said, caught up in the enthusiasm.

"It is not a victory yet. They will be back," Ichiro said. He sighed. "And they will not be so foolish next time."

Matsuo frowned, and then nodded agreement. "Yes, you are right. No doubt they will return."

"Send out scavengers to recover the arrows and other weapons, including armor," Ichiro said. "We will need all the weapons we can, and I expect Taira will not try anything for a while, at least."

"What of the wounded?"

"Let those who can walk go free, but I do not think we will find many wounded this time."

"What next?" Shizuka asked, coming to Ichiro's side.

"For myself, some breakfast. I'm hungry," he said. "You can join me if you wish."

———

Ichiro watched the last man re-enter the castle about two hours later. Lost in thought, Ichiro had left a cup of green tea resting unfinished and cold in his left hand.

"Your tea is cold," Shizuka said.

"What?" he said.

"Your tea. It is probably ice by now."

He brought the bowl to his lips and sipped. "Ah, yes, so it is at that."

"You have been positively glum all through this meal," Shizuka said. She picked up a bowl of steaming *udon* and sucked the long, flat noodles into her mouth.

"I fear I have trapped us. *Shika-traganai*. It cannot be helped, I suppose."

"So what is to be done?" she said, wiping her mouth with a sleeve.

"Only what I have done. What else is there?" Ichiro got to his feet. "I have work to do."

Outside he saw the Dojo brothers counting the stockpile of weapons collected from the dead. "Well over five hundred dead," Yomiyoshi said enthusiastically.

"Yes, quite amazing we were able to recover so much in such a short time," Hiroshi said.

"Good, very good," Ichiro said. But although the enemy casualties were high, he knew the numbers of Taira's dead would have to be higher still to cause the *daimyo* any real harm. "Do you have those sacks I asked Matsuo to bring from Edo?" Ichiro asked.

"Yes, but I don't understand..." Hiroshi said. He stopped and smiled. The younger Dojo had clearly realized what Ichiro had in mind. "Of course, it is so obvious. My men will have them filled and in place by afternoon."

""Place them on the outer wall. I do not think we will need then now, but evening is another matter," Ichiro said.

It was late afternoon when Taira's army was again sighted. A scout on horseback roared through the open gates, his lungs fairly bursting as he shouted the alarm.

From the ramparts Ichiro could see the dust cloud the enemy raised as it approached. "I want archers at either ends of the main wall," he said. "And bring out all the logs and boulders the scouts gathered."

"They are ready," Takemitsu said.

"What next, General?" the younger Dojo asked.

"We do nothing," Ichiro said.

"What? Nothing?" the elder Dojo exclaimed. "But what of the men in the woods?"

"They will hold their positions for now. We will do nothing, not even make a sound, until I say so," Ichiro replied.

"It shall be done," Takemitsu said.

A deep silence filled the *chiro*. Occasionally a man would cough or someone's whisper would echo unintelligibly off the walls. But the only other sound was the sharp, staccato snap of the banners flapping in the wind.

Ichiro watched the approaching army through Noshida's spyglass. It was a fine brass instrument of Italian manufacture. Noshida said an English sailor had given it to his family 300 years before. Noshida said he did not know what had been of the Englishman, though.

Ichiro raised it to his left eye. Through the spyglass, he could see the approaching army trailing a thick brown cloud behind it. The cloud, more natural this time, still resembled some malignant creature.

Ichiro found it hard to judge the army's size, but it seemed to him somewhat smaller than the initial attacking force. Perhaps the loss of so many men had taught Taira it was unwise to sacrifice mobility for sheer numbers. The necromancer was clearly not a good general, but he seemed to be learning. And Taira had obviously learned to keep troops in reserve, Ichiro realized.

He tried to estimate how far away the enemy were, but gave up and cursed the spyglass's limitations. "I wish I had some binoculars," he muttered.

"You wish you had *what*?" Shizuka asked as she came to his side.

"Nothing, just nonsense," Ichiro said quickly. He knew that wishing for the refinements of 20th century warfare was futile. He would have to make do.

Ichiro raised the spyglass back to his left eye in time to see two riders break away from the army's mass and ride toward the castle. The two stopped about seventy-five meters from the outer wall. One rider rode forward to the base of the wall.

"You within! Lord Taira demands your surrender," the rider shouted. "You cannot defeat us! There are one hundred of us for each one of you. We have food and water for months. You cannot have more than enough for a week!"

Silence greeted him from the castle.

The second warrior rode forward. "Come out and face us honorably in the open!" he called. "Better to die in battle than to starve within four walls. Come out! Our swords are sharp. We will be merciful and quick."

Again silence greeted the challenge.

The riders reined their horses about nervously, waiting for a response. When it did not come, they wheeled about and rode back toward the main army, which had now halted about three hundred meters away.

Ichiro watched the column open down the middle to let the riders pass through. The two were obviously taking the news that the castle was empty to Taira himself.

But Ichiro knew Taira was not so easily fooled.

The minutes passed with aching slowness. The breeze carried the fragrance of pine and camphor trees to Ichiro's nostrils.

An auspicious scent, he thought. His ancestor Kusinoki's name meant "camphor tree." Ichiro hoped the fragrance was a reassurance from Hachiman. More likely, it simply meant there were many camphor trees nearby.

Taira's forces parted once more to make way for riders. Five horsemen this time rode toward the *castle*. Joining the two original warriors were two other *samurai* and Taira himself. The five came to within thirty meters of the walls and halted.

Taira reined his horse slowly toward the wall. The necromancer and his mount were resplendent in gold armor bound with red cords.

Ichiro noted that the *daimyo's* helmet and gauntlets were of a foreign design; no doubt a gift from Van der Lieuw. *How many gifts had the damned sea captain given Taira?* Ichiro wondered.

"Minamoto-no-Ichiro," Taira called. "You are a reasonable man. Don't be a fool. Your martyrdom and that of your men will not save the emperor. My army will crush yours like so many gnats on a summer's day."

He reined his horse about, forcing the nervous animal to stay in place. "Surrender the sacred sword and I will spare your life," Taira said.

"You can lead my armies, general, when I am emperor, and

shogun too!" the *daimyo* continued. "You would not be the first Minamoto to join with the *Heike*. There are great worlds to conquer, General. You could lead my armies to victories in Japan and China. All Asia will fall to us. Together we could even conquer the effete Europeans.

"I await your answer, general. Will you join me or will you die?"

Only the roar of the wind and the snap of the flags replied to Taira's request.

Still trying to get me to join him, Ichiro thought. The audacity of the man, and the foolishness, too. Ichiro felt his fingers tighten on his sword hilt, felt the intricate carved patterns bite into his palm. He had a desire to plunge his sword deep into Taira's heart, but, oddly, he also pitied the *daimyo*. Ichiro suspected Taira was losing control of his powers.

Why else would Taira make such an offer when his forces are so clearly superior to mine? Ichiro thought. But he did not have answer. *Do you know why, Hachiman?* he asked silently.

The *kami* did not answer.

"Very well," Taira at last said. "Then you shall die, general. How unfortunate." The *daimyo* reined his horse about and rode back toward his army, his four bodyguards around him.

"Forward! Forward!" Taira called. His soldiers advanced, rushing toward the *chiro* with a blood-curdling cheer.

"Do we respond?" Matsuo asked.

"Not yet, not yet."

Taira's men were now at the foot of the outer wall.

Their grappling hooks snaked over the top of the wall and the men ran besieging ladders up against it. The enemy troops began their ascent. Ichiro waited until the first soldiers were near the top.

"Now!" he ordered. "Now!"

Axe blades flashed in the sun as soldiers brought the weapons down on the hempen cables that held up the outer, false wall. The cables snapped, their severed ends whipping skyward.

Taira's men screamed as the heavy, wooden wall, weighted with sacks filled with earth, collapsed on them. Those not instantly crushed to death beneath it found their arms and legs trapped. Archers on the inner, real wall quickly dispatched the wounded while *ashigaru* hurled down rocks and logs on the fleeing.

Once more Taira's men beat a hasty retreat, and once more a cheer rose from the defenders.

Dojo Hiroshi laughed heartily and slapped Ichiro on the back in an uncharacteristic display of emotion. Even he, with emotions cold as ice, seemed caught up in the joy of the moment. "See, I told you what my archers could do. Taira's men run like whipped dogs from us. They won't be back."

"I wouldn't count on that," Ichiro said.

"I would. I would bet a thousand *riyo* on it," Hiroshi said, still laughing.

Then there was a loud crack and Hiroshi's laughter stopped short. His hand clutched his throat and blood bubbled between his fingers.

Ichiro caught Hiroshi as he fell.

Another crack sprayed splinters from the top of the wall. Ichiro knew immediately what it was. Taira had snipers with matchlocks placed on the nearby hills. "Get down!" he yelled to the archers.

Ichiro and an archer carried the dying Dojo behind the safety of a parapet. Hiroshi tried to talk, but nothing came out. Then his eyes bulged wide open in both shock and surprise at how quickly death came. His eyelids did not close.

A third crack and an archer, hit in the chest, tumbled backwards from the parapets. The other archers ducked below the top of the wall. Although the muskets were far from accurate, their bullets were still deadly when they hit their mark.

Ichiro knew Van der Lieuw had supplied Taira with the muskets, just as the Dutchman had provided Taira's armor. *Even after his death, the Dutchman was still proving deadly*, Ichiro thought.

Noshida crawled over to Ichiro. "Dojo?" he asked.

"Dead," Ichiro replied.

"He was my friend, he said softly. Noshida looked at Ichiro. "So what do we do?"

"For the time being, we hide behind our walls," Ichiro said.

Another volley of shots rang out, and another archer tumbled, mortally wounded, over the wall.

"Should I alert the cavalry, general?" Noshida asked.

"No, I don't want Taira to know they are there. They will hold their positions."

Ichiro watched two bowmen lower Dojo Horoshi's body to Shizuka and another archer who stood below the parapet. Musket balls splintered the wood above Ichiro's head. He ducked, and then saw Yomiyoshi rushing across the castle courtyard toward his dead brother. If what Matsuo had said about the young man was true, Yomiyoshi was in frenzy and was likely to do something rash enough to endanger them all.

Ichiro crawled toward a ladder and was down it in a flash. He caught Yomiyoshi as the Dojo tried to grab his brother's limp and lifeless arm.

"Who did this? Who killed my brother? " Yomiyoshi cried. He struggled against Ichiro, who held him back. The young man was strong, but Ichiro was stronger. Tears rolled down the Dojo's face as he stretched out his arm to touch his dead sibling.

"It's no use. He is dead!" Ichiro said. "You cannot bring him back."

"Let me touch him! Kiss him farewell!" Yomiyoshi sobbed. "He saved my life so many times." He freed an arm and reached across Ichiro's shoulder to touch his brother.

"General, let him touch Hiroshi," Shizuka said. "It can do no harm."

Shizuka was right, Ichiro realized. To deny Yomiyoshi this last right would do no good. He relaxed his hold on the young warrior.

Yomiyoshi hugged his brother's body tightly as Shizuka and the archer lowered the dead man to the ground. Yomiyoshi pressed his head to Hiroshi's chest. Great sobs racked Yomiyoshi's body, rattling his armor like skeletal bones. "Dear brother, what karma brought you to this fate? I should be dead, not you! Not you who were so wise."

Yomiyoshi looked up at Ichiro. His face was pale, ghostly white and streaked with his brother's blood. "Where are they, the men who killed my brother?"

"On the hill to the west. But it is foolish to attack them alone. They have muskets," Ichiro said.

Yomiyoshi stood up and drew his *katana*. "It wouldn't matter if they were *kami*, they will die for killing Hiroshi." He turned and ran toward the castle's rear gate.

Ichiro moved to stop him, but he felt Shizuka grab his arm. "No, let him go. He is obsessed with grief, and you cannot stop him. If he kills them, then he has his revenge. But if he dies, then that, too is what he seeks."

Sadly, Ichiro found himself agreeing with her. Dojo Yomiyoshi was beyond his help now, as much beyond it as Hiroshi. He whispered a quick prayer to Hachiman, and to Kannon, the *bodhisattva* of mercy, then turned his attention to his troops.

"Matsuo, how's the situation?" he called out.

"We had five killed, three wounded," Matsuo replied. "But Taira's men are still retreating."

Good, Ichiro thought. That meant the gunfire was meant to harass his archers and keep them pinned down while Taira's men fled. The *daimyo* was at a clear disadvantage with his men in the open, just as the *bakufu's* forces had been when facing Kusinoki on this same battle-field six centuries before.

The gunfire was sporadic now. Taira obviously had only a few muskets, and he was trying to conserve his gunpowder and shot.

Then a scream drowned out the musket fire. The gunfire stopped.

Ichiro dashed to the ladder and climbed to the parapet. "Noshida, what's going on?"

"I don't know," Noshida said.

"I can see a Dojo, but I don't know which one," an archer called. "He's on the hillside and he's coming back this way."

"Give me your spy-glass," Ichiro said to Noshida.

"Gladly." The man pressed the telescope into Ichiro's hands.

Ichiro edged his way along the parapet to the west wall. Not wanting to take any chances of being shot, he looked for a break in the stockade, and found one where a knothole about the size of his fist had been. He pushed the spyglass through the hole and looked out.

Yomiyoshi was stumbling down the hill carrying several bundles. Ichiro thought the bundles seemed vaguely familiar,. Yomiyoshi had sheathed his sword, and he seemed to have three muskets tucked under one arm. His helmet dangled from its chin strings and bounced crazily at each step he took.

Ichiro was amazed that Yomiyoshi moved so quickly, heavily laden as he was. *The man is obviously either possessed or quite mad*, Ichiro thought.

"Open the gate for Yomiyoshi!" someone cried.

The *ashigaru* responded swiftly, pulling the heavy gate slowly open. Yomiyoshi, running so fast he almost seemed to fly, stumbled through the gate and into the courtyard. He gripped his bundles tightly and walked resolutely to his brother's corpse, which now lay in a shallow trench with the other dead.

"You are revenged, Hiroshi, dear brother," Yomiyoshi cried. "Your soul can find the Pure Land now your killers are slain." He dropped the muskets to the ground. Then carefully Yomiyoshi placed the severed heads of the musketeers, still tied into their helmets, next to Hiroshi's body.

The sight of the severed heads shocked Ichiro. Although beheading a dead enemy was not unusual, there was a brutality in Yomiyoshi's actions that Ichiro found sickening. But no one moved to stop the crazed warrior.

"See, do you see whom you killed?" Yomiyoshi said, picking up a head and addressing it. "The great warrior Dojo Hiroshi!"

He turned the head's sightless eyes toward his brother's body. The head's helmet tumbled to the ground. "Now, watch over him as his soul seeks Nirvana in the Pure Land."

Yomiyoshi slowly, almost reverently, placed the first head on the ground. He repeated the ritual with each head.

Still no one moved to stop him. Every eye in the *chiro*, including Ichiro's, was fixed on Yomiyoshi, both stunned and fascinated by the man's madness.

At last Yomiyoshi lifted Hiroshi's corpse into his arms. He turned his brother's face toward the severed heads. "Here are your killers, brother. May they guide you well into *O-Emma-Sama's* realm, and may the *kami* rip out their tongues before he leads you to rebirth."

Yomiyoshi lowered the body back into the grave, and then he collapsed on the ground and wept.

Ichiro looked about the castle, and saw the men staring with disbelief, terror and shock at the scene before them. He knew what he had to do to bring them out of their horror; otherwise they would be lost to him.

Ichiro climbed down from the parapets and walked across to Yomiyoshi's side. Ichiro felt the bile rising in his gorge as he bent down and picked up a severed head by its dark, oiled black topknot. He held the head aloft.

"Hachiman has given us a sign and a great victory," Ichiro said. "Even one man alone can stop three of Taira's men. Many more lie dead at our gates. We will not fail the Emperor Saigo! *Banzai!*"

"*Banzai!*" Date Matsuo shouted. Someone else also took up the cry.

"*Banzai!*" Ichiro repeated. He could feel the energy flowing into him, the same energy he felt when the young and all too eager pilots prepared to die for their emperor. It was intoxicating and it was terrifying.

"*Banzai!*" more voices cried.

"*Banzai!*" he said a third time.

"*Banzai! Banzai! Banzai!*" The cry shook the very walls of the *chiro*. It echoed from the neighboring hills and merged with distant thunder to crack the sky. The heavens themselves seemed to offer a thousand lives for the Emperor Saigo.

But Ichiro knew even ten thousand lives might not be enough to guarantee victory.

CHAPTER EIGHTEEN

Ichiro watched the sun, now a bloated orange ball, as it dropped beneath the tops of the distant hills. He suspected Taira would not attack again until morning. The night seemed to discourage the *daimyo*, as if Taira did not fully control things when the moon was high.

But Ichiro also knew Taira was licking his wounds like a defeated cat, tallying up his dead and wounded and wondering how so few warriors in a shaky wooden fortress could inflict so much damage. The *daimyo* knew magic, and he knew the seductive attraction of political power, of that Ichiro was certain, but Taira knew less the ways of war and lesser still the hearts of men willing to die for justice.

Ichiro hoped he could turn that flaw against Taira.

"Yomiyoshi is asleep," Date Matsuo said, climbing up to the parapets to join Ichiro. "Yukio gave him a powerful draught. The monk said it was something you gave him."

"Good, the dreams may help him."

Matsuo shook his head. "I am not sure. Yomiyoshi's mind is quite distraught. I think he is quite mad."

"Perhaps." But Ichiro could not deny it. The death of his brother had quite unhinged Yomiyoshi. Even Ichiro feared the man could explode at any minute, killing, slashing, destroying without thought even those who were his friends.

But Ichiro elected to drive the idea from his mind. Death from a mad *samurai* was in some ways preferable to death at Taira's hands.

"We'll wait until just before dawn to attack," he told Matsuo. "Alert the men in the hills. Tell them to divide into two forces on either side of the castle."

"What will be the sign for attack?" Matsuo asked.

Ichiro pondered the question. A trumpet call might alert Taira. *It would need to be subtler, less obvious, like a gentlewoman dropping a handkerchief to attract a man's attention.*

The thought made him smile. "The Emperor has some handkerchiefs with a chrysanthemum *mon* on them. We send two messengers each with a handkerchief and instructions to tell the commanders to attack when they see us raise a banner with chrysanthemum."

"Good enough, General," Matsuo said. "Now you should sleep. I already have the men assigned for guard duty, but I don't think Taira will attack this night."

"Neither do I, but I have learned never to underestimate the enemy." Ichiro yawned, feeling his jaw almost crack from the effort. *Matsuo was right,* he had to admit. *Sleep was a good idea.*

But he could not sleep. Shizuka lay next him, her body warm and inviting. They had made love frantically, with the intensity born of knowing they could both die within moments.

Again Shizuka was the aggressor, caressing him with her mouth and her sex until he was dizzy. He convulsed as he came, holding her head between his legs, hearing her moan with joy. Then she had looked up, licked her lips, and curled up next to him, her arm thrown across his chest. She was asleep almost immediately.

The exhaustion that followed should have brought sleep, but it betrayed him. The fear that his plans would fail goaded his brain and drove the sleep from him. He had done what he could. There was nothing more to do until the attack itself.

"Hachiman, let me rest," he whispered.

As usual, the *kami* did not respond, but Ichiro closed his eyes, and dreams eventually greeted him.

Tamika awoke him just before dawn. "Hurry, General. The sun awaits us."

She cast on eye on the sleeping Shizuka before she left. If Tamika were jealous, she did not show it.

Dressed, Ichiro stepped out into the early morning air, which was bitingly cold. Moonlight filled the courtyard with a pale, pearl-like glow.

Many of the men were already mounted, ready for combat. *Ashigaru* sat on the ground, quietly sharpening the blades of swords and *naginata*.

Ichiro walked briskly past them, nodding sharply when a man smiled, bringing a finger to his lips to silence a man who wanted to greet him. There would be time for talk later, but not now.

Ichiro climbed the short ladder to the parapet. His right leg ached from the cold, but he knew the excitement of battle would soon make him forget his pain.

Matsuo and Noshida stood on one of the towers. Noshida had his spyglass out, looking for the first rays of sunlight to pierce the horizon. Matsuo held the Emperor's flag in his arm, waiting to signal the attack.

"Good morning, general," Noshida whispered. "Not long now." He offered the spyglass to Ichiro.

Ichiro accepted the telescope and brought it to his left eye. The spyglass was warm from having been inside Noshida's jacket, but the lenses fogged and Ichiro was repeatedly forced to wipe them with the sleeve of his jacket.

Nothing moved outside the castle. In the distance Ichiro could see the glow of fires from Taira's camp.

Dawn was just now crawling across the horizon. The sun appeared to struggle to bring light to the darkness. A few clouds glowed on their bottoms from the early light. The glow was growing, becoming a crimson incandescence that seemed to set the sky ablaze.

Even nature has trouble resisting Taira's damned magic, Ichiro thought.

Ichiro returned the spyglass to Noshida. "It is almost time," he whispered.

He descended the ladder and strode across the courtyard to his horse. As Ichiro mounted Luck, he could sense the anticipation the other men. They were ready and they would not be denied.

"General, we await the word," said a *samurai* next to Ichiro. Ichiro lucked up and saw it was Tamika.

"It will be good to be in battle again. It has been far too long," she replied.

Tamika carried a plum-leaf blade spear and a *katana* with a black leather handle. She smiled and adjusted her *so-men*. Behind the iron faceplate she looked like just another warrior. But Ichiro knew better.

For a moment he was tempted to tell her to stay behind, but he knew she would not. He also knew she was a better warrior than any man in his troop, and he owed his life to her. "I am glad you are here," he said.

"Good hunting, general," she said.

"Good hunting. So let us be off. It is time!" he said. Ichiro looked up that parapet and signaled with a clenched fist. Matsuo waved back and began running the Emperor's banner up the flagpole.

Ichiro turned to the guards. "Open the gate."

But even before the stockade gate was completely open the horsemen were pouring out onto the plain and riding toward the Ishikawa River. Tumultuous cries of "Banzai!" sprang from their lips, and many knew they would pay that price today. *Ashigaru* followed behind, spears ready.

From hillsides also came the thunder of horses' hooves as the first wave of horsemen rode down upon Taira's still sleeping camp.

Taira's men were unprepared for the assault. The horsemen, trailing a cloud of dust, easily broke through the enemy lines in every direction, sending the *daimyo*'s men scattering like cockroaches afraid of the light.

Some of the enemy tried to ride horses that were still tethered, and they quickly fell victim to sword and spear. Archers tried to fix arrows to unstrung bows and were cut down where they stood.

A few of Taira's men resisted the attackers. One man wielding a *naginata* charged Ichiro on the left. Ichiro deflected the lance easily, and on the back cut he severed its blade from its shaft. The attacker tried to recover his balance, but Kusinagi cut the man down like a scythe cut a sheaf of wheat.

Ichiro saw two men fighting over a single suit of armor. He spurred Luck toward them, then bore to his right, and beheaded the man on that side. The other man, still gripping the armor, tumbled to the ground. The headless corpse, which also held tightly to the armor, fell on top of the unharmed *ashigaru*.

A rider with a *jumonji-yari* bore down on the *ashigaru* and dispatched him with a thrust to the chest. "An excellent move, general," the rider said.

It was Tamika.

"I think we've down enough damage here," Ichiro said. "Tell the men to prepare to return to the castle." Before he heard her acknowledgement, Ichiro turned Luck back toward the campsite. He realized instantly it was a mistake.

Four *harquebusiers,* their matchlock muskets raised, fired as one as he faced them. A bright yellow cloud, with four thin tongues of pure flame, filled the world.

Ichiro dove to his left side, jerking hard on Luck's reins. He felt one musket ball rip through the sleeve of his jacket, heard another whiz past his right ear. A third glanced on his right shoulder plate.

But the last one struck Luck near the neck. The horse whinnied once in pain, stumbled, and fell. Ichiro flung himself to the ground and rolled once, coming to his feet.

Ichiro was now at the musketeers' mercy, in the open with only his sword to protect him. He charged them as they reloaded, hoping to catch them before they could reload, fire again, and turn him into a crimson mass, Hachiman's protection notwithstanding.

He hit them as they tried to raise their weapons. The first man fell, stabbed in the throat, as he tried to bring his musket to his shoulder. Apparently wiser than his compatriots, the second *harquebusier* turned and fled. The third, his matchlock damaged, tried to use his rifle as a staff while the fourth tried desperately to force powder and ball into the weapon's long, thin barrel.

Ichiro easily deflected the third man's initial blow. He could feel Kusinagi bite into the wooden stock of the musket. But his own attack was deftly blocked, sending up a shower of sparks as blade met barrel.

From the corner of his eye, Ichiro saw the fourth man's struggling to relight his match, which had gone out. But in that brief instant the third man counterattacked, lunged, and caught Ichiro in the chest with the musket butt. The blow staggered Ichiro, forcing him backwards. The musketeer pressed his attack and charged, now swinging the gun like an axe.

Ichiro planted his foot and thrust.

The musketeer, unable to stop, ran onto the sword blade. The man stood for a moment, startled. He looked down at the blade imbedded in his chest, then looked at Ichiro. The musketeer's mouth opened wide in surprise as the life left him.

Ichiro pulled Kusinagi from the man's chest just in time to see the fourth man, his match lit, raise his weapon. But the shot never came.

As he watched, Tamika's lance caught the man in the back, lifted him from his feet and deposited him face down in the dirt.

"*Arigato,*" Ichiro said, breathing heavily. *Once again, I am indebted to that damned woman,* he thought.

"Your horse is back on his feet, general. It is time we were away. Taira's men are regrouping," Tamika said.

Ichiro looked up and saw Luck coming toward. The horse was bleeding from a wound on his right shoulder, but otherwise seemed unhurt.

Ichiro mounted. He shouted to one of his horseman who had a horn. "Sound a retreat," he ordered.

"Yes, general." The man brought the horn to his lips and blew. Its harsh notes resounded triumphantly across the plain. Hearing the horn, Ichiro's warriors finished their business and headed back to Asakawa Castle.

"A good day, general," Tamika said once they were back in the fortress. "Taira will think twice before attacking again."

"I am not so sure," Ichiro said as he dismounted.

Now that the battle was over, he found himself resenting what Tamika had done for him. For now he was in her debt and would have to repay the obligation. "Your *giri* rides heavy on me. How am I to repay the debt?"

Tamika undid her *so-men* and stared at Ichiro. There was pain and anger in her eyes. "How can a warrior who cannot be killed by a mortal man owe his life to me? Yes, you will repay your obligations soon enough, general, but I owe you *giri* for freeing me from Taira's spells. How am I to repay that?"

Ichiro felt chastened. Tamika was right, he realized. The debt he owed her was small, compared to that which she owed him. "You are right. I am a fool, and for that I am sorry."

Tamika at first showed no expression, then a smiled formed on her lips. She reached out and clasped his arm. A tear formed at the corner of her right eye, then rolled down her cheek. "There will be time for apologies later, Minamoto-no-Ichiro, if we are still here, if there is still a Japan. Perhaps we are all fools. But your apology still humbles me."

"It is better to be a fool in righteous cause than a hero who serves only himself," the Emperor said. He came to Ichiro and hugged him. "I saw you both from the tower. You were magnificent. May Japan always have such magnificent fools."

"The Emperor will never run short of those brave enough to fight and die like cherry blossoms," Ichiro whispered.

Yes, magnificent fools like me, he thought, *who has trapped his army in a flimsy fortress against an army whose leader possesses power greater than any other mortal. I am a magnificent fool who wonders if his cause is indeed righteous or could possibly succeed, just like the young fools I trained to fly who then climbed aboard flimsy aircraft and crashed into American carriers. A hero is only a fool who has survived*, he thought.

It was foolish to stay here now, he realized. He had to flee, to find that battlefield which would give him the advantage. But now how to survive long enough to find that place? How to deliver a blow to Taira that would cripple the *daimyo* and allow Ichiro's army to escape? The answer eluded him.

CHAPTER NINETEEN

Taira held back throughout the next day. Now stung twice, the *daimyo* was forced into caution, despite all his magical powers. But Ichiro also suspected that Taira had plans of his own, and that worried him.

Ichiro watched Taira as the *daimyo*, riding his dragon over his camp, directed his forces as they built fortifications. The enemy had relocated their camp and its fortifications on the opposite side of the Ishikawa River, using its waters as a natural moat. These fortifications would clearly resist the next massive attack Taira clearly seemed to fear.

No matter, Ichiro thought, *one massive assault was more than suffi-cient. Now it was time for the fox to nip at Taira's heels, to snap the daimyo's tendons and leave him hamstrung, at least for a while.*

Ichiro collapsed the spyglass onto itself and thought a moment. He had two days, perhaps three, before Taira's numerical superiority finally overwhelmed the *chiro*. He had to use that time well and leave the *daimyo* with a hollow victory when it came. Ichiro tried to recall what strategy Kusinoki had used both at his own Akasaka Castle and at the Battle of Chihaya. But the thoughts would not come, not just now.

Ichiro had ordered the bodies of his dead, now numbering thirty-three, salted and partially buried in the shallow trench where Dojo Hiroshi lay. That much he could at least copy from Kusinoki, when the time came. Ichiro hoped Taira was not a student of history, or even this simple diversion would prove in vain.

———

Date Matsuo woke him the next morning. "General, bad news."

Ichiro rolled over, rubbed his eyes. "What's happened?"

"The water has ran out," Matsuo replied. "Taira's men must have found the streams and conduits which fed the *chiro* and diverted their flow."

"Came we rebuild them?"

"Yes, but it would take time, and it would do us no good. Taira has poisoned the springs and the wells."

"How much water do we have in the castle?"

"Enough for three, four days. Longer if we ration it."

Damn! Ichiro thought. *This ruins everything.* Taira could simply wait him out now. Ichiro would have to take the offensive and send the *daimyo* reeling long enough for his men to escape. Again, he had no choice.

"You knew this would happen, Hachiman, yet you did nothing," he said to himself. "But it is not for you to answer, is it? It is for me to choose. And you knew that, too, didn't you?"

The *kami*, as usual, failed to reply, but Ichiro knew, somehow, that Hachiman was smiling.

Ichiro called his commanders together for a war council. The men sat cross-legged on the bare ground. Each sipped tea or chewed rice cakes or tore pieces from a hunk of smoked fish. But it was far from a banquet. They ate from hunger, from need and from knowledge that food would soon be a luxury. And they ate because they preferred not to talk.

"The cavalrymen must be withdrawn tonight. We cannot endanger them further," said Ichiro, breaking the silence.

"A wise move," Matsuo said. The others gave their approval with nods or grunts. "But where should they relocate? To Edo?"

Ichiro shook his head. "No, further north. To Matsumae on Hokkaido, near your family's lands."

"But that will leave Edo and the Shogun exposed to Taira's army," Matsuo protested.

"I think not," Noshida said. "Taira will not attack Edo. It is not the city he wants, it is Ichiro's sword. Why attack a city when your goal is Kusinagi? If he succeeds in gaining the sword, then he will attack Edo. But if he obtains Kusinagi, we will all be dead anyway."

Ichiro smiled, pleased because Noshida so clearly grasped the situation. "Good thinking, Noshida," he said. "Now, how soon can we withdraw the horsemen?"

"I could have them out by tonight," Matsuo said.

"No, I think morning will be fine," Ichiro said. "I have some tasks for them first. Can you get them to fell some trees and position them along the hillside?"

"It will be done," Noshida said.

Ichiro turned to Shizuka and Tamika. "How many *ninja* do we have among us?"

Shizuka smiled slyly. "I thought you would have guessed by now. There are twenty, counting me."

"More than enough for what I have in mind," he said. "Taira felt the tiger's bite yesterday. Tonight he'll feel the fox's. Smaller, but just as painful." He turned to Shizuka. What weapons will you need?"

"We have plenty of swords, knives, staffs and ropes, but we could use some *testsu-bishi*," Shizuka said. She reached produced some triangular-shaped thorns from a pouch at her side. "I would prefer iron caltrops, but there are plenty of thorns like this in the countryside."

She tossed it to Matsuo, who instinctively caught it and let out a howl. He pulled the thorn from the base of his thumb and sucked at the wound.

"An iron *tetsu-bishi* would have gone to the bone, but these are just as effective on a bare foot and will do in a pinch," she said. "All I need is to have some men to collect these thorns."

"Well, when Taira's men step on those, they won't soon forget the pain," Ichiro said.

"*I* won't soon forget pain either," Matsuo said, stilling rubbing his injured hand.

The others laughed. *Good*, Ichiro thought, *best to laugh now, keep the spirits high. A proverb said fools laughed at adversity, while heroes wept.* He did not care who laughed now, for he knew weeping would come soon enough.

The afternoon was scorching, in start contrast to the cold of the previous days. Ichiro suspected the *daimyo*'s magic had somehow disturbed the weather, and Taira seemed incapable of controlling it. Most of the soldiers avoided the heat by taking time to sleep, curling up in a shady corner or under a tent flap. Many slept, but Ichiro suspected that few of them dreamed.

Taira's men also surrendered to the heat. If the *daimyo* had little control over the weather today, then he had even less over his men's behavior, Ichiro thought. He could see some of Taira's soldiers bathing in the Ishakawa River. Some poured pails of water over each other. The water seemed to vaporize as it touched the men's skin.

Suddenly Ichiro realized how hot it felt. He could feel streams of perspiration pouring down his own back. Ichiro collapsed his spyglass and descended the ladder from the watchtower.

At the watchtower's base was a water barrel. Although Ichiro knew the water was precious, he was unable to resist his urges. He cupped his hands and splashed water over his face. He let the water roll down his neck until it drenched the front of his short jacket. The water was warm from the sun, but it still seeming cooling. Ichiro imagined it vaporizing as it touched his skin, as the river water had seemed to steam away from the backs of Taira's soldiers.

After a moment, he took a gourd from the barrel's side, dipped it in, and then drank. The water was sweet to his tongue, sweeter even than the plums he had picked from his grandmother's garden. He tried to remember when water tasted so wonderful. When he did remember, it saddened him.

The American fighter planes had caught them escorting bombers near Guadalcanal. Wave after wave the Americans came, tearing his comrades apart. The enemy always seemed able to find freshly fueled and armed aircraft from their carriers. Ichiro shot down two Wildcats and a Corsair that day, firing until his guns were empty and their barrels buckled from the heat.

But he could not stop the Americans from mauling the bombers like wild dogs savaged sheep. His fuel low, his guns empty, he ordered his men to retreat. Three bombers and five fighters, one trailing smoke and oil all the way, made it home. He had stepped from his plane exhausted, weary, his head throbbing. A corporal had thrust a tin cup of water into his hands. He had mumbled his thanks and swallowed greedily. Then, too, the water had been sweet.

"Don't drink it all, general. Leave some for me," Shizuka said.

"Sorry, I was thirsty," he apologized.

She smiled. "I have good news."

"Yes?"

"My spies tell me Taira is hurting. He has five thousand men still left, but is losing many to defections."

Ichiro shook his head. *Shizuka called that good news? Five thousand. A small army, but still ten time more than we have*, he thought. "What about casualties?"

"About two thousand dead, another thousand wounded. We've hurt him well, general."

"What about Taira himself?"

"My spies say he stays in his tent most of the time. His little jaunt on his dragon was simply to survey the terrain. His own men think the *daimyo* is ill."

Power and magic are dangerous drugs, Ichiro thought. *They can gnaw you like cancers and suck the life from you.* "Then perhaps we should pay our respects if he is ill. We will be unexpected guests, of course, but not uninvited."

Shizuka stared at him. "You have a plan, Ichiro, yet you won't share it. But surely you can tell me?"

"In time," he said, surprised again that she had called him by his name.

She snorted. "*In time!* Well, either you can tell me, or I will stay out of your bed."

Ichiro laughed. "That, my love, would be a small loss." He was amazed to see her blush for the first time since he had met her, apparently embarrassed that he had called her his "love."

But she quickly regain her composure. "If you do not tell me, I shall order my *ninja* not to cooperate." She crossed her arms and spread her legs in a gesture of defiance.

Ichiro frowned. No doubt Shizuka could do just that. Although he knew she would not sabotage his plans, he also knew her ultimate loyalty was to herself. But without her and her command of the other *ninja* his plans would fail.

He had no choice. He told her the plan.

Shizuka's eyes widened in disbelief. "The mirror and the jewel? Are you sure he has them?"

Ichiro nodded. "Taira keeps them in a wooden chest he carries with him. If he obtains *Kusinagi*, then all the Imperial regalia are his, and no one can stop him."

She shook her head. "I don't know, general."

So it was general *once again, now that it was business*, he thought.

"But we can try, even if it kills us," Shizuka said.

"I assure you, Shizuka, if we don't try, it *will* kill us."

"So what am I to do first?"

"First you must teach Tamika and me some of your *ninja* tricks."

Shizuka frowned. "You're not coming along are you? A commander should stay behind."

"A commander is a soldier, too. And I want the pleasure of personally taking Taira's trophies out from under his nose."

"Very well, it is your funeral."

"Dear Shizuka, it could well be all our funerals, with no one left to mourn us."

In the hot afternoon sun Shizuka drilled Ichiro, Tamika and a half dozen other soldiers in rudimentary *ninja* weapons, tactics and tricks. She showed them how the *tekagi*, or iron bear-claw, could stop a sword blade. She showed them the smoke grenade, the blowgun, and the *kyoketsu-shogi* or knife and ring. Then she demonstrated several *mudras*, special hand-positions to focus the mind's power, and the skills of non-movement so as to blend with the background like a ghost.

Ichiro was an apt pupil.

"You learn quickly, general," Shizuka said admiringly.

"You are an adept teacher, and even Hachiman would approve," he said politely. *But even the worst student learns much when he is desperate,* Ichiro thought.

She grilled her students mercilessly until each could snag his opponent's sword with a *kyoketsu-shogi*, until each was adept with the *bo*, or quarterstaff. Ichiro quickly learned to anticipate the movement of Shizuka's *bo* and to avoid entangling his sword with her knife and ring.

Then she blindfolded him and showed him how to move with the scabbard of his sword balanced on his sword-tip. Ichiro held the scabbard cord between his teeth so he could probe the darkness with it. Should he encounter someone he could release the cord and have his sword ready before his opponent could even unsheath his weapon.

It was late afternoon when Shizuka had finished with him. The sun was low in the sky. Sweat drenched him and his muscles both ached with exertion and tingled with anticipation.

"Well done," she said, admiringly as he removed the blindfold.

"So?"

Shizuka smiled. "We attack."

———

The night was overcast. Thick clouds obscured the stars' feeble light. Even the moon 's glow was a dull yellow behind the clouds.

"Perfect weather," Shizuka said. She sat up on the *futon*. "We couldn't have asked for better."

"If it holds," Ichiro replied.

"What?"

"Smell the air. A storm is coming." He stroked her arm.

She smiled. "Let it rain when it will. I think we may be long done with our business before the first drop falls."

"Perhaps, but the weather holds for no one."

"Then we'd best hurry."

The majority of the army slept, grateful for the long respite from battle, and glad to escape the surprising autumn heat. Only a small contingent prowled the parapets, their eyes watching for the enemy, but their bodies wishing for their beds. The *ninja* sat meditating in the courtyard, preparing their minds for the assault.

"Where's Tamika?" Ichiro asked.

"I haven't seen her," Shizuka said.

A noise came from the Emperor's tent, and Ichiro turned in time to see Tamika pushing the flap aside. She stood for a moment, illuminated by an oil lamp, as she tied her up her jacket and short pants. Through the tent flap Ichiro could see Saigo lying asleep on a cot, his kimono flung open. The young man's body glistened in the lamplight. Ichiro could also see Saigo's manhood subsiding. Tamika's thighs also glistened as she pulled on her short pants. She stopped for a moment, found a napkin, and wiped herself before she continued dressing.

Ichiro smiled. *So the Emperor finds Tamika attractive,* he thought. *Somehow, Hachiman had a hand in this. Still, she is only one woman,* he said to himself, directing the thought to the kami. *Saigo may yet prefer other young men, you know.*

Hachiman declined to respond.

Tamika, still fastening her jacket, stepped toward Ichiro and Shizuka. She slipped her sword into her *obi*, oblivious to their presence.

"We were waiting for you," Ichiro said.

She stepped back, startled, but quickly regained her composure. "General, how good to see you. A lovely night for a walk to Taira's camp, don't you think?"

"Yes, quite lovely."

Matsuo saw them off through the gate, a score of black clad, nocturnal predators who found the night a pleasing time for hunting. "Good luck," Matsuo said.

"The goose is unaware, and the fox shall find his meat most sweet," Ichiro replied.

Outside the *chiro*, the *ninja* met with two scouts who guided them across the hillside to a small ridge that overlooked Taira's camp. The *daimyo's* tents covered a large expanse of ground. Dozens of campfires glowed in every direction, like huge and grounded fireflies.

Ichiro found the fires unwelcome. It made it more likely that the guards to spot the *ninja*. Ichiro almost wished it would rain now and drown out the crackling flames. He could almost taste the moisture in the air. But rain, too, would prove disastrous. To attack now was the only choice.

The *ninja* were divided into groups, each with its own assignments. Four were to destroy Taira's gunpowder stocks and take some kegs of the explosive back to the *chiro* for Ichiro's use. Six were to poison the water barrels and to set fire to the supply tents. The others were to hobble horses, strangle guards and spread general confusion. while Ichiro, Shizuka and Tamika would try to take the mirror and jewel from Taira's own tents.

None of it would be easy, Ichiro knew. He gripped the hilt of his short sword. It failed to reassure him as Kusinagi did, but he had left the *tachi* with Matsuo so if he died here, the sword would not immediately fall into Taira's grasp.

Shizuka reached out and squeezed his forearm. The unexpected gesture was one of both reassurance and affection. "General, it is time."

They slipped down the hillside with little more noise than wind-blown leaves on a stone path. Ahead, they heard the boisterous laughter of soldiers drinking, soldiers whoring with camp followers, soldiers forgetting the pain of defeat by losing themselves in general debauchery. Untended campfires burned to embers before the *ashigaru's* tents. Occasionally, a trooper stumbled from a tent to piss or shit or vomit, but always he returned to the celebrations. Those men left to guard the camp showed little interest in their work. They too wished to guzzle *sake* with their compatriots and to pump themselves into a whore's willing body.

Taira's army appeared to be collapsing of its own weight, plunging toward chaos and destruction. The *ronin*, those bandits and thugs on whom the *daimyo* relied, would fight only for the promise of coins and pillage. Discipline clearly sat ill with them. Yet, moved by the *daimyo's* magic, they could prove a formidable force, Ichiro knew. If animal instincts drove them individually, they moved with malevolent purpose as a whole, an earth-scorching and merciless juggernaut.

Ichiro knew they were a microcosm of a world under Taira's rule. The forces of chaos--of wanton, indiscriminate annihilation--would level everything in their path until nothing remained. Then they would turn upon themselves and destroy even that vestige of humanity. *Can I stop this?* he thought. *Can they be defeated? Or am I foolish to even consider it?*

Ichiro knew the answer. He signaled the *ninja* to advance.

The first sentry never knew what killed him. The blowgun dart caught him full in the throat, and he collapsed like a paper lantern.

The second guard tried to scream as the knife entered his spine, but a forearm across his mouth muffled the cry. The warning shout gurgled to the guard's lips. Blood dribbled down his chin.

The sentries now disposed of, the *ninja* slipped through the opening in the perimeter and entered the enemy camp. Dark as the night itself, they moved unseen, unheard.

Ichiro, Tamika and Shizuka slipped toward a large tent near the camp's center. The tent, obviously Taira's, stood out from the soldiers' dwellings. It sat on a raised wooden platform. Carefully potted *bonsai* trees surrounded the tent. Lanterns were carefully placed at even distances around the platform's edges. It was an odd island of stability amidst the chaos. The old gods still demanded order and still required ritual obedience, even when they fought to destroy it. Taira was their obedient priest.

Guards with *naginata* held tightly in both hands stood unmoving at the four corners. Their faces were hidden behind fierce *so-men*.

Ichiro somehow knew instinctively that these sentries were inhuman. Whether they were alive or dead was another matter, and not one he was inclined to find out.

"What do we do?" Shizuka whispered.

"I don't know," Ichiro said. He had no answer. "It is time like this that I wish I were drunk like everyone else." Then it occurred to him. "Speaking of getting drunk, why don't we get some *sake*."

"Are you mad?" Shizuka said through clenched teeth.

"No, I don't think he is," whispered Tamika, "not if I understand what he's planning."

"All right, general, so you're not mad? So what do we do?" Shizuka asked.

"As I said, first we get ourselves some *sake* from a cooperative soldier who needs some drinking companions."

They found their man a short distance away. He staggered along and under one arm he carried a large jug of *sake*, from which he took frequent swigs. Between swallows, he sang, at the top of voice, a song extolling the virtues of Osaka women. Ichiro instantly recognized the man as the same soldier they had heard singing in Kyoto. Neither time nor liquor had improved his voice.

Ichiro waited until the man took a swallow and then decked him with a blow from a short *bo*. As the man fell, Ichiro caught the *sake* jar and handed it to Shizuka. He took up the soldier's song, taking great pains to match the off-key notes and erratic rhythms.

"You sound awful," Shizuka said.

"Would you rather I sing on key?" he replied, pulling on the man's jacket and helmet and mumbling a few incoherent lines. "Then everyone would be suspicious."

"Have it your way," she said.

Singing at the top of his lungs, Ichiro staggered toward the guards. He punctuated each verse by pretending to guzzle the *sake*, although he let only a few drops past his lips. It was a particularly bad variety of rice wine, but Ichiro suspected the soldier had been so drunk so as not to care. Each verse and swallow brought him closer to the guards. He watched them carefully, but his antics failed to produce a reaction from them. They remained as rigid as statues.

He sighed and staggered toward one guard. "Friend," he said and threw an arm around the sentry's shoulder. "Has our beloved lord kept you from enjoying yourself tonight? Come, come, friend, we'll all die soon anyway, so let's celebrate! I have plenty of *sake*." He thrust the jar under the guard's nose.

"You are drunk," the guard said in a voice that whirred and whistled like clockwork.

"So I am drunk, so should we all be, with so many of our friends dead."

"I do not drink," the guard said. "You must leave. Lord Taira wishes not to be disturbed."

"Does he now?" Ichiro said. "I should think so, probably embarrassed by how he wastes his men against that pitiful fort. I think I should talk to him about it." He stepped toward the wooden steps that led up to the tent.

The guard brought the point of the *naginata* against Ichiro's chest. "Go away. Lord Taira is not to be disturbed."

Ichiro pushed the spear away. "I'll have you know Lord Taira thinks very highly of me." He saw a second sentry moving toward him, spear at the ready. The guard moved with a slight jerking motion, like a poorly manipulated *bunraku* puppet.

"What is the problem?" the second guard asked, his speech as stilted as the first's.

"This man is drunk. He wishes to see the *daimyo*," the first guard replied.

"It is my right," Ichiro said. "Otherwise he'll kill us all." He swung his arms in a grand gesture, as though bringing the *sake* jar to his lips. Instead, it crashed heavily into the first guard's head. The jar shattered, spraying everything with liquor and ceramic shards.

As he finished the blow, Ichiro rolled to the ground, ducking under the *naginata* of the first guard as it tried to impale him. But the spear instead penetrated the chest of the second guard.

"I am hurt," the second guard announced flatly. Metal ground on metal as something in the sentry's chest groaned and snapped.

The first guard's *naginata* shaft caught in something and wrenched upward. The spear dislocated that sentry's arm, which dropped useless to the *sake*-drenched creature's side.

The *sake* apparently also caused some damage as sparks suddenly flashed under the first guard's armor and smoke curled from his neck. The first guard, now totally immobile, still clutched the *naginata* with its other arm and was pulled over as the second sentry finally collapsed. Something black and shiny, like oil, poured from the second guard's wound.

"Hurry," Ichiro said. Shizuka and Tamika followed him up the steps to the *daimyo's* tent. They slid past a few paper screens and then entered the main area, where they froze in their tracks.

Sitting quietly sipping a cup of tea was Taira. Beside him was the chest containing the sacred mirror and the sacred jewel. Two guards from his *go-umawarishu* stood next to him. Other members of the *daimyo's* personal guard quickly moved to block the escape routes.

"Good evening, General," Taira said. "I've been expecting you. I do hope you'll stay for tea." The *daimyo* laughed as he raised his cup to his lips.

CHAPTER TWENTY

In the torchlight, Taira appeared more drawn and cadaverous than before. Ichiro knew the *daimyo's* magic had become less overwhelming than when Taira had created the forest outside Jimmukei Monastery. Ichiro wondered if Taira now had to use most of his magic just to keep his army in line, or perhaps to hold back whatever forces of disorder gave Taira his power. Whatever it was, it seemed to slowly drain energy from the *daimyo*.

Ichiro had seen something like that in the leaders of his own world. The more power they sought, the more power controlled and, ultimately, consumed them. Taira was no different.

For a moment, Ichiro pitied the *daimyo*. It was *hoganbiki*, sympathy for the victim. And Taira was truly a victim of his own intrigues.

"I have expected you would try to assassinate me," Taira said.

Assassination? Ichiro was startled. The thought had never crossed his mind. *So Taira is now irrationally fearful as well,* Ichiro thought.

"I especially thought you would try to kill me, Tamika," the *daimyo* said. "I knew one day, you would break my spell and want me dead. But I did not think you would handle revenge so clumsily, although you did slip by my sentries more easily than I anticipated."

"The guards. They are not human, are they?" Ichiro asked.

"They are not even living creatures," Taira said, smiling slightly. He placed his cup on his tray, and a servant refilled it. "Actually, they are quite elaborate machines powered by small *mononoke*. I had a *banruku* master in Osaka build thirty of them for me. After he was finished, I had his throat cut so he could not build more for other warlords."

The *daimyo* frowned. "In retrospect, a regrettable error on my part. Now ,I cannot replace or repair any that are damaged or destroyed, such as the two you so cleverly eliminated."

"So you thought a machine might do what your undead warriors, women, and demons failed to accomplish," Ichiro said.

Taira sighed and raised his teacup and sipped. "Ah, good tea," he said. "Well, I confess the thought occurred to me, but although the machines are quite strong, they are slow, and not especially quick-witted. Still, they amuse me, and they have their uses." He set the cup down and clapped his hands once.

Two guards moved forward and grabbed Shizuka and Tamika. The women struggled against the machines' vise-lip grips, but to no avail. When Ichiro drew his sword to free them, two guards moved to block him.

"I would try nothing rash, general. My machines can easily rip the arms from those pretty women," Taira said.

As if to demonstrate, the two machines began to straighten out each woman's left arm until it could stretch no further. Ichiro watched help-lessly. He could see perspiration break out on Tamika's forehead, but Shizuka remained calm.

Then Tamika screamed.

Ichiro heard the sound of bone cracking. "Enough!" he shouted and turned to Taira. "What do you want of me?"

"You know as well as I."

Of course, Ichiro thought, *there could be nothing else.* "Kusinagi is safe, where you will never find it."

"Ah, such a shame," Taira said. He placed his teacup down on a lacquered tray and toyed with a sweet rice cake. "You are a harder nut to crack than I thought, general. I'll give you that, but I know you have only two hundred men, at most, left in your *chiro*. I have five thousand, and could easily produce five thousand more. The *shogun* is already fleeing north to Matsumae, so my spies tell me. He knows he cannot resist me. Yet you still do. Why?"

"Because someone must, and I have no choice," Ichiro replied.

Taira smiled. "But you do have a choice. You may live as my general, or die as a fool. So why not give me your sword. I need a warrior of your skill, and you will find what I offer you pleasing, as Tamika once did."

He turned toward her. "Before she saw fit to betray me like a disobedient *akita,* a bitch fit to be whipped."

Tamika spat at Taira, but the guard again stretched her injured arm. She cried out in pain.

Ichiro felt her pain stab him through and through.

"You can avoid her fate, General, just by surrendering. Imagine, Minamoto-no-Ichiro, together we could conquer Korea, China, India! There is no end to it!"

Ichiro sighed. "All right, Taira, I'll give you my sword!"

"Traitor! Bastard!" Tamika yelled, but the guard covered her mouth with a huge metal hand.

"Good, good. I'm glad you finally see my point of view," Taira said.

But as the *daimyo* rose, Ichiro reached into his jacket and unleashed his *kusarigama*. The weapon's cord, weighted by an iron ball, wrapped itself tightly around Taira's neck, and Ichiro jerked it back.

The rope around his throat brought the choking Taira to his feet. The *daimyo's* fingers clutched at the cord in a vain effort to loosen it, but Ichiro drew Taira in like a fisherman with a large catch. He grabbed the *daimyo* around the throat and placed the tip of his *katana* in the small of Taira's back.

"Yes, Lord Taira. I'll give you my sword, in your spine, if you don't release the women."

The guards moved to rescue their master. Ichiro took a step back and pressed the sword tip in deeper. "Stop them or I'll cut your spine now," he hissed. "A simple act of just slipping my blade in. I can cripple you first that way, paralyzing you. But you would still feel the pain before I killed you."

The guards moved closer.

"Stop, stop," Taira said, each word half-choked in his throat.

The mechanical sentries stopped.

"Tell them to release the women."

Taira hesitated. Ichiro dug the sword in further.

"Please, you are cutting skin!"

"Tell them."

"Release the women," the *daimyo* said.

The guards obeyed instantly. Both Shizuka and Tamika collapsed to the floor, Tamika crying out as she landed on her injured arm.

"For a moment, I almost agreed with Tamika and thought you'd sold us out," Shizuka said to Ichiro. She stared up at the guard. "You stretched my patience to the limit," she said, rubbing her sore shoulder. She had lost none of her wit.

"I was not going to let them disarm you," Ichiro punned. He was pleased for once that he could top her clever tongue, but, granting their situation, also afraid it might be the last time. "Tamika? How are you?"

Shizuka helped Tamika to her feet and they came to Ichiro's side. Tamika still clutched her arm to her chest, and her breath came in great sobs. "It's not broken, but the pain is unbearable if I move it."

"Now what, *samurai*?" Shizuka said.

Ichiro nodded toward the box. "The mirror and the jewel. Get them."

The *ninja* leaped nimbly between the two automatons. Paralyzed by the threat to their master, they did nothing to stop her. Shizuka opened the chest, tucked the two relics into her jacket and came to Ichiro's side.

"Good," he said. "Now we can leave. Back out very slowly."

"You're a damn fool, Minamoto," Taira said. His face was red from trying to breath against the cord. "You'll never escape my camp. I have things stronger even than my little puppets."

"No matter, Taira, even they won't harm you. You are our passport from the camp. Your life for our lives. A fair exchange, I think." Ichiro pulled the cord tighter around Taira's neck. "Now, let us be off!"

Just then the camp's gunpowder supply exploded.

CHAPTER TWENTY-ONE

The blast battered the tent. The walls flapped, ripped apart and burst into flame. The mechanical guards tottered and fell. Some lay on their backs like turtles, flailing their useless limbs.

Ichiro gasped for breath and tasted the bitter flavor of gunpowder and cordite. His head pounded with the rhythm of his heartbeat. His eyes burned from the smoke. He struggled to his feet.

All around him was chaos.

Taira lay unconscious nearby. Blood trickled from the corner of the *daimyo's* temple and from his ears. Taira had probably hit his head as we fell, Ichiro realized.

Ichiro touched his own temple and felt a small cut, the blood warm and moist. *Taira's body must have shielded me from the blast,* he thought.

Someone groaned nearby. Ichiro turned to see Shizuka sit up, shake her head, and spit out a mouthful of blood. "You and your damned explosions, general. I hope O-Emma-Sama blows you up when he has you at the gates of Hell." She spat again.

"Where's Tamika?" he said.

"How the hell should I know?" Shizuka said.

"I'm here," Tamika said feebly.

She was propped up against the inert body of a sentry. A long, blackened, wooden splinter protruded from her left leg. The trousers around it were torn and shredded. A thin trickle of blood oozed down her pale flesh as she tried to pull the splinter free.

Without thinking, Ichiro went to her, grabbed the splinter, and pulled it loose.

Tamika screamed and fainted. Blood pulsed from the wounded and spattered across the floor. Too late, Ichiro realized the splinter had nicked an artery.

"What a fool I am," he said. He quickly tore a length of cloth from his leggings and tied it just below Tamika's knee. He carefully tightened the tourniquet using the same splinter that wounded her.

Ichiro looked around for something for a bandage. *Taira's jacket, that would do,* he thought. "Shizuka, rip the sleeve from the *daimyo's* jacket."

"What?" she said, crawling toward him. Then she saw the wound. "Damn you, *samurai,* you may have doomed us. She'll surely loose the leg at least!"

"Just do as I ask and get me the cloth," he snapped. "I need to make a bandage."

Shizuka stared at him a moment, and for the first time he saw pain in her eyes. Then she shrugged and scuttled crab-like to Taira's side. The *daimyo* groaned as she cut away the cloth. "Probably the kindest thing he'll ever do, give his clothes to a poor injured woman. Too bad he's not awake to appreciate it."

"Hurry up!" Ichiro hissed.

Shizuka sliced away the sleeve with her *katana.* ""It's a shame just to cut his clothes. Why not let me cut his throat while we're at it?"

"Now is not the time," he said. "Taira alive will serve us well for the moment. If he dies, all could be lost."

She handed him the cloth. "What do you mean, all could be lost if he dies?"

"I'll tell you later." Ichiro carefully folded the silk and pressed it against Tamika's wound. He tore a strip of cloth from her legging and used it to bind the makeshift bandage. Tamika groaned as he tightened it and the tourniquet, but the flow of blooded abated.

"Help me get her to her feet," he said.

The two struggled to raise Tamika upright. She was almost all dead weight, but at last they had standing between them.

"Now where?" Shizuka said.

"To the *chiro*," Ichiro replied. "Or to our deaths."

Confusion reigned in the enemy camp, and that suited Ichiro well. The three blended in well in the chaos.

Taira's soldiers dragged companions from the wreckage of collapsed and burning tents, from under mountains of supplies and from beneath dead horses. Other men wandered around dazed and confused.

Although Tamika was unconscious and quite heavy, Ichiro and Shizuka managed to carry her some distance before they ran into the guard.

"Hey, where are you going?" he shouted. The man was nervous and menacing. He waved a plum-leaf blade spear in front of him, but always keeping it aimed at Ichiro's heart.

"Our friend is hurt. We're trying to find help."

In the light from the fire Ichiro could see the man furrow his brow. "Help, huh? Then why are you going toward the enemy camp?"

"The enemy camp? We didn't know that," Ichiro lied. "The explosion knocked us unconscious, and we must have been turned around."

The man seemed to relax a moment. "Well, perhaps so." Then he noticed their clothes. "*Ninja!*" he shouted. "There are *ninja* in the --"

The guard never saw Shizuka reach into her jacket, pull out a *shuriken* and send its razor sharp edge into his throat. Before the man could pull the blade out, Shizuka drew her *katana* from its scabbard. The guard's head tumbled to the ground, the shuriken still embedded in his throat..

Shizuka wiped the blade of her *katana* on her leggings. "Let's go."

"Just how many weapons do you have?" asked Ichiro, astonished.

"More than enough," she replied coolly. "In this world, a woman would be foolish to go about unarmed."

He could not deny that.

"Shall we go?" she said.

———

Once across the Ishikawa River, they were free from Taira's men, but Nature herself was not their ally. River water swirled about their legs, grabbed their ankles, and tried to pull them under. Ichiro nearly stumbled once, but caught himself and pressed on. Reaching the other side, they fell to the ground, gasping like beached fish. Each breath they took stabbed their chests.

"We'll go up into the trees," Ichiro said. "It will make it harder for them to follow us."

By now Tamika had regained consciousness, but with only one good leg and an injured arm, she could not move well. Adding to their problems were the brambles that tore them, the rocks that refused to bear their weight, and the stars, which gradually hid themselves behind storm clouds and denied them what meager light was left.

Then the rain came. A few hard droplets pelted them at first, but soon drenching sheets beat them without mercy. Each drop struck them like a *kendo* master's bamboo sword might strike an inattentive student.

It was almost a miracle when the *chiro*'s gates, looming unreal against the sky, at last appeared through the downpour. Ichiro pounded on the gate with the last ounce of his strength.

"Who goes there?" a familiar voice asked. It was Date Matsuo.

"It's General Minamoto," Ichiro shouted. The effort made him dizzy. He had so little energy left.

"General...oh my god! " Matsuo said. "Open the gates, open the gates. It's General Minamoto!"

It seemed like an eternity before the gates opened and they staggered inside. Hands sprang from the darkness to catch them before they fell. Ichiro looked up and saw the smiling face of Matsuo.

"General, we thought you were dead. We saw the explosion and the fires," he said.

"You give up too easily," Ichiro said hoarsely. He took a step, his legs buckled and several hands reached out to steady him.

"Tamika's leg," he said. "The wound is severe."

"She will be taken care of," Matsuo said.

"Good," Ichiro said. Then he passed out.

———

Yukio pressed a bowl of tea into Ichiro's hands, and he swallowed it in one gulp, not caring that it was hot enough to scald his throat. The tea revived Ichiro immediately, restoring warmth to aching body.

Nearby, Tamika lay on a stack of futons, their cloth stained with urine, dried blood and pus. Her wounded leg was raised slightly and seemed the color of dead fish, a translucent white. Only a black patch of caked, dried blood on a new bandage and a thin line of red running down her calf indicated the leg was still alive.

Her face was pale, resembling porcelain by torchlight. She labored at each breath, barely sucking air through bluish lips. Occasionally, her eyelids fluttered, and she uttered a low moan.

"The wound is severe, and she has lost much blood," said a *samurai* who had been trained as a physician. He was plump, balding and had a stringy moustache that drooped from the corner of his upper lip.

Yukio sat next to the *samurai*. He was pressing cold cloths to Tamika's feverish forehead.

"Has the bleeding stopped?" Ichiro asked.

"Yes, just barely. But even a simple movement could reopen it. You are fortunate she didn't die on the journey back to the castle."

"That may have been Hachiman's work," Ichiro said.

"Perhaps," the doctor said.

"Can you treat the wound?" he asked.

The *samurai* shook his head. "No, the wound is too deep. We can only hope the bleeding has stopped and the injury does not become infected. But if it does, I would have to amputate her leg. I fear she would die from the operation itself."

"Couldn't you cauterize the wound?" Shizuka asked.

The doctor gave her an irritated look. "The injury is to an artery. I could seal the outer wound. But the inner wound could still reopen, and she would bleed to death internally."

Ichiro accepted a second bowl of tea and sipped it carefully. Cauterization reminded him of the time he had burned a hole in Lord Akiyama's bamboo screen to demonstrate Kusinagi's power.

He sat bolt upright as the thought hit him. *Kusinagi! Of course! Dangerous it might be, but it was the only alternative.* Ichiro got to his feet.

"Where are you going?" Shizuka inquired.

"I have a plan. I am going to get Kusinagi."

"What? Are you planning to cut off her leg?" Shizuka asked, her voice a little shocked.

"By no means," he replied. He went to his tent, found the sword where Matsuo had hidden it, and returned. Once back in Tamika's tent, Ichiro unsheathed Kusinagi, tossing the scabbard onto an abandoned *futon.*

Ichiro carefully cut away the dressing and exposed the wound. Thick red blood pulsed to the surface of the perfectly round, dull gray hole. Carefully, he placed the tip of Kusinagi against the wound and pushed slightly.

The sword blade slid in easily. Tamika's skin folded back and rolled away from the sword until the injured artery was exposed. Even in the flickering yellow torchlight he could see the wound--a small, ragged nick. It spewed blood with each beat of Tamika's heart. Death moved slowly here, but each trickle of blood meant an ocean of pain.

Ichiro gritted his teeth and forced Kusinagi against the artery.

"Stop! What are you doing?" the physician cried, reaching for Ichiro's arm.

Ichiro stopped the man him dead with a cold stare. "Leave me alone. This may be the only way to save her."

The man moved back, cowed.

Ichiro eased the sword tip against the artery. It touched the blood vessel, and an odor of burning flesh filled the room. But the nick was sealed, and no more blood leaked out. As he carefully withdrew the sword, he could see new, pink flesh folding itself back into place. Kusinagi came from free of the wound, and the lips of dead gray skin closed against each other, to be replaced by pink scar tissue.

The leg seemed instantly better. As the blood pulsed through the repaired artery, the tissue regained its color and health.

The physician, his eyes wide in amazement, examined the wound. "A miracle! Healed on both sides! I would not have believed it had I not seen it!"

Ichiro suddenly felt dizzy. He eased himself to the floor. Kusinagi weighed heavy in his hand. His breath came in short gulps. Ichiro realized Kusinagi had drawn energy from him, had focused his thoughts and strength to cauterize the wound.

Suddenly he understood why Taira needed the sword. It was not just because Kusinagi carried significance as part of the imperial regalia. It was because, with it, the *daimyo* could focus all his powers, perhaps even control the door to the other worlds for as long as he desired.

The thought chilled Ichiro. He had to get Kusinagi away from here and from Taira as soon as possible. The temptation to toss the sword back to the sea crossed his mind, but he knew Taira would find it there. And Hachiman had given him the sword for a greater purpose.

He searched for a plan, and one slowly came to him. While the physician babbled and others came to see the miracle, Ichiro slipped passed them and into the muddy courtyard. Dawn still waited beyond the horizon, but the storm had broken, and a few stars glistened feebly in the sky.

His body was tired, but his mind was troubled. He need time to think, to develop his plans. Climbing to the parapets, he stared out across the starlit valley and out toward the river and the distant horizon.

"Aren't you tired?" Shizuka said, sliding up next him. "I saw you wandering this way and I followed. I was concerned," she said, answering his unasked question.

"I can't sleep," he said.

"Thinking and plotting again, no doubt. You think too much, general."

"Someone must."

"Damn you, Minamoto," she said softly. "Your plans will kill you before they're finished."

He laughed. "You forget I can't be killed by a mortal man. Now, you, on the other hand, could be in serious trouble if my plans fail."

"That's precisely what I'm afraid of," she said with a smile. She stared over the valley and tears came to her eyes.

He reached out to touch her, to stroke her hair. But she was distant and sad.

"Only two other *ninja* returned," she said. "Six were captured, the rest were killed."

"They are as good as dead," Ichiro said.

She nodded. "Taira will be quite creative, I'm sure. Boiling in oil, I wonder. Or perhaps flaying them alive?"

———

The answer came with the dawn. The mist lifted to reveal six crucifixes on the far bank of the Ishikawa. The crosses stood stark and lonely on the riverbank.

Through the spyglass, Ichiro could clearly see the dead *ninja*. Each had had his wrists and feet nailed to the crosses. Their bodies flopped forward, lifeless, held up only by short lengths of cord tied to the arms of the crucifixes. Arrows, the quills of porcupine, bristled from the *ninja*'s chests.

Repulsed, Ichiro turned his gaze away. "So, Taira, Van der Lieuw taught you another new trick while he was here." Ichiro whispered a prayer to the Amida Buddha for the dead *ninja* and hoped they would be reborn in the Pure Land, far away from cruel *daimyo* and from Dutchmen like Van der Lieuw, and from all sailors and saviors.

"The pit is ready. We just put the last of the charcoal in," said Matsuo as he came up the ladder to the parapet.

"How are the men?"

"Half have already slipped away and are heading toward Matsumae."

"Good. We'll wait until nightfall, then send out the rest. Ten men will stay with me."

"Good, I will find nine volunteers."

Ichiro frowned. "Nine? I said ten."

"Surely I will stay with you?" Matsuo said.

Ichiro shook his head. "No, I want you to lead the first group. You will go with Shizuka and Tamika to protect the Emperor Saigo and the royal regalia."

"General, I demand to fight by your side," Matsuo protested.

"No," Ichiro said softly, but firmly. "You are too valuable. The men trust you and will follow you. Lead them to Matsushita. I will you join you later.

Matsuo was crestfallen. He brushed back a tear, sighed, and then nodded sadly. "Very well. May you have good fortune, General. If you don't, we are all lost."

Ichiro smiled. "As long as Hachiman sees fit to need me, I will survive. And as long as Taira needs Kusinagi, I will survive. I promise you that."

"That I'm glad to hear," Matsuo said.

"Have the men set the mines yet?" Ichiro asked.

"Yes, all along the road and at the tree line. The mortars are also set."

"Good, then the men can prepare the walls. Tell Dojo Yomiyoshi and Noshida they will stay. I expect one more attack from Taira, probably tomorrow morning. He will wait until we're thirsty before he moves. I will delay him long enough so you and the others can escape."

"It shall be done," Matsuo said, bravely hiding his disappointment.

Ichiro felt tears of shame well in his eyes. He did not deserve such loyalty and friendship.

————

The day seemed to stretch endlessly from morning till afternoon and, as Ichiro expected, Taira did nothing. The *daimyo* was waiting, preparing his men.

Meanwhile, Taira's precautions allowed Ichiro time to prepare his escape. The soldiers who were preparing to leave filled jars with what water was left, but there would be plenty for the defenders who would remain. Many of Ichiro's fitted themselves with armor and the banners of the enemy. Others prepared the fort for the final assault Taira was bound to launch.

Before sunset Ichiro talked with Tamika as she prepared her saddlebags for the journey. ""How is the leg?" he asked.

"It hurts, but I'm glad of it," she said stoically. "The pain means I will not lose it." Two *ashigaru* helped her onto her horse, but she seemed unsteady in the saddle.

"I have something I wish you to guard," he said. He undid Kusinagi and its scabbard from his sash and held it out for her.

Tamika said nothing, but her eyes glowed with amazement. She reached out for the sword, but held back, wavering in her saddle. "I cannot," she said.

"You are the only one whom I can trust with Kusinagi," he said. "The sword knows your hand. It will be safe with you. So will the mirror and jewel."

"And we'll guard her well," said Shizuka, reigning her dapple gray up beside Tamika. Yukio, on small brown mare, followed behind Shizuka, carrying a small bundle containing the rest of the regalia.

"And if Taira finds us, the mirror and the jewel will join the sword at the bottom of the sea. Along with the *daimyo's* head. I promise that," Shizuka said.

Ichiro smiled. "Arrogance I've come to expect, Shizuka, but such a boast is new."

She scowled. "It is a promise, not a boast."

"See that you fulfill it then, if the occasion arises."

The scowl became a smile. "You have my guarantee, *samurai*."

"And see to it that you take care of yourself. My other sword now and then requires a sheath. I don't wish to lose that, either."

Uncharacteristically, Shizuka blushed.

"What's the matter, does the cat have your tongue?" Ichiro joked.

She narrowed her eyes, but her cheeks were still red. "I promise not to lose the scabbard, if you promise not to lose the sword."

Ichiro laughed so hard his stomach hurt. "I promise I will die before I relinquish my hold on that weapon."

The exchange baffled the young monk. ""I don't understand. I thought Tamika had Ichiro's sword. So why does Shizuka have the scabbard?" Yukio asked.

"It's not important, Yukio," Tamika said gently. "You will have you answer soon enough. Now it's time to pray for us all and hope our karma will keep us alive."

"But I still don't understand," Yukio protested.

"Permit me," said Matsuo, bring his horse up to Yukio's right side. He leaned across his saddle and whispered into the monk's ear.

Yukio listened, then his jaw dropped open, and he too turned red. "I see," he said. "I see."

"I trust you do," Matsuo said, laughing.

"Enough laughter. You'd best be off," Ichiro said.

The guards opened the gate to the darkening sky and, with Shizuka leading the way, the four rode out. As he passed through the gate, Matsuo turned his horse about and shouted, "See you in Matsumae. My cook will have some special *sushi* and *udon* noodles for you."

"See that he does," Ichiro replied. But he wondered if this was an appointment he would fulfill. He climbed to the parapet and watched them disappear into the fading red light of evening. He felt more alone than he could remember.

All around the parapet stood mannequins in suits of armor. They stared fixedly toward Taira's camp as Ichiro did. Their nearly human form sent a chill up his spine, and he sensed a void, all around him.

He felt it within and without him. It went beyond *in* and *yo*, beyond chaos and order, and it filled him with doubt. *Is this mu, what the Buddhists mean by emptiness?* he thought.

Had he done right? he wondered. Or was his resistance to Taira a futile act? Was it so terrible to let chaos win? Was it worse than the horrors men could inflict? Then, instinctively, his hand dropped to his sword hilt. Although it was not Kusinagi, it comforted him.

Ichiro knew that Taira was the only force holding back the chaos. The *daimyo* had opened the portal to the other worlds and needed its powers for his own purposes. But only he could close the door and keep chaos in check.

Ichiro realized that was why Taira held back from too many reckless attacks. It was why he needed the mirror, sword and jewel. Their powers would balance that of the chaos. Together they would hold back the flood.

But once opened, could the gate be closed? Perhaps not. As each day passed, Taira grew weaker and the opening must grow more and more.

But for how long? Ichiro thought. Taira was only human, only mortal. There would eventually come a day when the *daimyo's* strength would fail. Chaos would first overwhelm Taira and then all Japan. Disorder would pour forth like a *tsunami* to destroy everything in its path until all the universes were destroyed.

Pity for his enemy filled Ichiro. It was almost tempting to give the *daimyo* the three relics in order to stem the tide. But Ichiro knew power seduced Taira, and the mirror, sword and jewel would only corrupt him further. And it would not hold back the chaos forever.

But do I know how to use the relics properly? Ichiro thought. There had to be an answer, or Hachiman would not have chosen him for this task. If there was no answer then everything *was* futile. For perhaps once the door was opened or the deed performed, there was no way to whistle it back like an obedient dog.

A chill once again crept up his spine. "Hachiman, is there an answer?"

A lightning bolt arched across the sky and thunder, like deep laughter, rolled from the hilltops.

"Everything is set," said Noshida calling up from the foot of the ladder.

The words brought Ichiro back to reality. "Good," he said. "And what about the cannon?"

"It's loaded with all the gunpowder the *ninja* could steal," Nishoda said, climbing the ladder and coming to Ichiro's side. "Mind you, it's not much of a weapon, and I doubt the barrel will hold, but it should do some damage before it blows itself apart."

"What about the charges?"

"There's enough to start a few fires, and we've got plenty of charcoal to get things going."

"Do you have enough to keep the bodies burning in the pit?"

"Yes, and none too soon. They're starting to produce one awful stench."

"We won't have to endure that much longer," Ichiro said. "Have you selected who will stay behind to inform Taira of our demise?"

"Akutigawa volunteered. He's young, strong and can tell a pretty convincing story. He'll have no problems."

"Good," Ichiro said. He hoped the young *samurai* would take himself. Otherwise, there was no point to Ichiro's plans.

"Do you think Taira will attack soon?" Noshida asked.

"Soon enough, soon enough," Ichiro said. *After all*, Ichiro thought, *Taira has no choice.*

———

The attackers moved relentlessly, and mechanically, forward with the sun's first rays. They moved as if they had learned nothing from the repeated retreats, as if it had not driven even a modicum of fear into their brains. But then this army was mindless, fearless and unthinking because it was inhuman.

Ichiro had suspected Taira had lied about how many robots he possessed. But the number marching toward him impressed Ichiro. At least two hundred of the machines, each driven by its own demon, moved in rigid lock step, their spears held out like the spines of a huge porcupine.

They appeared to be a suicide force intended to batter itself against the *chiro*. They would take the full force of arrow, spear and musket ball, and still surge forward, virtually unstoppable. Taira's human forces would roll in behind them, ready to mop up the last resistance.

Why Taira had left these permanently obedient and brave soldiers in reserve puzzled Ichiro. Perhaps the *daimyo* underestimated the strength and resolve of the *chiro's* defenders. Perhaps it was simply more convenient to waste men in battle until the robots would be more effective against a weakened enemy. Or perhaps Taira was overly cautious and unwilling to waste expensive and irreplaceable weapons until victory was certain.

But now the *daimyo* probably thought victory was still uncertain, and he was desperate. If Taira knew his forces would face only eleven men, he would no doubt have changed his strategy. But now it was too late.

"Are they close enough?" Noshida asked.

"Not yet," Ichiro said. "A little closer and we can destroy more of them at one time."

The machines marched on, spear points held aloft and gleaming in the buttery morning sun.

"Let's hope your men used that gunpowder well," Ichiro said. "Fire!"

Noshida unfurled a red flag and held it over his head.

At the signal, flames erupted from the hillside. Burning logs crashed into the enemy ranks. The fiery timbers smashed some machines. Other machines, pinned beneath the burning wood, tried futilely to extricate themselves.

But no screams, no cries of help came from the wounded soldiers. Instead, their comrades rapidly closed ranks and continued on in eerie silence toward their objective.

"Not good," Noshida whispered. " There's still far too many of them."

"Don't worry. We have plenty of tricks left," Ichiro replied. "They're within range. Now."

Noshida signaled a man in the courtyard. The soldier pulled a short lanyard. The ground beneath the machines erupted as dozens of mines detonated. The explosions shattered the puppets' ranks, tore limbs from machines and sent pieces of metal flying.

"Much better," Noshida said.

But again the enemy regrouped. Now only thirty remained, but even that reduced number would still overwhelm the few men Ichiro had left. He had only one final line of defense and he had to use it. "Open the gates," he ordered.

Two men pushed open the huge gatefolds, exposing the cannon's maw to the enemy. A third man lit the fuse and then the three darted for safety. The fuse sputtered and spat as it sped toward the gunpowder, but there was no guarantee the cannon, cut from stone, with its barrel hollowed out, would hold under the force of the blast. Already, it seemed to Ichiro that the hemp cords wrapped around the barrel were straining and threatening to break.

Ichiro and Noshida ducked behind the sand-filled bodies of two mannequins. The mannequins offered little protection if the cannon exploded, but Ichiro knew that, if the weapon failed, they were all dead men anyway. *Hachiman, if you ever intend to intervene, now is the time to do it,* Ichiro thought.

The enemy reached the gate. The cannon roared. It spat out a long tongue of red flame. Bits of rock and scrap iron leaped from the barrel. The projectiles mowed down the machines like a scythe slicing stalks of ripe millet.

The roar echoed in Ichiro's ears. Blood pounded in his head. The gray smoke stung his nostrils and burned his throat so badly he found himself nearly choking.

But through the dense haze he saw the cannon had completely decimated Taira's robots. Pieces of shattered machines lay scattered at the gate and beyond. Some machines, torn in half or having only a limb or two left, twitched briefly, and then were still.

A single robot, bereft of head and right arm, remained standing. Its left leg was caught in the wreckage of its compatriots, and it marched relentlessly in a circle. Unable to free itself, it still tried to finish its mission.

"What a stink," Noshida said. "I almost think I prefer the dead bodies."

Noshida was right, Ichiro realized. The stench was horrible. It probably originated from the *mononoke* that powered the robots, but there was no time to speculate now.

"We must be going. Time to give Lord Taira our regards," he said.

Noshida whistled shrilly. A single soldier, obviously Akutigawa, raced across the courtyard with a burning torch in hand. When Akutigawa reached the pit, filled with the decaying remains of friend and foe alike, he placed the torch against the wood, charcoal, and paper surrounding the bodies.

Two other men with torches joined him, setting other parts of the pit aflame. The fire spread quickly, and soon acrid and oily black smoke curled toward the sky. An odor of charred flesh merged with that of smoke and gunpowder and filled the courtyard.

Akutigawa turned toward Ichiro and shouted, "Farewell, general. We'll see you in Matsumae!" Then he sprinted away to set off the remaining charges placed around the *chiro*.

Ichiro and Noshida descended the ladder to the courtyard where a man waited with horses. A second man opened the smaller gate at the rear of the stockade.

"Scatter like rice grains in the wind," Ichiro ordered as he mounted his horse. "We'll meet again in Matsumae!" He dug his heels into the horse's flanks and rode through the gate. He did not look back even when a series of explosions indicated that the charges had done what Taira could not and had reduced the fortress to rubble.

CHAPTER TWENTY-TWO

Ichiro drove the horse hard until it pulled up lame about two hours after they left the castle. He dismounted and patted the animal's lathered sides to calm it. When he thought it seemed less agitated, he checked the horse's left foreleg.

He cursed what he found. The horse had thrown a shoe and cracked a hoof. It would not carry a rider for some time to come.

Seeing he had no alternative, Ichiro tethered the horse to a pine tree where he hoped a farmer would find it. He removed the saddle and buried it under a rotting tree trunk. If he was lucky, Taira's men would never locate it. Then he tossed his saddlebag, which contained the last of his provisions, over his right shoulder and walked north toward Matsumae.

By midday, the sky had darkened rapidly. A scent of rain permeated the air. The odor suggested something more than a simple storm. Ichiro suspected a typhoon was rolling in.

He remembered a similar storm as a child. The typhoon acted like the destructive spirit of a dead child. It lashed the walls of their home, smashing windows and doors, and ripping the roof from the building with an anger he had never seen in nature. Terrified, his mother had clutched him to her bosom, singing lullabies and rocking gently back and forth. But the storm had fascinated him, and he wondered what act of Man had caused the *kami* to be so mad. He hoped this typhoon was not angry at him, and, more importantly, that it was nature's work, not born of Taira's magic.

Ichiro pushed the thought from his mind and wondered if the ruse had worked. If Taira, for even one minute, believed Akutigawa's tale of how the defenders all committed *seppuku*, it would be enough of a delay to help Ichiro's fleeing army. Surely the burned bodies among the rubble would cause the *daimyo* to spend some time searching for the remains that might be Ichiro's.

But Ichiro also knew he had purchased just a short delay. Taira might search the rubble for proof, but he would not be fooled for long. Then the *daimyo* would resume his quest, even angrier at being cheated of his prize.

Yet each moment Ichiro purchased from Taira's hesitation was precious. He had to use it well and not waste it.

A raindrop' hit him squarely across the face. It was followed by another and another. A jagged yellow lightning flash split the sky from horizon to horizon.

The storm burst fully upon him. The rain pelted his face and the wind lashed at him, tearing at his body, trying to drive him to ground. Ichiro pressed on, determined to go as far as possible.

Just ahead, only about thirty meters away, a small farmer's cottage suddenly appeared. It was small and seemed abandoned, but it offered welcome shelter from the storm.

Part of him urged caution. A still, small voice in his head warned Ichiro that to stop was to risk death. Taira's men were unlikely to ride out the storm. They would press forward, and so should he, the voice said.

But another part said survival was slim if he tried to best the storm. It was not a mortal man, and Ichiro was not immune to its power. If he fought it, he would have little strength left, and Taira's men would easily catch up with him.

Ichiro listened to that other voice and went to the cottage door. He knocked. "Hello!" he shouted above the wind. There was no answer.

He knocked again and again no one replied. Ichiro pushed the door.

It groaned on old hinges and swung slowly open. He entered, closing the door behind him.

The wind still raced through an open window on the far wall, and some rain spat through cracks in the door and through the window, but overall it was dry and warm.

Ichiro saw a small oil lantern on a low table illuminated by the lightning. He had nothing to light it with, he realized. *No matter*, he thought. *Better not to have any light.* It might give away his location to Taira's men in way the way radar echoes had told American bombers where to find the fleet at Leyte.

Ichiro tossed his saddlebag onto some straw mats and lay down. He had forgotten how tired he was. His bones ached. "I'll close my eyes just for a bit," he told himself aloud. But he quickly fell asleep.

———

He dreamed he was back in his Zero, his body aflame with aviation fuel. He was a human candle tumbling toward the sea. Pain stabbed his mind, and then he hit the water. He felt his limbs being ripped apart, but he felt free, his mind passing through some sort of gate.

He remembered the *koan* he had learned as a pageboy in the Buddhist monastery. *The hubless wheel turns.* He had meditated zealously on the *koan*, but he always believed he could never achieve the states of *satori* which came so readily to the other students and acolytes. After he had asked permission to leave the monastery, he was resigned to failure. But he had tried one more time and felt the world fall away into nothingness. And he wept because that bliss of *satori* would now be forever be denied him.

As his body flew into pieces, he rediscovered it, but too late. Is this a dream of your making, Hachiman? Ichiro asked as the waves overwhelmed him.

The *kami* laughed. *We are all dreams of our own making,* Hachiman said. *Who told you otherwise?*

The dream world fell away. Everything fell away.

———

A shaft of buttery sunlight skewered Ichiro's eyes awake. He lay still for a moment, adjusting to his surroundings. So he was not dead, not scattered like dry leaves across the Pacific. But was he alive?

Then he realized where he was and the question of his existence was irrelevant. He sprang to feet and grabbed his saddlebag. How long had he slept? he wondered. Probably too long, and that meant Taira's men had closed in on him. There was no time to eat or drink. He had to leave now.

The arrow slammed into Ichiro's shoulder as he stepped through the doorway. The saddlebag caught the brunt of the shock. He staggered against the jam. Searing pain ran up his arm. As he reached up to pull out the arrow, he saw a bamboo stave flashed toward his head. He managed to raise the saddlebag to block it, only to catch a second stave across his mid-section.

The blow drove the air from Ichiro's lungs, and he doubled over in pain. More staves pummeled him across the back and shoulders and along the side of his head. He saw himself racing toward the ground, out of control. The earth sprang up to meet him and he landed with a sound like a sack of wet grain.

Ichiro tasted the wet black soil, a bitter, acrid taste mingled with saltiness. The saltiness came from the blood pouring from his nose and lips. He realized he was choking on it. He coughed, and saw foamy red drops spin away before his eyes.

Something like the claws of a huge bird of prey grabbed him and pulled him up from the ground. Standing unsteadily, he felt something slammed into his stomach. His body wanted to double over, but the claws, which held him fast, refused to let him.

"That's enough," a familiar voice said.

The claws released him and he dropped like wet laundry. The pulse pounding in his temples nearly deafened him.

"Pick him up," the voice said.

Ichiro knew that voice. Whose voice was it? The claws firmly clasped his arms and dragged up against the hut, where he was rudely tossed.

He raised his head, and with blurry eyes could make out a handful of *ashigaru* and *samurai*, including three or four with wooden *kendo* swords and bamboo staves. They were obviously the thugs who had beaten him.

He spat out a mouthful of blood and ran his tongue around his mouth. No teeth broken or missing, and his jaw just seemed bruised. Ichiro was thankful for small blessings.

Nearby, he saw a man on horseback moving slowly toward him. The man looked down at him. "An excellent move, general. For a moment you had me fooled. But you forget, I, too, am an educated man. I also know of Kusunoki Masushige's stratagems."

Now Ichiro recognized the voice. "I regret my plan was less than totally successful, Lord Taira," he muttered through split lips. "Yet, you admitted it almost fooled you."

"Well, I confess to failing to recognize it at first," Taira said. "My anger at being cheated of your death blinded me to that, I suppose. Fortunately, I recalled I had a book about your illustrious forebear. It was most enlightening. I regret not reading it earlier. It would save us both this entire farce we have been obliged to perform."

The *daimyo* dismounted. He walked slowly toward Ichiro, then bent down and stared him face to face.

Ichiro smelled the stench of death on Taira's breath. It was a rancid and sweet odor that nauseated Ichiro. "Now, general, kindly give me Kusinagi, and I will assure you your death will be swift and painless, quite unlike the beating my men gave you."

Ichiro stared into the *daimyo's* eyes and saw the fear of a trapped animal. Taira's desperation grew each second. The man was clearly terrified of the destruction he faced without the sword to give him the power to control. But the *daimyo's* fear offered Ichiro a chance to gain time for his army.

He smiled, half-amused by and half-pitying Taira.

Surprisingly, Taira also smiled. But it was a grin of fear. The *daimyo* pulled the sword and scabbard from Ichiro's *obi*.

For a moment Taira stared at the weapon, holding in front of him with both hands. He seemed like a child with a new toy, his eyes wide with wonder. Ichiro hoped the Edo sword maker"s work was convincing, if only for a while longer.

"At last," Taira said. "At last, it is mine."

The *daimyo* eased the counterfeit Kusinagi from its sheath. He ran a finger along the polished steel blade and along the *horimono* near the hilt. Then his smile of wonder changed to one of puzzlement, followed by rage.

With growing apprehension, Ichiro realized that another of his plans had failed.

Taira turned Ichiro with anger burning in his eyes. "This is not Kusinagi!" he shouted, flinging the false weapon aside. He dropped to his knees and grabbed the front of Ichiro's jacket. "Where is the sword?" the *daimyo* demanded.

"I don't have the sword," Ichiro admitted.

The *daimyo* shrieked and brought his open hand crashing into Ichiro's face.

The blow knocked Ichiro sideways. Fresh blood ran from his nose and into his mouth. His cheek stung and he felt his left eye swelling shut.

"Where is Kusinagi?" Taira screamed, grabbing Ichiro by the shoulders and shaking him violently as if to rattle the information out.

"I don't know," Ichiro said.

Taira flung him against the wall. Ichiro's head hit the stones with a crack, but by now he felt little pain.

"I could kill you now, you know!" the *daimyo* yelled, getting to his feet. Taira's face was red with rage, and his clenched fists shook uncontrollably. Perspiration rolled down his face.

"Yes, you could kill me," Ichiro said slowly. "But remember, no mortal man may kill me. Unless you are now immortal. Or already dead."

The insult infuriated Taira. He drew his *katana* and lunged for Ichiro's heart. But the sword point struck something solid and failed to penetrate.

Ichiro felt the cold metal of his last talisman, which hung from his neck, as it pressed deeply into his chest. It had saved him.

Startled, Taira drew back and lunged again. The medallion, apparently with a mind of its own, moved to deflect the attack. Furious, the *daimyo* swung the *katana* at Ichiro's head. Ichiro rolled to one side to evade the blow. The sword hit the hut's stone wall and smashed itself to pieces.

Defeated, his eyes filled with tears of fury, Taira flung the broken sword's hilt over the hut's roof. "Put him on a horse and take back to camp! I will make him tell me where the sword is!" He turned from Ichiro and stormed back to his horse. Mounting, Taira pulled sharply on the reins, causing the horse to whinny in pain. "I will make you will give me the sword, Minamoto, I swear I will!"

The *daimyo* reined his horse about and galloped down the hillside. Three *samurai* followed close behind their lord.

Two *ashigaru* grabbed Ichiro and pulled him to his feet so brutally he thought they would twist his arms from their sockets. He was pushed up onto a weary, bow-backed dapple-gray. His hands were tied to the saddle by a ham-handed *ashigaru* who had a puffy, tanned face and a mouth missing several teeth.

"A little easy on the wrists," Ichiro muttered.

The man gave Ichiro a gap-tooth grin and pulled the rope tighter.

Well, there was no bargaining with this fellow, Ichiro thought.

The *ashigaru* barked an order to the other men, who had mounted equally broken-down nags. Then the man slapped the flanks of Ichiro's mount and sent it in the general direction of the Ishikawa River and the ruins of the fortress Ichiro had abandoned barely a day before.

The journey back seemed intended to cause Ichiro the most pain. Each step the horse took produced a corresponding stab of pain in Ichiro's bruised and bleeding flesh and a low groan from his lips. *Maybe Taira should have killed me,* Ichiro thought. *It could not be much worse than this.*

To distract himself from the pain, he thought about the Zen *koan*. *So when does the hubless wheel turn?* he wondered. He turned it over and over in his mind, even though he knew the proper answer was supposedly *mu*--nothingness. But he was aware that to merely know the answer was not to *know* the answer.

As he wrestled with the *koan*, he found time seemed slipped away. The pain vanished away with it. Ichiro was aware of his breathing, of his heartbeat. The world took on a humming vibrancy. He had never noticed how green the pine trees along the mountain path were, or how brown the rain-soaked soil. Each note of the songbirds' melodies danced in his head.

Then he noticed the environment changing. His captors were taking a different path down the mountain. No longer were they heading toward the Ishikawa River and the fortress. The land was unfamiliar, yet Ichiro felt a kinship with it. He did not recognize it, but somehow he knew where they heading.

The land flattened out into a broad valley, and by evening they had reached a narrow river that flowed leisurely toward the sea. Ichiro knew now they were near the Hokkaido Post Road, and not far from the point where he left the road on his original journey to Edo. He also knew their eventual destination--Taira's *yashiki*.

They crossed a river, a tributary of the Ishikawa perhaps or a fork of the stream that ran through Getsuyu's village, Ichiro thought.

The gapped-toothed *ashigaru* shouted to his men, and they halted by a riverbank. Dismounting, they quickly set up camp and started a fire to prepare their dinner. They untied Ichiro from his horse. He wanted to rub his raw wrists, but the soldiers pulled his arms behind him and retied the ropes. They pushed him against a tree and left him alone to watch them cook their glutinous white rice and silvery-white bits of fish in greasy, blackened iron pans.

Ichiro grew hungry, his mouth watering from the smell of hot oil, rice and fish. How long had it been since he had eaten? He couldn't recall, but his stomach, with a deep growl, remembered all too well. He could no longer resist its protestations. "I would like some food," he said.

The *ashigaru* ignored him and went about their work. One of them placed a jar of *sake* into the fire's white coals. Another scooped dollops of hot food into several dirty brown wooden bowls.

"I would like some food," he repeated. "I am hungry."

The ham-handed man turned his head toward Ichiro. "You can shut up," he said, shaking a fat finger at his prisoner.

"Lord Taira will not like it if he discovers you haven't fed me," he said.

The *ashigaru* put down his bowl, picked up a stave and walked toward Ichiro. "There is only food enough for my men, not for the likes of you."

"If your lord wants me alive, you'd better feed me."

"I told you to shut up," the man said. He swung the stave at Ichiro's mid-section.

It was the move Ichiro had waited for. He fell backwards, then kicked out with his left leg.

Thrown off-balance by the force of his own stave hitting empty air, the *ashigaru* caught the full force of Ichiro's counterattack. The blow landed in the man's stomach, just under his ribs. The man groaned and bent double as the wind was driven from his lungs.

Ichiro wasted no time. He got to his feet and, as the man tried to staggered away, Ichiro crashed his head into the *ashigaru's* fat face.

The man groaned and sprawled headlong into a small red shrub. Blood rolled from his nose and mouth, and Ichiro could see the man's smile would now be minus a few more teeth.

Breathing heavily, Ichiro leaned against a tree and saw the other *ashigaru* walking toward him. One had his dagger drawn. Now he realized how foolish he had just been. *Well*, he thought, *they can't kill me, but they can certainly cause me great pain.*

The *ashigaru* with the dagger spun Ichiro around and pushed him face first into the tree. Then the soldier carefully cut the ropes that bound Ichiro's wrists. The man turned Ichiro around. A second soldier thrust the remains of their leader's meal into Ichiro's hands.

"Thank the *kami* that someone finally put that pig Imae in his place," one man said.

"Should I cut his throat now?" another said.

"No, let's just throw him in the river. Everyone knows he can't swim. Then we can tell Lord Taira that when we tried to ford the river, Imae fell from his horse and we couldn't save him," the man with the dagger said.

"Good enough," the second replied. He and another man began dragging the hapless and unconscious Imae to a fate his men obviously believed was well deserved.

"Thank you for the food," Ichiro said to the man with the dagger.

"Don't thank me," the man said. "Lord Taira will reward us well with you in one piece, but if you die, he will have us gutted and our skin tanned and painted for a new screen."

The man's words sickened Ichiro. He was alive only because these men preferred that Imae not damage valuable merchandise. And they had let him do their dirty work in disposing of their hated leader.

He stared into the mass of sticky, burned rice and bits of crumbling fish in his bowl, almost wanting to throw it aside. But hunger overcame him. He dug his hands into the food and sucked it from his fingers in greedy gulps.

Sated, sleep came easily, even in the cold and wet mountain air. But Ichiro's dreams were of starving fish feeding on the bloated, drowned body of Imae as it drifted slowly toward the sea.

CHAPTER TWENTY-THREE

The valley even grew more familiar to Ichiro as the next day wore on. When they passed the remains of a small village, Ichiro remembered it all too well. The ruined fishing traps still stood upright against the current, but new grass covered the burned millet fields, and the air was fresh.

How long had it been since he was here, A month or two? A month seemed about right. Amazing how it had changed already. The new grass suggested that Taira's magic had found a formidable foe in the simple cycles of nature. *Or is it just a respite because the daimyo's concerns were elsewhere?* Ichiro thought.

The soldiers had retied Ichiro's hands to the saddle, but the knots were looser than those Imae had fastened. Ichiro found he could control the horse's movements after a fashion and could even move in the saddle. He looked toward the village, and could see the shrine to the Amida Buddha where he had faced the first of Taira's ploys. But there was no sign of Getsuyu, the *jito*. Indeed, there was no sign of human life at all.

Ichiro hoped Getsuyu was still alive, but just in case the *jito* was indeed dead, Ichiro whispered a prayer to the Amida Buddha in hopes his friend would see the Pure Land.

The village disappeared all too quickly as they entered the nearby hills, but it was not long before Taira's *yashiki* came into view.

In contrast to the first time Ichiro had glimpsed it, the small castle seemed forlorn and surprisingly sad. No soldiers, other than a bare handful, camped in the *tensho*. The garden, once bright with color, seemed overgrown and tangled, like the events Taira sought to control. Chaos ruled here, twisting everything to its own designs.

Taira's equerry, looking older and more careworn, came from the stables to handle the horse. He mumbled to himself, scratched his scraggly black beard, and spat on the ground.

"How are your horses, friend?" Ichiro said. "It's been a while since we talked."

The equerry gave him a puzzled look. After a moment, the shock of recognition crossed his face and he smiled. "Why, general, I'm so glad to see. you How is your horse?"

"Far from here, I'm afraid. But well."

"Good, a fine animal," the man said.

"Enough chit-chat," the *ashigaru* leader said. He cut Ichiro's hands free of the saddle, but ropes still tightly bound his wrists. The man and two other soldiers dragged Ichiro from the horse.

The *ashigaru* pushed and prodded him up the steps toward the main house. The stairs groaned under their weight, and musty, brown dust rose with each foot that trod on them. The *bonsai* trees at the doorway were gnarled and bent, their leaves yellow and dry.

Ichiro was amazed at what he saw. Everything seemed to be aging at a rapid rate, collapsing upon itself. An odor of damp decay pervaded the air.

A hand pushed hard on Ichiro's back, driving him through the entrance. He landed heavily. Pain erupted throughout his injuries. With a groan, he rolled over into a sitting position, and came face to face with Taira.

The *daimyo* wore lounging robes and sat on several thick cushions. His right arm lay across a carved teak armrest. He drummed his fingers rhythmically.

"So good to see you again, Lord Taira," Ichiro said, trying to be civil.

But the *daimyo* was unamused. His face was chalky and his black eyes burned with inhuman fire and fear. Wrinkles formed tangled webs at the corners of his eyes. Two furrows, like deep streambeds, cut their way from the sides of his mouth to the sides of his nose. Taira's skin sagged like that of an old man, which he seemed to be rapidly becoming.

Taira's decline matched the steady decay in the house. Once lavish paper and bamboo screens were tattered and torn. Paintings flaked and cracked. On the tray before the *daimyo* was a cup of tea with a thin, green surface of scum. The cakes next to the tea showed traces of blue and black mold.

"I know now you sent the sword along with Tamika," Taira said. He tongued nervously at a moustache that was now flecked with white and gray hairs.

"Your intelligence sources are good, but do you know where they are bound?" Ichiro said.

"To the north. The Shogun and his men ride to join them," Taira said flatly. There was a weariness in the *daimyo's* voice. He appeared tired of the chase.

"Edo is wide open, then," Ichiro said. "You could march right in."

Taira scowled and brought a clenched fist down on the armrest. "To hell with Edo! I must have your sword. Will you tell me where they are bound, or must I force it from you?"

Ichiro shook his head. "No, I will not tell you."

The *daimyo* shook with rage, barely able to control himself. "Damn you, Minamoto, why do you continue to resist? I can offer you so much!"

"You can offer me nothing."

"Take him away," Taira yelled to the *ashigaru*. Three foot soldiers dragged Ichiro to his feet. "I will soon make you talk, general. And you will regret that Hachiman blessed you so. You will *beg* me to kill you. I promise it!"

The *ashigaru* dragged him from the room. They hauled him, unresisting, across the courtyard until they came to a stone hut without windows. One soldier unlocked the hut's heavy red cedar door. The other two dumped Ichiro unceremoniously inside. He fell several meters down and landed on some wet straw, brown with mildew. The soldiers closed the door, but before the darkness closed in on Ichiro, he glimpsed the dungeon's previous occupant, who still resided there. The huge grin on the skeleton's yellowing skull suggested he was glad to see Ichiro.

The feeling was not mutual.

Ichiro sat down on the straw, trying to ignore its rancid odor. *What to do?* he wondered. He doubted there was anything edible in the pit, other than the straw, and he did not have the bovine stomachs required to digest *that* even if he had wanted to. His body was still aching and sore from the beatings and the long ride, so exercise was pointless. Sleep seemed a likely possibility.

No, he told himself. The day was still too young for that. Meditation was appropriate. He anticipated torture at Taira's hands, and he had to discipline his mind to face the ordeal. Also, he had found the calming effect of the mediation had brought an order to his soul which had helped him survive the ride.

He remembered as a youth the stories of the rebellious *samurai* Toyama Mitsuru, who had disciplined himself so well, he could sit *zazen* motionless for hours on a winter's day even as frost formed on his beard. Ichiro's favorite tale of Toyama was where he challenged a Zen monk to a meditation contest. Both sat motionless for five days, neither eating, drinking, sleeping, nor even moving a finger or opening his mouth. Disheartened, the priest finally gave up.

"Well, if Toyama could do it for five days, then surely I can do it for a few hours more," Ichiro said to himself aloud.

Ichiro tucked his clubfoot under him and placed his left foot across his right thigh in a half-lotus position. It was not perfect, but it would do. He closed his eyes and thought of the *koan* the old abbot had given him. *When does the hubless wheel turn?* echoed in his head.

Then Ichiro sensed something cold and smooth slide across his leg and into his lap. A cool tongue slithered across his wrist, tasting the saltiness of his perspiration. A second something eased its way over his left thigh. A third noisily moved through the straw.

He could not tell if the snakes were poisonous, but he suspected they were. Taira obviously had introduced them into the pit from some hidden passageway. There were at least three, but he suspected there were more.

Taira must have learned of my fear when he probed my mind at Getsuyu's, Ichiro thought. His mouth was dry. He licked his lips. He could feel his heart rate rising. He thought of the *koan* and tried to keep his pulse under control.

A chill wind rolled through the bottom of the door of the hut and tumbled into the pit. Ichiro gritted his teeth and tried not to shiver. The snakes, sensing the cold, were attracted to his body to keep themselves warm, he realized. The one in his lap seemed to be asleep. The other two had also found niches next to his body.

An excellent move, Taira, he thought.

"I am glad you appreciate it, general," came Taira's voice echoing in Ichiro's head. "You play *go*, so I am surprised you did not expect it."

Even a good gamesman stumbles, Ichiro thought.

"Then savor my gambit. Perhaps we can discuss it in the morning," Taira said. "If you are alive."

The voice vanished.

Ichiro swallowed softly. Don't move, he told himself. This would not have bothered Toyama, he reassured himself. A snake stirred, pushed its head into the fold of Ichiro's jacket. It slipped over Ichiro's shoulder and went down his back.

Ichiro's breath came slowly and shallowly, and his heart seemed determined to beat itself to death against his ribcage. He forced himself to think of the *koan*.

When does the hubless wheel turn?

The snake draped itself around Ichiro's neck, and another searched for warmth up his jacket sleeve. Cold sweat rolled down Ichiro's back and down his arms. Snake tongues darted out to gather the salty liquid.

When does the hubless wheel turn?

The *koan* focused his thoughts. His breathing began to regulate itself, his heartbeat slowed. He began to visual a gate, the gateless gate of *satori*. He did not know where it led, but he worked toward it, knowing it meant freedom.

The snakes, warm in their niches, quickly fell asleep. All but one; it probed the creature generating such warmth. Its tongue tasted his skin, gathering information. It was contemplating attack.

Ichiro sensed the snake rising up before him. He turned the *koan* in his mind. The gate danced before him.

The hubless wheel turned.

The snake raised itself up, hissed, and struck.

Ichiro entered the gate.

The world fell away, and he was somewhere else, and he was drowning.

The world was all water, shining pale blue under a hot sun. Ichiro's lungs strained for air. He kicked his legs madly, trying to reach the surface, which seemed only tantalizing centimeters away. Suddenly, he broke through, sucking in a huge dollop of air before the waves crashed down on him and drove him under.

The air refreshed Ichiro. He battled his way back to the surface. He breathed in air and cold brine. Never a good swimmer, he still forced his legs to keep himself afloat.

In the distance, he saw an island bobbing on the surface. In the spray, it glistened like a tantalizing emerald, shimmering green and gold. He began swimming toward it, each stroke straining his body. His heart seemed to be in his throat, trying to leap free of him. His lungs felt like they were being crushed by a tremendous vice.

Ichiro's feet struck bottom. A huge wave caught him and threw him high into the air. He crashed heavily onto the beach. Exhausted, he lay there, gasping for breath.

The thunder of waves and what seemed like gunfire and explosions in the distance filled his ears.

Where was he?

He did not know.

He did not care. Spent, he could only think of the *koan*. He lost consciousness.

The hubless wheel turned again.

CHAPTER TWENTY-FOUR

A thin shaft of light crept through a hole in the hut's roof. By that light Ichiro, saw he was no longer in the pit, but on a ledge at the other end of the hut. The ledge, he saw, was narrow, barely half a meter wide. How he got there he did not know.

His clothes, mysteriously drenched, reeked of salt. *Sea salt, perhaps?* he wondered. In his dream he remembered swimming. *Was it possible that he had swum to the ledge from the bottom of the pit?*

That seemed highly unlikely. He sat up and shivered in his wet clothes. A cold wind had snaked its way under the hut's door and through the hole in the roof.

He eased himself to the edge and looked into the pit. What he hoped to find were the handholds he had used to climb the pit walls.

What he saw was the twisted forms of ten snakes, all drowned. They lay in a pool of water about ten centimeters deep at the bottom of the pit. Their dead bodies resembled ornately colored ropes of ruby, emerald, gold, and azure. Little flecks of yellow straw floated past the dead serpents, almost taunting them.

"Then it wasn't a dream," Ichiro said. Somehow he had solved the *koan*, but the answer had not been *mu*. It was not nothingness as he thought he understood it. He had entered the gate, and it had taken him...somewhere.

He had no time to contemplate the answer. The door of the hut burst open.

Light flooded Ichiro's eyes. "A fine way to treat your guests," he snapped. "First you try to drown them, then you blind them."

Silence greeted him. Ichiro's eyes adjusted to the light, and he saw Taira standing in the doorway.

Taira stood motionless, his black robes making him resemble an ebony statue. In his right hand the *daimyo* clutched a fan, almost crushing it. Then his entire body shook with rage. He screamed and flung the fan at Ichiro.

It hit Ichiro's shoulder and bounced harmlessly away into the pit to join the serpents.

"I don't know what magic you used to avoid my snakes, but you will pay, Minamoto!" Taira screamed. He gestured at the ledge Ichiro lay on.

The ground shook beneath Ichiro and the ledge disintegrated. He reached for a handhold, but his fingers closed on loose earth. He fell feet first into the pit, landing with a splash. Above him, the door slammed, and once more, darkness filled the hut.

The water now came up to the middle of Ichiro's calf. He sat down. To his surprise, he found the water was warm. Had he been digging, trying to get out, and had somehow tapped into a thermal spring? He did not know how that was possible, yet somehow it seemed more likely than his passing through the gateless gate into some other world. Still, he remembered swimming. He did not recall digging.

He pulled off his wet clothes and smelled them. There was indeed an odor of salt water and seaweed about them. It made no sense, no sense at all.

Ichiro wrung out his clothes and hung them to dry on several exposed roots he could make out in the half-light. He doubted they would dry completely, but being naked in the hot warm was preferable to freezing in wet clothes.

When they dried, he decided he would try to climb from the pit, even if that was impossible. He clutched the talisman for luck and felt his fingers touch something else. Yes, of course, he remembered the strange stone the doctor had given him, the stone that wa supposed to absorb poisons. Ichiro was glad he had it. He feared it might prove useful all too soon.

Ichiro shivered involuntarily and sat down in the heated water to stay warm. *Strange that winter seem to have arrived so early,* he thought. *Were the forces of chaos drawing the heat from the world and bringing the eternal winter of disorder?* he wondered. *Was this Taira's real legacy, to conquer a world only to have lost to the glaciers of a new ice age? That would be justice.*

He felt something roll up against his leg, and sprang to his feet with a start. He reached down and picked up the snake. It repulsed him and he started to throw it out of the pit. Then he hesitated.

Once, on some nameless atoll where he was stationed, the soldiers had tricked him into eating roast snake. When he learned what it was, he was sick the next day, but now his stomach rumbled and he felt the pangs of hunger. There was no telling when Taira would feed him.

Ichiro used his fingernails to tear off the snake's head and to strip the skin from its body. The taste was sharp and bitter, but the meat was hot and steaming, and pulled easily from the bone. He sucked it down ravenously.

Sated, he flung the remains of the snake from the pit and sat down. He sighed with relief. Another snake rolled up against his body, but he ignored it. It would be a meal for another day.

As there was little else to do, he decided to try to meditate again. He knew it was a vain hope, but perhaps he would find the gate again and, with it, a means of escaper.

But nothing came of Ichiro's efforts. The hubless wheel did not turn this time. He wondered if he had found the gate only because the snakes threatened his life, and because one had struck.

Tired, he lay back in the water, his head against the side of the pit. Ichiro did not recall sleeping, but he remembered waking to the sound of soldiers arguing. A blast of freezing wind and sleet came through the hut door as it opened. A soldier in a heavy winter coat and thick leggings came in. He carried what appeared to be rope coiled at his side. A second soldier follow him.

"You down there," the first soldier called.

"Don't bother," the second complained. "He's probably frozen to death by now."

"No, I'm still alive," Ichiro shouted.

"See, I told you," the first soldier said top his companion. He looked down toward Ichiro. "You down there, Lord Taira wants to see you."

"Why?" asked Ichiro.

"How should I know. I only follow orders," the soldier said. "I am sending down a ladder for you." The man uncoiled the rope ladder at his side, fastened it to a hook in the hut wall and tossed it down the pit.

Ichiro caught it and tugged. It seemed firm. "Wait," he said. "I have no clothes. Mine are all wet. I'll freeze if I don't have dry clothes."

"Go get him a jacket and some trousers," the first soldier said to the second.

"Why should I go?" the other protested.

"If he dies, Lord Taira will have our heads pickled with his dinner cabbage," the first replied. "That is why."

The second man, grumbling, left. He returned after a while with a bundle of clothes, which he tossed down piece-by-piece.

Ichiro dressed quickly and climbed the ladder. At the top he faced his two rescuers (or executioners, he was uncertain what they were) who gave him a heavy blanket to keep him warm and a pair of thick sandals.

"Get a move on," the first soldier said. "I'm freezing my plums off out here."

Outside, sleet battered the hard, frozen ground. A thin film of pale white ice covered the grass and turned bushes and trees into grotesque crystal sculptures. The three men, bent against the cold, walked as quickly as possible to the *yashiki*. The footing was rough, and twice Ichiro found his balance tested as he hit icy patches of ground.

He caught himself once against a *gekko* tree. His eyes fell on a small beehive. A single insect, slowed by the cold, moved with difficulty to the hive entrance. Ichiro had an idea. Although he didn't have a sword, he now could have a weapon.

"Hurry up," a guard shouted.

"I'm sick," he lied. As he doubled over in mock pain, Ichiro grabbed the beehive and broke it off the branch. He pretended to retch as he slipped it into his kimono. "Now, friend bees, do not sting me until I need you."

"Come on," a first soldier said. "Sick or not, you're to see Lord Taira."

"I feel better now," Ichiro said. He smiled. The bees, warmed by his body, were starting to stir.

Once inside the main house, the two guards hustled Ichiro to a set of small rooms in the back. "This is where we leave you," said the first soldier.

If so, they had left him in a veritable paradise compared to the pit. Fresh clothes--including a bright blue-and-gold formal *kimono* decorated with elaborate red and white embroidery of Chinese design--were laid out for him.

He noted with some amusement that there was a large cedar tub filled with steaming bath water in the room. "Well, another bath would not be unwelcome."

Ichiro undressed, soaped his body and climbed into the tub. The water was hot and steaming, and stank of sulfur. That did not surprise him, somehow. He sank back in the water, letting it soak away the stiffness and pain in his muscles and bones. "You stink like your *daimyo,* but your warmth is more welcome," he told the water.

He had barely begun to feel better when a panel slid open. Six women entered the room. Their presence at first startled him, but then he recognized them as Taira's wives and daughters. They resembled a set of unpleasant dolls, their faces uniformly grim behind deathly white make-up. Their mouths were bright red frowns, their eyebrows high, arched black slashes above their eyes. One older woman, perhaps the primary wife, came forward and bowed slightly.

"Our lord and master awaits you for dinner," she said, exposing fashionably blackened teeth, teeth that looked as though they could tear human flesh. There was a smell of decay about her, an odor no perfume could mask, and which even overcame the stink of the sulfurous water.

"Tell your master I will join him shortly, when I am dry."

She paused, then nodded, as if accepting the circumstances. Then she clapped her hands. Two other women, probably daughters, came forward. They carried towels, which they placed next to the tub. One daughter then went to gather Ichiro's old clothes.

The beehive! he thought. "No!" he said, half-rising from the tub.

The two women stopped. "But, honored sir, our lord has provided new clothes," the older woman said.

"Please, my clothes hold many heirlooms of my family. Allow me to remove those heirlooms, and you may take dispose of my old clothes."

The women stared at Ichiro. *Oh, god,* he thought, *they're expecting me to climb out of the tub and to dress myself before them.* That certainly wouldn't do, not if his plans were to work.

"I come from the south," he lied. "In my home province, it is customary for a bather to dress himself in solitude, to have time with his thoughts."

The women didn't move. Ichiro held his breath, then the older woman nodded slowly.

"Very well, but we must wait outside to escort you to the dining hall," she said.

Ichiro waited until the women had left before heaving a huge sigh of relief. He climbed from the tub, dried himself and put on the new clothes. Yet as he dressed, he wondered if the opulent clothes were just another part of Taira's trickery. *A trap, a spell, perhaps?* he thought.

Well, he had his own trickery to demonstrate for the *daimyo*, although admittedly less magical. He tucked the beehive into one billowing sleeve of the kimono and the stone into the other.

Ichiro slid the panel open. The women watched him carefully. Their black eyes resembled the eyes of a family of tigresses who were observing their prey before striking and devouring it.

Ichiro bowed slightly. "Shall we go? Your master, I'm sure, is tired of waiting."

The old woman sneered, but said nothing. They escorted Ichiro to the main hall. Two guards, the same ones who had brought Ichiro from the pit, stood leaning on *naginata*. The sentries straightened up when they saw the women.

The old woman walked straight to them. "I could have you flayed alive for such laziness. His lordship would enjoy that. We haven't had good entertainment in some time." She glanced at one guard. "Let us in."

The guard nervously reached across and slid the panel open. The old woman stepped inside. One of Taira's daughters touched the soldier's elbow, then slid a finger down his forearm to the wrist. "Yes, such fine flesh. Pity, I would so enjoy a flaying," she said. She moistened her crimson lips with the tip of a thin black tongue.

An involuntary chill rolled down Ichiro's spine. He saw that both sentries were pale with fear. But the daughter only laughed, tossed her head, and passed through the panel. The other women followed.

The women stepped to each side of the entranceway as Ichiro came through. He could see torches flickering in the hall. Their light covered everything with a cold, buttery glow. Tapestries of a European design hung along the walls to keep out the freezing wind. The tapestries were probably Van der Lieuw's gift.

Nearby, a small group of musicians performed background music on *biwa*, Chinese *pi'pa* and *shakuhachi*. The music was horridly dissonant and painful to hear.

"Welcome, honored guest," said Taira. The *daimyo* sat at the head of a group of banquet guests.

As Ichiro entered the banquet, guests stopped their gossiping, and all eyes turned toward him. Each guest sat at his own small table. Ichiro recognized some of the other guests, including Lord Akiyama, some lesser nobles, some hangers-on from the Imperial Court, and some performers from the kabuki. *All sycophants, without the loyalty or courage of someone in Edo,* he thought.

"I was not so welcome yesterday," Ichiro said coldly.

"Ah, but that was yesterday, and I have seen my errors," said Taira. "I trust you will forgive my indiscretions." He gestured toward an open space next to his seat. "Please, come, eat."

Ichiro took his place at the table. "But remember, Lord Taira, I am not your dog."

Taira seemed hurt by the remark. "Ah, true, but if one should be a dog, one should choose a rich and powerful master," the *daimyo* replied.

Ichiro detected an odor of *sake* about Taira. He's drunk, Ichiro realized. And a pathetic, maudlin drunk, too.

"Ah, here comes our meal," Taira said. He clapped his hands in obvious delight.

Servants carried in several trays containing bowls of a bean-curd soup called *suimono,*, a plate of fish balls, a platter of fish grilled in *shoyu,* and small bowls of *su-no-mono,* sea slugs in vinegar. There were also bowls of *chawan-mishi.* The odor of the shitake mushrooms and vegetables even made Ichiro's mouth water.

Yet when the food was placed before him, Ichiro could see something was desperately wrong with it. The grilled fish, or *hachi-zakana,* looked diseased and malformed. Tumors speckled the creature's flesh, which itself was a glistening silvery-gray. The sea slugs were a pale translucent white, and resembled hideously fat maggots floating in a rice vinegar ocean

While the vegetables, too, looked distorted, their appearance was less disturbing to Ichiro. He brought his bowl of bean curd soup to his mouth and sipped. The taste and odor nearly made him retch. There was a flavor of death and decay to this food. He found himself missing the taste of the snakes in the pit.

Ichiro pretended to cough, reach into the sleeve of his kimono and pulled out the poison-stone. He coughed again and slipped the stone into his mouth, using his tongue to position it again his cheek.

He noticed the guests were staring at him. "A chill," he said. "The weather is not good for me."

"Ah, well, soup should warm you up," Taira said, his speech now a little slurred. "Eat, eat."

Ichiro forced himself to swallow the soup. He could not imagine even a starving man enjoying this food, yet he watched the other diners ravenously tearing into the meal, stripping fish cleanly to twisted bones, and grasping sea slugs between chopsticks and sucking them down whole. Sauces and bits of fish dribbled down the guests' chins as they ate.

The diners released little sounds of pleasure at each morsel. The sounds were nearly as sickening to Ichiro as the food itself.

Ichiro forced down what little he could over three courses and washed the taste from his mouth with *sake*. The liquor seemed immune to the horrors of the rest of the meal.

"You have not enjoyed my food, General? Does the taste offend you," Taira said, a long frown on his pale features.

"By no means, my lord," he lied. "But I have been in field so long, I am afraid such food is too rich for me."

Taira smiled, exposing teeth just showing the start of rot. "You are a good general, Minamoto, but a terrible liar. But I forgive you. At least you are not a glutton like my others guests."

The servants returned with large blue ceramic plates, which they displayed to each of the diners. On each plate was a wheel of *sashimi*. The raw fish was thinly sliced and arranged to form lotus blossoms, cranes in flight, or white foxes.

Ichiro recognized the dish as *fugu*. Eating the puffer fish was a gourmet's delight, but also a risk. Unless it were cleaned properly, the flesh of *fugu* was deadly poison. Ichiro recalled seeing a neighbor die from eating improperly cleaned *fugu*. "A terrible death," his father had said. "The mind remains clear, but the body grows numb. Soon, you cannot sit up, then you cannot speak or move. Finally, you cannot breathe."

Ichiro hoped the stone would give him sufficient protection against the poison.

"Ah, now for the best dish of the feast," Taira said.

The guests cooed and murmured over the puffer fish.

Ichiro remembered a *senryu* verse. *Last night he and I ate fugu. Now today we carry his coffin.*

Taira smiled, as if reading Ichiro's mind. "Ah, Minamoto, those who eat *fugu* are fools, I know. But those who do not eat *fugu* are also fools."

"So, Taira, if I know you, all is not as it seems."

The *daimyo* nodded. "You know the game well, *samurai*." Taira turned to his guests. "Ah, friends, now for the fun. Among all our delicious *fugu* is one piece which retains the fish's poison. Enjoy,

enjoy, for it may be the last meal for one of you!" He laughed heartily.

And oddly, so did the other guests. Their chopsticks jumped for the paper-thin meat as the servants brought it to them.

Ichiro hesitated.

"Eat, eat, Minamoto," Taira admonished.

"What do you expect me to do if I do eat it, Taira?"

"Why, I expect you to *die, samurai*," the *daimyo* replied. "Wouldn't that be an irony, Minamoto? You cannot be harmed by any other mortal man, but you could, by chance, select the poison morsel and die by your own hand."

"Who am I to deny you such a pleasure," Ichiro said. He reached for a sliver of fish, dipped it in a mixture of soy sauce, *wasabi* horseradish and red pepper, and brought it to his lips. The gelatinous flesh had a delicate taste, subtle and elusive. *Well*, he decided, *if I am to die, let it be with a wonderful taste in my mouth.*

Ichiro swallowed, ate a second portion, and waited for the poison, if there were any, to take effect. How would it be? he wondered. Numbness, a tingling perhaps? Would the breath catch in his throat?

The clatter of chopsticks interrupted his thoughts.

Across the table, Chiharu Ohmori, a *kabuki* actor and favorite of Lord Akiyama, grew pale. The actor's eyes were wide with fear. He tried to speak, but his tongue seemed frozen in his mouth. Ohmori's breathing grew labored and harsh.

"Alas, how unfortunate," said Taira. There was genuine disappointment in his voice. He turned to Ichiro. "I had so hoped you would get the tasty morsel. But I forgot Chiharu's love for fugu. Well, now we shall see his final performance."

The actor fell to one side, then rolled onto his back. His body convulsed and shook violently for a moment, then was still.

Taira's wives and daughters gathered round the body as one, caressing Ohmori's limbs, running their hands over his still warm chest.

The daughter who had terrified the guards brought the actor's hand to her lips. She licked the fingers with a thin, dark tongue, then sucked them one at time. She drew a slender index finger into her mouth and her jaw flexed. There was an audible snap, and the hand came from her mouth, minus the finger. She chewed with relish, a thin trickle of blood running down her lips.

"Not fair," cried another daughter. "She'll have eaten all the tasty portions before we have had a chance at him."

"Now, my lovelies, you must not fight over him," Taira said. "There is plenty for all of you, but take him to your chambers to enjoy your meal."

The six women grabbed the dead actor by his legs and dragged him out of the hall. At each step, Ohmori's head bounced to-and-fro like a child's ball.

Ichiro felt a chill run up down his spine. The wrong piece of *fugu*, and it could have been his body the women would dine on, his finger chewed as delicately as *sushi*, his eyes sucked out like sugar plums, his genitals held in chopsticks to be dipped in horseradish sauce and slipped daintily between bloodless lips.

Taira leaned over to him. "Once they were lovely, you know. Now they are unholy things," he said.

Ichiro sensed fear in the *daimyo's* voice.

"Their appetite is insatiable. Even I sleep in dread of them, my own flesh! The guards now protect me as much from my own family as from you and your associates."

"You have my sympathy," Ichiro said.

Taira stared at him for a moment. "Yes, I suppose you do sympathize." The *daimyo* turned back to his dinner guests. "Ah, poor Ohmori, such response to his last performance. The critics shall eat him alive."

The guests laughed, but it was forced laughter.

"But come, come, my friends, let us enjoy the remainder of our meal," Taira said. "We've yet to have dessert."

"Permit me to provide that," Ichiro said, seizing his chance. He pulled the hive from his sleeve and smashed it open on his plate.

Enraged, the bees swarmed about the diners' heads, stinging indiscriminately. Ichiro grabbed a pair of chopsticks, knocked a bee from his cheek, and jumped across the table as best he could. His leap sent one guest flying, and he pushed aside a second diner who rose to stop him.

"Guards! Don't let him escape!" shrieked Taira, his arms flailing like windmills to beat away the insects. But the more the *daimyo* struggled, the more the swarm seemed attracted to him.

The guards entered the hall, their spears ready for attack. The first guard lunged toward Ichiro. But Ichiro side-stepped the attacker, grabbed the *naginata* by the shaft and thrust the chopsticks into the *ashigaru's* unprotected throat.

Instinctively, the man loosened his grip on his lance and brought a hand up to pull the weapon from his neck.

Ichiro took the opportunity to twist the naginata from the guard's grip. Now off-balance, the guard fell heavily, his neck covered in blood.

Ichiro saw the other guard out of the corner of his eye, and was barely able to deflect the man's lance thrust. He and the *ashigaru* now faced each other. Ichiro feigned an attack toward the man's face. The guard raised his lance to parry, and Ichiro spat the poison stone.

The projectile hit the man in the right eye. The sentry staggered backwards, his hands going to his face.

Ichiro swung the butt end of his lance around and rammed it into the *ashigaru's* mid-section. The man collapsed like a sack of rice.

By now, the diners were racing for protection from the bees, but two seemed intent on stopping Ichiro. "I would like to oblige you, but I must be going," he said. He cut the rope supporting a tapestry, and the huge cloth collapsed on the attackers. In falling, the tapestry revealed a thin wooden wall leading to the outside.

Ichiro threw himself against the wall. There was a resounding *crack* of snapping wood, and Ichiro tumbled into the garden. Lanterns filled the area with a soft light, and he could see the gate that opened out toward the hills. He ran toward it, hearing the massed footsteps of guards entering the hall behind him.

He wondered if one of Taira's ancient *kami* might be in residence at the gate this evening, but at this point, Ichiro decided he would risk the wrath of a god rather than end his escape attempt.

Ichiro was just outside the garden gate, headed toward several horses tied to a large camphor tree when the first arrows tore into the ground about him. He grabbed the reins of a large bay mare, mounted the animal bareback and kicked his heels into her flanks.

Startled, the horse wanted to bolt, but Ichiro pulled tight on the reins and turned her in what he remembered was the direction of Getsuyu's village.

Behind him, he could hear the shouts of angry foot soldiers and what could also have been the cries of enraged dinner guests, but soon he was out on the road, and all Ichiro could hear were the sounds of pounding hooves and the relentless drumbeat of his heart.

CHAPTER TWENTY-FIVE

Ichiro had not ridden far when he suddenly felt something tighten around his neck and chest. His lungs strained for air and his throat burned. He felt the amulet around his neck trying to push back against the tightness.

Something grabbed his right wrist.

Ichiro looked down and saw the sleeve of his kimono methodically trying to pull his hands away from the reins. "Damn you, Taira," he muttered through clenched teeth,"so you bewitched the clothes!"

He grabbed the cloth of the sleeve with his left hand, trying to pull it away. The silken folds entangled his fingers, but he managed to free his hand before it became trapped.

Then, like a cocoon, the other sleeve quickly wrapped itself about his left arm. Ichiro forced his left hand toward the *naginata* in a scabbard on the horse's saddle, but the sleeve tightened and pulled his arm back.

The horse galloped on, now increasingly out of Ichiro's control. He could see the fear in its eyes; saw the flecks of saliva on its thin black lips. His right hand had a tenuous grasp on the reins.

Straining, Ichiro forced his hand toward the spear. His fingers fell short. I won't let Taira's tricks defeat me, he told himself. He gritted his teeth and concentrated on edging his hand forward.

The fingertips touch the *naginata's* shaft, but the horse's wild galloping kept the spear bouncing out of his reach. He found it harder to breath now, and feared he would black out before he succeeded. He remembered passing out once in a dogfight over Leyte. He'd spun wildly out of control, and when he came to, he was scarcely 600 meters from the ocean.

He tried to remember how he pulled out of that dive. He eased his hand forward. Pain tore into his shoulder as the kimono tried to hold him back. His fingers curled around the spear, but it bounced away. He remembered how he had clutched the joystick between his legs, forcing the plane around, kicking the flaps and aerilons until it was stable and he had started to climb. He held onto the horse with his legs and pushed his hand forward with all his strength.

Ichiro felt the shaft hit his palm. His thumb and fingers locked around the spear just as the reins pulled free of his right hand.

He tumbled backwards from the horse, his hand still tight around the *naginata*. He hit the ground heavily, knocking what breath remained in him from his lungs. He was dazed for a moment, but he quickly clambered to his feet.

The kimono had loosened its grip for a moment. A thought skimmed passed Ichiro's consciousness. Perhaps the clothes were not clothes, but were some creature or demon capable of assuming any shape. It would have lain dormant until ready to attack.

The fall may have stunned it, he realized. Ichiro used the naginata to cut the *obi* from his waist, then tossed the weapon aside and tore the *kimono* from him. He had almost freed his right hand and arm when the robe awoke.

Ichiro screamed as it bit into his arm. *The little bastard has teeth!* he thought. He balled his hand into a fist so it wouldn't take a finger. Then the other sleeve wrapped itself around Ichiro's left leg and tried to pull him down.

Grimacing, he dropped to one knee and grabbed the *naginata.* The blade whistled as it slashed through the sleeve around Ichiro's foot, severing the cloth completely from the kimono.

A horrible shriek split the air, a scream of indescribable pain. The kimono released Ichiro's hand. He stumbled back, then regained his balance. The scream still echoing in his ears, Ichiro thrust the *naginata* into the center of the *kimono*.

The robe -or creature, whatever it was- unleashed a deafening cry and wrapped itself about the lance. It tried to pull the *naginata* free, but then it collapsed into a formless mound of cloth. Decay set in almost immediately. A rancid and pungent smell assaulted Ichiro's nostrils as the cloth dissolved into a thick, milky slime. The slime glowed faintly in the dark.

Ichiro pulled the spear from the thing. Using the *naginata* for support, he tried to catch his breath. His lungs burned and his head swam. Suddenly, he remembered the other clothes Taira had provided.

He ripped the *juban* from his back, and flung the short jacket to the ground. The trousers followed. He reached for the *shita-obi*, but fell back in excruciating pain as the loincloth constricted itself about his testicles. It also shrieked as he cut it in half with the *naginata*.

His pain faded after a moment, but Ichiro was too tired to move. He stared at the sky, letting the sleet pound his face. His skin goose-pimpled and his teeth chattered, but these were minor inconveniences now. In fact, they were positively refreshing.

"Well, now I'm both horseless and naked," he said aloud to himself. He got to his feet, using the *naginata* as a walking stick.

Now which way is Getsuyu's village? he wondered. No matter, I know where Taira's camp is. Any direction away from there is fine by me.

He struck off toward the rising moon, knowing he would have to find shelter soon or freeze to death.

———

The river, its rolling waters black and thick, looked familiar, he thought. A broken fishing trap, bobbing next to a jagged and twisted tree limb, confirmed it. Getsuyu's village was nearby.

The sleet had stopped, and the first flickers of dawn rose above the hilltops. The huts stood eerily still and quiet in the soft grey moonlight.

There was no sign of any cooking fire, nor did any lantern glow behind rice paper windows. The village was dead, more dead than when Ichiro had first seen it less than a month before.

He crossed the bridge and walked slowly down the muddy dirt road that ran through the village. The silence was deafening. Nothing made a noise, not a bird, not an insect, not even the wind.

Ichiro came to the shrine of the Amida Buddha where he first met Getsuyu. Now, I recall that Getsuyu's house was in this direction, he said to himself. He found the *jito's* house more easily than he expected. He pushed the door. It fell inside with a dull thud.

"Getsuyu? Are you in?" Ichiro called. "It is me, Minamoto-no-Ichiro."

No one answered.

He stepped inside. The hut seemed empty, as if it had been abandoned ages ago. Dust covered everything, including the cooking pot. *That seems strange,* he thought, especially because it had not been that long since he had been in Getsuyu's home.

Something crunched under his foot. He knelt down and found the shards of a *sake* jar. The neck of the jar, the stopper still inserted, stood upright in the dirt of the floor. The broken ceramic saddened Ichiro. He remembered Getsuyu pouring warm rice wine into his cup and discoursing on Taira and dragons. "What tales I could tell you now, old man, to pay you back for your kindness," he thought aloud.

He dropped the shard back into the dust. A heavy folding screen, its red lacquered bamboo now faded and peeling, blocked the entrance to the other half of the hut. Ichiro pushed it aside.

They lay side-by-side, Getsuyu and his wife, under a large, heavily stained old *futon*. Their mummified remains suggested they had been dead a long time. In death, they seemed at peace, with her head on his shoulder and his now paper-thin arm around her. The skin on their faces was brown and crusty. Their lips were drawn back in a semblance of a contented smile.

Ichiro slumped against a wall and cried. "I brought this on you," he said to the corpses. "Taira did this because you sheltered me. Forgive me!" He wept uncontrollably, each tear expressing his loss.

Composing himself, he began a search for things he could use. In a dusty chest he found men's clothes. The jackets and trousers were worn and musty smelling, but they would do. Getsuyu was a little smaller than Ichiro, as he remembered, but the *jito's* kimono and loincloth fit well enough. Ichiro found a long jacket and pair of trousers that were not too uncomfortable. There was also a quilted outer robe for the cold weather, as well as *tabi* and wooden sandals.

In a sealed jar he found some roasted millet and rice, still as fresh as the day it was harvested. There was also some pickled daikon. Ichiro decided not to cook a meal there, fearing Taira's men would spot the smoke from any fire. Instead, he took Getsuyu's old cooking pot and wrapped it in a bundle with the food.

As he tied up the cloth, he noticed something shining embedded in the dirt. It took only a moment to free the object.

It was a small mirror. Ichiro spit on the glass and wiped away the remaining soil. He looked at the mirror and saw a strange face staring back at him. The face had long hair that was wild and knotted. A thick, scraggly beard and two long, tangled moustaches adorned the lower half of the face. A pair of weary, almost wise, eyes stared back at him.

Ichiro smiled. The reflection returned the smile.

"Well, Taira's men are looking for you, my friend," he said to himself. "Perhaps a change in your appearance is in order."

Ichiro found a razor in Getsuyu's chest. There was water in the Amida Buddha's shrine, he recalled, so he took his bundle and *naginata* and went there.

Shaving off his beard without hot water and lather was a problem, but he remembered equally difficult shaves back at the airfield. He managed the operation without once cutting himself. Shaving his head proved easier, once he removed the hair on his neck.

Ichiro rinsed the razor in the water trough and then carefully tossed the hair clippings to the wind.

He glanced in the mirror to admire his handiwork. "Now I am a wandering mendicant, an old monk," he said, running his hand first over his bare chin then over his gleaming scalp.

To complete his disguise, Ichiro found a large basket, once big enough to completely cover his head. Using the razor he slice away some of the weaving to provide eyeholes. He placed the basket over his head and glance at himself in the mirror. What stared back at him was the image of a *kumoso*, a monk of emptiness who had renounced this life.

A weight seemed lifted from his mind. For a moment his mind returned to the airfield shrine where he had prepared himself for death. He thought that he had understood *mono-no-aware* then, but he knew now he was mistaken. Then had he clung to death as a release from his pain and from the curse of sending young men to their deaths. Now, hounded and hunted, running naked, he knew he also had caused a great pain even to those who helped him. That was true *mono-no-aware*.

Lying in Taira's pit, he had found reality slipping from his fingertips. Even his hatred for Taira fell away. *Was that satori, then?* he thought. *Is this enlightenment? Or I am just weary?*

Ichiro glanced up at the statue of the Amida Buddha and smiled. "I want you to make sure Getsuyu and his wife are reborn in the Pure Land," he told the figurine. "And if I die, you make sure I am reborn there, too," he added.

The statue remained solid, unmoving. But the position of its hand in a *mudra* of compassion suggested Ichiro's wish would be fulfilled.

———

Ichiro had just left the shrine when he saw the riders crossing the bridge. There were five of them, obviously just a small patrol, and they seemed weary and tired of searching. He recognized none of the men.

"You there, monk!" the lead rider shouted.

"Yes, honored sir, how can I help you?" Ichiro said.

The rider reined his horse up next to Ichiro. He was a large, corpulent man with a sunburned face ringed by a corona of coarse black hair. "We're looking for a *samurai*, a prisoner of Lord Taira's who escaped."

"I have seen no one but you all day," Ichiro replied.

The man stared at Ichiro with small, rodent-like eyes. "Say, who are you, monk? Why do you hide your face?"

"Me?" Ichiro said, placing a hand on his upper chest. "I'm just a poor pilgrim who has renounced this world and who seeks enlightenment," he lied, finding a certain pleasure in that. "I am bound for a Jimmukei Monastery, which is not fair from here. My name is Kochi."

"Just a monk, eh?" The man's eyes focused on the *naginata*. "If you are a monk, why is it you should go abroad armed?"

Ichiro bowed his head. "Alas, although I am nothing more than a monk, with no worldly possessions, there are still those men would not hesitate to rob even me." He demonstrated a few quick moves with the *naginata* to show the rider that he knew how to use the weapon. "I usually say a few prayers for the poor fellows afterward."

"So would you say prayers for me?" the man quipped.

"I think you are not a man in need of prayer," Ichiro replied. He saw a chance now to distract the men. "But for a few coins, I might be willing to make an offering for you, to insure that you find what you are seeking."

The man grinned. "You are quite something, monk." He reached in his jacket and pulled out some coins, tossing them at Ichiro's feet.

Ichiro knelt down carefully and picked up the coins. "Many blessings on you. And while it is true I have seen no one today, someone has been in this village. I went to the village master's house. The *jito* is dead, but there is evidence of a man who has been there not long ago. Perhaps he went to the south. The Tokaido Post Road is not far away, just over that ridge." Ichiro gestured toward the burned millet fields he had first crossed to reach the village.

The man turned in his saddle. "The monk says Minamoto was here. He's probably headed toward the Post Road."

The others turned their horses about and recrossed the bridge.

"I am much obliged, monk. Say some more prayers for this Minamoto. He'll probably need them," the man said. He took another coin from his jacket and threw it at Ichiro's head.

Ichiro snatched the coin from the air. "You be can sure I will do so."

The man took off after his companions.

Ichiro put the coins in his bundle. The money would come in handy later, when he had a chance to make a real offering.

The hubless wheel turns, he thought with amusement. For a

moment, the landscape around him seemed to shimmer and threatened to dissolve. The five riders grew increasingly out-of-focus.

Ichiro smelled and tasted salt spray. Then the world was solid once more, and the riders were gone. But the experience bothered him. Was it a power inherent in himself, or was it another product of Taira's tampering with chaos? He needed to know, and he hoped the abbot of the monastery could tell him.

————

The path into the hills was well worn and gave Ichiro little trouble, not that it mattered, because he felt exhilarated, and even the roughest, most pock-marked road would not have bothered him. He had seen nothing which suggested that Taira's men were still after him. The nearer he came to the monastery, the more orderly things seemed. The sun at mid-afternoon was a dazzling gold. He took off the basket and felt the air, cool and pleasant, on his freshly shaved scalp. He had a sense of being somehow reborn.

Ichiro remembered many of the hills and landmarks from his first visit to the monastery. He looked forward to seeing the abbot again.

Near the crest of the hill he spotted a small grove of plum trees. Much of the fruit had fallen to the ground or rotted on the branches of the horribly twisted trees, but here and there he found a few fruits still intact, red and sweet.

After he ate his fill of plums, having sucked the juice from his fingers, Ichiro sat with his back against a plum tree. The sun, now just above the horizon, warmed his face. In the distance he saw what appeared to be two large birds circling in the sky.

The birds' movement was hypnotic and, combined with a full belly, made his feel sleepy. "I'll rest a moment, then continue to the monastery," he told himself.

Ichiro had barely closed his eyes when he heard the loud beating of heavy, leathery wings. A sudden sharp wind kicked stinging sand and dirt into his face. He kept his eyes shut. Whoever it was that wanted to disturb his rest would introduce himself soon enough.

"What have we here, Jiro?" said a high-pitched voice.

"A lazy damn monk, Akiku, come to steal our plums, then scold us for clinging to earthly things," a second, slightly deeper voice said. Wings fluttered.

A sign of anger? Ichiro wondered. *Or frustration?*

He opened his eyes. Standing over him were two large bird-like creatures. He had seen *tengu* in the illustrated books he had read as a child, but this was the first he had ever seen in real life.

He smiled, amused at their vaguely comical appearance. The *tengu's* heavy, leathery brown wings ended in long, slender clawed hands. They had huge thin beaks and their bodies were covered in thick, brown feathers. Each wore a coat of woven leaves and tiny cap on its head.

Ichiro also noticed each creature had one hand resting on the hilt of a short sword. Although they looked foolish, the *tengu* possessed a reputation both as bandits and as deadly swordsmen. It was even said that Yoshitsune had learned the art of *kendo* from the *tengu*, Ichiro recalled.

"The vile hypocrite. Look at the plum juice on his fingers. See where it has dribbled down his chin," said the first *tengu*, the one called Akiku. It was the shorter of the two and had yellowish speckles on its beak.

"I say let us teach him a lesson," the one called Jiro replied "Let us beat him till he screams."

"That would hardly seem fair," Ichiro said, rising and supporting himself with his *naginata*. "I apologize for eating your plums, but I was hungry, and they were so cold and so sweet."

"That's what all men say," Akiku shrieked. "And they rob us blind!"

"I am sorry to have caused you injustice," Ichiro said. He took one of the coins from his kimono. "Perhaps this will make amends."

Akiku slapped the coin from Ichiro's hand. "Human money! We have no need for worthless metal!" it hissed.

"We'll take what you owe us!" said Jiro. It sank a taloned hand into Ichiro's shoulder.

On reflex, Ichiro snapped the shaft of the *naginata* upward between the creature's legs.

The *tengu* howled in pain. It doubled over and fell on its side, its hands covering its injured genitals.

"So it's a fight you want," Akiku said. The *tengu* drew its *katana* and lunged at Ichiro.

Ichiro parried the attack with the *naginata*, then counterattacked. The *tengu* flapped its wings and took off, barely avoiding the thrust. It flew over Ichiro and landed behind him.

But as Ichiro turned to parry a second attack, the *tengu* leaped over him again. Its thin, scaly foot shot toward Ichiro's head. He tried to duck, but the *tengu's* foot caught him full on the shoulder, knocking him from his feet.

Ichiro scrambled to his feet. The *tengu* spun about in mid-air and flung itself at him. Ichiro parried the creature's sword attack. It kicked out at him again, but he grabbed the *tengu's* leg and pulled.

Startled, the creature tried to kick with its other foot and slashed at him with a free hand, but Ichiro caught it by the wrist. The *tengu*, now with only one wing free, became unstable. Ichiro snapped his arms down and the creature crashed heavily to the ground.

He sat on its chest and placed a sandaled foot on its throat. The *tengu* tried to struggle. "If you move, I'll break your neck like a chicken's," Ichiro said.

He glanced at the other *tengu*, the one called Jiro, who was now sitting up. Its hands were still firmly planted over its crotch. "And if you try anything," Ichiro said "I will make it far more painful than a kick in the balls."

The *tengu* howled again, not relishing a repeat of the pain. "All right," Jiro said. "We surrender. You can have the damn plums."

"They weren't ours anyway," Akiku admitted. "It's a wild plum grove."

"I thought as much," Ichiro said. "But that wouldn't stop you from waylaying a stranger for a bit of fun, now would it?" He took his foot from Akiku's throat and stood up.

The *tengu* sat up, rubbing its throat. "Those plums may not be ours, but you lied too. You clearly are no monk."

Ichiro picked up the *tengu's* swords. "I never said I was a monk.

You assumed that." He slipped the two *katana* into the waistband of his outer robe.

"I will just hold on to these so you won't be tempted to bother any other travelers," he told the *tengu*. "Now, if you will excuse me, I must reach Jimmukei Monastery before dark."

"You'll have long walk then," Jiro said. It gingerly got to its feet, still wincing in discomfort. "Jimmukei monastery disappeared about five days ago."

Ichiro turned to face the creatures. "If this is another of your tricks, I will have your heads."

"Oh, no, no, *samurai*," Akiku said. "My brother tells the truth. One morning it was there, then by afternoon it was gone, every block and every stone and every roof tile."

"And every monk," Jiro added.

"I don't believe you," Ichiro said.

"I promise you, in the Buddha's name, it is no lie!" Akiku said.

"Then take me there," Ichiro said.

"Why should we, after the way you treated us? Who are you anyway?" moaned Jiro.

"I am Minamoto-no-Ichiro, descended from the great Yoshitsune," he said.

The *tengu's* eyes grew wide with fear, and they suddenly flung themselves at Ichiro's feet. "Oh, forgive us, master," they cried.

Their reaction stunned Ichiro. "Forgive you? What do you mean?" he asked.

"Our ancestors taught the great Yoshitsune," Akiku said. "They vowed loyalty forever to the Minamoto clan."

"And now we have betrayed it," Jiro wailed.

"No, you did not betray that loyalty, because you did not know who I was," Ichiro said. He noticed the sun was dipping below the horizon. "But you can make up for it. Take me to Jimmukei Monastery."

"Gladly," Jiro said, but Ichiro sensed the reluctance in their voices. Or was it fear?

CHAPTER TWENTY-SIX

The tengu carried Ichiro toward the monastery, but from the air he could see the creatures had not lied.

Even in the dying evening light, it was obvious the monastery had vanished. Left behind was a huge area of bare, brown earth, and only a few scraggly plants. Around the edge many large trees looked like the victims of a typhoon. Some trees lay on their sides, uprooted, while others were neatly stripped of foliage.

It looked like some giant hand had simply reached down and plucked the building from the face of the earth.

"Take me down," he said.

The tengu slowed their flight, circled the area once, and, hovering, lowered Ichiro to the ground. Then they too landed.

"See," Jiro said. "Gone, but who knows where?"

"Come on, Ichiro-san, you've seen the truth. Now let us leave," Akiku said.

"No, I need to know why this happened," Ichiro replied. He walked toward the open ground.

The closer he came to the area, the more Ichiro was convinced that this was not Taira's work. Everything had disappeared; not even a single building stone could be seen, but he knew Taira would have delighted in totally destroying the monastery and leaving its charred and shattered ruins behind as a warning.

He walked to the center of the ground. From here he could see the tengu had started a fire and were preparing to cook some of his rice and millet. He pitied them now. They clearly feared this place. "I would too," he said to himself, "if I were they."

His eyes fell on something glistening in the last of the day's sun. Ichiro knelt down and picked it up. It was a white stone, one of Hachiman's symbols.

Ichiro smiled. He took the stone in his hand and assumed a *zazen* position. He let his mind relax and began controlling his breathing in the way he had learned when a pageboy. *So*, *Hachiman*, he thought, *what happens when the hubless wheel turns?*

The world fell away.

Sunlight surrounded him. He sat on a pathway of white stones. Around him was a moss-carpeted forest shrouded in mist. In the distance he saw Jimmukei Monastery. He could hear the low, deep sound of chanting issuing from within its walls.

To his side he heard the sound of footsteps. Ichiro turned and saw a wraith-like apparition: a small man dressed in a broad-rimmed straw hat and priest's robes.

Abbot Kobori smiled. "Ichiro, welcome. We've been expecting you."

———

The monks' chants formed a single, overwhelming drone note. Ichiro could feel the note humming in his own chest. *It was a sound*, he thought, *that could shatter mountains.* Or hold a monastery in a place between universes.

Ichiro sat with the abbot in his chambers. The abbot sipped tea. Ichiro could see the strain and weariness in the man's face.

"So what is this place? The Pure Land?" Ichiro asked.

Abbot Kobori laughed. "Perhaps. Perhaps not. Everything is illusion, and so is this. So is the Pure Land, if you wish. But this place will protect us for the time being.

"We have chanted continuously for six days. At first I feared it would not work, then the world outside shimmered and dissolved, and we were here."

"Why did you leave?" Ichiro asked.

"We thought it wise to protect the Dharma from Taira's destruction."

Ichiro felt a tinge of anger. "You ran away, to save yourselves then?"

Kobori shook his head. "No, even this will not save us. We cannot stay here long without chanting. We each take turns, but eventually we will falter. Then we and our monastery shall return either to our proper world or to a chaotic universe. A small matter, I suppose." He sipped tea.

"I don't understand," Ichiro said.

"Each universe is like a living creature," Kobori said. "It is in balance, and to maintain that balance, it rejects that which does not belong. To keep something there requires a strong spell, like the strength of a *kami*."

"So that is what is happening to me," Ichiro said with a sudden realization. "In Taira's pit, I briefly returned to my own world."

Kobori nodded. There was sadness in his eyes. "The spell that held you in Nihon grows weak as chaos increases."

"But then why doesn't the universe reject Taira's demons? They, too, are from outside," Ichiro asked.

The abbot set his cup down. He sighed. "When a disease is strong enough, it overcomes a body that can no longer resist. So it is now. Chaos is on the point of overwhelming the universe."

"So why does it reject me?"

Kobori shrugged. "The universe resists where it can, even in futility. The spell weakens, and you are gone. The universe will survive only when the door between the worlds is closed."

Ichiro thought for a moment before asking his next question. "*Roshi*, am I right in assuming that it is Taira himself who must close that door?"

The abbot smiled. "You are wiser than I thought, Ichiro. Yes, he must close the door, but it must be soon. It is near the end of the twenty-eighth day of the lunar cycle."

Of course, Ichiro thought. On that day Taira must stay awake all night to purge his body of poisons. But as he had seen, the poisons in Taira, in the world, were so strong now that the *daimyo* might be unable to purge them.

"He will die that night," Ichiro realized, "and then no one will be able to close the gateway."

"Yes," the abbot said. "You understand."

"How long before then?"

"Three days," Kobori said.

"And long will it take me to reach Matsumae?"

"On foot, four days."

Ichiro cursed. "Then all is lost, *roshi*."

"No," the abbot said. "There is a way. Do you still have the final talisman the goldsmith made for you?"

"Yes, but how did you know?"

Kobori raised his hand for silence. "I know many things, but enough. Near the monastery is a cave. You will find what you need there."

The abbot gave Ichiro directions, then set down his teacup. "Now it is time for you to go."

Ichiro nodded. "The hubless wheel turns."

"And we are powerless to stop the Law of Karma," the abbot added.

The scene before Ichiro shimmered and flickered. He watched the abbot's image fade and dissolve. He saw the monastery turn to black sky and the stars become a whirlpool, but after a moment the stars and sky returned.

They were different stars and a different sky.

"He's back!" Jiro cried.

"Thank goodness!" Akiku added.

Ichiro could see the red of glow of morning in the east. "How long was I gone?"

"All night," Akiku said. "We were afraid you wouldn't return."

"We looked up and saw you covered in this yellowish glow. Then we heard a thunderclap, and you vanished," Jiro said.

"Where have you been?" Akiku asked.

"Perhaps the Pure Land," Ichiro said with a soft smile, "and perhaps not."

The *tengu* both looked puzzled. "The Pure Land, or maybe not?" Jiro asked.

"Think of it as a koan," Ichiro said. "Now, do you know of a cave not far from here?" He gave them the directions.

"Yes, we know of that cave," Akiku said. "But I would not wish to go there. It is a bad place."

"Good, then we shall be off," Ichiro said. He handed the *tengu* back their swords. Once more, he had no choice. It was three days to certain destruction.

The *tengu* did not protest. They apparently knew they also had no choice.

———

Keeping his balance with the *naginata*, Ichiro scrambled over a rocky outcropping. An icy rain was falling, and it made his footing precarious at best. The *tengu*, even clumsier on foot than he was, lagged behind.

Ichiro surveyed the cave while he waited for them to catch up. The cave formed a narrow black mouth running vertically among a massive outcropping. Loose soil from above had rolled down into a crack formed at the side of an overhang. In that soil, some twisted gray trees and a variety of blue, red, and green lichens had taken hold.

Ichiro saw some jagged gray objects at the mouth of the cave. The objects looked ragged and weather-beaten, but they were too distant to clearly make out. The rain only made his attempts to see more difficult. He wished he had the spyglass now.

Akiku came to his side. Jiro was not far behind.

"I'm freezing," Akiku moaned. "Terrible weather."

"Let us return when it's warmer," Jiro said.

Ichiro had to admit the *tengu* were right about the weather. The sleet and icy rain stung his skin, and was especially unpleasant on his bare scalp. For the first time he missed his hair. "I am going up to the cave. I want you to fly to either side of the opening."

Akiku started to protest, but Jiro said, "It's no use complaining. Do as he says."

The *tengu*, swords drawn, flew from the outcropping. Akiku ensconced herself behind a twisted pine tree to Ichiro's left. Jiro hid behind an upthrust boulder on the opposite side.

Ichiro moved cautiously toward the cave. The rock was now slick with ice, but his sandals seemed to grip well enough on most of the surface. The sleet stung his face like hundreds of tiny needles. He tried to remember what creature in legend was associated with icy rain.

As he approached the cave, Ichiro could finally see what the objects at the cave mouth clearly were. A crushed human rib cage, bits of cloth still stuck to it, was the nearest. Beyond it were scattered arm and leg bones, not all human. A human skull, missing its lower jaw, seemed to stare intently at him. Another skull, cracked open like an eggshell, lay next to it.

Ichiro edged toward the bones. The ground was covered in loose stones and he had to use the *naginata* as a walking stick to steady himself. He could see no weapons among the carnage, neither helmets, swords, nor spears. He wiped sleet from his face.

Then he saw it. A single woman's comb dangled from a stunted bush, and beneath it was a woman's ragged, torn wide obi.

Perhaps I should feel better that thing prefers women, he thought. He decided to move around the periphery, toward Akiku. Whatever was in the cave, he would rather not meet it head on.

Ichiro had taken about three steps when he slipped on a patch of ice. The loose stones underneath, not yet cemented by the sleet, slid free under his feet. Ichiro jammed the *naginata* into the ground to steady himself, but the shaft of the lance snapped with a gunshot-like crack that resounded off the nearby hills.

From inside the cave, something roared in response.

It was a roar like thunder, and it pounded Ichiro's head. Clutching the remnant of the ruined *naginata*, he covered his ears and dove for cover behind a large boulder. Ichiro could feel the sound beating on his body with each echo. A new roar followed the echoes from the cave.

He looked up in time to see the dragon at the cave's mouth. Ichiro remembered the creature, with its tiger's head and serpent's body, from the time he faced Taira in the village square. It was Taira's dragon.

Yet something was clearly wrong with it. Large open sores lined its flanks, and its left shoulder and the side of its neck displayed grey, leprous patches devoid of scales. The dragon was in obvious pain. Enraged, it sniffed the air with mad intensity, its large, round nostrils alternately flaring open and closing. Its long, forked tongue darted between black lips, tasting the air for the intruder.

Ichiro pressed himself close to the boulder, hoping the dragon had not seen him. He reached into his jacket and fingered the last talisman. He had to get it around the dragon's neck. The abbot had said the cave would contain what he needed, but he had not told Ichiro it might require a great deal of work to obtain.

Ichiro cursed breaking the *naginata*. Now it was about as valuable as a ragged sail was to a ship in a typhoon.

He noticed the rocks to his left were not quite so jagged as he first thought. They were also positioned so as to shield him from the dragon's view. If he could climb to the top he could edge himself around to the overhang above the cave mouth. That might give him a chance to get the medallion on the creature.

Ichiro turned back to see where the dragon was and came face-to-face with its huge, foul-smelling maw.

It roared and lunged for him. As he fell back, he jammed the *naginata* blade into the dragon's neck. The blade slid cleanly into a bare, grey area on the dragon's right side.

The dragon screamed and backed away from Ichiro. It tried vainly to dislodge the lance, but it could not get a talon around the stump of a shaft.

Ichiro scrambled toward the rocks, climbing as best he could. As he reached the top, he saw the two *tengu* flapping about the dragon's head. While they could not use their swords to seriously injure the dragon, they were able to keep the creature occupied.

As he watched, the dragon turned to face Akiku, only to have Jiro dart in from the other side and jab the creature in the flank. The dragon shrieked, sat on its haunches, and lashed out with its front talons at Jiro, but Akiku kicked the back of its head. It spun about and snapped, but its jaws fell on empty air.

"Hurry, Ichiro-san," Akiku shouted. "I don't know how much longer we can occupy it." But as the *tengu* spoke, the dragon cuffed her. Akiku tumbled through the air. She regained her balanced just before she would have crashed into an outcropping.

Ichiro raced along the overhang that ran along the top of the cave. As he unfastened the chain holding the medallion, he knew he would have to jump onto the writhing creature's back, but the dragon was too far away.

"Akiku, Jiro, force the dragon back toward the cave!" he shouted.

Akiku responded by stabbing the creature in the neck, just above the naginata, which remained firmly implanted in the creature's flesh. As the dragon went for Akiku, Jiro repeated the attack on the opposite side.

The dragon lashed out with a foreclaw and snapped its tail like a whip at the two *tengu*, but it also retreated a short distance.

Jiro flew to an outcropping, picked up a large stone and heaved it. The projectile hit the dragon square on the chest. It howled and withdrew further. While it occasionally snapped its sinuous head at an attacker, the dragon also kept retreating toward the safety of the cave.

Ichiro poised himself as the dragon came into range. Gritting his teeth, he jumped.

He landed just behind the dragon's neck. The force of the impact knocked the dragon forward, and Ichiro felt himself sliding off the creature. He dug the fingers of his right hand under a thick fold of scale and tried to wrap his legs around the dragon's body.

The dragon, surprised by the attack, shook itself violently. Ichiro held on for dear life as the creature bucked and shook itself. The *tengu* tried to draw its attention, but the dragon displayed a single-minded intention to dislodge its unwelcome rider.

Ichiro had managed to slip the chain around the dragon's neck. He now held an end in each hand, but he needed to fasten it for it to be effective. But his grip on the chain was now the only thing holding him onto the dragon.

He brought his hands together, digging his feet into the dragon's flanks, feeling the skin on his shins and feet being rubbed raw by the creature's scales. Then he saw that the dragon's neck was too thick at this point to allow the chain to completely pass around it. He would have to move up the neck, but that risked loosing the tenuous grip he had. *Then again, what choice do I have?* he thought.

Pushing with his feet, he made slow progress. He pressed himself close to the dragon's back, digging his heels in where he could as it bucked and shook. He felt his hands coming closer together around the dragon's neck, but it was not enough.

The dragon bucked less now, in part because the *tengu* were wearing it down. Then it shook itself hard, and Ichiro held on tight to keep from being bucked off.

He fixed his eyes on the chain. It was not much more now, only a hair's breadth. He forced the hook into the loop, watched it catch.

The dragon reared, slamming its back against a rock face. Ichiro hit the hard surface with a glancing blow, and it knocked the breath from his lungs. His legs lost their grip.

Terror seized him. His right hand was trapped between the chain and the dragon's neck.

The dragon shook violently, tossing Ichiro like a rag doll. Pain seared his shoulder as the muscles and bone twisted and stretched. The chain shifted, and his hand came loose.

Ichiro hit the ground heavily, like a bag of millet, his legs and arms akimbo. The landing left him breathless and paralyzed. He stared up at the icy rain and watched the claws and fangs of the dragon descend toward him.

The hubless wheel turns, he thought. *I've failed you, Hachiman.*

He waited for the talons to sink deep into his chest. The world melted and went black. He tasted sand and sea and a hint of something like Death.

"Well done, Ichiro-san!" several voices all said at once. One voice sounded like Akiku's, , but he also heard the sound of Abbot Kobori's, voice, and of Hachiman's, too.

He wanted to disagree, but his lungs and chest hurt too much. His right shoulder and arm throbbed. He took a breath.

The world swam into view. Akiku and Jiro knelt next to him. Ichiro thought the *tengu* were smiling, but he had no idea what a *tengu's* smile looked like. "So the dragon killed you, too, then?" he asked.

Akiku and Jiro both laughed, a pair of warbling high-pitched gurgles.

"By no means, Ichiro-san," Akiku said.

"See for yourself," Jiro added.

The *tengu* raised Ichiro to a sitting position. He winced as they touched his shoulder, but the pain seemed to be subsiding. The pain vanished completely when he saw the dragon.

It lay quietly licking a sore patch on its left foreleg. The talisman glistened on its chest, exuding a warm, white glow. As Ichiro watched, the dragon's sores and gray areas retreated, to be replaced by healthy skin and new, shining scales.

"Help me up," he said to the *tengu*.

Akiku and Jiro got him to his feet. He walked unsteadily toward the dragon.

The dragon looked up at him, pain in its eyes. The *naginata* remained planted in its right shoulder.

Ichiro reached out and stroked the dragon's neck. The skin was warm and smooth.

"Forgive me," Ichiro said. He grabbed the broken shaft of the lance and pulled it out.

The dragon did not flinch.

In fact, it didn't seem to feel the pain at all.

Ichiro watched the wound left by the naginata close and seal itself. After a few minutes, it had vanished completely.

"There is a saddle and bridle in the cave," Akiku said. "As well as many things I would prefer not to mention."

"May they be reborn in the Pure Land," Ichiro replied. "Bring me the saddle."

The dragon calmly allowed Ichiro to cinch the saddle to its back, and it did not protest as he placed the harness over its head and the bit in its mouth. He stroked its head as he would a horse's snout. It gently nudged him.

"We have a long ride ahead," he said.

"A long ride?" Jiro asked. "To where?"

"To Matsumae," Ichiro said. "We have an appointment there."

CHAPTER TWENTY-SEVEN

The air tasted of salt and spray.

Ichiro pulled back on the reins. The dragon rapidly flapped its heavy, leathery wings to hover in place. Leaning back in the saddle, Ichiro could see a wide expanse of sea—the straits of Tsugaru Kaikyo, which separated the northernmost tip of Honshu from Hokkaido.

"Where is Matsumae?" asked Jiro. He hovered next to the dragon, his wings beating madly to stay in place.

"Down to the northwest, on that stretch of land," Ichiro said. "The castle should be visible soon."

Ichiro remembered visiting the castle--or its copy in his world--when he was a boy. Built in 1601 by Tokugawa Ieyasu, it was the most northerly feudal castle in Japan. He recalled it as wind-swept, cold, sad and lonely.

He let off the reins and then tugged gently. The dragon began its descent through the sparse cloud cover.

The descent was a peculiar experience for Ichiro. It combined some of the worst traits of both flying an aircraft and of riding a horse.

It had taken him a while to learn the subtler aspects of dragon flight. One, after all, rarely called on a horse to take to the air or to bank slowly and then descend for a landing.

Once they were below the clouds and into the bright, clean sunshine, Ichiro spotted the fleet, which the Shogun and Matsuo had assembled. It was a formidable armada, consisting of several war-junks, Korean-style turtle boats and a variety of small junks and fishing smacks.

"You have done good work, my friends," he thought aloud. "Let us hope it is sufficient."

"Ichiro-san, what is that?" Akiku cried. The *tengu* pointed toward the horizon.

Ichiro looked up. A rainbow of bright, intense colors carved a swath across the sky. One end extended up beyond the clouds, toward the sun, while the other seemed firmly planted in the earth a short distance north of the castle. It was no ordinary rainbow, Ichiro knew. It was thousands of years old and he knew it held the answer to many questions.

"That," he told the tengu, "is the Bridge to Heaven."

Ichiro circled the castle once, watching the multi-colored banners of the allied clans flapping in the breezing. The *samurai* and *ashigaru* cheered. With the two tengu acting as wingmen, he carefully brought the dragon to earth in the courtyard.

As the warriors continued to cheer, the dragon responded by standing up on its hind legs and roaring.

Even though Ichiro struggled to stay in the saddle, he smiled because he knew what the roar was.

It was a cry of freedom.

Two soldiers came out to take the dragon's reins. Akiku and Jiro helped Ichiro from the saddle.

Shizuka, Tamika and Yukio ran out to greet him. Matsuo and the Shogun were not far behind. Shizuka, for once unrestrained, threw her arms around his neck and hugged him. The others slapped him the back, their faces shining with huge grins.

"Welcome, General," the Shogun said. His face was a broad grin. "The army awaits your command."

"We will seek the Bridge to Heaven," Ichiro said. "I believe it holds some answers to our questions." Then he sighed with relief. "But first, I would like some tea and some food, and a chance to rest. I have had a hard flight."

"The Ainu are suspicious of anything we do," Matsuo told Ichiro. Matsuo had told Ichiro that he and his father and two brothers regularly came to Matsumae as part of their feudal duties. He had thought it wise to befriend the Ainu and not treat them as savages like most Japanese.

"Of course, I can't blame them for being suspicious," Matsuo said. "Whenever we Japanese come to Hokkaido, all we seem to bring is war or men intent on stealing their island's resources."

"I have never seen an Ainu," Ichiro admitted. Like every school-boy, he knew the aboriginal people of Hokkaido were supposed to be hairy and barbaric, and worshiped bears. The men's faces were covered in whiskers except for their eyes and mouths, and the women tattooed black moustaches on their upper lips for beauty. How much of it was true, he could not say.

The two men rode side-by-side down a well-worn path. A small, mounted contingent followed behind. Shizuka, Tamika, and the Emperor were also part of the train. Shizuka and Tamika came because Ichiro could not refuse them the opportunity to see the Bridge to Heaven. Saigo came because the Shinto priests in the castle said the *kami* would be insulted if the Mikado, a *kami* incarnate, were denied a pilgrimage.

The train also carried the two other sacred relics to be dedicated at the shrine. Ichiro once more had Kusinagi in its familiar place by his side.

Ichiro looked up at the arching rainbow. Unlike other rainbows, it did not seem to grow dim as they rode toward it. Its colors remained strong and clear even in a cloudless sky. Ichiro had to admit the sight was awe-inspiring, but to be so close to heaven was also disturbing.

They rode past silvery flooded paddies of green ripening rice as well as some fields planted with what appeared to be sugar beets. In the distance, Ichiro saw the dark blue-green of cool weather forests of pine, birch and larch. It seemed most of the land was covered in trees or cultivated fields. Only the snow-capped and cloud-enshrouded peaks of gray and brown mountains broke up the expanse of green carpet.

"There's the kotan that guards the Bridge," said Matsuo.

A short distance ahead was a collection of straw huts, grain houses and animal pens that made up an Ainu village. The kotan residents were busy at their labors, but they soon stopped work when they saw the approaching soldiers.

"Their jito is a reasonable fellow," Matsuo said, "but he also trusts no one from Matsumae except for me, and I'm not sure how far that trust extends."

A large, barrel-chested man appeared at the top of road. Several other Ainu joined the man, some carrying fishing spears and others bearing scythes and other farming tools. Ichiro sensed the Ainu suspected a trick and were prepared to fend off any attack.

The train drew up short of the village. "We'll go no farther," Matsuo said. "I don't wish to upset them, because I've seen what the Ainu can do with those fishing spears. Most unpleasant."

There was a strained silence as each side watched the other carefully. The Ainu jito appeared to being sizing up the opposition and calculating how long it would take to annihilate them. Ichiro suspected the Ainu could accomplish it quite quickly and efficiently.

"They look nasty," Tamika said, riding up to Ichiro's side.

"I suspect they think the same of us," he replied.

"I think we should approach on foot," Matsuo said to Ichiro.

Matsuo dismounted and handed his reins to another *samurai*. Ichiro did likewise, handing his reins to Tamika.

"Shigeru-san, how is the crop this year? As plentiful as the dowries of your daughters, I hope?" Matsuo said, starting up the road.

The *jito* laughed.

"Matsuo, you are just like your father, much to your mother's sorrow." He walked toward Matsuo. Two younger Ainu were at his side.

The *jito* was a stocky, well-muscled man, with pale, leathery skin. He was not as hairy as everyone had told Ichiro the Ainu were, but he was hairy enough. A coarse, wiry beard covered his face, and similar hair covered the back of his hands and the exposed portions of his chest.

The man wore a quilted robe decorated with embroidered geometric patterns. The *jito's* head was adorned with a headdress made of what seemed to be woven straw and bear fur. Large rings dangled from his earlobes.

The younger men at his side were taller, but also stocky and well-muscled. One had a short beard, while the other had only a faint amount of curly facial hair. Like the *jito*, they had earrings in both ears.

"It has been too long, Shigeru," Matsuo said.

"Yes, long enough that I can recall when you had two eyes," Shigeru replied.

"One is still good enough to enjoy the beauty of the ladies," Matsuo said. He turned to Ichiro. "General, this is Shigeru, the village head-man. Shigeru, this is General Minamoto-no-Ichiro. We seek your help."

The *jito* raised a thick eyebrow. "Our help?" he asked suspiciously. "Since when has the army of Nihon bothered to ask our help?"

"We seek the Bridge to Heaven," Ichiro said. "Can you take us there?"

The Ainu shook his head. "You ask too much, general. Yes, we can take you there, but you would displease the Bear-Goddess. She would destroy you."

"Unless..." Matsuo said with a smile.

"Unless you appease her with a feast," Shigeru said. He grinned. "You understand us well, Matsuo."

Matsuo turned to Ichiro. "We have no choice, but a bear-feast is not unpleasant."

Ichiro smiled, then laughed. "After the last dinner party I attended, Matsuo, I can assure you, a bear-feast will be more than pleasant."

———

The *jito*, with a contingent of most of the adult Ainu, both male and female, led Ichiro's party on foot to the Bridge of Heaven. The base of the bridge was a ruined stone temple, once a shrine to the brother and sister *kami* Izanagi and Izanami. The bridge, Ichiro recalled, was formed after the two deities had stirred the ocean with a spear and formed the islands of Japan from the chaos.

The light from the rainbow was dazzling, especially where it ended in a shallow pool within the shrine. The light merged into a dazzling white sphere just above the water. But as they watched, the light began fading. As the sun set, the Bridge to Heaven slowly vanished.

The pool glistened with the last light of the setting sun and with the milky rays of the waning moon. In another two days even that light would vanish with the new moon, Ichiro knew. If Taira succeeded, then it was likely the shrine would never again reflect light of any kind.

The Ainu lighted torches and started cooking fires. Before long, meat and fish were sizzling over the burning logs. Jars of sake, bamboo wine, and other alcohol passed through many hands. The villagers ripped off hunks of meat with their teeth and washed it back with huge mouthfuls of liquor.

"The Ainu call drunkenness 'Supreme Bliss'," Matsuo said. "After what we've been through, I'm inclined to agree," Matsuo said. He passed a *sake* jar and a skewer of smoked salmon to Ichiro.

"You have seen a bear-feast before," Ichiro said. He sipped the sake. It was warm and refreshing. So was the salmon. "So what do we do?"

"The Bear Goddess will take her time in coming," Matsuo said. "Since we may have a long wait, the best we can do is to enjoy ourselves."

After a while, an older Ainu, a village elder, began to sing. He told of how the salmon-folk took human form to mate with humans, and how a fisherman fell in love with a salmon-woman. He refused to give in to her wishes to stop fishing, and she returned to the sea. Then one day, he speared a salmon heavy with roe. When he placed the fish on the ground, it transformed itself into his wife, now with child. His spear had pierced her through the heart, and she died in his arms. In grief, he vowed to never again fish for salmon.

Ichiro found himself moved by the tale, even though he had to rely on Matsuo to translate the unfamiliar Ainu into Japanese. This was not the tale of a barbarian, but of a civilized human, he had to admit.

The singing continued as a young woman, her upper and lower lips heavily tattooed, sang the bawdy tale of the love of the great tortoise-god of the sea for the owl-god of the mountain and what children this union produced. The Ainu, now suitably inebriated, roared with approval.

As the laughter died down, an Ainu beat on a small skin drum. Several men and women began a mad, whirling dance. Two Ainu men gathered Tamika and Shizuka into the whirling circle, and even Saigo joined in. To the Ainu, the emperor was simply another man, not a divine ruler. For Saigo, however, to be treated so casually seemed to be a great relief.

Eventually Ichiro was pulled into the dance, and he made a great effort to follow the steps even as he struggled not to limp or stumble. As the alcohol took effect, Ichiro found Time collapsing upon itself. The dancing itself seemed to collapse Time, making the seconds and hours run faster.

Eventually, the revelers began dropping out one by one. They gathered themselves around the dying embers of the cooking fires and slept.

Ichiro sat down beside a sleeping Shizuka and picked up a sake jar. It was empty, which saddened him. "The feast is over," he said, "and the Bear-Goddess did not appear. Perhaps we were not celebrating enough to please her."

He felt a warm tear roll down his face. His head hurt. He lay down beside Shizuka and placed his arm around her.

"Bear-Goddess," he whispered. "I am disappointed you would treat the end of Nihon and the universe so lightly." After a moment, he fell asleep.

His drunken dreams ended abruptly when someone screamed.

Ichiro sat up, his hand instinctively going to Kusinagi. He heard a commotion near the temple. There was the sound of tree limbs and undergrowth snapping. Ainu shouted and yelled, then a deep, angry growl pierced the night. Birds, awakened by the noise, fled the treetops in fright. Their terrified cries added to the commotion.

"What is it?" he asked.

"The Bear-Goddess comes," said Shigeru.

Ichiro tried to stand, but found himself still groggy. His head throbbed. Through foggy eyes, he could see the flames of fires and torches flickering distortedly next to the temple where the Ainu had gathered.

He staggered toward the temple. The cold, wet air quickly revived him, but he was amazed that the night's earlier debauchery had had little ill effect on the natives.

Most of the Ainu were now in the woods. Their torches danced like huge, orange fireflies as they ran. Some beat drums and others blew a variety of noisemakers. But over the din Ichiro could hear something large, very large, crashing through bushes, tossing up undergrowth, and breaking branches and twigs on the forest floor.

Ichiro noticed that both the sound and the torches were getting closer. The Ainu were driving the Bear-Goddess, or whatever it was, into the clearing.

Suddenly, something burst from the woods. Ainu scattered in all directions and gradually formed a circle around the dark, huge thing.

"The Mother! The Mother of Gods and Men!" the Ainu chanted.

In torchlight, a huge brown bear stood heaving and trembling. The creature took in huge gulps of air, wheezing at each breath. There was a musky odor to the animal, a smell that spoke of mountain earth, forest air, and spring water. It stood up on its hind legs and bellowed.

Ichiro realized the bear was more than huge; it was gigantic. It stood nearly two-and-a-half times the height of a human, with legs as thick as a young birch and large, heavily clawed hands. He could also see the bear was an old female, with loose, blackened dugs and sparse fur along her belly.

Shigeru shouted something in Ainu. The chanting stopped. Everything was silent except for the crackling of torches and the heavy, tired breathing of the bear.

Ichiro looked around. He saw all too quickly that the Ainu had encircled him as well. He stood alone in the ring with the bear.

"Matsuo," he called, "what did the *jito* say?"

Matsuo forced his way passed several Ainu and came to Ichiro's side. "He said 'Let the Mother judge the visitors.'"

"Which means?"

"They believe the bear will decide our truthfulness," Matsuo explained. "If we are worthy of entering the temple, she will leave. If not, she will kill us."

Ichiro looked at the ring of Ainu around them. "I suppose running would do us no good?"

"Not unless you would prefer impalement on an Ainu spear."

"I see," Ichiro said. "Well, I think I have nothing to fear anymore." He strode slowly toward the bear, his arms extended, hands out.

The bear, unsure of Ichiro's motives, stepped back. She swung a paw toward him as a warning and growled. Her mouth displayed large and well-worn yellow teeth.

"Mother of gods and men," he said softly, "the *kami* Ojin Tenno Hachiman sent me here because Nihon and all the world is in danger. The Bridge of Heaven holds many answers to our problems."

The bear dropped to all fours as if to attack.

Ichiro closed his eyes.

After a moment, he opened them. The bear crouched before him. It sniffed his body, its large black nose twitching nervously.

Ichiro reached out a hand to touch the animal. The bear started, but made no move to strike. He stroked its head. The fur was thick, but fragile. The animal's skin was loose, dry, and inelastic. This was an old bear, he realized, but how old, he could not venture to guess.

Perhaps this is the Bear-Goddess, Ichiro thought, caressing the bear's fur. "Mother Goddess," he said softly. "If you love your children, you know that I tell you the truth. I must know the answer. I have no choice."

He looked down and saw the bear was gone. The Ainu began shouting. Ichiro caught a glimpse of the bear plunging back into the darkness of the forest and the night.

"The Bear-Goddess has decided" Shigeru shouted. "The visitors speak the Truth. They may enter the temple at dawn."

Ichiro felt giddy. He suddenly felt as old as the ancient she-bear. He released a great sigh and the tension rolled from his mind and body. "Thank you, Hachiman," he whispered.

———

The Bridge to Heaven slowly reappeared as the sun, red and warm, peeked over the eastern horizon. Even as faint as they were now, the colors of the Bridge dazzled the eye and took one's breath away. Each of the seven colors of the spectrum was of the most intense hue it could be, the brightest that could be found in the universe.

Then the colors hit the pool in the shrine. Ichiro averted his eyes as the pure white fireball of light expanded. The others, too, looked away. After a moment, the fireball receded to a steady, pulsing glow. Ichiro thought it seemed alive.

"What will you do?" Shizuka said.

"I don't know," he replied. "I have no idea what will happen." He fingered the hilt of Kusinagi to reassure himself.

"The time is right," said Shigeru. "You must go now."

Ichiro took a deep breath. What would he ask the kami? Or would he even need to ask a question? Or was it already played out? Only the *kami* and perhaps the Buddha knew the answer.

He walked toward the temple. As Ichiro approached the building, he could almost smell the age of the structure. The Ainu had not built this shrine, but neither had the people of Nihon. It had an air of antiquity about it, an odor of eternity. For a moment, Ichiro thought the temple was older than the world itself, and that it must have existed even before the universe was born.

The glow over the pool seemed to grow stronger as Ichiro approached. It seemed to pulse with a swifter and stronger rhythm. He reached the first step of the shrine. He smelled old stone and ancient wood. Ichiro tasted Time itself.

But as he moved to the first step, he found himself paralyzed. He was as rigid as a statue, unable to move anything except his eyelids and his lungs.

What is happening? Ichiro thought with panic. He tried to will himself to move. Nothing happened.

"Do not resist, Ichiro-san," a voice said in his head. It was Hachiman. "You have done all that I could have asked of you, but this is one task that is not yours to complete."

Ichiro felt a hand at his side, felt Kusinagi and its scabbard being withdrawn from his obi. Another hand touched him lightly on the shoulder. It was a touch of reassurance.

Then Saigo and Tamika stood before him.

Ichiro saw that Tamika cradled Kusinagi in her arms. The emperor carried the sacred jewel in one arm and carried the sacred mirror of Ameratsu in the other. They moved like creatures possessed by some supernatural power, their bodies glowing.

Ichiro could see an otherworldly love and compassion in the pair's eyes. They smiled gently, and nodded toward him. Then they turned and walked into the shrine.

As he watched, Saigo and Tamika removed their clothes and stood naked in the glow. Tamika now held the jewel and the mirror, while the emperor held Kusinagi over his head.

They placed the relics on the vine-covered altar of the shrine. They bowed to the four directions, then, holding hands, the two stepped into the pulsing ball of light.

Although the light nearly blinded him, Ichiro kept his eyes on the globe. He saw Saigo and Tamika embrace, then lie down in the shimmering pool. They began to make love.

The glow grew intensely bright. Ichiro screwed his eyes closed to shut out the light, then suddenly, whatever held him released its grasp. He tumbled to the earth.

Strong hands helped him to his feet and pulled him away from the temple.

"What's happening?" asked Shizuka.

"I have no idea," he replied.

"We were watching you, then suddenly you seemed frozen," said Matsuo. "Then all of us seemed powerless to move, except for the emperor and Tamika. They gathered up the sacred relics and started toward the temple. No one could stop them."

Shizuka grabbed his arm. "Look!" she cried, pointing to the temple.

The three watched in amazement as the ball of light began to fade. At last, it was reduced to a warm red ember. Waves of heat radiated from it.

Within the crimson glow, something moved. Its silhouette was black, like an Indian shadow puppet. It appeared vaguely human as it stepped from the boiling fires.

The glowing ball vanished. Beside the pool stood a tall, thin creature, a *futanari*. It stood naked, its smooth and nearly hairless muscular body glistening in the morning sun. Long, shiny tresses as black as ebony fell to its shoulders and down its back. Its face was delicate, both handsome and beautiful. On its upper body were smallish, conical breasts with dark nipples, but between its legs were both a fully formed penis with testicles and a vagina.

The sacred jewel, on a thin golden chain, rested between the being's breasts. In one arm it cradled the sacred mirror; in the other, Kusinagi. All three relics glowed with an unearthly sheen they had not previously possessed.

"We thank you, Minamoto-no-Ichiro, for uniting us again," the being said.

"Who...who are you?" Ichiro asked.

"You knew us as the Emperor Saigo and the warrior-women Tamika, and so we shall be again one day," the being said. It moved slowly down the steps and stood before Ichiro.

"But we are also Izanami and Izanagi," it said. "Once we created this floating world, but Izanami died as she gave birth to Fire. Long have we remained apart, beloved sister and brother, one in heaven and the other in the underworld., but you have reunited us, you have restored balance to the universe. For that, you have our thanks."

The man-woman leaned forward and kissed Ichiro gently on the lips.

Ichiro did not resist. The futanari's lips were strong and gentle, sweet as cherry blossoms. Ichiro's body trembled with confusion. "What should I...should *we* call you, beloved *kami*?"

The being smiled. "Call me Inyo, because I am both man and woman, order and chaos." Inyo placed Kusinagi in Ichiro's hands. "Now, beloved Ichiro, there is still work left to be done. Only when you complete it will we, sister and brother, husband and wife, be totally reunited. Then we shall return your Mikado and his consort."

"I would gladly die a thousand times to please you," Ichiro said.

"Your single life, returned to us whole with victory, is our desire," Inyo said.

"*Arigato*," Ichiro said. He could think of nothing else to say.

"To the glory of the emperor and to Nihon!" Matsuo shouted.

"For the Mother-Spirit and Father-Spirit," the Ainu *jito* cried.

The Ainu and *samurai* responded as one. Their cheers shook the treetops and echoed off the nearby mountains.

CHAPTER TWENTY-EIGHT

"The *tengu* say Taira has reached the harbor across the straits," Date Matsuo told Ichiro and the shogun. The men sat on thin cushions and *tatami* around a low table located in Ichiro's quarters in the castle. A map of the area was spread across the table top. "He appears to be finding all the ships he can to mount an invasion."

"Did Jiro and Akiku say how many men Taira appears to have?" Ichiro asked.

"They guessed there were perhaps two thousand, maybe twenty-five hundred," Matsuo replied.

"Then he seems to have lost more men," Ichiro said.

"How many did he have at Akasaka?" the shogun asked.

"We estimated five thousand," Matsuo replied.

"Good, with our seven thousand, the odds are in our favor," the shogun said.

"Only if we can defeat him today or tomorrow," Ichiro said. "If Abbot Kobori is correct, that is all the time we have. Our numbers will matter little if Taira holds out beyond that, let alone defeats us."

"I see," the shogun said. "Well, then we better make certain we waste no time. I'll have the ships and their crews prepare today for an attack tomorrow."

"Good," Ichiro said. "And Matsuo, you drill the troops today. We'll rise before dawn tomorrow and board the vessels."

"So it is to be the Battle of Dan-no-Urra once more," Matsuo said with a grin. "I would have imagined that after eight hundred years the Minamoto and the Taira would have decided to fight their last battle on land this time."

"Just remember, Matsuo, that the Minamoto have always had the superior seamen," Ichiro replied.

"If I do forget, I'm sure you will remind me," Matsuo said.

"Well, then, shall we meet again this evening to report on our progress?" the shogun asked.

"Agreed," both Matsuo and Ichiro said.

———

After Matsuo and the shogun had left the room, Ichiro sat quietly staring at the map. How many kilometers had he traveled, he wondered. A thousand, two? Did distance even matter, since it was time which was the commodity he lacked so sorely?

He knew this time he could not afford to be conservative, to be defensive. His attack had to be aggressive, forward, more than daring if he was to have any chance to catch Taira and close the gateway between the worlds.

And there was another problem. Where was the gateway? Only Taira knew.

Ichiro sighed and ran his left hand over his head. The sensation of feeling his bare scalp still surprised him. *Well, perhaps I will renounce the world soon enough,* he thought. *Now is as good a time as any.*

He reached for a cup of tea on a lacquered tray set next to him. The tea was cold, but Ichiro did not mind. The liquid's warmth was not important enough to bother with now.

"Ichiro-san?" a voice said.

Ichiro looked up to see Yukio standing in the doorway. The monk look tiny and fragile in his heavy, quilted jacket. There was a worried look on Yukio's face.

"Yes, Yukio, what do you need?" Ichiro gestured for the monk to enter. Yukio sat across the table from him.

"I must talk to you about something," the monk replied. "Something which bothers me."

Oh, no! Ichiro thought, *the poor boy is going to express his undying love for me.* "Well, what is the problem?"

"Last night I was sitting outside playing the *biwa*," Yukio said. "Everyone was asleep, except for a few guards. I felt lonely, with all of you away, and the music made me feel better."

"Yes?"

"As I was playing, I heard a voice say that my music was beautiful. I looked up and I saw a man and two ladies with him."

"Did you recognize them?" Ichiro asked, sitting up with interest.

"No. They were very strange. They were all dressed in white. Even the man, who wore armor," Yukio replied. He looked down at the floor. "You may think I am telling tales, but I swear they seemed like silk. I could even see stars through their bodies."

Ichiro grew concerned. Either the monk was imagining things, or it was possible that Taira was trying a new ploy. But what it was Ichiro could not guess. "Did they say anything?"

"They asked for you," Yukio said, licking his lips nervously. "I told them you were away. They seemed very sad, and said they would come back tonight to find you, then they vanished."

"Did anyone else see them?"

"No," the monk said. Yukio wrung his hands. "I asked a guard who was nearby, but he said he had not seen anything. I am afraid, Ichiro-san."

"I would be too, Yukio," Ichiro said. "I think you have seen ghosts."

"Ghosts? But whose?"

Ichiro had an idea of who they were, but he could not be sure. All he knew was that ghosts traditionally were dangerous beings. "I don't know," he said. "But we must stop them. They said they would return tonight, so we will wait to greet them."

"What do you know of ghosts?" Ichiro asked Shizuka as they ate a meal in his rooms.

"Ghosts? A funny question, coming from you," Shizuka said. She popped a ball of glutinous rice into her mouth.

"Well, what do you know about them?" Ichiro asked. He sipped a bowl of *miso* soup.

"Ghosts have poisonous breath that can drive a man mad or kill him, and it is said they must have a human to guide them in this world, or they will wander aimlessly about," she replied. "Why do you ask?"

Ichiro told her what Yukio had said.

"Do you think then that they are Taira's ancestors come from the grave to kill you?" Shizuka said.

"Taira is desperate. The ghosts are not mortal men, so they might prove good assassins, and his own ancestors would be the most eager to help him," Ichiro said.

"And they have chosen Yukio as their guide."

"Yes, obviously" he said."

"How do you plan to stop them?"

"I don't know." Ichiro put the soup bowl down. "Unless you have a suggestion."

Shizuka laughed. "Why ask me? Because *ninja* can disappear like a ghost?"

Ichiro smiled. "That thought had entered my mind."

"I am no good at magic," she said, "but I think I know of a way." She told him.

"It will have to do," he replied. "Or I am a dead man."

———

Yukio fidgeted as two soldiers with calligraphy brushes and ink painted Buddhist prayers on his naked body. "The paint is cold!" he protested. "And you press too hard with the brushes."

"Stop moving, you'll smudge the prayers," Shizuka said.

The monk lay still and let the men draw ideograms on his back and buttocks. Prayers already covered his head, neck and arms.

Ichiro pitied Yukio for the indignities he was enduring, but there was no choice. The monk was apparently the part of the gateway through which the ghosts could enter this world, according to Shizuka. If the ghosts could not find Yukio, then they would not be able to find Ichiro either.

"Will it work?" Matsuo asked Shizuka.

She shrugged. "Who can tell?" she said. "But the prayers are supposed to render him invisible."

"He hasn't disappeared yet," Matsuo noted.

Shizuka glared at him. "He'll be invisible only at night and to the ghosts as well. I hope."

The soldiers had now painted prayers along the backs of Yukio's legs and feet. When the ink was dry, more prayers would be added to Yukio's chest, face and abdomen.

"Ichiro-san, I am scared," Yukio said.

Ichiro placed his hand on the monk's shoulder to reassure him. "I am scared, too, Yukio. But we have no choice. And I am sure the Buddha's prayers will protect us all."

Yukio smiled. "I will try to be brave, Ichiro-san."

"Good," Ichiro replied, returning the smile. But he felt uneasy, and he only hoped he could prove as brave as the young monk when the critical time came.

―――――

The night sky over Matsumae was cold and as clear as crystal. Ichiro found he could easily make out several constellations, as well as many individual stars. The stars suggested a serenity to the universe which Ichiro did not share at that moment.

"It is almost midnight," Shizuka said. "We shouldn't have to wait much longer."

"I hope not, for Yukio's sake," he said.

Ichiro and Shizuka had hidden themselves behind several crates of supplies so they could watch Yukio.

The monk himself sat near the main gate, but the prayers and darkness had rendered him nearly invisible now. He was playing a plaintive tune on the *biwa*. Ichiro recognized the melody "The Song of the

Seashore." Yukio gave it a grace and sadness that plucked Ichiro's heartstrings and belied the obvious fear the young monk felt.

"He plays beautifully," Shizuka said.

"Yes, he does," Ichiro replied. He sat down and leaned back against the crates. "If you don't mind, I am going to get a little sleep. Wake me if something happens."

Ichiro's eyes had barely closed when he felt Shizuka shaking him. "Wake up!" she hissed. "Something is happening!"

He scrambled to his feet. "What is it?"

"Look," she said, pointing to the gate.

Three pale forms appeared to be passing through the very wood of the main gate. They were indistinct at first, just shapeless white images about the height of a man.

But as Ichiro and Shizuka watched, they saw the forms coalesce into shape. The forms were a man in armor and two women who looked like noble ladies. The man looked old and aristocratic. One woman was middle-aged, while the other was quite young. The three were as translucent as rice paper. Ichiro could see the timbers of the gate through their bodies.

The man's armor was of a very old-style from the Heian period, as were the women's kimono and hairstyles. It was just the sort of clothing and armor the Taira would have worn before they were defeated by the Minamoto eight hundred years ago.

"Who are they?" Shizuka whispered.

"I think it is Taira Kiyomori, his wife Nii-no-Ama and his daughter , the mother of the child emperor Antoku who was drowned at Dan-no-urra," Ichiro said. "They were the greatest of Taira's ancestors."

The three ghosts looked around the courtyard. "I hear lovely *biwa* music, but I see no musician," the ghost of Kiyomori said.

"Our friend the young monk said he would be here," Nii-no-Ama said.

"He promised he would be here," Kenrei-mon-in said.

Shizuka grabbed Ichiro's arm. "Oh damn, those idiots forgot his ears!"

"What?" Ichiro looked toward where Yukio sitting and his heart skipped a beat. The monk was completely invisible, but floating in mid-air, seemingly unattached to any body, were Yukio's ears. The ears almost glowed in the moonlight.

Ichiro's hand went to Kusinagi's hilt, but Shizuka pulled him down behind the crates.

"Are you mad, *samurai*?" she hissed. "Those ghosts are here because they want to kill you. If you try to save Yukio, the ghosts' breath will poison you and you will die, idiot!"

Ichiro wanted to argue, but he knew she was correct. "So what do we do?"

"There is nothing we can do, except hope they do not see his ears," Shizuka said gently.

Ichiro closed his eyes and nodded. Again, he had no choice. He rose slowly and looked over the edge of the crates. He watched the three ghosts moving in a circle, apparently still looking for Yukio.

"It is unfortunate that our young monk is not here," the ghost of Kiyomori said.

"Still, I do hear music," said the ghost of his wife.

"Look!" cried the ghost of his daughter. She pointed toward Yukio. "How strange! Two ears floating in the air."

"Yes, quite strange!" said Kiyomori. "Well, perhaps we should take those ears back to our dear descendant, so he will know we at least tried to find the Minamoto."

Kiyomori walked over to Yukio. The ghost took hold of the monk's ear and jerked quickly.

Ichiro averted his eyes. But he heard not a sound from Yukio, no scream of pain.

"Fine ears," said Kenrei-mon-in.

"I wonder whose they are?" said Nii-no-Ama.

"Who knows? But ears can never replace the head of A Minamoto," said Kiyomori. "Come, we must go now. The hour is late and we must be across the sea before dawn."

With that, the three ghosts turned and passed through the main gate.

Ichiro ran from behind the crates before Shizuka could stop him. He could see Yukio lying motionless on the ground. Where the monk's ear had been was now a red, raw wound.

Carefully Ichiro picked up Yukio and cradled the monk in his arms. Yukio's eyes fluttered. Then he saw Ichiro, and he smiled broadly. "Ichiro-san, I was brave. It hurt when they tore off my ears, but I didn't cry out." Then he lost consciousness.

"Bandages, get bandages!" Ichiro yelled.

Shizuka grabbed a nearby guard and, yelling orders, she sent him off to get help. She came to Ichiro's side. "Ugh! Those wounds are ugly," she said. "Who would have thought a ghost could be so strong!"

The guard returned with three other *ashigaru*. Shizuka recognized one as one of the men who had drawn the prayers on Yukio. She grabbed him by the jacket and shook him. "Idiot! You forgot his ears, damn you!"

"Ears are small," the man protested. "It's difficult to write prayers on them. The ink smears!"

Disgusted, Shizuka pushed the man to the ground. "Idiot!" she cried. "Well, get him to the doctor and have his wounds bound."

The men picked up Yukio gingerly. The monk moaned.

"Careful, damn you," Shizuka shouted. "Or I'll make you all pay dear for any injuries you cause him."

After the men had left, Shizuka sat at Ichiro's side. "He was brave," she said.

"Braver than I am," Ichiro said, feeling ashamed and powerless. "I could never be that brave. Even I would have cried out."

"Yukio loves you," Shizuka said. "Love sometimes gives a person more strength than we can understand."

"I owe him a debt I can never repay."

Shizuka snorted. "Damn you, *samurai*, always thinking about repaying obligations. Can't you see Yukio was repaying the debt that he owed *you*? Being with you has brought him adventure, excitement and love. He repaid that debt the only way he knew how, by risking his life and being brave to help you."

Ichiro shook his head. Again, she was right. "You are wiser than you let on, Shizuka. And I am more a fool than I thought."

"Fools do not risk their lives to save what they love, whether a man, a woman, or a world," she said.

Ichiro looked up at her. He did not speak for a moment, because he could not deny the truth in what she said.

"Tomorrow," he said finally, "tomorrow, a fool will try to save the world. What choice does he have?"

Shizuka smiled sadly. "None, none at all," she said

CHAPTER TWENTY-NINE

A stiff, freshening wind blew in from the north. It tasted of salt and of the very soul of Hokkaido. The sea was choppy, but only a few of the waves would pose a problem for the emperor's fleet, and especially not for the flagship, a war-junk called the *Asama-kan*.

"A good omen, this wind," said the Shogun. He held onto the rigging of the *Asama-kan* to steady himself on the ship's gently rolling deck. "Hachiman is with us."

"He has never been against us," Ichiro said. His body ached from its injuries, but the anticipation of battle eased the pain. "But, yes, the omen is good."

"We make our own omens, *samurai*, let us not forget that," Shizuka added. She fingered the hilt of her sword. "Hurry up, *daimyo*, I'm growing impatient," she yelled to the wind. "Let us settle accounts now."

Ichiro smiled. He pulled Noshida's spyglass from the man's sword belt and scanned the horizon. There was still no sign of Taira's ships, but he knew they were out there. The *tengu* said that about one hundred ships of various sizes had left port that morning, but nothing further was known because the vessels had disappeared into a fog bank. Ichiro suspected the fog bank was not natural.

He surveyed the emperor's fleet. About three hundred ships rode forward on the wind. They included several Chinese-style war junks like the *Asama-kan* and three large turtle-ships based on Korean designs. Date Matsuo commanded one of those turtle-ships. The remaining vessels ranged in type from merchant sampans to small fishing boats. If battles were won on numbers alone, then Ichiro knew he should feel confident with a three-to-one advantage. But Taira's magic could easily reduce that numerical superiority to nothing.

The beat of leathery wings caught Ichiro's ear. Overhead the two *tengu* hovered briefly, then landed on the deck by Ichiro's side. "Minamoto-san," said Jiro, "Taira is just over the horizon. You should be in range shortly."

"His ships are having difficulty moving against the wind and the currents," Akiku added.

Ichiro collapsed the spyglass. "Good." He called to a young sailor. "Signal the fleet. Tell them 'East Wind, Rain'."

The sailor, grinning, grabbed a signal flag and clambered up the rigging. As the other ships saw the message, their crews unleashed a thunderous cheer.

"Now we shall see how powerful Taira really is," the Shogun said.

"Or how weak we are," Ichiro added grimly. He shivered against the cold spray now filling the air.

A fog bank roiled from the horizon, its thick gray clouds almost boiling from the sea itself. From the leading edge of the bank appeared the first of Taira's ships, a war junk. A second ship, an ungainly merchant sampan, followed.

"Call the men together," he said to Shizuka.

It took the *ninja* but a few moments to gather the *samurai* and *ashigaru*. As he looked out over them, he could see the eagerness in their young faces. They were hungry for battle, a hunger untempered by the actual face of battle, a hunger that had yet to experience the horrible stillness and silence that would follow.

Ichiro's heart wept, knowing some of these men would not return to their loved ones. "You know your duty. Set fire to as many of the enemy as you can. If you can board his ships, disable the rudders so he'll drift with the tide, but remember, you fight for Nihon and the Emperor Saigo."

"May we die a thousand deaths for the emperor!" a young *samurai* shouted. "Banzai!"

"Banzai!" the others said, taking up the cry. Soon the shout came from every ship of the fleet. The men seemed heartened by cheers.

But the battle-cry made Ichiro remember young students who were dressed in flight suits and helmets, their silk scarves streaming in the wind. He saw them taking a final cup of sake in the Emperor's name and shouting "Banzai!" before scrambling into decrepit aircraft. *Strange,* he thought, *why can't I recall their faces?*

"You look too grim, *samurai*, for one who is supposed to inspire great acts of bravery," Shizuka said.

"I have seen many acts of bravery, Shizuka," he said with a faint smile. "They produce few survivors. I will inform the honorable Inyo that Taira's ships have been sighted."

The war-junk's cabin was small, but comfortable. Inyo had insisted on accompanying the fleet, rather than waiting at the castle. The *kami*, wearing a heavy red and blue brocade kimono, sat cross-legged on thick *tatami* covering the slatted wooden floor. Inyo's right arm reclined on a heavy ebony armrest. The sacred jewel and mirror lay before the *kami*.

"Your majesty, Taira's fleet has been sighted," Ichiro said, bowing. "We are preparing to engage them."

Inyo nodded. "Good, beloved general. May victory be ours, but if not, I am prepared." The *kami* produced a short dagger from within the kimono. It was a *wakizashi*, a dirk used for *seppuku*. "This body will not fall, living, into Taira's hands. You must also sink this ship should defeat be imminent. The sacred relics must never reach the *daimyo's* grasp, even if all else is lost."

"It shall be done, your majesty," Ichiro said. He turned to go.

"One moment, before you leave," Inyo said. The *kami* rose and came to Ichiro's side.

Ichiro felt Inyo's arms about his neck, felt the *kami's* head against his shoulder.

"As Saigo and Tamika, as both man and woman, we have loved you, Ichiro," the *kami* said. Inyo's eyes were moist. "Should you die, our grief will be immense."

He caressed the *kami's* head and shoulders, then gently eased himself from Inyo's arms. "I also love you, but all things pass, your majesty. Someday, you will forget me as well."

"As gods, we cannot forgot you," Inyo said.

"When you are once more Saigo and Tamika, I will be a memory soon enough," he replied

He left the cabin and did not look back.

———

Taira's ships, two abreast, bore down on the Imperial fleet. The *daimyo* now had the advantage of the strong current in the strait, but the powerful north wind drove Ichiro's ships with equal fervor.

Ichiro raised his spyglass and thought of Admiral Togo at Tsushima defeating the Russian Baltic fleet in 1905. It gave him an idea. "Bring the ships around," he ordered the helmsman. "We're going break off, then cut across their bows and encircle them."

The ship lurched slightly as the rudder was turned hard to starboard. The bow dived briefly under the crest of a wave, with seawater washing across the deck. High in the rigging, sailors struggled to control the sails and prepared to tack against the wind.

Ichiro held onto the railing to steady himself. "The fate of the empire depends on this," he said to the shogun. "Let us do our utmost, then."

"And when have you done less, my friend?" the shogun said.

The *Asama-kan* continued hard to starboard, but gradually it righted itself. Behind it, the other ships repeated the maneuver until they all seemed to be sailing diligently away from Taira's ships. Ichiro mentally counted the minutes the ship sailed on this course. "Now, hard to port," he ordered.

The ship lurched and went bows under again. The *Asama-kan's* hull groaned from the strain. The sailors now reversed their efforts with the sails. As the war-junk came about, it was almost parallel with Taira's ships.

I hope Taira is wondering what I am doing, Ichiro thought. *May he be confused just a little while longer, please, Hachiman.* He watched as the *Asama-kan* began to pace the *daimyo's* ships. "Now, straighten her course."

It was a calculated risk, he knew. It might have been wiser to order all the ships to turn together, but this maneuver would let him take advantage of both the current and the wind once he completed the encirclement. Slowly the *Asama-kan* and the rest of the fleet cut in front of Taira's ships.

"A perfect crossing of the 'T'," Ichiro said, suddenly exhilarated. Soon he would order another turn to starboard and began the encirclement. "Admiral Togo would be proud," he said.

"Admiral who?" Shizuka said.

"An old family friend," he lied.

She looked down and shook her head. "Sometimes you baffle me, *samurai.*"

Ichiro laughed. "I'll explain later," he said. He turned the helmsman. "Turn to port and we'll sink them."

The helms flung the steering oar hard against the hull. The sails flapped noisily as they caught the wind. Then, without warning, the wind vanished and the sails collapsed, heavy and slack. The ship began to drift in the current despite the helmsman's effort to control it.

"What's happening?" Shizuka asked. "Why did the wind die out so suddenly?"

Ichiro, cursing under his breath, brought the spyglass to his eye. "Every one of our ships is dead in the water, or drifting!" He turned the glass to the *daimyo's* fleet and cursed. The sails of Taira's ships, tacked against the wind, still billowed and fluttered.

"It's Taira. He's used his magic to still the wind," Ichiro said. "Break out the oars," he yelled to the crew.

Sailors and *samurai* ran to the center of the *Asama-kan* and began distributing long, heavy *yulo*. The oars were quickly in their davits and men were exerting great effort to keep the ship's stern pointed in the direction the wind had last blown. The other ships quickly followed suit.

"If Taira hits us now, we're in for it," Ichiro said. The *daimyo*'s boat continued to bear down on the Imperial fleet. As Ichiro watched, a Taira war-junk rammed a small sampan which was struggling with the current. The sampan broke in half, tossing men and weapons into the sea.

Most of the *samurai*, clad in heavy armor, quickly sank beneath the waves, but Taira's archers dispatched the *ashigaru* and sailors who struggled to swim. Hungry sharks took advantage of the drowning men's plight.

The sea turned crimson.

More and more of Taira's ships collided with Imperial war-junks. Grappling hooks flew between the ships and *samurai* and *ashigaru* on both sides boarded the respective enemy vessels.

The sea was rapidly awash with banners, weapons, and sinking, burning ships, but the cries of the drowning and the moans of the wounded were lost amidst the sound of battle cries and clashing swords and spears.

Ichiro heard a loud crack! Something screamed across the sky. A moment later it landed to the side of the *Asama-kan*, producing a fountain of water that drenched Ichiro and most of the oarsmen. There was another explosion, and something ripped through the ship's mainsail.

Ichiro turned to see a large war junk approaching on a collision course. Prominently displayed on the ship's bow was a banner bearing Taira's *mon*.

"So, your flagship appears, does it, Lord Taira?" Ichiro asked rhetorically.

In answer, a large puff of white smoke appeared at the enemy vessel's bow, followed by a sharp report.

An explosion rocked the *Asama-kan*'s starboard side. When the smoke cleared, several oarsmen lay dead. The wounded cried out in pain.

When magic fails, cannon succeeds, Ichiro said to himself. *The weapon was no doubt yet another of Van der Lieuw's presents to Taira,* he thought.

Another cannon ball roared overhead.

Suddenly the cannon-fire stopped, and there was the sound of cracking and splitting wood. A turtle-ship, driven by oars, had rammed the *daimyo*'s vessel amidships. Through the smoke and spray, Ichiro saw the turtle-ship's banners and flags. It was Matsuo's ship.

The appearance of his friend heartened Ichiro. "Archers! To the front!" he shouted.

The few bowmen Ichiro had on board went to the bow and unleashed a hail of arrows on Taira's crew. The deadly rain drove Taira's cannoneers from their guns. A similar barrage from archers on the upper deck of Matsuo's otherwise enclosed vessel kept the *daimyo*'s men from boarding the turtle-boat.

"Bring the ship about, helmsman," Ichiro shouted. "We'll come along side Taira's ship and board her."

Slowly the oarsmen, with great grunts and groans, rowed the *Asama-kan* forward against the strong current Each stroke of the oars brought the vessel tantalizingly closer to the enemy ship.

"Just a little farther," Ichiro said through clenched teeth. He felt the stern of the ship come around slightly, felt the *Akama-san* start a slow descent down the crest of a wave. Her bow crossed that of Taira's vessel, and then she was parallel to it.

The archers provided a withering fire that prevented Taira's men from manning their guns. By now, Matsuo's men had left the protection of their ship and were streaming over the railings of the *daimyo*'s boat. Sword clashed with sword, *naginata* with palm-leaf blade spear.

"Launch the grappling hooks," Ichiro cried.

Ashigaru whipped the hooks about their heads and heaved the grapples across the narrow strip of water now separating the two vessels. As each hook bit into the wooden deck and railing of the enemy ship, the *ashigaru* began reeling in the cables.

Wood groaned. Some cables snapped. Then at last, the *Akama-san* shook heavily as she collided with Taira's ship. Shouting battle cries, *samurai* and *ashigaru* poured over the railing. The first across fell to the blasts of *harquebuses*. At each explosive crack of the muskets, a line of soldiers collapsed.

"Archers!" Ichiro shouted.

The bowmen found easy prey in the *harquebusiers*, who were unprotected each time they reloaded their weapons.

Under the unrelenting hail of arrows, the *harquebusiers* gradually retreated toward the stern of the ship. They left many comrades behind.

By now, *samurai* and *ashigaru* fought hand-to-hand, rendering the archers useless. The bowmen tossed their bows aside, drew swords, and leaped across to the enemy vessel.

Ichiro raised himself up on the rigging, one foot firmly on the rail. He watched the rise and fall of both ships' decks, waiting until the *Asama-kan*'s rose slightly higher than Taira's ship. Then he jumped.

The enemy deck rose up to meet him. Ichiro landed heavily, almost stumbling. A hand caught his arm and steadied him. He looked up and saw Shizuka's smiling face.

"I thought you would need some help," she said.

"I'd be a fool to refuse it."

He drew Kusinagi from its scabbard. "Shall we go?" he asked, but Shizuka already had her sword drawn and was wading into the fray.

At Ichiro's side, a *samurai*'s throat exploded in crimson cloud as an enemy *naginata* found its mark. Ichiro parried another lance, snapping its shaft. Kusinagi's blade continued on into the chest of the enemy warrior. The man died at Ichiro's feet.

Blood and seawater now drenched the deck, making the footing unsteady at best. A *samurai* lunged at Ichiro, but slipped and impaled himself on an *ashigaru*'s palm leaf spear. Two *samurai*, clenched tightly in hand-to-hand combat, tumbled over the railings to their mutual deaths beneath the waves.

Ichiro and a handful of *ashigaru* forced several enemy *samurai* toward the ship's stern. The enemy, realizing they were trapped against the railing, flung themselves overboard rather than surrender. Their heavy armor dragged them under and they vanished even before Ichiro could look over the railing into the black, swirling waters.

The path to the stern, and to Taira himself, was now open. What few warriors remained fought valiantly, but they fell beneath the onslaught of spear, arrow, and sword.

Kusinagi tasted blood and sang. Ichiro's arm ached from the effort, but he moved without thinking now. His weapon thrust, slashed, and parried, and he was oblivious to the blood spattering him. Taira was his only goal now.

"They're escaping!" someone shouted.

Ichiro looked up to see Taira and several nobles, including Lord Akiyama, as they prepared to descend rope ladders to a waiting sampan, which had somehow slipped behind the flagship. A detachment of men with *harquebuses* guarded the *daimyo*. Their musket fire had already left several *samurai* and *ashigaru* sprawled dead and dying.

But the *harquebusiers* were retreating with their *daimyo*. Only Lord Akiyama, having difficulty walking, remained. He had three retainers with him, and they were bravely trying to hold off Ichiro's men. One man fell to an arrow in the back. Another retainer ran to the rope ladder to help Akiyama down to the sampan.

There was the sound of gunfire, and the retainer clutched his chest. Blood from a musket-ball wound ran between his finger. He took one step forward and fell.

Ichiro turned to see that some of his men had captured muskets and had learned how to fire them. But he also saw that the sampan was moving from the ship, heading away from the battle. He ordered his men to halt their attacks.

"Cowards! Traitors!" screamed Akiyama as he reached the railing. "Taira! You have betrayed me!"

"You're a fine one to speak of betrayal, Lord Akiyama," Ichiro said, stepping out in front of his men.

Akiyama turned about, a look of horror on his face. The white make-up made the noble look even more like a ghost than when Ichiro had last seen him at Kyoto.

Akiyama's last man stood between Ichiro and the noble. Despite the fear on his face, he held his *naginata* ready to defend his lord. The sight of the loyal warrior was both pitiful and pathetic.

"It is time to surrender, Lord Akiyama," Ichiro said.

"I will not accept defeat, general," Akiyama said. He glanced furtively about, then spot an anchor and chain that lay at his feet. The noble quickly wrapped the chain about his waist and held the anchor over his head. "I shall smash the skull of any man who attacks me."

A *samurai* moved forward to stop Akiyama, but Ichiro thrust out his arm and held the man back.

"No," he admonished the soldier. Ichiro took a step forward. "You are defeated, my lord."

The retainer stepped toward Ichiro, menacingly thrusting his *naginata*. "Stand back, *samurai*," the man said.

Kusinagi sang.

The blade took off the man's left arm at the elbow. He looked at the stump with a look of stunned amazement. The expression remained on his face as his head hit the deck and rolled against the railing.

"Damn you, Minamoto!" Akiyama shrieked. He raised the anchor to strike.

An arrow struck the noble full in the throat. He stumbled back against the railing. He tried to speak, but nothing came out. A crimson bubble formed on his lips, burst, and sprayed his chalky features.

The anchor fell from Akiyama's arms, and both went over the side of the ship. Ichiro lunged for the noble's body. He caught a fold of Akiyama's *sotai*, but the cloth tore through his fingers.

Ichiro tried to find the noble's body beneath the water, but all he saw were sharks. Their dorsal fins cut the water in a frenzied dance. He looked down at his hand and saw the ragged fragment of black silk.

In spite of Akiyama's treachery, Ichiro found himself admiring the noble's courage at the end. He doubted that death had redeemed Akiyama, but Ichiro tossed the piece of silk onto the sea and whispered a prayer to the Amida Buddha.

Ichiro felt a hand grab his shoulder and shake him.

"Wake up, *samurai*! The day is ours, but Taira is escaping!"

He turned to see Shizuka pointing out to sea. There was a bow in her hand.

"An excellent shot," he said.

"Worth it for Akiyama, damn the man," she said. "But Taira is getting away."

Ichiro shook his head. "No, he's not getting away. He only believes he is." He yelled to his men. "Cut the *Asama-kan* loose. We have a fleeing deer to catch."

———

Ichiro stood in the bow of the *Asama-kan*. All around him Taira's sampans and war-junks blazed, sank, or struck their colors and fell to the Imperial forces. Others ships, now empty, drifted aimlessly away, rocking mournfully on the wave as the wind and current drove them farther out to sea. The sea itself was flecked red from the blood of the dead and from the many banners and insignia from the destroyed ships. The bobbing debris reminded Ichiro of autumn maple leaves floating on the many ponds near Kyoto.

However, his eyes did not linger long on the remnants of the battle. Instead, his gaze remained fixed on the distant form of Taira's fleeing sampan. The sampan struggled against both tide and wind. High above the ship the two *tengu* flew, dogging the vessel and keeping it in sight for Ichiro.

Through the spyglass, Ichiro could see men battling with oars and trying to maneuver with torn sails that flapped impotently in the wind. It seemed as if even Taira's magic had at last abandoned him.

By contrast, Ichiro's men had tacked well against the wind and their yulo moved in smooth rhythm. The *Asama-kan* bore down on the fleeing sampan as relentlessly as a tiger bore down on its prey. Gradually, the war-junk drew even with the enemy vessel and began to keep pace with it.

"Soon, Taira, soon you will have nowhere to go," Ichiro said aloud to himself. He clutched the rigging with an angry hand, moving back slowly to the helm, his eyes fixed on the enemy. *If I could make you sail faster, dear ship, I would,* he thought. "Keep her steady, helmsman," Ichiro shouted.

The young sailor held tight to the steering oar. "The current is strong, general," he said. "I am doing all I can to keep us moving forward."

Ichiro smiled and clapped the man on the shoulder. "It won't be long before that won't worry us."

"General, the enemy is trying to turn away," another sailor called.

"Bring us about to port and take us across their bow," Ichiro said.

The helmsman flung himself against the steering oar. High above in

the rigging other sailors danced nimbly about to keep the sails tacked
to the wind. Slowly the bow of the *Asama-kan* began to move to port.

"What are you planning? To ram him?" Shizuka said. She held on
to the railing to keep her balance.

"If we must ram him, we will, but I would prefer he simply surrender," he said.

She snorted derisively. "Taira will never surrender."

"So we ram him, then."

The sea grew choppy, and the sky had darkened considerably. The
cold wind bit into Ichiro's already wet skin, chilling him further.

"A storm," Shizuka said. "Just what we don't need."

"Yes," he said. "But is this Taira's storm or Nature's?" Or has Chaos
already taken control?

Ichiro watched the sampan start to turn tightly, trying to evade the
huge warship. The smaller ship shuddered slightly as it angled along
the crest of a wave and was twisted by wind and current.

The sampan hung for a moment on the wave crest, then turned
sideways, rolled down the back of the wave, and came close to capsiz-
ing. The port railing went under the water, then the ship righted herself
suddenly. It shook violently, like a giant *akita* shaking itself after a
bath. Like water droplets from the back of a dog, three sailors were
flung from the rigging into the sea.

The helmsman and sailors of the *Asama-kan* also struggled to steer
their ship. The ship rocked wildly in the heavy seas. A second sailor
joined the helmsman to keep the steering oar steady, while sailors
descended from the rigging, fearful they would end up like the men on
the sampan.

Now the sampan was almost perpendicular to the *Asama-kan*, and
it could not move quickly enough to avoid a collision. The warship
continued its turn, a maneuver that rapidly brought it alongside the
sampan.

Ichiro smiled sadly. "There is no escape, Lord Taira."

Although walking on unsteady legs and clutching the rigging for
safety, *samurai* and *ashigaru* readied grappling hooks. The *Asama-kan*
pressed in on the sampan, but oddly, the enemy crew did not respond.

Ichiro held tight to the rigging himself, his foot planted on the rail for additional stability. He saw only a few men on the deck of sampan. Trying to keep the sea from sweeping them overboard, most of the men clung to the rigging and to the railings. The enemy helmsman, like Ichiro's own, held tightly to the steering oar. Even at a distance, Ichiro could see the sheer terror in the man's face.

Ichiro looked for Taira and saw the *daimyo* in the stern. The noble stood unmoving in the hatchway of the cabin. Ichiro was unsure why, but somehow he knew Taira was overwhelmed by the powers he had unleashed. The storm was no longer the *daimyo*'s to control.

The sea had grown so heavy now that waves lifted the *Asama-kan* high above the sampan, then brought it crashing down like a hammer trying to shatter bamboo. Then the waves would repeat the process with the sampan, raising it almost as high as the *Asama-kan*'s topsails.

The enemy ship seemed to fall from the sky. It landed heavily, listing precariously to starboard. A wave smashed the sampan's stern, and something broke with a loud crack! As the ship righted itself, only the stump of the steering oar remained. The helmsman had vanished, washed overboard.

The sampan, now completely out of control, slipped sideways and collided with the *Asama-kan*.

The blow shook the war-junk. Rigging snapped. Wood screamed and shattered.

Ichiro felt the rigging slip from his fingers. He screamed in horror as the deck disintegrated into splinters beneath his feet, and he plunged headlong through empty space.

CHAPTER THIRTY

I chiro landed heavily on the deck of the sampan. The ship rocked, flinging him against the railing. For a moment, all the breath in his body fled. Stars rolled away before his eyes, but they were not the constellations he had seen when he was at the monastery in that other place.

He instinctively wrapped an arm about the railing and tried to get to his feet. Although the ship appeared determined to keep him on his knees, Ichiro finally managed to steady himself.

But what Ichiro saw as his vision cleared distressed him. The sea had now pushed the two ships apart. The *Asama-kan* had fallen behind the sampan, and it now battled swells and waterspouts. Her sails, ripped and torn, resembled sheets of drenched rice paper impaled on chopsticks.

He tried to whisper a prayer for the crew, but words failed him.

"What luck!" a voice said. "I had given up all hope, and yet the gods delivered you to me!"

Ichiro turned to face Taira. The *daimyo* stood on unsteady legs in the stern hatchway. His feet and arms were widespread, pressed against the heavy wood opening for support. His face was pale and haggard. There was madness in his eyes.

Or was it simply fear? Ichiro thought.

"Give me Kusinagi!" Taira yelled. "With it I can control the chaos, I can stop this storm!"

"I thought the storm was not yours," Ichiro replied. A swell burst over the railing, nearly knocking him from his feet. He came up sputtering, and with the odd feeling that the wave had deliberately attacked him.

"You sensed it," Taira said. "It wants to kill you."

"So I did not imagine it," Ichiro said. He tried to keep his feet.

"This storm is the center of the chaotic vortex," Taira said. "At its apex is the doorway between the worlds. I first opened it to gain my powers."

"It has grown since then," Ichiro said.

"To my regret, I could not stop it," Taira said. "But with Kusinagi I know I can control it. Please, give me the sword!" he pleaded.

"No," Ichiro replied, his hand going to the sword's hilt.

As if in response to his refusal, another wave smashed into Ichiro. It seemed to grab at his obi, trying to tear Kusinagi from him. He tightened his grip on the sword.

"The storm won't be denied," Taira said.

"You have no more men to stop me," Ichiro said. He saw a length of unbroken rigging and wrapped his right arm in it. "And the storm will have to take the ship, and you as well, if it wishes to destroy me."

The *daimyo's* arm shot out suddenly, his finger outthrust like an arrow. "Don't taunt me, Minamoto. I still have powers left, powers enough to destroy you."

"This is the sixtieth day, Lord Taira," Ichiro replied. "If you don't close the gateway tonight, the demons will overwhelm you, and everything will be destroyed. You know that well."

Taira shrieked. The cry, born of anger and frustration, pierced the air and tore at Ichiro's ears. The ship itself seemed to shake even more from the sound.

"You are a fool, general!" Taira screamed. "And you will pay. The spirits of my ancestors will see to that!"

The *daimyo* flung his arms skyward. Lightning tore across the sky and a huge wave crashed over the sampan.

Ichiro clung to the rigging as the wall of water battered him against the railing and shook him like a dog shakes a wet cloth. As the sampan steadied itself, Ichiro could see the wave had deposited three crabs on the deck. He knew the creatures all too well.

The *heike* crabs were large and flat, with four long, thick legs and four, thin short legs. But it was their shells that mattered more. In each of the three Ichiro could see a human face. Each face was said to be that of a Taira warrior who had died at *Dan-no-ura*. The crabs themselves carried the *samurai's* restless spirit, waiting for the day the Taira would be avenged upon the Minamoto. If the legend were true, then these creatures had come a long way from the Inland Sea to achieve their goal.

"Crabs, Taira?" Ichiro said, trying to maintain what courage and strength he had left in his gradually tiring body. "Do you intend to destroy me with these pitiful things?"

"Your mockery has gone far enough, Minamoto," Taira said. He glared at Ichiro with the eyes of a fanatic.

"Eight hundred years ago, your kindred killed the honorable Sukemori, Arimori and Yukimori."

"My ancestors did not kill them, Taira," Ichiro replied. "They tied weights to themselves and leapt into the sea rather than be the prisoners of Yoshitsune and Yoritomo. They died honorably."

"They were cursed by the Minamoto!" Taira shouted, almost spitting the words. The scars on his cheeks caused by Ichiro's sword glowed red with his anger.

"For eight hundred years, they have walked the bottom of the sea, eating the filth of other creatures, waiting for revenge," the *daimyo* said. "Now they shall have it!"

A cold blue light enveloped the three crabs. Slowly the creatures changed shape, growing, and metamorphosing. The light expanded until it was as tall as Ichiro. Then suddenly it vanished.

In its stead stood three warriors dressed in ancient armor, but they were not ordinary *samurai*. Though each stood on two strong legs, all possessed six arms, and each arm held a wakizashi. What had once been claws that had sifted through sand and waste for food would now seek only Minamoto blood.

Eight hundred years was a long time to wait for revenge, Ichiro had to admit. But he intended to make them wait for any revenge, as he unsheathed Kusinagi. "Of the thirty-six ways to fight, the best is to flee," an ancient proverb said. Now Ichiro understood its wisdom, but Ichiro also saw a way to halt the crab-warriors. He stood between them and Taira. If he could threaten the *daimyo* directly, then perhaps the creatures might hesitate to attack or Taira might panic. That could give him the chance to force the *daimyo* to shut the gateway.

In either case, if I remain here, I'm likely to die, he thought. The crab-warriors were definitely not mortal men, not if they had waited eight hundred years for this moment. Slowly, Ichiro edged his way along the railing toward the stern, fearful that the waves would again smash him to the deck. But the deck was strangely steady now, even though the sea raged around it. Ichiro suspected Taira was using the last of his magic to hold the sampan still, in order to aid his ancestors.

But the warrior trio walked with deliberate speed toward Ichiro. They appeared in no hurry. Their quarry could go nowhere.

Ichiro backed slowly toward the hatchway, which was only a few arm lengths away now. But as he turned, he saw that Taira had disappeared into the ship's depths.

Ichiro cursed, but before he could follow the *daimyo,* one of the warriors stepped between him and the opening. A section of railing at Ichiro's side exploded into splinters as a sword smashed into it.

Ichiro ran up the short steps to the sampan's raised stern, which now offered the only escape, but once he was there, Ichiro knew he had also trapped himself. Two of the warriors moved to block the two stairs, while the third approached him, swords whirling for battle.

Ichiro backed himself toward the railing, making certain that neither of the other warriors could move behind him. His mind raced, trying to find a new escape route. His foot caught in something, and he nearly stumbled. He caught hold of the broken steering oar and kept his balance.

But as he caught himself, he caught sight of a small anchor and rope lying next to the jagged, splintered other half of the steering oar. The memory of Shizuka's *ninja* lessons came racing back. *So what if it isn't a kyoketsu-shogi, it will do,* he thought as he resheathed Kusinagi and snatched the anchor up.

The first warrior now approached Ichiro, making a great show of flashing his weapons. He resembled a picture of the evil Hindu goddess Kali that Ichiro had seen once in Burma. The warrior's blades danced about his head, each of the six arms making a circle that rotated first one way, then the other.

The effect was hypnotic and clearly intended to mesmerize a victim, but Ichiro kept his eyes on the creature's chest, avoiding the dancing swords. He wondered if the warrior's armor were metal or simply formed from the shell of the crab. *If it is only shell,* he thought.

He whipped the anchor and rope about his head, keeping his eyes on the warrior's head and chest. The arms came in, went out with each circle. Ichiro waited. He saw the arms move in toward the warrior's body, preparatory to changing direction.

The rope leaped from Ichiro's hands. The anchor snagged one of the creature's arms, then tangled another, and then a third. Ichiro snapped the rope around, throwing a loop over the warrior's head and yet another arm.

The warrior thrashed about, trying to cut the anchor cord with a free blade.

Ichiro pulled the rope taut, which drew the arms together into a confused clutter. Blades struck each other and, out of control, hacked off their master's own hands. As the rope tightened, the warrior spun about and was carried into Ichiro's arms.

Ichiro caught the warrior about the waist, lifted him from his feet and drove him against the broken stump of the steering oar. A loud crunching sound, like a crab's shell smashed underfoot, filled Ichiro's ears as he felt the oar pierce the warrior's armor.

The warrior, resembling a giant insect impaled on a long brown pin, shook briefly, then, his eight limbs curled inward, and he was still.

Before the others could react, Ichiro quickly undid the anchor and its rope and turned to face them. Chastened by the fate of their comrade, they moved cautiously toward him. Their weapons remained steady. They had apparently learned that the dancing blades would fail to hypnotize their prey.

Ichiro would have to choose between the two, but neither seemed a particularly appealing opponent. *A good swordsman hides his intentions,* he thought, *but a ninja would divert his. Ennyu no jitsu,* Shizuka had called it.

Ichiro looked down at the remainder of the steering oar. He snatched it up, remembering how he had played *beisoboru* as a boy. The shaft was as long he was, but Ichiro found he had little trouble handling it.

He waited for the warriors to approach, but they kept their distance. They hesitated, as if each expected the other to make the first move. That was to Ichiro's advantage.

Each time one moved toward him, Ichiro would feint with the oar, force a retreat, then turn to face the other as it moved in closer. Yet the warrior's faces were impassive, betraying no emotion, no hint as to their intentions. That made Ichiro's task difficult.

He had decided, because of how he held the oar, that the warrior to his right would first draw his fire. As they drew closer to him, Ichiro counted the steps separating them. He drew a breath, and feinted to his right.

The warrior on that side stepped back. Ichiro rotated on his left foot and stepped into the swing. The oar came around just as the other warrior started to lunge toward Ichiro.

The warrior saw its mistake too late. The oar struck it fully on the side, the force of the blow carrying it into the railing. Its armor buckled and cracked, and shiny ichor spilled from the breaks. Two arms now hung useless at its side. Crippled, it managed to stay on its feet, trying to turn so as to press an attack.

Ichiro unsheathed Kusinagi and stepped around the warrior. He brought the sword down in an overhead cut. The two pieces of the warrior, the inhuman flesh flaky and white, tumbled to the deck in total silence. There was no blood, only a clear, shiny fluid that reeked of fish and of the sea, but Ichiro did not take time to ponder it.

The second warrior, momentarily caught aback, suddenly pressed an attack. Ichiro grabbed the anchor and whipped it as best he could with his right arm.

The heavy metal caught the last warrior full on the chest, making him stagger. One arm was tangled in the rope, but the creature quickly cut itself free.

Ichiro took advantage of the delay to race down the steps and throw himself through the hatchway. Sputtering oil lanterns dimly lit the hold itself. The hold stank of carp, oil, and sweat, of cormorants and night soil. A narrow corridor ran down the center, with smaller rooms to either side.

Ichiro ran the length of the corridor, checking each room. Each was empty, until he came to the sixth.

In the pale flickering light, he saw a stack of harquebuses and matchlock pistols, as well as musket-balls and gunpowder. A *samurai* lay cowering next to the weapons. He did not notice Ichiro, but wrapped his arms about himself in fear. Perspiration poured from his forehead.

"Oni!" he whimpered. "Demons! All around me! Everywhere! Attacking me!"

Ichiro grabbed a harquebus, loaded it with gunpowder and a musket ball, and tamped it down.

The warrior entered the room before Ichiro could remove the ramrod or light the match.

"Demon!" the other *samurai* screamed as he saw the six-armed being. "*Oni!*" Crazed with fear and terror, the man flung himself at the crab-warrior. "Die, *oni*, die!" he shrieked.

The warrior's swords made short work of the man, who fell back, a bloody corpse. With its *wakizashi* hungry for more blood, the being turned toward Ichiro, but the distraction gave Ichiro time to reach for one of the oil lamps and light the weapon's serpentine match. As the warrior stepped toward him, Ichiro brought the serpentine to the musket's touchhole. The gunpowder in the touch flared up, then ignited.

The musket belched a jet of flame. Gunsmoke filled the room. The ramrod leapt from the muzzle and struck the warrior full in the chest.

The impact drove the crab-thing back into the corridor. It crashed against the opposite wall, the wood cracking noisily from the blow. Using two of its hands it tried clumsily to pull the ramrod from its chest, but with its fingers and its swords all parts of its body, the being could only press the ramrod between two palms.

Ichiro tossed the musket aside and away from the gunpowder. He unsheathed Kusinagi and stepped into the hall.

Seeing Ichiro, the warrior stopped its futile efforts and turned to face Minamoto. "I will tend to that later," he said in a thick, wheezing voice. "I should have suspected Minamoto trickery."

"So you speak?" Ichiro said with surprise.

The warrior nodded slowly.

"Whom do I have the honor of addressing?" Ichiro asked.

"In life I was Taira-no-Yukimori, a proud warrior of a noble line," the warrior said softly. "I was cousin to the brave Sukemori and Arimori. Many are the campaigns we fought together, until the Minamoto tricked us at Dan-no-ura. We three tied ourselves to anchors to drown ourselves and vowed we would gain revenge. Eight hundred years we have waited, and now Sukimori and Arimori are gone from my side again. But I will not fail them."

Ichiro thought he saw tears form at the corners of Yukimori's inhuman eyes. The warrior's pain moved him.

"Noble Yukimori, I am Minamoto-no-Ichiro, descended from Yoshitsune and from Kusunoki Masashige. Be it known that no mortal man may kill me, for I am blessed by Hachiman himself." He found the words of the traditional introduction came easily to his lips, which surprised him.

"May this be your last contest, Minamoto," Yukimori said. "I will avenge my cousins."

The warrior moved forward clumsily, his six short swords ready, but his body in pain from the protruding ramrod. Yukimori tried to lunge, thrusting his three right hand swords, but the attack was pathetic, and in the tightly enclosed corridor, his six arms had no space to maneuver.

Ichiro parried the three swords easily, and his counter-attack severed two of the warrior's hands. Yukimori cried out in pain. It was a loud, long cry borne of eight centuries of frustration.

"Damn you, Minamoto!" he hissed. Yukimori brought his three uninjured left arms forward, but one sword lodged itself in the wooden bulwark of a cabin. The force of the blow brought his entire body around.

Ichiro thrust and Kusinagi penetrated Yukimori's throat. The warrior beat feebly against the sword's blade with his one good right hand, but Kusinagi glowed and pulled the life from him.

"I have failed you, my cousins!" Yukimori gasped. "To crawl on my belly for eight hundred years only to die like this!" He jerked spasmodically, his body pulling free from Kusinagi. Yukimori tumbled backwards, landing with his arms and legs akimbo. His eyes, yellow and empty like two cooked eggs, stared at the ceiling. His arms and legs began to curl inward, like a crab's.

Yukimori wheezed once, gasped for air, and was still. His armor cracked at the seams and started to decompose now that the magic was gone.

Ichiro turned his eyes from the sight and tasted bile in his mouth.

Someone screamed nearby.

The sound seemed to come from toward the bow. It was a man's voice, shaken with terror. Ichiro recognized the voice. It was Taira's.

Ichiro stepped over the liquid mass that had been Yukimori and edged down the corridor. The boat shook violently and threw him against the wall. The sampan now pitched heavily from side to side, forcing Ichiro to brace himself against the bulwarks.

Taira's magic is failing, Ichiro thought, *and he can no longer keep the ship steady.* As if in answer, the ship' bow dived steeply and then shot up suddenly, nearly tossing him backwards. Oil lanterns jerked on their mounts, but fortunately none fell.

Ichiro pressed forward. Taira's cries grew more frenetic. Ahead of him was a dull, grey glow. There was an electric smell to the air. The glow appeared to come from behind a heavy sliding screen.

He reached out for the screen. The ship lurched, sending him crashing into a bulkhead. "So, you don't wish me to enter, eh?" he said. "Then, by all means, you must excuse me if I do."

Ichiro flung himself against the screen and tried to brace his feet against the walls of the corridor. He forced his fingers against the edge of the screen and pulled. The screen resisted, pushing back against him. He felt it catch his fingertips and he winced with pain, but he also increased the pressure. The heavy screen creaked, then, with a piercing shriek, it slid open and from its tracks.

A howling wind caught Ichiro full in the face, and the dull, gray glow became an intense white light.

"Damn you, go back! Return!" Taira screamed. "I am your master, you are not mine!"

Ichiro squinted his eyes against the wind and light and stared into the opening. What he saw took the breath from his lips and made his heart race.

Taira stood in the middle of a swirling maelstrom. He held his hands up, trying to force back a mass of...things.

Bone-white they were, and as thin and as translucent as rice paper. Although they seemed to change shape constantly, Ichiro could discern several grotesque oni.

Their heads festooned with tremendous horns and their loins girded with tiger skins, the *oni* bared ghastly yellow teeth, as if hoping to tear Taira's throat from his body. Red-haired *shojo* from the depths of the sea and human-like ghosts with serpentine necks burst from the mass, screaming and shrieking. Eel-like *namazu* swirled in the air and tried to wrap themselves about Taira's body, only to collapse back into the churning, bubbling mass.

Behind the creatures of chaos, Ichiro could discern a wavering shape, a black and pulsing emptiness. He knew it was the *Oni-Torii*, the demon-gate between the universes, the pathway to *Yomi*, and the world of disease, decay, destruction and darkness. Through it poured the inhuman things that Taira had called forth, waiting to boil out into the world and to destroy everything in their path.

And only the power of the *daimyo* kept the demons at bay, but Ichiro knew it was the sixtieth day. Taira needed to rest because the poisons built up through his magic had weakened him. And the *daimyo* clearly would not last long enough to regain his strength.

Ichiro unsheathed Kusinagi and stepped through the doorway.

A demon with a long snake's body burst from the mass and flew at him, baring long yellow teeth. Ichiro waited until it was almost on him before he thrust Kusinagi into its gossamer chest.

The *oni* screamed as Kusinagi's steel touched it. The sword drank the demon's strength, pulling it into the tip of the blade. Kusinagi vibrated slightly, as if it had converted the chaotic energy into something more orderly. Ichiro sensed that the sword was growing stronger, more deadly.

The horimono burned red hot with the energy even after the last wisps of the demon vanished into the sword. The sword's glow surrounded Ichiro with a crimson aura, an aura he knew would protect him. *But for how long?* he thought. *For how long?*

He strode toward Taira. Several demons broke from the chaotic mass only to be sucked into Kusinagi as their comrade had been. Ichiro felt the sword vibrate with power each time it consumed an oni. It was power he welcomed, for he knew, instinctively, that he would somehow need it later.

A *namazu* leapt free, its needle-sharp teeth intent on Taira's throat. Instead it met Kusinagi and was absorbed.

Taira looked up at Ichiro. The *daimyo's* face was almost as bone-white as the demons, and his eyes were deep black caverns of fear. "I can hold them only a short time," he said with difficulty. "What a fool I am! They used me. Now they have moved the ship to point to the northeast."

The northeast, Ichiro thought. *That was the direction in which no traveler wishes to depart because destruction lies that way. The direction of the Oni-Torii and of Yomi.*

"You must close the gate," he said.

"I have no strength," the *daimyo* protested. "It is all I can do now to keep them at bay."

Ichiro slashed at the vortex. He jumped back as an electric shock ran up his arm. His hand went numb and he almost let go of Kusinagi.

"It wants Kusinagi," Taira said. "Without the sword, you are easily defeated."

"We shall see if they succeed," Ichiro said. He snapped his wrist, Kusinagi sang and a ghostly being with a snake's neck was sucked into the sword.

"Come with me," Ichiro said, helping the weakened *daimyo* to his feet. "I will help you close the gate."

Ichiro whispered a prayer to Hachiman for success, and hoped his plan would work. If not, then they were all doomed. He forced his mind into a state of no-mind. *When does the hubless wheel turn?* he thought.

The world outside the *Oni-Torii* vanished. Ichiro and Taira fell toward the seething, cavernous mouth of chaos. They hung suspended in space, balanced between the worlds, only the *daimyo's* magic keeping them from being sucked into the demon-gate.

Ichiro could see a huge jeweled iron screen to the side of the *Oni-Torii*. The *amado* was embellished with *kanji* script spelling out Buddhist and Shinto prayers. The screen was decorated with strange engravings of mythical creatures and kami.

"The *Jigoku-Amado*," Taira said. "'The Door to Hell.' The prayers on the screen hold back the chaotic forces of Yomi. I used spells to break the locks which held it closed and I slid it open just a bit."

"No one can open such a door a little bit," Ichiro said.

"So I have learned," the *daimyo* said. A coughing fit racked his body. Ichiro held Taira as the spasms subsided. They fell closer to the *Oni-Torii*.

Ichiro realized the *daimyo's* spell was failing, and Taira was dying.

"I cannot hold out much more," Taira gasped as the fit passed. The *daimyo* wiped spittle from his thin, cracked, and dry lips. He stared at Ichiro, a puzzled look on his face. "Why are you doing this? You could have killed me many times. Why didn't you?"

Ichiro tried to speak, but the words would not come. *What could I say?* he thought. *That I let him live because I know he must close the Jiguko-Amado?*

"The Buddha spoke of compassion for all living things," he said finally. "Perhaps I cannot do less."

Taira did not respond for a moment, then nodded his head. "I underestimated you, general," he said. He looked toward the demon gate. "I underestimated many things, it seems."

The *daimyo* coughed again. He clutched his throat and fought for air.

The mouth of chaos drew them closer.

"You must close the gate," Ichiro said again.

"Impossible," Taira replied with the feeble wave of a hand. "Too weak."

"I will help you."

Taira smiled. It was a sad, weary, defeated smile. "Very well," he said. "But you are a fool, Minamoto."

"Fools do what heroes fear to do," Ichiro replied.

They slowly descended toward the hell-door. Ichiro felt themselves rotate slight, orienting themselves so they were aligned with the Jiguko-Amado. With the ease of a cormorant's feather, they settled to earth beside the door. Taira collapsed at Ichiro's feet.

Ichiro looked up and his breath was taken away. The *Jiguko-Amado* towered above him, so high he could barely see the top. It was at least a thousand times taller than a human.

He lowered his gaze, and at the edge of the door, he could see the swirling maelstrom of Yomi. Taira's spell still held the demons back, but just barely. The spell was as thin as onionskin. It had grown thinner and appeared torn in places. The spell-wall bulged like a balloon whenever an *oni* or a *namazu* tried to crash its way through.

Ichiro lifted Taira to his feet. "How do we close the *Jiguko-Amado*?"

"The screen slides as smoothly as the Ishikari River flows to the sea," the *daimyo* said. "It was breaking the seal which held the screen that was difficult. Sealing it again may be impossible."

Ichiro looked up at the hell-door and could not imagine how it could move so easily. He placed his shoulder against it and pushed. It did not move.

He grunted and pushed again. The door remained motionless.

"It slides as easily as..." he started to say angrily, then stopped as Taira reached up and placed a trembling hand against the cold iron. The *Jiguko-Amado* moved as Taira, weak and exhausted, stumbled and fell.

Ichiro moved behind Taira and helped the *daimyo* stand. He placed his hand next to Taira's and pushed. The hell-door slid effortlessly, then Taira's hand slipped from the iron and the *Jiguko-Amado* came to a sudden stop.

"I can go no further," the *daimyo* said.

"You must!" Ichiro said. He watched an *oni* throw itself against the spell-wall, stretching it almost to bursting. "We have no choice."

Ichiro took the *daimyo's* hand. Its fragility shocked him. So thin it was, the skin like dried leaves, with huge bruises resembling ink blotches. The bones were thin, like those of a small bird.

Gently, Ichiro placed the hand against the screen and held it as the two pushed. The *Jiguko-Amado* groaned as if in pain, then glided forward. The screen moved easily as Ichiro watched the demons batter themselves. He hoped the spell would hold.

The door came to an abrupt halt.

Ichiro stopped himself to keep from colliding with Taira. He was about to reach for Taira's hands when he saw *daimyo's* fingers still clutched the iron screen. Taira himself, gasping for air and drenched with perspiration, leaned against the door for support.

Someone else held the *Jiguko-Amado* in place, Ichiro realized.

He looked up in time to see a large object hurtling toward them. He pulled Taira down just as it sailed over them and crashed to earth.

It was the carcass of a piebald horse, its skin flayed backwards from its body. The horse was followed by mounds of flying excrement and urine, and by a mass of dead toads.

Ichiro shield his face against the onslaught and its foul, choking odors. His mind ran back to his schooldays, trying to recall who in legend was associated with flayed horses and plagues, and he remembered Kusinagi. The sword was taken from the bowels of a dragon slain by a warrior of destruction, a warrior who flayed a piebald horse backwards to terrorize Amaterasu, the *kami* of the sun.

That warrior god had tried to drive Amaterasu's light from the world. He had failed then, but now he was trying once again to bring darkness of chaos to the world.

Ichiro stepped out from his shelter at the edge of the iron screen. A rain of urine filled the air. A massive turd struck him in the chest, spattering. Ichiro kicked aside several dead toads that landed at his feet.

"Susa-no-wo, surely in a million years or more you could have created something better than a flayed horse, piss, and turds to announce your presence?" he shouted.

The foul storm stopped as suddenly as it had begun.

From behind the other side of the *Jiguko-Amado* a figure emerged. Ichiro's heart skipped a beat when he saw the being.

For it was indeed *Take-haya-susa-no-wo-no-mikoto*, known to all Nihon as Susa-no-wo. Susa-no-wo, his brave, swift, impetuous, male augustness; Susa-no-wo, the kami banished from heaven for his cruel antics and the kami who had conquered the chaos of Yomi for his own kingdom. And now he sought revenge against the all heavens and all the earths.

CHAPTER THIRTY-ONE

S usa-no-wo, clad in an ancient style of kimono, stood with his arms crossed in a gesture of defiance. (*Or was it fear?* Ichiro wondered.) The *kami* was twice the height of any human. His face resembled a frog's, and his skin was pale white, like the inside of an oyster shell. A long, scraggly beard adorned his chin. Centipedes moved among the long hair that was as bluish black as an iris and braided across his shoulder in the Chinese fashion. A single dull yellow eye burned in a deep socket.

Ichiro stood frozen in awe for a moment. Then he noticed Susa-no-wo was staring past him at Taira, who was slumped, gasping, against the Jiguko-Amado.

"You disappoint me, Taira," Susa-no-wo said. His voice was thin and whining. He tapped an iron war fan against the palm of his left hand. "I offer you all the powers of Yomi,,even wed you to my lovely daughters, and still you fall back on your pitiful human ways like a penitent Buddhist."

Susa-no-wo spat. His saliva struck the ground and boiled like acid. Then he noticed Ichiro.

"So you are Hachiman's little tool, then," the *kami* said petulantly.

His single eye fell on Kusinagi. "I see you also have my little jewel. I remember when I tore it from the eight-forked dragon of Koshi."

Susa-no-wo cried with rage and anger. "Like a fool, I sent it to my sister Amaterasu, thinking I could win her favor and return to the seven-fold heaven."

He spat again, this time just in front of Ichiro. "I should have known she would give to a mortal."

The ground bubbled and smoked at Ichiro's feet, but he did not flinch. He was both puzzled and intrigued by Susa-no-wo. The *kami*, for all his powers, seemed more a blustery windbag than ruler of chaos.

"I am no ordinary mortal," Ichiro said. "My name is Minamoto-no-Ichiro, honorable Susa-no-wo. I am descended from the great Yoshitsune and from the loyal Kusunoki Masashige."

The *kami* snorted, and made a dismissive gesture with his fan. "Honorable ancestors do not make one honorable. Just look at those descendants of my sister's, those pitiful humans who dared called themselves Mikado of all Nihon."

Ichiro smiled. "Nevertheless, I am as honorable as they, for I have fought loyally for the Emperor and have driven your servant Lord Taira to this fate."

Susa-no-wo seemed unimpressed. He preened his beard with fingers that had no fingernails.

"If you don't mind, honorable *kami*, I have work to tend to," Ichiro said. He turned and started back to help Taira.

"Stop! I command you!" Susa-no-wo shrieked.

Ichiro turned again and saw the *kami*'s face was now bright red, with black lines of stress defining the muscles along his misshapen skull. Susa-no-wo thrust his iron fan toward Ichiro and it shook uncontrollably with his rage.

"Humans! Such insolent creatures," Susa-no-wo said, the acid spit flying in huge droplets from his twisted lips.

"I have no time for insults," Ichiro said. He found himself having a hard time believing this *kami* was so powerful. *Susa-no-wo whines and sobs like a child,* he thought. He started back toward Taira.

The *daimyo* raised his hand.

Ichiro spun about, unsheathing Kusinagi in time to deflect a blow from Susa-no-wo's iron fan.

The *kami* pressed another attack at Ichiro's head. Ichiro moved to parry, but Susa-no-wo feinted and the side of the fan caught Ichiro in the side and sent him flying.

He landed against the horse's carcass, which cushioned his fall. Ichiro rolled to his feet and his lungs gasped for air, but he was pleased to see Kusinagi still firmly clenched in his left hand. "An excellent move, honorable Susa-no-wo," he said, his ribs hurting at each word.

The words barely touched the air when Susa-no-wo, screaming wildly, flung himself at Ichiro.

The iron fan sped toward Ichiro's head, but he rolled aside, feeling the air from the weapon as it swept past his ear. He came to his feet, ready to attack, but Susa-no-wo easily parried Ichiro's slashing cut. The iron fan beat back the sword as though it were straw.

Ichiro brought his sword under the fan and tried a point attack against the *kami*, but again Susa-no-wo parried the blade.

The force of the attack sent Ichiro off-balance. As he tried to steady his balance, Susa-no-wo's hard-calloused hand caught him across the shoulder blades. The blow drove him into the ground, and he tumbled toward the *Oni-Torii*.

The demon-gate, like an all-devouring maw, seemed to rush toward him. The surface Ichiro slid on appeared frictionless and he could find no grip, no way to slow himself. The faces of hungry demons grinned out at him from behind the rice paper-thin spell holding them back, a spell he knew would not prevent him from passing into the world of Yomi.

Then he saw the track on which the *Jigoku-Amado* rode. It was a long, thin black line of metal, glistening as blue-black as Susa-no-wo's hair. Ichiro knew if he could only get a foot out, he might stop himself. He twisted as best he could and thrust his right leg straight out.

His foot hit the rail, and a searing pain shot up his leg from the ankle to the knee. The force twisted him about, and his upper chest slammed against the *Jigoku-Amado*.

The air burst from his lungs, yet Ichiro held on tight to Kusinagi. *Or was the sword holding on to him?* his racing mind thought.

He rolled on his back with a groan and saw Susa-no-wo, in the shape of a huge, heavily-clawed red dragon, descending toward him. Susa-no-wo, his black hair unbound and flowing down his now scaly back, landed on Ichiro's chest and shrieked in triumph.

The *kami*'s steely black dragon claws glistened moistly. Susa-no-wo brought his talons down against Ichiro's throat and casually stroked the skin there.

"So, mortal, it is time for you to die," Susa-no-wo said. "A pity, because while Hachiman chose well, even he could not foresee your failure. But I will not kill you just yet, not just yet. First I want to see your fear."

Susa-no-wo brought his face down close to Ichiro's. He could smell the *kami*'s foul breath, like a thousand rotting, bloated corpses. Acid spittle rolled from the lips onto Ichiro's armor where it bubbled, etching the lacquer and burning through the cords holding the armor plate together. Ichiro tried not to think what would happen if the spittle touched his skin.

The *kami* laughed and shook his huge head with delight. A length of unbound hair fell to the ground near Ichiro's left hand, near the blade of Kusinagi.

Ichiro remembered Lord Akiyama's screen. He edged the sword over slightly.

"Are you not terrified, mortal?" Susa-no-wo said. "Fear is the ultimate chaos, the chaos of the mind?" To emphasize his point, he drew the edge of a claw along Ichiro's chin.

Ichiro felt the claw rip his skin. He clenched his teeth against the pain.

Susa-no-wo raised the claw to his lips and licked off the drops of blood. "Like a fine plum wine," the malevolent *kami* said. "I shall enjoy drinking your blood."

"Not before Kusinagi drinks yours," Ichiro said. He thrust his sword into Susa-no-wo's mass of hair. The strands smoldered and burst into flame.

Susa-no-wo, startled, screamed and tried to beat out the flames. He rose up from Ichiro's chest, leaving his own underside exposed.

Nearly blacking out from the pain, Ichiro sat up and thrust Kusinagi into Susa-no-wo's midsection.

The *kami*'s dragon body went stiff, and he screamed. Susa-no-wo reverted to his own form, but the sword remained lodged in his belly. He reached for it, to pull it out, but his calloused, fingernail-less hands came away blackened and burned from the blade.

Susa-no-wo tried to speak, but could not. There was surprise in his eyes, but not fear. Even as the sword drank his essence, the *kami* remained defiant to heaven.

Still gripping the sword, Ichiro struggled to his feet. His head spun, and when he tried to place his weight on his right leg, a stabbing, agonizing fire drove itself up his spine and seared his brain. He fought for consciousness. The blackness tried to grip his mind, but it slipped away. His eyes grew more focused.

Yet even as his vision cleared, Ichiro was uncertain if what he saw happening was real.

Kusinagi vibrated violently in his grasp. The sword's entire blade, not just the *horimono,* glowed a bright red. The heat was intense, and Ichiro felt it scorching his face and hand, but he could not release Kusinagi. It seemed bonded to him.

Still impaled on Kusinagi's point, Susa-no-wo began to loose substance, becoming ghostly. The *kami*'s body, drained of energy, collapsed upon itself like a piece of *origami.* He folded slowly, neatly into a tiny square that folded again upon itself, and then was sucked into the blade. Only a tiny wisp of black smoke remained.

Ichiro tumbled forward as the *kami* vanished. He hit the ground and rolled onto his back, exhausted.

"Minamoto," someone groaned. "Help me."

Ichiro tried to sit up. The pain from all his injuries almost overwhelmed him, but he forced himself not think of it.

He looked toward the *Jigoku-Amado* and saw Taira lying prone on the ground. Blood was on the *daimyo*'s lips, and his breathing was shallow.

With great effort, Ichiro rose to his feet, sheathed Kusinagi, and staggered to Taira. His head spun and his temples throbbed as he reached down to help the *daimyo* up.

"Susa-no-wo? He is dead?" Taira whispered hoarsely.

Ichiro shook his head. "I think not. I think he is simply trapped in Kusinagi."

"No matter then," Taira replied. "We have failed. The gate is open, and I can go no further."

"We haven't failed yet."

Ichiro carried Taira a few steps and leaned him against the iron screen, but the effort of moving the *daimyo* had drained him. He had to pause to catch his breath. His heart pulsed in his chest.

"I have come too far to be defeated now," he said. Ichiro put one arm around Taira's waist to hold him up and placed the *daimyo's* hand against the *Jigoku-Amado*.

"Now, push!" Ichiro said.

Metal groaned on metal, a dull, thick sound. Then slowly the *Jigoku-Amado* moved.

From the corner of his eye Ichiro could see demons still trying to break free from the spell holding them in Yomi. Each time they seemed to stretch the barrier to its limit, only to have it spring back. But it would not hold much longer.

Then Taira slipped.

The *daimyo* tumbled between Ichiro's feet. Ichiro tried to keep from landing on Taira, but could not. Instead he crashed shoulder first into the *Jigoku-Amado* and then was tangled up with Taira.

But as he hit the *Jigoku-Amado*, he felt the iron screen start to slide effortlessly. He watched it roll the final distance to seal off the passage to Yomi.

The *Jigoku-Amado* slammed shut with a bright, clear ringing sound. The sound reminded Ichiro of Buddhist temple bells, bells celebrating great joy.

Ichiro untangled himself from Taira. "We've have done it!" he said jubilantly.

Taira shook his head weakly. "Do not celebrate so quickly," he said, his voice barely a whisper. "You must seal the gate, or the *oni* will be able to open the gate when the spell fails."

"How do I seal it?" Ichiro asked, grabbing the *daimyo* by the shoulders to hold him up.

"There is a latch on the bottom," Taira said.

Ichiro closed his eyes and groaned. "Hachiman," he said, addressing the *kami*, "if I had know what you would put me through, I would gladly have frozen." He gently lowered Taira and slowly made his way to the Jigoku-Amado.

Only now did he really see how large the iron screen was. Just to look up at it gave him vertigo. But rather

than stare at its heights, he concentrated on the screen's lowest edge.

He ran his fingers over the carvings and the Buddhist and Shinto prayers, searching for whatever might be the latch. And at each touch he could feel the *Jigoku-Amado* move ever so lightly as the *oni* and other denizens of *Yomi* threw themselves against it.

But he try as he might, he could not see the latch. And it seemed to him the *oni's* furious endeavors were growing in intensity and strength. It could mean only one thing: Taira could no longer hold the spell.

Frantically, Ichiro ran his fingers along the edge. His heart raced and he could feel the perspiration rolling down his back and legs.

Then he saw it.

Located at the leading edge was a long, thin depression, about as wide and long as a sword. In the depression were raised carvings, horimono that matched those on Kusinagi, only in reverse.

Quickly, he unsheathed his sword. The blade still glowed with Susa-no-wo's energy. Carefully Ichiro placed the blade into the depression, feeling for where the horimono matched.

He felt something grab the sword. It locked Kusinagi in place. The blade began to glow, first a soft yellow and orange, then red-hot, silvery-blue and finally white-hot.

The energy rolled up his arm and tossed him aside, tearing Kusinagi from his grasp.

Oh, no, he thought, fearing an *oni* had somehow survived and wrenched the sword from him. *Have I failed again?*

But what he saw told him otherwise.

Kusinagi's glow blinded him. He could not believe the metal was so hot and yet did not melt. Then the glow exploded, sending a fireball around the edge of the *Jigoku-Amado*. The fireball rolled rapidly along the screen's perimeter, leaving a wake of red-hot flame behind it. Ichiro watched its progress in amazement, feeling the heat on his face and chest as it rolled around the first three corners and down the final side of the screen.

As it touched Kusinagi's blade to complete the circuit, it stopped, then slowly died away. The wake it had produced glowed brightly for a few more moments, then also died away. Kusinagi dropped from the depression, clattering noisily on the ground.

Ichiro approached the *Jigoku-Amado* cautiously. He snatched up Kusinagi and quickly resheathed the sword, then he touched the edge of the iron screen. Smooth, warm metal greeted his fingers.

The gate was welded shut in its rails. It would not move now, no matter how hard the oni beat themselves against it.

But how? Ichiro thought. Then it came to him. All the energy that Kusinagi had drawn from all its victims, including Susa-no-wo, had been stored up within the sword for later use, like a battery. When he had placed Kusinagi in the depression on the *Jigoku-Amado*, the sword had released all that energy and the heat had sealed the screen.

Ichiro raised Kusinagi slightly in its sheath and touched the blade. Drained, it was ice-cold now, colder than he could ever remember it being. He sighed and felt the strength leave him. He leaned against the *Jigoku-Amado*, wondering how he was able to stand at all.

Then he saw Taira standing unsteadily a short distant from him. A dagger lay in his hand. Ichiro recognized the weapon. It was his.

He looked down and saw the empty sheath. He realized Taira must have obtained it when they had fallen together. He cursed his luck, but he saw that Taira was hardly in any shape to do him harm.

"Honorable lord,' Ichiro said. "The spell still protects me. No mortal man can harm me, and you are in no shape to try."

"It is not for you, Minamoto," Taira said. He dropped heavily to his knees, steadying himself with his free left hand. "It is for me."

Before Ichiro could react, Taira pulled open his kimono and plunged the *wakizashi* into his abdomen. The *daimyo's* body stiffened with the first wave of sharp, mind-clearing pain. Taira's eyes grew wide, as if he had suddenly realized some deep truth. Blood ran in a bright crimson stream down the length of the blade and onto his fingers.

Ichiro staggered toward him. "Why!" he cried, tears rolling down his face. "Why?" He grabbed Taira by the shoulders and held him upright. He stared into the *daimyo's* eyes and saw weariness. And emptiness, the *mu* of *satori*, of enlightenment.

Taira swallowed with difficulty. "I have done much wrong. I must make amends. And if I remain alive, I will be tempted to open the gate. The *oni* know that." He grimaced and doubled over with pain, but still drove the sword deep into his bowels. He gasped. "Only with my death can that be prevented."

Blood bubbled at his lips. "Do me a last favor. Be my *kaishaku*."

Ichiro found himself weeping uncontrollably. He had fought this man and nearly died for it, yet he could not hold back the pity and compassion he now felt for Taira. It was *hoganbiki*, sympathy with the defeated.

"Will you be my *kaikashu*?" Taira again asked.

"Gladly," Ichiro said. In almost one motion he took a deep breath, stood up and unsheathed Kusinagi.

"*Kiai!*" Taira said with a last breath, tears in his eyes.

"*Kiai!*" Ichiro replied in the proper fashion as Kusinagi, a blue flash, split the air.

There was little blood. The head rolled from the body and came at last to an upright position facing Ichiro.

"May you be reborn in the Pure Land," Ichiro whispered.

Taira's eyes blinked once, then a smile crossed his lips, just briefly, and he was dead at last.

Ichiro felt the ground move. He looked around him. The *Jigoku-Amado* had vanished and in its place was the hold of the sampan. The ship pitched violently onto its side and then righted itself with equal force.

The twisting ship buffeted Ichiro, tossing him against the hull. Pain shot though his injured ribs and ankle. He struggled for balance, trying to stay upright while not placing too much weight on his injured leg.

Ahead, still lit by swaying lanterns, lay the narrow corridor, but as he stepped towards it, a lantern fell from its hook. It shattered on the wood decking, the oil igniting instantly and flaring up. The floors and walls of the corridor quickly caught flame and engulfed the other lamps, which added their fuel to the fire.

Well, once again, I have no choice, he thought. He turned to the other end of the hold. A small, dimly lit corridor led to the bow. He started toward it, but a glance over his shoulder told him the fire was spreading rapidly and could easily catch up to him.

He walked, half-crouching to lower his center of gravity and prevent a sudden movement of the ship from pitching him to the side. He felt like a crab, scuttling across a beach as the waves crashed behind him, ready to smash him to pulp.

The hold rapidly filled with thick, acrid smoke. The lacquered finishes of the walls and timbers caught flame quickly, and burned intensely. Ichiro's lungs burned and ached. He stumbled, crashing headfirst to the deck. As he rose, he saw the smoke rolling toward him. If he did not move quickly, the gases would ignite, and the flames would flash over him.

He gritted his teeth and tried to clear his mind, to think of the hubless wheel, but the stabbing pain brought him back to this world every time he thought his mind had found the proper channel.

When he reached the corridor, he was gasping for breath, his eyes watering and burning. The stink of flame and death greeted his nostrils.

The sampan lurched and went bow under. A torrent of cold water poured into the open hatch, nearly knocking Ichiro down, but he kept his balance. The salt spray refreshed him, encouraged him.

A short ladder reached up to the deck. He grabbed the handhold just as another wave crested the bow. The water crashed over him as the bow lifted, trying to throw him back into the hold.

His lungs, burned and battered, now struggled to find air in the spray. He placed his left foot on the ladder, then his right. It seemed like such slow progress, but he knew he could go no faster. *One foot at a time*, he thought, *one foot at a time.*

He reached the top of the hatch and flung himself onto the deck. Below, the fire and gases ignited with a terrible roar, blowing open hatches and belching thick black smoke and yellow flame from every seam.

"There he is," he heard a voice said.

"Where?" came another.

"Near the bow," the first voice said.

The voices seemed to come from overheard. As Ichiro raised himself to look, a wave battered him into the deck, driving his left cheek into the rough decking, but by now he was both too numb to feel anything, and too filled with other pain to recognize any more injury.

Ichiro lay groaning, ready at last to die. He could hear the flames consuming the lower decks, reducing the ship to ash. Soon, the upper decks would follow, and he with them. Ichiro did not mind dying. He had always wanted his ashes cast out at sea.

He heard the sound of leathery wings beating the air. Ichiro looked up and saw the tengu land on the rolling deck. They came to him and helped him to his feet.

"Leave me alone," he said. "The ship is sinking. Save yourselves."

Akiku took hold of Ichiro firmly under the arms. "Don't argue, general. We've come to save you."

She flapped her wings, lifting him from the deck. "Damn, you're heavy, general."

Jiro caught Ichiro by the feet. "He didn't have armor on last time, remember?"

Ichiro wanted to resist, but he was too weak. "The demon-gate is closed. I have finished what I came to do. Let me die now."

"Not if we can help it," Jiro said.

The two tengu beat their wings furiously, raising Ichiro high into the air. Beneath them, Ichiro could see the flames pouring from every aperture of the sampan. The base of one mast had caught fire, and some of the sails, the edges charred, burned like dried summer grass.

The hull of the ship groaned noisily, expanding from the fire's heat. As Ichiro watched, the sampan began to list heavily. Steam rose from the burning timbers as seawater quenched the fires. Then, as slowly as a dancer in a *Noh* drama, the ship rolled completely over and slipped quietly beneath the waves. Only bits of burning debris bobbed about in its wake.

Ichiro closed his eyes and turned his face away. He whispered a prayer to the Amida Buddha for Taira's sake.

A short distance from where the sampan sank, the Asama-kan rode lightly on the gently rolling sea, but the storm had done more than its share of damage. He could see sailors moving among the rigging, repairing sails and spars.

Others worked to repair the damage caused by Taira's cannons and from the collision.

"Not much further," Jiro said.

"A good thing," Akiku said. "I don't think I could carry the general much further."

A gust of wind caught them, twisting them apart and in turn making them twist Ichiro. He grunted in pain, but the sharpness of it brought him from the dim edge of unconsciousness.

"Easy, damn you," he groaned. "I'm not a piece of furniture."

Jiro laughed. "Don't worry, general, we'll get you down without another scratch."

Ichiro swallowed with difficulty and licked his dried, burned lips. He wondered how his face looked. Angry red, probably, but probably not blistered. That really didn't matter because all his injuries had resolved themselves into a single, dull throb. His mind sought relief in unconsciousness, but not yet, he told himself. Not just yet.

As the approached the ship, Ichiro saw *samurai* and sailors gathering in a small group to receive him. Someone had brought out a futon or two to set him on.

The tengu dropped slowly toward the Asama-kan. They hovered briefly above the group, then lowered Ichiro into a mass of upraised hands.

"Careful now," Akiku said. "He's a little bruised."

Ichiro felt the hands gently catch hold of his back and shoulders, then lower him to the futons.

"Welcome back, general," the shogun said. He stood over Ichiro, his helmet under one arm. "What news?"

Ichiro closed his eyes, took a deep breath and sighed. "I have the honor to inform the Shogun Tokugawa Yoriyoshi that the *Oni-Torii*, the source of all our troubles, is sealed."

"And Taira?"

"The *daimyo* is dead, by his own hand and mine. Tell the Emperor that the world is safe."

"Long live Emperor Saigo!" a *samurai* shouted. The shout carried the length of the *Asama-kan* and was picked up by the other warriors.

But Ichiro did not hear it. When the final words left his lips, he had lost consciousness.

CHAPTER THIRTY-TWO

The initial impact stunned Ichiro. He instinctively gasped for air but inhaled water instead. Pressure built up in his chest and in his throat as his body demanded he breathe, while simultaneously preventing him from gulping water. His body doubled over, Ichiro felt suspended in space, but his eyes, even as his vision clouded, told him he was submerging farther beneath the golden, glistening, sunlit surface. A stabbing pain expanded behind his eyes and in his ears as the water pressure steadily rose.

He had a mounting sensation of choking as the frigid salt water seeped into his agonized lungs. Ichiro, his body wracked with pain, knew he was dying.

Yet as the dark waters engulfed him, Ichiro found himself strangely calm and unafraid. As his body screamed and spasmed, his mind became clear, and even serene. He had been here before, he remembered, in another place and another time, too long ago and too far away to be important now.

Finally, his body touched bottom and settled easily into the muck and slime on the sea floor. The pain slid from his body just as a snake shed its old skin. His arms and legs seemed as flaccid as boiled *soba*. Ichiro sensed his body merging into the waters and the ooze of the sea bottom. The gentle waves rocked him and he felt himself flowing with the current and the tides. *This,* Ichiro thought, *must be <u>satori</u>, the enlightenment that carried one to merge with the universe and discover, no, **become**, <u>nirvana</u> itself.*

The darkness engulfed him, but he found he was filled with joy and anticipation.

Ichiro heard breakers crashing on a beach. His eyes fluttered open and soft, buttery light flowed into them.

"Ah, you are awake," a familiar voice said.

It was Hachiman. "I was concerned that I had actually killed you this time. Unintentionally, of course."

The world before Ichiro slowly grew less opaque and murky, then came into sharp focus. He could see he was lying on a beach, but it was a strange beach. The sands were crimson like blood, glistening and sparkling. Waves rolled up the beach and then retreated back to the sea. The roiling waters were the color of obsidian, tipped with silver-caps. And the sky, well, the sky was golden, cloudless and sunless.

Supporting himself on his forearms, Ichiro raised himself up to a sitting position.

Sitting next him was Hachiman, now in the form of Maitreya, the laughing Buddha. A broad smile ran cheek to cheek on the kami's round face. "Welcome to the Pure Land," Hachiman said.

"It is not what I thought it would look like," Ichiro said.

"But it is what *I* thought it would look like," Hachiman said, laughing heartily. Seeing that Ichiro did not seem to find this funny, Hachiman waved his hands and the landscape and sea became like the beaches and sea off Tokyo Bay, but there was still no sun in the sky. Ichiro got to his feet and noticed the Pure Land was as translucent as porcelain. He could see stars and galaxies and myriad worlds eddying beneath his feet, and it startled him.

"The Pure Land sits above the universe," explained Hachiman, who now sat in a lotus position and floated gently in the space before Ichiro. "Those who dwell here look down on the worlds with compassion."

"I see," Ichiro replied. "So I am now here to watch helplessly, but with compassion, as the tragic events of karma unfold before me?"

Hachiman chortled with satisfaction. "Oh, no, not helplessly,' the *kami* said, gleefully clapping his hands. "I knew I had made an excellent choice when I found you."

"What do you mean?" a puzzled Ichiro asked.

With a laugh, Hachiman unfolded his legs, stood upright and came to Ichiro's right side. He put his arm on the *samurai's* shoulder. "There is much to talk about, Ichiro, much work for you to do for those who dwell below."

"Work to do?" Ichiro asked. "Such as?"

"There will be time for that later. All the time in the world," Hachiman replied. He gently pushed Ichiro up the beach and toward a strange structure that suddenly appeared near the horizon. "But first, let me show you your new home. You will soon come to miss it when I send you on missions."

"Now, there is much for us to see," Hachiman added, with a laugh, "and we haven't got all day, you know."

Even Ichiro had to admit that he found that amusing.

END

www.ingramcontent.com/pod-product-compliance
Lightning Source LLC
Chambersburg PA
CBHW051313250626
47155CB00007B/2305